Praise for Paul Gitsham

'Brilliant book . . . Heart-stopping finale'

'I do love this series'

'Paul never lets you down'

'Beautifully written, well plotted and well researched'

'Up there with the best series'

T0337223

PAUL GITSHAM started his career as a biologist working in the UK and Canada. After stints as the world's most over-qualified receptionist and a spell ensuring that international terrorists hadn't opened a Child's Savings Account at a major UK bank (a job even duller than working reception) he retrained as a Science teacher.

Also by Paul Gitsham

Web of Lies

PAUL GITSHAM

ONE PLACE. MANY STORIES

HQ
An imprint of HarperCollins*Publishers* Ltd
1 London Bridge Street
London SE1 9GF

www.harpercollins.co.uk

HarperCollins*Publishers*
Macken House, 39/40 Mayor Street Upper,
Dublin 1 D01 C9W8
Ireland

This paperback edition 2023

1

First published in Great Britain by
HQ, an imprint of HarperCollins*Publishers* Ltd 2023

Copyright © Paul Gitsham 2023

Paul Gitsham asserts the moral right to be
identified as the author of this work.
A catalogue record for this book is
available from the British Library.

ISBN: 9780008395346

To my beloved wife, Cheryl.
We did it!

Prologue

The woman hunched over the workbench straightens with a groan. How long has she been working? She's so tired, she can't even remember. She looks at the pile of finished boxes, then at the far bigger pile awaiting assembly, and feels a wave of despair.

Christmas is half a year away, but she'll need to fulfil her orders months before then. She has to. It's her last throw of the dice; the culmination of years of scraping by, building her reputation, garnering positive reviews. First at the kitchen table, then at a second-hand dining table in the garage, and now in the cheapest rental unit, on the dodgiest industrial estate in Middlesbury.

If she can prove herself this Christmas, they can finally move forward; the banks will start listening again, and they can put all this behind them and start living like a family once more. Her eyes flick towards the picture above the bench: four crudely drawn stick figures representing the centre of her universe.

She's exhausted; all she wants to do is go home and sleep. But it's too early. She has to hit her daily target. Miss it tonight and she'll have even more to do tomorrow.

She wistfully remembers her university days: all-nighters fuelled by endless cups of coffee made with three spoonfuls of harsh, supermarket-brand instant coffee. Foul-tasting, even with milk and sugar, but effective.

Those days are long gone. Caffeine no longer does the job.

Opening a drawer, she pulls out a small tin marked "paperclips" and unscrews the lid. She has to be careful; she needs enough to get her through the next two hours, but not enough to stop her sleeping when she finally makes it home.

Just the one line, she decides; although she makes it a generous one.

The knocking on the door makes her jump.

Who the hell is that, this time of night? She hastily wipes her nose, screws the lid back on the tin and drops it back in the drawer.

More knocking.

During the day, she works with the door propped open to let in more light, but not at night, when the occupants of the other units have gone home.

Crossing the workspace, she peers through the narrow window next to the door.

She recognises a familiar outline.

'What are you doing here?' she starts to ask as she turns the handle.

The words die in her throat . . .

THURSDAY 16TH MAY

Chapter 1

'Louisa Greenland, thirty-one years old, missing since Tuesday night.'

Detective Chief Inspector Warren Jones projected a headshot of a dark-haired woman with pale, lightly freckled skin, onto the briefing room screen. 'Her husband, Ben, reported her missing yesterday afternoon, when the nursery for their youngest child contacted him at work to say she had been sick and needed to go home. Louisa is the primary contact, but her phone was switched off. He picked up his daughter and took her home and could find no sign of his wife. He went around to the industrial unit she rented for her cosmetics business and found it locked. None of the tenants from neighbouring units recalled seeing her that day.'

The question was immediate and predictably from Detective Sergeant David Hutchinson, who always got his hand up first. A transplant from Newcastle, "Hutch" specialised in organising door-to-door canvassing; he'd worked at Middlesbury for longer than anyone cared to remember.

'Why didn't he notice she was missing first thing?'

'Apparently, Louisa has been working very late for the past few months, and her husband is a light sleeper, so she is staying in the spare bedroom. He gets up with the kids and does the school and nursery run; Louisa works from home during the day and picks them up. For the past few months, she's then left her husband in charge for the evening and walked to her unit and worked until the early hours.' Warren gave a tight smile. 'We'll be looking into the state of their marriage as a matter of course.'

'Why has it come our way?' asked DS Mags Richardson. 'She's been gone, what? Thirty-six hours? Surely it's still a missing person inquiry.'

'An overabundance of caution perhaps, but there are enough inconsistencies for them to bring us in,' said Warren. The Missing Persons Unit's careful approach was understandable. The previous year the team, based at Hertfordshire Constabulary's headquarters in Welwyn Garden City, had failed to escalate the disappearance of a vulnerable victim. Several months had passed before her body was found, during which time her killer had been free to murder again. The subsequent inquiry into those failings, and another poorly handled disappearance, had been brutal, almost claiming the scalp of Camilla Wong, the inspector in charge.

'At first glance, Louisa's a prime candidate for somebody who's decided to take off for a while. She's had mental health episodes previously, including post-partum depression, and has been under significant pressure for the last year. Her husband claims their marriage is fine, but their sleeping arrangements suggest that might not be entirely true. Her unit was locked, its alarm set, and her bag wasn't there. A search of the premises revealed a quantity of cocaine; she has struggled with addiction issues in the past.

'All that being said, she is regarded as potentially vulnerable. We have been called in because of some worrying indications.'

He ticked the reasons off on his fingers. 'First, she is a devoted mother and normally leaves her phone switched on. According to the network, it was turned off shortly after midnight on the Tuesday and hasn't connected since. Its last location was her unit.

'Second, her laptop was still sitting on her workbench. She always takes that home.'

He uncurled another finger. 'Third, she had a number of important phone calls scheduled for yesterday afternoon. She runs an online business called "P@mper by Louisa", selling handpicked cosmetics. Earlier this year, she secured a contract to supply the Holistics Spa and Gym chain with Christmas beauty hampers for their gift shops. If it all went well, she hoped to expand her business further. She was said to be very excited about it.

'Finally, there is evidence to suggest that she left abruptly. She is extremely organised, bordering on the obsessive, and working to a tight schedule. She set herself a target of thirty completed hampers each night, the number needed to fill a shipping crate. The latest crate was only half filled, but she had already prepared everything necessary to complete the remaining hampers. Her husband is adamant she is the sort of person who won't leave a job half done.'

Looking around the room at his colleagues' faces, Warren could see his own unease mirrored. Missing Persons had been right to contact CID; something didn't smell right.

* * *

Ben Greenland opened his front door before the doorbell finished sounding.

'Have you found her?' he asked immediately.

'No, I'm sorry, Mr Greenland, we have no news yet. My name is Detective Sergeant Karen Hardwick with Middlesbury CID. May I come in?'

'CID?' Greenland swallowed. 'Don't you investigate murders? Does that mean you think . . .'

Behind him, PC Kevin Lederer, a family liaison officer who Hardwick had worked with before, laid a hand on the man's shoulder, gently leading him back indoors; his voice was soothing. 'Not necessarily, Ben. CID are detectives. They're the best placed to assist Missing Persons with the search.' Hardwick noted he avoided using the word "investigation". An "investigation" was scary; it implied something had happened that needed investigating. On the other hand, a search was positive; it meant that they were hoping to find her.

The familiar sound of a Disney movie drifted in from the living room; the couple's two daughters, Pippa aged three and Molly aged five. Ben's mother was currently entertaining her grandchildren. The door to the living room opened, and a dark-haired woman about the same age as Greenland came out.

'Ben? Is everything OK? Have they found Louisa?'

'And you are . . .?' asked Hardwick.

'Caitlin. Caitlin O'Shaughnessy, I'm a friend of Louisa and Ben's.' She spoke with a soft, Irish accent. 'I just came around to see if he and the girls were OK.'

'There are no updates, I'm afraid,' said Hardwick. 'Would it be possible to speak to you?'

'I was just leaving,' she said. 'But I can give you my details.'

Hardwick noted them down. O'Shaughnessy turned to Greenland and gave him a hug. 'Call me as soon as you hear anything,' she whispered, before shouting goodbye into the living room and leaving.

Hardwick took a chair at the kitchen table opposite Greenland, accepting his offer of a coffee. 'I know you've been through this already, but I'd like to hear it first-hand from you,' said Hardwick. 'Tell me about Tuesday.'

Greenland nodded tightly. Hardwick could see the impatience on his face, but he forced himself to speak. 'It was a normal day. I left for work at my usual time, just after eight a.m. I dropped the kids off at nursery and school on the way. Louisa was still asleep.'

'In the spare room?' interjected Hardwick.

'Yes, she's been working until the early hours. She sleeps in there so she can get a lie-in and not disturb me when she comes in.'

'And where does she work?'

'The Forest End Industrial Estate. She rents a lock-up to run

8

her online cosmetics business.' Middlesbury had a number of industrial estates within the town's boundaries. Forest End was one of the less salubrious.

'Did she visit there during the day?'

'I don't know. Some days she does; other times she works from home. She prefers to do paperwork at the kitchen table, so she can run the washing machine and prepare dinner. The unit's only a short distance from here, so it's no big deal for her to pop down there for a couple of hours to pack some hampers. Either way, she picked up the kids at their normal time and brought them home. I arrived home at around half-five.'

'And how did she seem to you?'

He shrugged. 'Normal.'

'She didn't mention any worries?'

'Nothing.'

'What about the last few weeks? Anything unusual?'

He puffed his lips out. 'Look, the last few months have been hard work. P@mper has only really been ticking over for the past couple of years. She sells her gift hampers online – eBay, Etsy, Not On The High Street, Amazon – the usual places. She was getting great ratings, but sales were stubbornly low. She started off working out of the garage on her own, but eventually needed more space, so she hired the industrial unit. She was keeping up with the workload, but only breaking even. Then in January, she landed the Holistics contract and things went crazy. She's hoping to take on a couple of people to help her over the summer.'

'How does she get there?'

'She walks. It takes about fifteen minutes.'

'Even late at night?' asked Hardwick, keeping her voice neutral.

Greenland shifted in his seat. 'She doesn't drive. Sometimes she calls a taxi . . . normally she texts to tell me she's on her way home, but Tuesday night she didn't.'

'What time does she usually come home?' she asked.

'About two a.m. It depends.'

Hardwick smiled encouragingly. 'Depends on what?'

'On what she needed to do that evening. She tries to do thirty hampers most nights to fulfil the Holistics contract, but before she assembles them she needs to prepare everything. She makes her own scented candles and bath bombs, and each hamper has a handwritten insert. Plus, she's still building hand-selected hampers for her online clients. They take a lot more time and effort than the identical ones for Holistics, but they are the customers who built her reputation, and she needs to look after them.'

'Going back to Tuesday, walk me through what happened after you dropped the kids off.'

'Just a typical day. I worked until five, then drove home. Louisa was already in.' He looked up at the ceiling briefly. 'She'd made a cottage pie. The girls were in the living room watching a film. I tidied the kitchen, whilst Louisa went and spent some time with the girls. Then we ate and I loaded the dishwasher as Louisa bathed the kids. She then left to go to work. That's the last I saw of her or spoke to her.' His eyes filled with tears.

Hardwick gave him a moment to compose himself. 'What time was that?'

'About seven. Look, I've already told everyone this.'

'I know, but sometimes people remember new details and I always prefer to hear it first-hand,' Hardwick reassured him. 'Please carry on.'

'I put the girls to bed. I read to Pippa until she fell asleep, then Molly and I did a bit of reading practice, before she went to sleep also.'

'Do the girls sleep in the same room?'

'Yes. Maybe when they're older, and we can afford to move house . . .'

'Did they get up in the night?'

'Not that I recall; they're both pretty good.'

Hardwick made a note to look into having a specialist interview

10

the two young children. She'd also have someone speak to their teachers and other carers; it was amazing what kids overheard sometimes. 'What did you do then?' she continued.

'Nothing much. I pottered about in the kitchen, sorted some laundry and set the timer on the washing machine. Then watched a bit of TV, until it was time for bed.'

'What did you watch?' asked Hardwick, casually.

'The footie on Sky. West Brom v Villa in the Championship play-off.'

'What time did you go to bed?'

'About half-ten. I watched the ten o'clock news, read for a bit and I guess I was asleep by elevenish?'

Hardwick made a note in her pocketbook. 'And did you sleep through until the morning?'

'Yes. The alarm goes off at quarter to seven. I got up, made the girls breakfast and did the school run, then went to work.'

'And you are sure your wife wasn't home?'

'I have no idea. I don't disturb her; I let her lie in.'

'Did you try to call Louisa during the day?'

'No, we were snowed under at work. I planned to give her a ring at lunchtime, but Pippa's nursery called about midday and said she had a temperature and had been sick. That's when I checked my mobile and saw Louisa hadn't texted when she finished work like she usually does. So I picked Pip up then drove home. The house was empty, so I called Lou's mobile and it went straight to voicemail. Pip was a bit sleepy, but she was OK, so I drove around to Lou's unit, but it was all locked up and the garage next door said they hadn't seen her. That's when I called the police.'

'Do you know if she came home at all?'

'I don't think so. The dishwasher was still full, and the washing machine needed emptying. She usually leaves her cereal bowl to soak in the sink, but it wasn't there, and the only coffee cup was mine from breakfast. She also makes a point of making the girls' packed lunches when she gets in. Crazy, I know, that time of night, but she likes to put a little note in there. Their lunchboxes were still empty that morning . . . she's never forgotten before.' His lip started to tremble. 'Something must have happened to her Tuesday night.'

Hardwick gave him a sympathetic smile. 'I realise this must be difficult, for you, but what was your wife's state of mind? How was she feeling in the days before she went missing?'

He wrung his hands together. 'She was stressed, and she was very tired, but she was also excited, you know? She's worked so hard over the past couple of years and finally, it was going to pay off. The contract with Holistics was a really big deal. They said that if her hampers sold well over Christmas, they would consider stocking them permanently and even using some of her products in their spa therapies. Then she could consider renting somewhere a bit nicer, perhaps even opening her own shop.' He rubbed his face. 'Longer term, I was going to cut back at work and help her run the business.' He gave a bleak smile. 'Everything was going really well.'

Hardwick chose her words carefully. 'We know Louisa had some mental health challenges in the past. Do you know if she had been struggling at all recently? Perhaps found things a bit overwhelming?'

He shook his head vigorously. 'She had some difficulties a few years ago, but the last bout of depression was postnatal, after Pip was born. She had a few dark months, but her GP was brilliant. Since then, she hasn't needed any medication and, like I said, she was excited about the future.' His voice became more earnest. 'Lou has never been afraid of hard work. Back at university, she was the queen of the all-nighter. She loves a challenge. That's why I can't see her walking away now, leaving things unfinished.' He gestured towards the living room. 'And she would *never* leave me and the girls. Never.'

Hardwick met his gaze. 'Ben, my colleagues have searched Louisa's unit and we found a quantity of what appears to be cocaine. Was Louisa using drugs?'

Greenland's shoulders slumped. 'Shit,' he said quietly. 'I thought we'd dealt with that.'

'I need you to be honest with me, Ben,' said Hardwick. 'We're very worried about Louisa. We are aware she had some problems in the past.'

He sighed. 'No, you're right.' He swallowed. 'Back at university, we liked to party; Louisa especially. She's always been all or nothing. That was fine at uni, but when we left and started working, it nearly cost her her job. She sought help and stopped the cocaine and the drinking. As far as I know, she's been clean since then.'

'So no drugs at all?'

He bit his lip. 'We occasionally have a little weed now and again, just to unwind after a hard week, but nothing stronger. I still have the odd pint with my mates, but we never have booze in the house.'

'Do you know where she got the cocaine?'

'No, idea,' he said quickly.

'Where do you get the cannabis?'

'Just a mate,' he mumbled.

Hardwick waited, but he looked down at the table and remained mute.

'If Louisa did decide to leave for a while, perhaps to clear her head for a few days, do you know where she might go? Any places that are special to her, or friends she might stay with?'

'No, just the ones I told the constable from the Missing Persons Unit about. And I had another look at the wardrobe and bathroom. None of her clothes are missing, her overnight bag is still there, and her toiletries are all in the cupboard. Her contraceptive pills are in her bedside drawer; she'd never leave without those.'

A sudden squeal came from the lounge, followed by a muffled adult voice admonishing somebody to "play nicely".

'I'm sorry, Sergeant, I have to go and deal with that.'

'Of course.' Hardwick handed over her card. 'If you think of anything at all, please let me know, or speak to PC Lederer.' She gave him a smile. 'I promise you, we will do everything in our power to find Louisa.'

Hardwick saw herself out, whilst Greenland and Lederer headed to the next room to put an end to whatever drama was unfolding between his daughters. Sitting in her car, she called the station. DI Tony Sutton answered.

'I've just spoken to Ben Greenland. He's lying.'

Chapter 2

'Why do you think he's lying?' asked Warren. He was perched on the table opposite Tony Sutton and Karen Hardwick's workspaces.

'He says that Tuesday night he watched Villa playing West Brom on Sky, followed by the ten o'clock news before going to bed.'

'Nice one, Karen,' said DS Richardson, approvingly.

'Good spot,' echoed Sutton.

They all waited expectantly, Sutton not even bothering to hide his smirk.

Warren gave a sigh. 'OK, I'll bite. Why is that significant?'

'The game kicked off at eight, but it was a draw, so they went into extra time,' said Hardwick, 'and when that wasn't enough, they had a penalty shootout.'

'That's when the teams take it in turns to kick the ball at the goal, until one of them misses,' supplied DS Pymm helpfully, from behind her trio of extra-large computer screens.

'Thank you, Rachel, even I know how a penalty shootout works,' said Warren. His lack of interest or knowledge of football was a frequent source of amusement for his colleagues. 'So, what you're saying is, the game will have ended after the ten o'clock news?'

'Yes,' said Hardwick. 'Robbie watched the match and it went on well past ten. He doesn't support either team, but you couldn't have pried him off the sofa with a crowbar.'

'It was the play-offs,' confirmed Richardson. 'No way would he turn over and watch the news instead of seeing how the match ended.'

'Could he have been mistaken?' asked Warren. 'I agree that by the sounds of it, the match was pretty memorable, but he could be getting his days confused.'

'Possible,' said Hardwick, 'but he remembered who was playing. And there are other things bothering me. Like the whole thing about the text messages she sends when she leaves the unit.'

'That's been worrying me also,' interjected Pymm. 'I've gone through her phone records, and she sent one to her husband each night at about two a.m., give or take a half-hour. Without access to her phone or his handset, I can't tell what the messages say, but they are never replied to.'

'His wife is leaving work in the early hours of the morning, and he claims to have been asleep,' said Hardwick. 'His alarm goes off before seven, so I can't imagine he's lying awake each night until he receives that message.'

'He says he's a light sleeper; perhaps he just wakes up, reads it and then goes back to sleep?' said Sutton.

'That doesn't sound normal to me, Boss,' said Richardson. 'There's no way my husband would go to sleep if he knew I was walking home by myself that time of night, especially in the area around the Forest End Industrial Estate. Something's not right with that marriage.'

'He said she sometimes catches a taxi,' said Hardwick.

'I have no record of her calling any local cab firms,' said Pymm. 'If she was getting a lift, then she did it via an app. That should be on her bank statement.'

'I agree, this doesn't add up,' said Warren. 'If she was planning to leave him, then she'll have needed money. I think we have enough to justify a warrant for both of their banking and phone records.'

He looked around at his team. 'Missing Persons have got the ball rolling, but something feels wrong here. I spoke earlier to DSI Roehampton and she agrees. Without second-guessing Missing Persons, who will continue to treat her as missing, potentially vulnerable, we will be running in parallel, treating it as a suspected murder. Better to stand down if she turns up unharmed, than find we've missed opportunities to investigate if it does turn into something more serious.'

He turned to Hutchinson. 'Hutch, I want you to organise door-to-door along their street and the most obvious routes to and from the industrial estate. See if anyone has any gossip about their marriage, if they saw her that night, or can confirm she usually walked that way. Check if anyone has CCTV.'

He addressed Richardson. 'Mags, get the Video Analysis Unit ready for incoming. Until we know otherwise it's a live investigation, potentially with a life in danger, so front of the queue, please. Also pull in ANPR and traffic cams from the area surrounding their house and the industrial estate. If she was taken against her will, then there will probably have been a vehicle involved.

'Karen, I want you to coordinate interviews with friends and family. I also want you to work with Hutch to interview the owners of the neighbouring units. Secure any CCTV and get a feel for how well they knew her and her husband. If anything makes the interviewer's nose twitch, I want it called in immediately. For all we know, she could be tied up inside one of the other units.' He turned to Sutton. 'Tony, be ready to deal with any applications for search warrants. They might be time-critical.'

He returned to Pymm. 'Rachel, run any names, phone numbers and licence plates through the computer and see if anything interesting pops out. Bring in additional indexers from Welwyn if necessary. We need everything loaded onto HOLMES as quickly as possible.'

Pymm was the team's "officer in the case", working with a team of civilian indexers and exhibit officers. She was in charge of keeping HOLMES2, the case management database used in major inquiries, up to date. She was also a specialist in data analysis and took charge of scrutinising electronic evidence, as well as querying the Police National Computer for any recorded incidents relevant to persons involved in the case.

'Anyone know what time Moray is due in?' asked Warren.

'Any time now,' said Hardwick.

'Tony, bring Moray up to speed and then work with Missing Persons on the victimology. Whilst you're at it, speak to Kevin Lederer. He's been supporting Ben Greenland for the past twenty-four hours. See what he thinks.' He paused. 'Janice, what can I help you with?'

'I have Andy Harrison on the line,' said Janice, Warren's unofficial PA. 'He thinks you might be interested in what they've found at her unit.'

Warren smiled. 'I swear he's psychic – I was just about to ask for an update on the forensics.'

* * *

DSI Ashley Roehampton was at a conference down at the force's headquarters in Welwyn Garden City, so Warren decided to go and see what had caught the attention of Forensics for himself. It was rare for an officer of Warren's rank to visit crime scenes, and practically unheard of for them to conduct interviews, but Middlesbury CID was unique. The merger of Hertfordshire, Bedfordshire and Cambridgeshire Constabularies' Major Crime Units had occurred under Warren's predecessor, but DCI Sheehy had fought to maintain Middlesbury's CID unit as a separate entity, operating as a "first response unit" dealing with Middlesbury and the villages in the northernmost part of Hertfordshire. That role had continued under the stewardship of Detective Superintendent John Grayson, but his retirement a little over a year ago had shone a spotlight on the department's status again.

So far, his replacement, DSI Roehampton, had largely continued Grayson's policy of allowing Warren free rein to conduct investigations as he saw fit, but she occasionally raised an eyebrow when Warren or Tony Sutton took the lead in interviewing suspects or witnesses. The unit had maintained its enviable success rate, but the ongoing budget cuts meant senior officers were again questioning Middlesbury's existence as an independent unit. It remained to be seen how hard Roehampton would fight their corner, especially if she was as ambitious as some believed.

The lock-up rented by Louisa Greenland was one of half a dozen in a row and was flanked by a double unit operating as a garage and body-repair shop, and a small business fixing garden equipment. Unlike her neighbours, she hadn't bothered to install a sign above the metal roller doors, which he noted were bolted to the concrete apron.

'The side door has a five-lever mortice lock, and a heavy-duty padlock fitted to the outside,' Crime Scene Manager Andy Harrison was explaining as Warren wrestled his way into a Tyvek scene suit. 'Her husband claims both the lock and the padlock were secured when he came around yesterday and there's no sign of forced entry.'

'Does that work?' asked Warren, pointing to the security camera angled at the door.

'Apparently so. Mrs Greenland had it fitted herself, along with an alarm. That was also set when her husband arrived. The husband can't remember the password to the digital video recorder, so the company is sending someone out. We're also trying to access the footage on the cloud server where it's backed up.'

Warren was surprised. 'The unit has internet?'

'Yes, along with electricity and running water. There's even a basic toilet.'

The two men entered the unit. It was little more than a concrete box, but Louisa Greenland had done her best to make it more homely, with the walls covered in children's paintings. Citrus mingled with lavender and the heavy smell of soap and a half-dozen other scents; Warren's eyes started to water. A folding table had a kettle, mini-fridge and the makings for tea and coffee. On the right side of the unit was an open door.

'A bathroom with a sink,' supplied Harrison.

Between the door and the front of the unit were dozens of sealed packing crates. A white-suited technician had already opened several.

'Completed hampers,' said Harrison. 'The current Mrs Harrison loves this sort of stuff; the bathroom's uninhabitable for twenty-four hours after her Sunday night relaxation session.'

As usual, Warren wasn't entirely sure if the rotund Yorkshireman was being serious or not.

On the opposite side of the unit were other opened boxes and piles of wicker baskets, stacked inside one another. The boxes were different shapes and sizes with a variety of shipping labels.

'Those contain the raw materials she uses to make her toiletries and build the hampers; we're doing an inventory.' He gestured toward the far wall. 'And I guess this is where she assembled everything.'

A sturdy work bench about four metres long had been erected. The wall behind was covered in photographs of Louisa and the two girls; Ben must have been behind the camera. At one end were a couple of wicker hampers, filled with packing material. Nestled within them were what appeared to be candles and an array of coloured soaps. A flat rectangle wrapped in gold foil had a dark label, pronouncing it to be vegan, ethically sourced, eighty-five per cent chocolate. Very nice, Warren was sure, but as far as he was concerned, you couldn't beat a nice bar of Dairy Milk.

At the opposite end of the bench sat a closed laptop and a colour printer.

'It's pretty dingy in here, but those seem like overkill,' said Harrison, pointing to a pair of free-standing lights, similar to the ones found in a photography studio.

Standing in the centre of the room, Warren did a slow rotation. The unit was more or less what he would expect for a small, one-woman business operating online.

'What was it you found, Andy?' he asked.

Harrison produced a small torch and shone it on the door-frame. A yellow scene marker, a little over a metre from the ground, pointed to a tiny red dot.

'Blood?' asked Warren.

'According to the peroxide test, yes. And a quick squirt of luminol has found a few more spots on the floor, which were cleaned up.'

Warren felt the familiar tightening in his gut. It wasn't entirely unexpected, but like everyone, he'd been hoping Louisa Greenland had just decided she needed a few days on her own and would turn up unharmed when she'd cleared her head.

'Don't read too much into it,' cautioned Harrison. 'The spots are tiny. Even if they are hers, they could be from weeks ago; she could have had a papercut or, given the Colombian marching powder we found, a nosebleed.'

'What else?' asked Warren.

Even behind the man's mask, Warren could see his features become more grave. He picked up a see-through plastic evidence bag. 'We found this blowing around on the floor.'

Warren squinted at the tiny fragment of paper. He'd forgotten his reading glasses again.

'Looks like confetti. Maybe it's packing material? Or from a hamper for a hen party?'

'Look closer,' instructed Harrison.

It took Warren a moment to focus on the tiny writing on the paper.

'Shit,' he breathed. 'Is that an AFID tag?'

'Yes,' said Harrison. 'Somebody fired a Taser in here.'

21

Chapter 3

'On the fence,' was PC Kevin Lederer's summary of how he felt after a day with Louisa Greenland's husband. 'On the one hand, he's saying all the right things; he appears to be genuinely worried and upset about her disappearance, whilst maintaining a brave face for the kids. On the other hand, I agree something isn't right about their marriage. I get the separate rooms bit; if she's working until silly o'clock every night, then I can see why she might camp out there.'

'But?' prompted Warren. He could hear the hesitancy in Lederer's voice over the conference call.

'I don't think he's telling us the truth about what happened Tuesday night. I'm pretty certain he didn't watch the football, for starters. I saw the match myself and tried to chat about it and he struggled to discuss it in detail.'

'And it wasn't the sort of match you'd forget,' said Warren, ignoring Tony Sutton's grin.

'I'm surprised you watched it,' said Lederer. 'I thought folks from Coventry went out of their way to avoid watching the Villa?'

'Well, you know,' mumbled Warren, before clearing his throat. 'Anyway, what else?'

'I've not seen anything overtly suspicious,' said Lederer. 'No freshly scrubbed surfaces or empty bottles of cleaning materials in the bins, but I'm sure he made a phone call yesterday evening on a second mobile.'

'What makes you think that?' asked Warren.

'I was sitting in the kitchen when he went upstairs to run a bath for the girls. I could hear they were in the bedroom from the thumps on the floor; they keep jumping off the bed and usually get a bollocking, but he just left them to it. Eventually, I decided to check everything was OK and found the bathroom door locked and the kids running riot. I could make out his voice over the running water. When I asked if everything was all right, it suddenly stopped.'

'Could he have been talking to himself?' asked Warren.

Lederer was completely unabashed. "I can't be sure, but I stood outside for about a minute, and it sounded like the ebb and flow of a conversation, although I couldn't make out any words and only heard his side.'

'Why do you think he was using a second mobile?' asked Sutton.

'Because when I went back down to the kitchen, his usual phone was plugged into the charger.'

*   *   *

'How's the shoulder?' Warren asked Moray Ruskin as the team assembled for their afternoon briefing.

'It's getting there. The physio reckons I can double my swimming and carry on increasing the weights. She'll see me again next month.'

'Glad to hear it,' said Warren, pushing down the feeling of guilt he experienced every time he was reminded of the cataclysmic events the previous year. Mistakes had been made, and deep down in the part of his psyche he admitted to only in the privacy of the therapist's office, he couldn't help blaming himself.

It was cruelly ironic. In the months before that day, he'd finally started to move on from the death of Gary Hastings. The lingering PTSD he'd suffered since that horrific night had started to recede, and he'd even been able to play with Oliver Hardwick, Karen's young boy – born after his father was killed – without feeling a sense of shame.

And now it was as if he'd gone back in time; the issues he'd fought so hard to overcome were back with a vengeance. At least the nightmares had stopped since moving out of the house.

Calling the meeting to order, he handed over to Tony Sutton.

'Missing Persons have done a great job helping with the victimology and we've uncovered a lot of new information. Louisa was born and raised in Nottingham and has an older sister, Stephanie, who she was very close to growing up. They were actually born just under twelve months apart, and so ended up in the same school year; they are physically similar enough that those who didn't know them assumed they were non-identical twins. In fact they were sometimes referred to as "the twins", even by those who knew otherwise.

'This closeness continued through their university years. They both attended the University of Middle England here in Middlesbury from 2005 and shared halls of residence and, later, digs. Louisa did Marketing and Business, whilst Stephanie did Law. It was here Louisa met her future husband, Ben, who is from Middlesbury. All three of them graduated in 2008. Louisa and Ben stayed in Middlesbury, whilst Stephanie moved to London to finish qualifying and start working as a solicitor.'

'What does her sister say?' asked Hutchinson.

'MPU interviewed her within a few hours of Louisa being reported missing. She hadn't spoken to Louisa for a couple of weeks and hasn't been up to Middlesbury for a month. She said her sister's business was taking off and she was working long hours. As far as she is aware, the relationship with her husband is sound.'

'Given what we now know, arrange for her to be re-interviewed,' ordered Warren. 'What about parents?'

24

'Both still live in the Nottingham area. They went through a nasty divorce when the girls were teenagers. Again, neither parent had any concerns, other than a bit of parental worry about her overworking. Her mother has been on holiday in Australia; she'll be arriving back sometime in the next twenty-four hours. We'll interview her properly then. Her dad is coming in tomorrow for another interview.'

'Make sure to ask about their thoughts on Ben,' said Warren. 'She's been missing nearly two days now; hopefully they'll be worried enough not to hold back any nagging doubts they were initially reluctant to share with the MPU.'

'The relationship with her sister doesn't sit quite right with me,' said Hardwick. 'They were in the same school year and survived their parents splitting up, and then instead of taking the opportunity to go their separate ways at university, ended up living together. That's a very close sibling bond. Yet Stephanie claims not to have spoken to her for a fortnight. They may not have been real twins, but I'm wondering if something changed recently?'

'I'd also ask her about Ben,' said Hutchinson. 'We've got follow-up interviews scheduled with her closest friends and some of the couple's mutual acquaintances. There's a lot of overlap, since they met at university. I'm thinking that we probe deeper; get any niggling worries out in the open.'

'I agree,' said Warren. 'Be considerate, but our priority is finding Louisa, or failing that, working out what has happened to her and who is responsible. We can worry about hurt feelings later. What about Ben's mother? She's been with him since he reported Louisa missing. What has she got to say about her daughter-in-law?'

'I just spoke to Kevin Lederer,' said Ruskin. 'He managed to grab a quick chat with her after Ben went for a lie-down. She was quite candid about Louisa's mental health issues and was worried she was stretching herself too thin. She says she thinks she's taken herself off for a few days, although Karen's visit has spooked her a bit.'

It wasn't surprising; up until now, the investigation had been coordinated by the Missing Persons Unit. Part of their job was calming worried loved ones, reassuring them that most people who disappeared returned of their own volition within a few days. The involvement of CID would feel like a sudden and ominous escalation.

'Did she comment on the couple's marriage?' asked Hutchinson.

Ruskin shook his head. 'Not really. She claimed that as far as she knew, everything was fine. But Kevin isn't convinced. He gets the impression Ben is a bit of a golden boy; he's not sure she'd be willing to speak out of turn.'

'However, a search of the PNC has turned up a couple of interesting things. Firstly, Louisa has a conviction for drink-driving. She wrapped her car around a lamppost back in 2015. Nobody was hurt, but their oldest, Molly, was in the car seat at the time. She was handed a ban and nearly given a suspended sentence, but agreed to take part in a drink-drive rehabilitation course and undergo counselling. The ban has expired, but she never took up the option to retake her driving test.'

'That would explain why she is walking to her unit late at night,' said Hardwick. 'But why didn't she retake her test? It would make things a lot easier. We should ask her husband directly. He admitted she'd had a problem with alcohol in the past, along with other substances, why didn't he mention the driving ban?'

'We'll do it when we get him in again,' decided Warren. 'What else did you find?'

'I did a search for Ben. There's nothing on the system in his name, but on a hunch, I expanded the terms to include his and her family members and turned up Darren Greenland, Ben's younger brother. He has several convictions for possession with intent to supply and shoplifting. He was also charged with assault and battery against a former girlfriend, back in 2014. The charges were eventually dropped through lack of evidence, after the victim refused to cooperate. His last known address is Middlesbury.'

'That *is* interesting,' said Warren. 'Ben refused to say who the couple bought their weed from, and Louisa had to get that cocaine from somewhere. We need to look into him as a person of interest. Let's find out what relationship he had, if any, with his brother's wife and find out what he was doing Tuesday night. What about social media?'

'Missing Persons have been trawling the major platforms since she was reported missing,' said Ruskin. 'They've identified four accounts so far; her husband isn't aware of any others.'

He read from a list. 'Her Twitter, Instagram and business Facebook accounts all appear to be used strictly for running P@mper; pictures of her products, testimonials from satisfied customers and links to her website and the various online stores she uses to sell her hampers. The platforms are playing ball; they've all given us access to her private messages. We've found nothing suspicious; everything is strictly professional. The last time she posted anything publicly was last week, sharing a five-star review from Etsy.'

'What about personal accounts?'

'Just the one, a personal Facebook. I've looked through her most recent posts and they are mostly memes and family stuff. She's not a big over-sharer. She's posted and liked a few inspirational quotes – you know the sort of thing, pictures of beautiful sunsets with trite sayings about how the struggle is worth it et cetera. I guess you could see them as cries for help, but I don't know if I'm reading too much into them. Certainly nothing jumps out. The last things she shared were on Tuesday morning: a picture of her girls dressed as Disney princesses and a quote about every parent's wish being for their kids to have the freedom to choose what they want to be in life. She hasn't liked or commented on anything since.'

'What about Messenger?' asked Warren.

'She uses it quite a bit; it looks like it's the primary method of communication she used to keep in touch with her old university

27

friends. They had some sort of reunion back in April. Missing Persons have already compiled a list of her most recent and most frequent contacts, and are arranging interviews.'

'OK, keep at it,' said Warren. 'Contact the Social Media Unit to get them to do some of the heavy lifting and coordinate with Missing Persons; don't reinvent the wheel.'

People Louisa's age were the first generation to have reached adulthood in such a connected world, living much of their lives online. But social media could be an incredible time-suck for investigators. Ruskin had completed advanced courses on its use, but it was important not to overstate its importance. Not everyone shared their innermost thoughts on public forums, and what was portrayed was often a distorted, idealised version of reality.

'What about WhatsApp or email?' he asked.

'We know of a business email account with a well-publicised address, a joint email account with her husband for managing bills and a personal email account. We're onto the relevant providers to get access. She also uses WhatsApp, but as you know it's end-to-end encrypted on the users' devices. Without access to her phone, or that of whoever she's been contacting, Facebook can't help us. Ben has shown us the messages he exchanged with her as well as any texts, but obviously we are limited to what he wants us to see. He could have deleted anything incriminating; we'd need a warrant to search his handset to have a hope of retrieving them.'

Witnesses so far had stated that there was no way Louisa would leave her children, and in the pit of his stomach, Warren believed them. But then again, the world was full of absent parents, and if she was undergoing a mental health crisis . . .

He forced his attention back. 'We'll bear that in mind, but I can't see us getting a warrant at this stage.'

* * *

'Missing Persons secured some CCTV footage from the most likely walking route between Louisa Greenland's house and her lock-up,' said Richardson. 'Hutch's team are trying to find some more.'

Warren leaned over her shoulder as she started the video.

'This is from 19.14 the night she disappeared.'

The footage was from a camera mounted on the front of a house, angled to cover the two cars in the driveway. The field of view overlapped with the pavement adjacent to the front fence. Louisa Greenland was wearing a white T-shirt over blue jeans. A grey backpack was slung over her right shoulder.

'She's walking in the direction of the industrial estate. That bag looks like it has a padded compartment for a laptop,' said Richardson. 'It's bulging slightly, so I'd suggest she has a jacket in there for later.'

'Her laptop was still in the unit, but there was no sign of the backpack,' Warren recalled.

Richardson switched to another video. It was from the same camera, but the weather had shifted from sunny to overcast. 'This is the previous day.'

The timestamp was 19.18. Louisa was wearing a light-brown jacket and carrying the same backpack; it looked emptier. Her jeans had been replaced with black trousers.

'We've found her walking this route, plus or minus twenty minutes, almost every day for the past three weeks.'

'It matches the location data for her phone,' Pymm added.

'And what her husband has told us,' Hardwick supplied.

'What about when she returns?' asked Warren.

This time the footage was in black and white. The timestamp showed 02.25 in the early hours of Monday morning; the day before she disappeared.

A woman of similar build, wearing what appeared to be the same clothing as Greenland, carrying a backpack, appeared from the opposite direction. She was walking more briskly.

'We've got footage from every night,' said Richardson. 'Except last Tuesday when it was raining hard. And the night she went missing.'

'Do the timings on the videos match her phone records?' Warren asked Pymm.

'Yes, she's captured on video between two a.m. and half-past each night. She sends a text message to her husband about eleven minutes before she appears on camera. The location data shows her phone leaves the unit within a minute of the text message being sent and typically arrives home fourteen minutes later, passing the location of the camera at roughly the time we see the woman we believe to be her.'

'So she texts her husband to tell him she's on her way, then leaves immediately,' said Warren. 'What about last Tuesday, when it was raining?'

'Judging by the speed her phone was moving that night, I'm going to suggest she travelled by car,' said Pymm. 'As usual, her husband didn't acknowledge her text, so I don't think she got him out of bed to pick her up. I assume she called a taxi using an app.'

'Presumably she will have given the industrial estate as a pick-up address,' said Warren. 'Rachel, as soon as her bank statements come through, I want you to identify the cab firm she uses. If she's using their app, she probably pays by credit card. If she did disappear voluntarily, then she could have used a taxi.'

'What if she doesn't use her card?' asked Pymm. 'Some firms still insist on cash. She could even have used PayPal.'

Warren rubbed his chin. 'In that case, we'll have to do it the old-fashioned way and contact the cab companies directly. Be discreet. It strikes me that very few people probably knew her routine, but a taxi driver who picked her up a couple of times, or just got chatting with her, might have spotted an opportunity. If we start asking around the cab firms, they might get wind of it.'

He turned back to Richardson. 'Are there any other routes she could have used to walk home? What about cameras on, or around, the industrial estate?'

'Answering your second question first, the units either side of her have external CCTV, but from the angle of their cameras, I'd say their fields of view barely overlap with the edge of her unit. You could easily enter and leave it without being captured. And any vehicles would only need to be parked a few metres away to be completely out of shot. We'll seize their footage to see if anyone was careless and wandered into view.

'Hutch's door-knockers are working their way outwards from the industrial estate. There are a couple of other roads she could have walked down, especially if she was walking somewhere other than home. I'll keep you updated.'

'When the footage is reviewed, ask the analyst to check and see if anyone is following her,' suggested Hardwick. 'On the way there and on the way back. If some weirdo spotted her on her daily walk, he might have decided to follow her to plan his attack.'

'Good suggestion,' said Warren. 'We'll also ask her husband if she ever mentioned anyone giving her the creeps.'

'We should also ask her female friends,' said Hardwick. 'You know how it is – being cat-called or perved at by random blokes is so commonplace she probably wouldn't even mention it to her husband, especially if she didn't want to worry him. But she may have gossiped about it with her girlfriends.'

Chapter 4

'Any joy unlocking the CCTV at Louisa's industrial unit?' Warren asked Richardson after finally grabbing a late lunch.

'Not yet,' she replied. 'We've issued a warrant to the cloud-hosting service; fortunately they're UK-based. A technician from the company supplying the digital video recorder is on their way to see if they can get into it. They've asked us to leave it *in situ* until they've had a go.'

'What happens if they can't unlock it?' asked Sutton.

'Pete Robertson's team will remove the hard drive and have a crack at it. If she's enabled the encryption, it could take a while. Which a cynic might believe is a convenient delay.'

'What's the situation with her laptop?'

'Again, Ben doesn't know the password. Pete's team are prioritising it, but the hard drive is encrypted,' said Pymm. 'However, it's just the off-the-shelf Windows encryption. His team have a few tricks they can try.

'But in other news, we've got a hit on the PNC. Guess who runs the one-man garage next door to Louisa's unit?'

'Go on,' said Warren making his way to her desk.

'Russell Myrie.'

'You're joking?'

'I wish I was. He uses his mother's maiden name, but it's linked to his real name on the computer. He got out eighteen months ago after finishing half his sentence. He set up his business a year ago. Basic repairs, resprays, after-market modifications, that sort of thing. He's not allowed to perform MOTs because of his criminal conviction, but it looks like he makes a tidy living. I notice he doesn't mention he is a registered sex offender on his Facebook page or advertise it on his website.'

'I'll bet,' said Sutton.

'I think we need a bit of a chat with Mr Myrie,' said Warren. 'I wonder if he'll be pleased to see us again, Tony?'

* * *

'I wondered how long it would be until you fucking turned up.'

Russell Myrie was a skinny man, with a shaved head, the shadow of its stubble marking the outline of his male pattern baldness.

'Good to see you too, Russell,' said Sutton.

'Well let me tell you what you want to know, then you can piss off and leave me in peace. I'm already losing business 'cause of your lot sealing off the area in your white suits.'

'Sorry to inconvenience you,' said Warren, flatly.

'So, yes I did know her. Yes she has been in here a few times to chat and yes, you can see my CCTV. No, I haven't kidnapped her and locked her in a dungeon. No, I don't have an alibi for Tuesday night and no, you can't poke around in here without a search warrant.'

'Ta da!' said Sutton, producing a warrant with a flourish.

'How about we do this down the station?' suggested Warren.

* * *

Russell Myrie was an arrogant prick. That was Tony Sutton's assessment, based on their previous encounters with him. Warren wholeheartedly agreed.

They'd first dealt with the man back in 2012. He'd been accused of several counts of rape and serious sexual assault, against multiple women. He was known to befriend his target, getting them drunk, possibly even drugging them, before going back to their place and having what he claimed was consensual sex. Apparently, his arrogance could be mistaken for self-confidence and even cheeky charm in the wrong light.

None of the rape charges were proven, but he was eventually sentenced to seven years for the sexual assault charges, which the judge had deemed serious enough to receive the upper end of the tariff. He had to sign onto the sex offenders register indefinitely and was subject to a Sexual Harm Prevention Order.

The two men knew from experience that Myrie would try to dodge their questions and play the innocent victim. They would need to be firm with him and let him know from the outset they weren't messing around.

'So basically, you've arrested me because of that bullshit back in 2012. Instead of looking for a real suspect, you've picked the low-hanging fruit.'

'A couple of things before we start,' said Warren. 'One, you aren't under arrest, as I have made clear repeatedly, and your solicitor has explained to you. You are helping with inquiries and are free to leave at any time.'

Myrie gave a snort. 'Oh, please, we all know that if I try to walk, you'll arrest me anyway. The only reason you haven't is you don't want the custody clock to start ticking. I'm not a fucking idiot.'

'The second thing,' Warren continued, ignoring the man's bluster, 'is that your conviction in 2012 wasn't "bullshit". You were convicted of multiple accounts of serious sexual assault and charged with several more.'

'Which he was acquitted of,' interjected Myrie's solicitor.

34

'Yeah, the bitches were full of it. They just got caught out by their boyfriends and complained they were raped to cover their own backs.' He gave a sneer. 'They weren't complaining the night I shagged them, I can tell you.'

The duty solicitor flinched but said nothing. Warren felt sorry for the woman. Representing such clients was part of the job, but he imagined that didn't make it any less unpleasant. He suspected she was glad to have opted for a trouser suit, rather than a skirt; Myrie had turned leering into a spectator sport.

'How well do you know Louisa Greenland?' asked Warren.

'Just in passing. She did most of her work in the evening after I finished for the day, but sometimes she'd come in for a couple of hours during the afternoon. She'd go outside for a cup of coffee sometimes and a bit of fresh air. Not surprising really – it smelt like a prossie's handbag in there, as my old man used to say.'

'And what did you speak about?' asked Sutton.

Myrie shrugged. 'Nothing important; she told me what she did in there.'

'You said she's been inside your unit,' said Warren. 'Why?'

'I'm a sucker for a damsel in distress,' he said, with a smirk. Warren and Sutton said nothing, just stared at him.

'The backrest was loose on her office chair. She asked if she could borrow a screwdriver to fix it. When it became obvious she wasn't really sure what she actually needed to do, I told her to wheel it over and I'd sort it for her; I figured it would be quicker.'

'And that was the only time she came into your unit?'

'Pretty much. Sometimes she'd come and watch me work whilst she drank her coffee and we'd have a natter.' He gave a leer. 'If you ask me, I reckon things weren't right at home; not getting the attention she needed.'

Warren knew exactly what Myrie wanted him to ask, but unfortunately, he saw no way to avoid the question. He deliberately made his tone bored. 'Did you and Mrs Greenland have any sort of romantic or sexual relationship?'

Myrie's leer became a big grin, as he stretched his back. He made a show of cracking his knuckles and then looking thoughtful.

'Is unrequited love romantic? Or just sad?' he asked.

Warren and Sutton made no comment. They'd played this game before; fortunately, Myrie had a short attention span.

'No. No relationship. I wouldn't have been averse; she was a good-looking woman – cracking pair of tits – but she restrained herself, and I'm too much of a gentleman.' He smiled again and looked at them for a reaction.

'Is a good-looking woman,' said Warren.

'Sorry?'

'Louise Greenland is a good-looking woman,' clarified Warren. 'You used the past tense. At present, this is a missing person inquiry, not a murder investigation. What are you not telling us, Russell?'

For the first time, the man's grin faltered. 'Nothing.'

'What do you know that we don't?' asked Sutton.

'Hey, now hang on, it's just a figure of speech. Is or was, what's the difference?'

Warren gave a shrug. 'I'm not a psychologist, obviously, but I've heard it said that when people feel guilty about something they've done, their conscience really wants to tell everyone. So they start making little verbal mistakes, accidentally releasing nuggets of the truth without realising.'

'It's called a Freudian slip,' supplied Sutton.

'Oh come on,' protested Myrie. 'Don't give me that psychological bullshit. OK, I knew her but only to talk to. Look at my CCTV; there's no way in or out of my garage without being recorded. She hasn't been inside there for weeks. And I've *never* been inside her unit.'

'Are you absolutely certain?' asked Warren. 'We have a full forensics team searching her unit. If you're lying to us, we'll find out.'

'No chance,' said Myrie. 'You'll find my fingerprints on her office chair, but that's it. In fact it was only a few weeks ago when I fixed it – the video might still be on the cloud server.'

'We'll do that,' said Sutton. 'To speed things up, can you tell us the type of security system you use?'

Myrie rattled off the make and model of his camera, and the service where he stored his online backup.

Warren and Sutton exchanged a glance. The set-up was identical to that used by Louisa Greenland.

∗　∗　∗

'What a nasty piece of work,' said Roehampton. She'd watched the interview of Russell Myrie over the live feed from the interview suite.

'Yeah, he was an arrogant shit back in 2012 and a few years in Parkhurst associating with other arrogant shits hasn't made him any better,' said Sutton.

'Score another victory for the parole board,' said Hardwick. 'Do you think they actually believe these bastards when they claim remorse and say they've changed?'

'Probably not,' said Roehampton. 'But they know what they need to say to get out of there. What do you think, Warren?'

'He's definitely on my list, but despite his past history, kidnap would be a massive escalation,' he replied. 'He also claims to have been home alone watching the football. He at least knew it had gone to penalties.'

'Which could just mean he's a better liar than Ben Greenland, or he took her after the final whistle blew,' said Pymm. 'I just got off the phone to Andy Harrison. They've found prints on the office chair matching Russell Myrie.'

'How long until they've finished checking his CCTV?' asked Warren.

'He gave them the password, so they're checking Tuesday night now,' said Richardson. 'They'll know within the hour.'

'Good. Then get them to go back over the rest of the footage. Let's see if he was telling the truth about that office chair and how often she went inside his unit. I want to know if their relationship was more than he claims. No CCTV inside, I take it?'

'No, just the external camera.' Richardson gave a grimace. 'Hardly a surprise; God only knows what he gets up to in there.'

'He seems very confident we won't find anything untoward on his CCTV,' said Roehampton.

'Don't be fooled,' cautioned Sutton. 'He was like that seven years ago; absolutely confident we'd not find any evidence linking him to the victims, but it was all a bluff. As soon as we presented him with what we had, he did a complete one-eighty and admitted to having sex with them, but claimed it was consensual. Mark my words, if we do find something, he'll have an explanation.'

'We need to test his alibi,' said Warren. 'Speak to his neighbours, see if he was in that night like he said. Can we access his phone records?'

'There's nothing listed under his name with any of the carriers,' said Pymm. 'Why am I not surprised he's an anonymous pay-as-you-go type?'

'What about his car, Mags?'

'I'll run it through the ANPR system and see if he was anywhere he shouldn't be.' She gave a frown. 'I'll also ask the Video Analysis Unit to check the registration numbers of any of the cars he was working on, in case he borrowed one for the night, or nicked its licence plates.'

'Good thinking,' said Roehampton, getting to her feet. 'I'll leave you all in Warren's capable hands. In the meantime, I have a budget meeting to go to.'

Warren kept his face neutral, yet again thanking his stars that he'd finally decided not to go through with his application for John Grayson's old job. Having observed Roehampton in her new role for the past year, he'd definitely dodged a bullet. There was no doubt in his mind what he'd rather be doing right now.

*   *   *

Warren arrived home shortly after ten p.m. Disabling the alarm with his key fob, he fumbled for the unfamiliar light switch. He'd lived here for over a month, but it still didn't feel like home. Maybe some carpets would help; they were due next week, followed shortly after by a new bathroom and kitchen.

Grabbing a plate from one of the cardboard boxes on the 1980s-vintage kitchen worktop, he made his way through to the lounge, and collapsed on the sofa – one of the few bits of furniture not in storage. He flicked on the TV, resting on its newly assembled stand. He'd promised himself he'd build at least a couple more bits of furniture before the kitchen fitters arrived. Tony Sutton had offered to come around and help him make some of the larger pieces of furniture that recommended two people. Although given the fun and games he'd had trying to put together the TV stand – supposedly a one-person job – he might need to round up a couple more pairs of hands. He wondered what Mags Richardson was up to; she and her husband had built a luxury garden office from scratch. He bet she wouldn't drop a hammer on her foot and spend two days limping.

He was pleased that the disappearance of Louisa Greenland was the lead item on the local news, and even more pleased the press conference given by Missing Persons had been edited to include everything they wanted out in the public eye, but none of the rather crass questions aimed at DI Wong's department's failures the previous year. Marcia Cooper, from the *Middlesbury Reporter*, had lost none of her ambition and charm, and by all accounts, the end of the press conference had been rather uncomfortable for everyone present, not least Ben Greenland. There was a time and a place for those questions, and frankly this was neither.

Warren tipped the chips and battered sausage onto the plate and added a large splurge of brown sauce. At least it was the low salt and sugar version. With nobody to nag him about his diet, he'd lapsed back into his old habits. He'd have to watch that.

The decision to let the MPU lead the public appeal was a strategic one. They still weren't certain Louisa had been taken against her will, although it was looking that way, and they were now proceeding on that assumption. However, revealing their suspicions at this early stage would tip off whoever was responsible. In the worst-case scenario, it might even make them panic and harm her.

The reasoning behind involving Ben Greenland at the conference had been threefold. His carefully prepared statement had stressed how much he and his family loved Louisa, and how much her little girls missed their mummy. That would hopefully invoke sympathy from the public and encourage witnesses to come forward, or in the best-case scenario, persuade Louisa to return.

Second, if she had been taken against her will, whoever had done so may be watching; if they were having regrets about what they had done, then it might just be enough to persuade them to release her, or encourage others with suspicions to do the right thing.

Finally, they wanted to observe Ben Greenland. Body language experts were poring over video footage of the conference. More than one killer had been unearthed when their behaviour in the immediate aftermath of a loved one's disappearance had caught the attention of the investigation team.

A creaking from upstairs made him jump. He relaxed again; it was just the house settling for the night, the sound amplified by the bare floors and empty rooms. He'd lived in their old house for so long the groans from the gas boiler and the sound of the fridge-freezer's compressor kicking in had become as familiar as his own breathing.

God, it felt so empty.

Taking his dirty plate and the balled-up chip paper into the kitchen, Warren grabbed a bottle of beer before returning to the lounge. The news had finished, replaced with *Question Time*.

A flat, cardboard box with a picture of a coffee table on it sat in the middle of the room, making him feel guilty. Before he could change his mind, he slit the tape with a pair of scissors. It was a coffee table. Surely, if there was one piece of furniture in the whole damn house that could be assembled by one person, in a reasonable amount of time, this was it?

FRIDAY 17TH MAY

Chapter 5

The eight a.m. briefing started exactly on time. Warren slurped his coffee, wincing as the hot mug stung the cuts on his fingers from the previous night's DIY efforts. At the back of the room, DSI Roehampton settled in; unlike her predecessor, she was at least polite enough to turn her mobile phone face down and give the speaker her full attention.

'Yesterday's press briefing hasn't yielded much in the way of useful information,' Warren started. 'There have been no new sightings of Louisa since Tuesday, so we'll concentrate today on interviewing her nearest and dearest. Given his offending history, Ben's brother, Darren, is a priority, but he is proving somewhat elusive; none of the people he shares a house with have seen him. That's not entirely out of character. There are reports he likes a pint in the Feathers pub.'

'Have we heard back from the body language experts yet?' asked Roehampton.

'Before lunch, I'm told,' offered Sutton.

'What about the AFID tag?' asked Hutchinson. 'Have they traced it back to a specific Taser?'

'No, unfortunately. The serial number on the confetti matches a cartridge from a batch stolen from the Chicago Police Department eighteen months ago. They're being sold on the dark web and are cropping up all over the world.'

'Have we got access to the Greenlands' bank records yet?' asked Roehampton.

'Yes, they came through this morning,' said Pymm. 'I'm going to take a look at them after we finish here.'

'If Ben is responsible, then either he bought the Taser on the dark web, or he handed over a bundle of notes in the local pub,' said Roehampton. 'Those things aren't cheap. Check for any suspiciously large cash withdrawals or credit card payments to unknown sources. See if he has used a cryptocurrency exchange to buy Bitcoin or similar. When are the forensics due back on the blood smears?'

'Hopefully by end of play today or first thing tomorrow,' said Sutton. 'Louisa's DNA is already on the database from her drink-driving conviction, so they can do an immediate match to see if it's hers.'

'PC Lederer thinks Ben might have a second mobile phone,' said Hardwick. 'Is there any way to tell if that's true? I presume it'll be a burner phone.'

Pymm gave a so-so gesture with her hand. 'In theory, yes. We could request a cell-tower dump, but it'll turn up every handset within fifty to a hundred metres of the tower, including most of their neighbours and probably anyone driving past. The data could have its uses, but we'll never get a warrant that intrusive based on what we've got so far.'

'We'll put in a retention request anyway,' ordered Roehampton. 'Then the data is available for us if we do get a warrant down the line.'

*   *   *

'No fingerprints from Russell Myrie anywhere in Louisa's unit, other than the chair back,' said Pymm.

Too much coffee, the previous night's chip supper, and increasing worry about the mother of two had conspired to give Warren a bad case of acid indigestion. He swallowed another antacid, avoiding Pymm's gaze. He knew a lecture was in his near future.

'Where are we with video evidence?' he asked.

'They've reviewed all of Tuesday and she doesn't enter Myrie's garage, nor do they interact anywhere within the camera's field of view,' said Richardson.

'That's not unexpected,' said Ruskin. 'He must know that, with his history, we'd come knocking on his door first. If he did snatch her you can bet he did it well out of sight of any cameras.'

'How is the analysis of the area surrounding Forest End and the Greenlands' road?'

'ANPR and CCTV haven't turned up anything of immediate use, including Russell Myrie's Volkswagen Golf, or any of the vehicles he's working on,' said Richardson. 'ANPR coverage is limited to major junctions, none of which are near that area. We've captured loads of cars travelling up and down their road between early evening and the following morning, but they are all side-on to the residential CCTV cameras, so no licence plates.'

'What about the Greenlands' Renault?' asked Sutton. 'He would have had to get to the unit and back somehow, especially if he had Louisa in the car with him.'

'No cars matching make, model and colour,' said Richardson. 'But it isn't the only way to Forest End. If he wanted to avoid any CCTV in their street, he could have nipped down one of the parallel roads. Hutch has a team securing more footage, but there are dozens of potential routes he could have taken if he was really crafty, and the number of cameras increases exponentially as you widen the search area.'

Richardson made a very good point. This all took resources. They hadn't even formally declared it a homicide, so that source of funding hadn't been unlocked. They would have to decide

47

what to do about that sooner rather than later. At the moment, her family still hoped she was just missing. The whole team were praying for a miracle, but the longer it dragged on, the less likely it was they'd have a happy ending.

'I've been looking through Louisa's bank and financial records,' said Pymm. 'This is her business account. As you can see, she's well into her agreed overdraft and hasn't been in the black for months. I've gone through her recent transactions and identified most of the entities she has dealt with.' She ran her finger down the screen. 'These are the direct debits paying for her industrial unit, water, electricity and broadband. Forest End may be a dive, but it isn't cheap.' She pointed to another entry. 'This is a standing order to her bank. It's the same each month, so I'm guessing it's a loan repayment.' She indicated another cluster of payments. 'These are the suppliers she uses for the raw materials for making her candles and bath bombs, and these are where she sources her hampers and the bathroom products and cosmetics she doesn't make herself. And this is a delivery company that she presumably uses to post the completed hampers to her customers.'

'I don't know much about internet selling, but that looks pretty normal,' said Warren. He waited patiently; he knew from years of working alongside Pymm that she wouldn't have called him over unless she had something interesting to show him.

'Her income seems to mostly come via a PayPal account. I've been onto her webpages and the remittance each time matches what she's charging for her hampers, minus a percentage I assume is the platform's cut and PayPal's commission. However, a few weeks ago, she also started receiving money from this secure payment service. I originally assumed that she'd just started selling her hampers on a new website and this was how they charged customers, but the sums she's receiving don't match what she usually charges on Etsy or Not On The High Street. Some of the sums she receives are as little as twelve pounds. Either she's

48

selling something else we don't know about, or the seller fees for this website are extortionate – we're talking over fifty per cent.'

'That's strange,' said Warren. 'Is there any way to trace her account back to the website generating the sales?'

'Not easily. The payment service is US-based. We can ask them, but I doubt they'll tell us. We'll probably need to get a warrant served in the US.'

'That'll never happen,' said Sutton, who'd wandered over to join them. 'Presumably she set it up on her laptop? If Pete Robertson's team can crack the encryption on her hard drive, we may be able to find it on there.'

'Well, it sounds like P@mper was struggling to make ends meet,' said Warren. 'Maybe the stress really was too much for her?'

'Or maybe the stress was too much for their marriage?' said Sutton, meaningfully.

'Definitely food for thought. Thanks, Rachel,' said Warren turning to leave.

'But that's not the most interesting thing I've found,' said Pymm, waiting until he'd taken half a dozen steps.

'Every bloody time . . .' muttered Warren as Sutton chuckled. Pymm loved to keep the best for last and Warren had fallen for it again. He returned to her desk.

Pymm scrolled further back. 'This is where she placed a bulk order for all her raw materials – far more than she does normally. From the date, I'm assuming that this is when she landed the contract with Holistics Gym. You can see there is no big cash injection from Holistics, meaning she needed to pay for everything up front. Presumably, it was pay on delivery. That's what pushed her into her overdraft. Up until then, her income pretty much matched her outgoings; some months she made a profit, other months a small loss. But with the interest on her unauthorised overdraft and her credit cards, she wasn't just struggling to make ends meet, she was heading for a crash.'

Chapter 6

Stephanie Hellard, Louisa Greenland's sister, had booked into a local hotel and was helping entertain her two young nieces at the Greenland family home when Karen Hardwick invited her to give a formal statement. It was Hellard who suggested they do so down the station. Hardwick wondered if that was to spare her nieces any more upheaval, or if she wanted to speak more candidly.

Up close, it was obvious why people who knew both Stephanie and Louisa could mistake them for twins.

'Lou has the other half,' said Stephanie when she saw Hardwick had noticed the small, broken heart tattoo with an "L" on the inside of her right wrist. 'Hers is on the left wrist and has an "S".'

'This must be a very difficult time for you,' said Hardwick. 'Has Louisa ever gone missing before?'

Hellard shook her head. 'Never. As I'm sure you're aware, we aren't really twins, but we're a lot closer than most sisters. Even if we haven't seen each other for a while, we can always text each other or call and we'll drop everything and answer.' Her lip trembled. 'She was my sister and best friend all rolled into one.'

'What do you think has happened?' asked Hardwick.

'I really have no idea,' said Hellard. 'But one thing I know, is that Lou would never walk out on Ben and the girls. She just wouldn't. Please, Sergeant Hardwick, don't waste any time waiting for her to come home. Something bad has happened to her.'

'I promise you, we're doing everything we can,' Hardwick assured her. 'But we can't entirely dismiss her leaving of her own accord. How are things at home at the moment?'

'I imagine you know by now their marriage wasn't perfect. Her new business has taken over her life and it's making things difficult, but she was loving the challenge. This contract with Holistics Gyms was going to be her big break; the sacrifices wouldn't be forever. There's no way she would have just upped and left.'

'Did she mention anyone that she was worried about? Perhaps a bit creepy, or who she'd had a run-in with?'

Hellard gave a little snort. 'You mean like Ben's brother?'

Hardwick said nothing.

'Yeah, he's a prize arsehole. I know he's tried it on with her a few times. He also tried his luck with me, but backed off when I reminded him I'm a solicitor and know exactly how to get him in a shitload of trouble with his parole officer.' She bared her teeth in a tight smile, and Hardwick was unsure whether to be impressed or scared.

'When did you last have contact with Louisa?' asked Hardwick.

'A couple of weeks ago? We had a chat on the phone, just to catch up.' Her face dropped. 'But we hadn't had a chance to meet up in person for weeks.'

'Why is that?' asked Hardwick. 'I'm told you were inseparable at university.'

'Nothing dramatic,' Hellard assured her. 'Life gets in the way sometimes. Louisa had the kids and was working those odd hours; my law firm has taken on several new clients.' Her bottom lipped trembled again. 'I was actually going to phone Tuesday night, but one of my clients rang up in a bit of a mess and I spent half the night trying to sort the bloody idiot out.'

'Is there a name for this client?' asked Hardwick casually.

Hellard gave a humourless smile. 'You know I can't do

that, Sergeant. But if you're looking for a way to confirm my whereabouts, he called my business landline back at my flat. But good luck trying to determine his identity – let's just say he's the sort of person who prefers not to register his mobile phone.'

'Just crossing the Ts and dotting the Is,' said Hardwick.

'Of course.' She paused. 'Look, I'm a solicitor, so I know you'll be looking very hard at Ben right now.'

'What do you think we'll find?'

Hellard said nothing, instead pouring herself a fresh glass of water from the jug on the table in the smart interview room.

'Ben is a sucker for a pretty Irish girl. He always has been; that's why Lou caught his eye back at university. Dad's originally from County Cork, which is good enough.'

Hardwick waited for her to continue.

'There have been occasions where Lou has felt a little . . . insecure, you might say. Nothing concrete, but she has had her doubts.' Hellard chose her words carefully. 'That being said, back then she had a bit of an issue with drink and drugs and she suffered from paranoia.'

'And what about now? Is she drinking or using drugs again?'

'Not that I've seen,' she replied. To Hardwick's ears, her words were chosen with the care of a solicitor.

'So you don't think there was anything to it?' Hardwick pressed. If Louisa was using cocaine again, it could have made her exaggerate anything that she thought she saw.

Hellard paused. 'I wouldn't say that,' she admitted. She cleared her throat. 'I'd rather you didn't share this with anyone, but I suggested that perhaps Ben's Wednesday night football training and pub visits might not be a great idea and that maybe now she was working each night, and Ben was caring for the girls, this might put an end to anything. Assuming there was anything to put an end to,' she added hastily.

'And could there have been?' asked Hardwick.

A long pause. 'Perhaps.'

'Can I ask your opinion of Ben?' Hardwick left the question deliberately ambiguous.

'He's a good man,' Hellard stated firmly. 'I truly believe that. As you probably know, we all met at university. I've known him as long as Lou has. If he has been playing around, I will be absolutely furious with him. But what I can say, with certainty, is that he loves Lou and she loves him. I know you have to do your job – and I've represented a number of clients over the years who've abused their partners, or worse. But I will tell you this for free: I don't believe Ben could harm a hair on Lou's head, nor do I believe she could have left those girls, and you are never going to convince me otherwise.'

*　*　*

Louisa Greenland's father, Domnall Keane, was a short, stocky man with thinning grey hair that might once have been the same lustrous black as his daughter's. Warren had opted to interview him. Her mother was due in later; Ben had suggested it might be better if they were interviewed separately, and if possible didn't bump into one another.

The man cradled his cup of coffee in both hands. His eyes were red, and his Irish accent, tempered by decades living in England, was gravelly. The smart interview room was designed to put visitors at ease. Its soft chairs and pastel shades were ideal for breaking bad news, comforting loved ones, and even interviewing traumatised witnesses and suspects. It now also served the best coffee in the building.

'Lou had her problems. A bit of depression when the kids were born and she liked a drink rather more than was good for her.' He looked rueful. 'She gets that from me, I'm afraid.

'But recently, things were looking up. She started this business, P@mper, a couple of years ago. Hand-made hampers full of smelly

53

stuff – you know, the sort of thing women use in the bathroom. She'd just landed a big contract with some gym company.'

'Do you know if things were all right at home?' asked Warren.

Keane shrugged. 'Far as I know. She was working long hours, but Ben's a good lad. He's stepped up and done his part, babysitting the girls each night, whilst Lou ran her business.' He corrected himself. 'Sorry, Lou's always on at me not to be so patronising. Ben's their dad, not a babysitter.' He looked at Warren's wedding ring. 'Sorry if I offended.'

'Not to worry,' said Warren. 'So, you think everything at home was OK?'

'Of course, why wouldn't it be? Lou always said everything was fine.'

'And her relationship with Ben?'

Keane smiled. 'Like I said, a great lad. She married well – sorry that sounds wrong. I don't mean the money, just that he's a really lovely bloke,' he corrected himself, looking embarrassed.

'What do you mean?'

'I mean she loved him and married him because he's a good man, not because his family are wealthy.'

'I didn't realise that,' said Warren. 'How do you define wealthy?' From the size of their house and the age of their car, the Greenlands appeared to be living on a modest income.

Keane gave a chuckle. 'Well I didn't ask to see his portfolio before I agreed to let him marry my daughter, but I know his father ran a very successful business, which his mother, Angelina, sold when he passed away.'

Warren felt his excitement rise. Could this be the motive for Louisa's disappearance? A kidnapping for ransom? It had been over three days; had anyone contacted Ben and asked for money? He thought back to PC Lederer's suspicion that Ben had a second mobile phone.

'Do you know if Ben has access to that money?' he asked.

'Not directly,' said Keane. 'It went to his mother; he'll inherit his share when she dies. She was very generous when they got married.' He chuckled. 'Saved me a fortune. But I know she is reluctant to give him a handout, unless he really needs it – not that Lou would take one anyway; she's determined to run her business all by herself. Giving him money would put his mother in a bit of an awkward position with Ben's brother.'

'In what way?'

Keane shifted uncomfortably. 'I'm not one to gossip, mind, but I'm sure you'll find out anyway. Ben's younger brother, Darren, is a bit of a troublemaker. He's been in and out of prison a few times.' He looked embarrassed. 'I don't know what went wrong there. Ben is such a lovely bloke, but Darren . . . well he's a wee shite. He's a junkie and hit his ex-girlfriend, from what I've heard. But family is family, and Angelina is a very fair-minded woman. If she gave Ben money, then she'd have to give Darren the same amount.

'Unfortunately, she knows that if she gave Darren any money, he'd just . . .' He mimed injecting into his arm. 'He'd be dead in a week. All very sad.'

'Did Louisa have much contact with Darren?' asked Warren. His mind was already filling with potential motives.

'I doubt it,' said Keane. 'I can't imagine they'd have much in common. You know what family is like; there are certain things you have to do, like birthdays and Christmas, but I can't see her and Ben choosing to socialise with him.'

Warren decided to change the subject and let his subconscious chew on what he'd been told.

'I believe Louisa has a sister.' He forced himself to use the present tense, determined to keep the tone positive.

Keane gave a short laugh. 'Yes, Stephanie. Completely different kettle of fish.'

Warren blinked. 'Really, I thought they were very similar?'

'Oh physically, they are. And Marianne and I somehow timed it so they both came along within twelve months and ended up in the same year at school. Not that we planned it that way.' He looked upwards and crossed himself. 'I still haven't decided if giving us two of them was God's reward to a good Catholic couple, or punishment for . . .' The well-rehearsed joke petered out as he realised what he was saying.

He took a deep, shuddering breath, before forcing himself to continue, his voice thick with emotion.

'By the time they were old enough to go to school, Lou and Steph were like peas in a pod. Everyone assumed they were non-identical twins. Lou was the youngest and she would follow Steph around like a puppy; not that Steph minded. We had a three-bedroom house, but the girls insisted we get bunk beds and let them both sleep in one room and turn the other one into a playroom. They were like that until they left for university. But personality-wise, they are completely different. I don't know if it's because she's the eldest, but Steph is a bit more serious. She was always going to be a lawyer. Lou was more creative and loved a good party. It was Marianne who convinced her to study some-thing sensible at university, like Business. Not that I had much influence by then.' He looked sad. 'Which is nobody's fault but mine; Marianne did a fantastic job with them. Anyway, Lou got her degree and used it for a few years, but the corporate world didn't suit her. She really wanted to be her own boss and put her artistic skills to use. She set up P@mper a couple of years ago. It's perfect; she gets to be creative, whilst the skills from her degree help her run her business.'

'Louisa and Stephanie remained close whilst they were at university, I believe?' prompted Warren.

'Yes, they both went to UME here in Middlesbury and managed to get placed in the same halls of residence in the first year, then shared a house for the next two years.'

'And that's where Louisa met Ben?'

'Yes, they were all in halls in the first year and he lived with them in the second and third year. I don't know when they

56

officially became an item, but his name kept cropping up and by the time they graduated, they were going steady.'

'Stephanie tells us she hadn't spoken to Louisa for a fortnight and hadn't been up to Middlesbury for longer. Given how close they were, that seems a little odd. Did something happen between them?'

Keane frowned. 'I'm not really sure. They always seem fine together whenever we all meet up. Look, what you have to realise is that their mother and I had a really messy divorce, but even before we finally split, we weren't in a good place.' He cleared his throat. 'Both of us have to take our share of the blame, but I'll admit it was mostly my fault. The girls were only young when things started to get really bad; I think we probably should have called it quits at least a year or two sooner than we did. We stayed together as long as we did for the girls' sake, but we really shouldn't have. Either way, it meant they relied on each other for support more than they should have.'

'When they finished university, Lou and Ben stayed in Middlesbury, and Steph headed down to London to finish her training and got a position with a really good law firm.' He smiled, the pride in his voice evident. 'Lou and Ben eventually married, and a year later Steph tied the knot.' A wave of sadness crossed his face. 'Unfortunately, that didn't work out. In the meantime, I guess they just drifted apart.'

'Going back to Louisa,' said Warren. 'Do you have any ideas why she might have decided to leave?'

'No, nothing.' His eyes started to fill with tears. 'That's why I'm so worried. Everything was great; why would she just disappear?'

Without warning, he grabbed Warren's hand. 'Please don't tell me she'll come home when she's ready, DCI Jones. I'll admit I'm not the best dad in the world, but a father knows when his wee girl is in trouble.' He dropped Warren's hand, looking embarrassed.

'I promise you, we're doing everything we can to find your daughter,' said Warren, his voice catching, the intensity of the man's emotion affecting him more than he'd expected. He couldn't bring himself to add "and bring her home".

'Thank you,' whispered Keane.

* * *

'We have a potential motive for Louisa Greenland's disappearance,' said Warren. He updated the team on what Domnall Keane had just told him.

'A kidnapping for ransom,' said Sutton. 'It would certainly answer a lot of questions.'

'It could also mean she's still alive,' said Richardson.

'If Ben is being extorted, then presumably he will have needed to ask his mother for the money,' said Ruskin. 'Should we bring her in for questioning?'

Warren thought for a moment. 'Not yet,' he decided. 'First of all, we need to confirm her father's story. I don't think he was lying to me, but he may be mistaken. If he is correct though, I've been thinking about who our suspects might be. Assuming it isn't a stranger who got wind of Angelina's fortune and decided Louisa and Ben might be the best way to gain access to it, it could be someone a lot closer to home, and we don't want her tipping them off.'

'You're thinking Darren?' said Sutton. 'Angelina may not want to give Ben any money, but I reckon she'd cough up if her daughter-in-law was kidnapped. Darren could be going through Ben or direct to Angelina. Maybe that's who Ben was speaking to on the phone in the bathroom, when Kevin Lederer overheard him?'

'Unless she keeps the money under her mattress, I should be able to access Angelina Greenland's financial records,' said Pymm. 'I can get the bank to flag me if there are any suspicious cash transactions.'

'Do it,' ordered Warren. 'But let's not just assume Ben is an innocent party in all this. He and Louisa are struggling financially; P@mper could really use a cash injection. What's to stop him staging Louisa's kidnapping? He then goes to his mum, cap in hand, and begs for her help?'

'Could Darren still be involved?' suggested Hardwick. 'He could do the actual kidnapping so Ben can stay home with the girls and build an alibi, then split the money?'

'That could work,' said Hutchinson. 'But at the risk of complicating things further, what about Russell Myrie? He's a shifty little sod; is it just a coincidence, or is he in on it? It would be a change in offending pattern, but if there's money involved . . .'

'Could he know Darren? They're both ex-cons,' suggested Sutton. 'He and Myrie may have cooked up this whole thing between them, with or without Ben's knowledge.'

'All those scenarios are possible,' said Warren. 'And finding Darren remains a priority. But there is one more we haven't considered. What if Louisa is in on the whole thing?'

Chapter 7

'I've just had a very interesting conversation with Louisa's bank manager,' said Pymm. 'Once I faxed over a copy of the warrant, she was very obliging.'

'Faxed?' said Ruskin. 'I thought they went out of fashion in the Seventies?' He shook his head. 'It's a good job there are still some of you oldies around – I wouldn't even know how to turn the machine on. Ow!' he yelped as Pymm's crutch caught him on the back of his calf.

'As I was saying,' said Pymm. 'The conversation was quite illuminating. Apparently, Louisa applied for an extension to her existing business loan when Holistics first contacted her, but they did a risk analysis and declined it. In her bank manager's view, P@mper was barely making the loan repayments for the initial business loan. Ben and Louisa had already remortgaged their house and were only making the minimum payments on two credit cards. The contract with Holistics, whilst potentially lucrative, had a sale or return clause. If they didn't sell all those hampers over the Christmas period, Louisa could potentially end up with a garage full of unsold merchandise. The bank manager advised against her taking the risk.'

'Did she say how Louisa reacted?' asked Warren.

'Not well. She was quite tearful, apparently. She admits she felt quite sorry for her, and suggested that if she were in Louisa's position, she would look into getting a part-time job to place the family on a firmer financial footing and run P@mper as a sideline.'

'It doesn't look as though she took her advice,' said Sutton. 'And it sounds as though Louisa wasn't entirely honest with her family about the outcome of her meeting at the bank.'

Warren was thoughtful. 'When did she receive the decision from the bank?' he asked.

'January 23rd,' said Pymm.

'And when did she order all those bulk materials?'

'February 5th.'

'That's barely a fortnight later,' said Warren. 'I'd be interested to know when she signed the contract with Holistics. It might give us an indication of her state of mind. Did she sign the contract, then find out she couldn't get financing? Or was she denied the bank loan, but decided to take the risk anyway?'

'And what if Ben found out she had just gambled their house and livelihood?' asked Sutton. 'Could that be enough for him to kill her?'

* * *

'Sir, we've got access to the cloud server storing the CCTV for Louisa's industrial unit.'

'What have you found?' asked Warren; Richardson's tone was grim.

'It's what we haven't found,' she said. 'There is no stored footage.'

'What do you mean?'

'Blank screen, no input.'

'You are joking?

'She had the basic subscription to the cloud service. The camera is set to ultra-high definition, so it gobbled her data allowance up

61

in fourteen days, and started overwriting older footage. Whatever was already on there has been replaced by a blank screen flashing "no input".'

'Wouldn't she have got a warning email or something?' asked Sutton.

'Only if she configured the system properly, and most people don't.'

'What about the physical drive?' asked Warren. 'Isn't the cloud service just a backup for whatever is on the hard drive?'

'The unit is the cheapest on the market. Its disk is even smaller than the cloud backup. Whatever it did record has been over-written.' Her voice became even more grim. 'But that's not the most worrying thing. The camera is working fine, but it's been disconnected from the unit.'

'How?' asked Warren.

'There's a network cable from the back of the recorder that supplies power and receives data. That's been unplugged.'

'Do we know when?' asked Sutton.

'Yes, the technician accessed the event log. The signal disappeared at 18.04 on April 15th. But like I said, she hadn't configured it to alert her by email. She didn't have a dedicated computer monitor and mouse for the recorder; she did every-thing via an app on her phone. Unless she checked it regularly, she'd never notice. And it doesn't look as if she even logged on to change the system time when the clocks went forward in March.'

Warren couldn't blame her. He and Susan had installed CCTV after the Delmarno incident some years before. After the novelty wore off, he hardly ever bothered to look at it, just trusting it was chugging away in the background. He'd installed a top-of-the-range system at the new house and had been diligently making sure it worked properly, but aside from using it to track a missing parcel thoughtfully placed in the recycling bin on collection day, he'd not accessed it for a fortnight.

'Assuming the cable didn't randomly fall out of its own accord, then somebody had to disconnect it from inside her unit,' said Warren. 'Get forensics to check the recorder and the cables for fingerprints and DNA.'

Chapter 8

It was clear that whilst Louisa got her dark hair from her father, she'd got her petite build from her mother. Marianne Keane had light blonde hair, streaked with ash grey. Her skin had the healthy glow of someone who'd just spent a fortnight in Australia, although worry and jet lag had left dark smudges underneath her eyes.

She cradled the coffee Warren had made her with both hands.

'Domnall was always a poor judge of character,' she said, her voice scathing. 'As soon as he found out Ben was a Manchester United fan, that was all he needed to hear.'

'I assume you weren't as taken with him?' said Warren. They'd spent the last few minutes talking about Louisa and reasons why she may have voluntarily disappeared. The one thing she and her former husband agreed upon, was that Louisa's previous issues with her mental health, and the stress she was under with her business, would not have been enough for her to take off without telling people. If nothing else, she'd never have abandoned her two daughters.

She took a long swig of her coffee, obviously choosing her words carefully. 'I don't doubt Ben loves her, and she certainly loves him, but he was, how shall we say . . . a bit of a charmer?'

Her tone of voice made it clear that it wasn't a compliment. 'Believe me, I spent enough years married to Louisa's father to recognise a man with a wandering eye, when I see one.'

'Do you think he was cheating on her?' asked Warren.

'I've never seen or heard anything concrete,' she admitted. 'But I've watched him when we're out; like how long he takes to pay for drinks if there is a pretty girl behind the bar. I remember one time, we'd all gone out for a meal to do some wedding planning. Ben took our food orders to the bar. I passed him on the way to the bathroom and he was chatting to the server – a pretty, little dark-haired girl; couldn't have been more than twenty. They both had their phones out. When he returned to the table he was all apologies, saying there was a queue. There wasn't – the place was half-empty.'

'You believe they could have been swapping numbers?'

'That's what I suspect.' Her lip curled. 'That was a little over a week before he got married.'

'Did Louisa ever say anything? Any worries on that score?'

'No. But then, the girls have never been very good at sharing that sort of thing with us.' A look of shame crossed her face. 'That's our fault – me and Domnall. When our marriage collapsed, the girls stopped telling us things; they just dealt with it between them.' She cleared her throat and blushed slightly. 'When Louisa started . . . you know . . . I knew nothing about it until Steph came to me and said she needed some extra sanitary products. I could see something wasn't quite right and when I asked her why she needed more already, she admitted that Louisa had gone to her for help.' Her voice caught. 'She said I had enough to deal with and didn't want to worry me. She was only thirteen. That's when I told Domnall enough was enough, and it wasn't helping any of us trying to fix our marriage.'

'Do you think that's why they went to the same university?' asked Warren.

'I've always thought so. Louisa received her offer of a place first and accepted immediately. Steph got several offers, some from really good universities. I'm certain she chose UME because that's where Lou was going. She was still being big sister.'

'When we spoke to Stephanie, we got the impression she and Louisa had drifted apart recently. Domnall wasn't really sure why. Do you have any insights?'

She rolled her eyes. 'That man wanders through life without a care in the world.'

'He seemed to think it was because Stephanie moved to London. Do you think it was more than that?'

'I think it was more complicated. I wouldn't say they necessarily fell out.' She paused. 'I think Steph is a little jealous of Louisa; perhaps even a little resentful. Not about money or anything – she's already a partner in a law firm and owns a flat in some swanky development in central London. But she was always the responsible older sister. Even at university, she looked out for her.' The woman looked a little self-conscious. 'I'm sure you know that a few years ago, Louisa had a bit of an accident after she'd been drinking. Steph arranged for a top-class lawyer, and she managed to avoid a custodial sentence. Louisa spent some time as an outpatient at a private clinic for people with substance issues; there's no way she and Ben could have afforded that.

'The thing is, Louisa was always the free-spirited one, and popular with the boys. It was probably inevitable she and Ben would get married one day, and I believe Steph felt jealous that Louisa seemed to get all the luck on that front.

'I think that was why she announced, out of the blue, she was bringing a plus-one we'd never even met to Louisa's wedding. It caused all sorts of problems with the catering and seating arrangements. That was in June. Christmas Day they announced their engagement, and within twelve months I was wearing another new hat.'

'I understand the marriage didn't last?' said Warren.

'No, and I think that caused some tension between the girls.

Louisa had reservations about Colin from the outset. He was twenty years older than Steph and had been divorced twice before. He already had several children from his previous marriages who Steph didn't get along with. He didn't want any more, and she couldn't talk him around. They were divorced within three years.

'To add insult to injury, shortly before they split, she was made a partner in the law firm she works at. The senior partner rebranded the firm as "Brindstocke and Hellard", her married name. He didn't want to do that again, so she has had to keep her married name and is reminded daily of her mistake.'

Warren winced.

'I don't think Louisa was insensitive enough to say "I told you so"', continued Keane, 'but I stumbled on them arguing the following Christmas after a few too many and Steph stormed off shouting: "Not all of us are lucky enough to have bagged our soulmate". It all seemed to blow over by the morning, but I can't remember them falling out like that before. Looking back, I think that's why they aren't as close as they once were.'

'Let's go back to Ben. I believe his family is quite wealthy,' said Warren, moving the conversation back towards what he really wanted to speak about.

'Yes, although you wouldn't know it,' she said. 'His father died when he was a child. He'd run a very successful haulage business. Angelina, Ben's mother, had a good job as a teacher and didn't want to give that up, so she sold the business and carried on living the way she always had.'

'What happened to the money?' asked Warren casually.

'Not a lot,' she said, with a bitter chuckle. 'I guess she paid off her mortgage, but she continued working. She took early retirement when Louisa and Ben had Molly, so she could enjoy the grandkids a bit more, but most it of ended up in the bank; Ben and his brother will get that one day, I suppose.'

'I understand Ben and Louisa were finding it hard work juggling childcare with them both working,' said Warren, choosing his words carefully. 'If it's not a rude question, can I ask why his mother doesn't babysit a little more, to take the pressure off?'

She gave a wry smile. 'Well, as much as Angelina enjoys being a grandmother, she's also enjoying her retirement. She jokes that she has no idea how she ever found the time to work.'

'Did she ever help Louisa and Ben financially?' he asked.

Keane looked a little uncomfortable. 'When they got married, she was very generous, but I don't think she's given them much more. It's a bit awkward for her. Ben's brother is a drug addict. Angelina is scrupulously fair to her boys; she'd feel obliged to give Darren the same as Ben, which wouldn't be a good idea.' She shook her head. 'The poor woman is in a terrible position. Giving Darren money would probably stop him committing burglaries and shoplifting, but I'm sure she knows that funding his drug habit is only going to kill him. I think she's offered to pay for rehab for him, but it doesn't appear he's taken her up on the offer.'

'What about a loan to help P@mper?' asked Warren.

'No. Louisa got an extension to her bank loan. She was determined to stand on her own two feet. I've always been very proud of her.'

Warren decided not to mention that Louisa's application to the bank had been refused. He could think of no reasonable justification for breaching her financial privacy at the moment.

Taking a deep breath, he decided to broach the elephant in the room. 'You and Mr Keane are quite confident Louisa wouldn't disappear of her own accord. If that is the case – and I say *if* – can you think of anyone who might have wished her any harm? Any worries that she mentioned?'

'I've been thinking about nothing else since I heard she was missing,' she said. 'And I'm at a complete loss. Louisa is popular and kind. She has a great circle of friends. She's made a few mistakes, but haven't we all? Nobody got hurt. I know you're probably looking into Ben right now, but as much as I distrust him to keep it in his trousers, I can't imagine him harming her.

Whatever their problems were, I know she loved him; she'd never have left him or the girls.'

She shook her head. 'I just can't believe it's happening again.'

Warren blinked. 'What do you mean?'

'It's like that poor girl Sinead back when they were at university.'

Chapter 9

'Sinead McCaffrey went missing in April 2008 from the University of Middle England. She was twenty-one and in the final year of her biology degree. She was the housemate of Ben Greenland, and Louisa and Stephanie Keane, as they were back then.'

Everyone in the briefing room sat up straighter. DI Camilla Wong from the Missing Persons Unit was a short, dark-haired woman in her late thirties. Her voice was quiet, but she commanded everyone's attention in the room. 'It isn't listed fully on the PNC, as it wasn't recorded as a crime, which is why it didn't come up in your initial search.'

She projected a photograph onto the briefing room wall. 'This was taken a few days before she went missing.'

The image was one of a dark-haired woman, petite and pretty, with hazel eyes and a sprinkling of freckles across her nose. She was smiling at the camera, holding a can of supermarket own-brand lager.

'I remember those days,' said Pymm. 'If I never see another can of that stuff, it'll be too soon.'

'She was reported missing by another housemate, Caitlin O'Shaughnessy, after she hadn't seen her for a couple of days,' said Wong, directing a scowl at Pymm. It was fair enough; Pymm's wit wasn't always appropriately timed. 'The housemates were starting their finals, so it wasn't unusual for them to not see each other for a while, but Sinead missed her regular badminton game, and her phone was turned off. Her study group were getting concerned as well. She wasn't a big social media user, this was 2008 remember, but she hadn't posted anything on Facebook for a few days. Caitlin found her parents' phone number back in Ireland and called to see if she'd gone home without telling anyone, but they hadn't spoken to her either.

'One of the lads in the house managed to get the door open to her bedroom, and found it empty, with the bed made and her bookbag and laptop still there. They called the university welfare office, who eventually called the police. Sinead is still listed as missing, although she was declared legally dead three years ago.'

'Why wasn't it recorded as a crime?' asked Sutton.

'No evidence of foul play,' said Wong. 'A partial record is listed on the PNC, but neither Louisa nor Ben are linked to it as they were just witnesses, which is why we only just discovered it. Unfortunately, a lot of students go missing around exam time. Usually they turn up in a few days; sometimes we find a body.

'Her personal tutor said Sinead had been struggling with her workload since before Christmas and had recently missed a dissertation deadline. He was concerned enough to put in a referral to the university welfare office who arranged counselling and managing workload sessions. Her GP prescribed anti-anxiety medication.

'Her course mates said she was very stressed and admitted that she had been self-medicating – drinking hard at the weekend and smoking a lot of cannabis to relax. Of course, that just made things worse. Her occasional Facebook posts in the run-up to the disappearance suggested she was finding it hard to cope. Her housemates confessed they knew she was struggling, but didn't know about the counselling and didn't realise things had got so bad. They were all in the same boat.'

'Were they living in halls at the time?' asked Ruskin.

'Unfortunately not. There were six of them renting a private house down Potter Street.'

Potter Street was a cheap area popular with students from UME. Warren doubted there would have been much in the way of CCTV. Wong confirmed as much.

'It was a little before my time, but I've reviewed our case file and a thorough investigation was performed. They did all the usual – medical, social media, bank accounts and phone records, but nothing came up; she simply vanished. She took her purse and keys with her, and one of the girls thinks she was wearing her favourite green T-shirt. We don't believe she had more than a few pounds cash.

'No witnesses remembered seeing her. The local cab firms denied she was ever a passenger, and the buses didn't have CCTV back then. We narrowed her disappearance down to a window of just over forty-eight hours. She was filmed leaving the university library, alone, with her bookbag and laptop at four p.m. on April 9th. Her phone left the network shortly after it arrived home and was found on her bedside table; the time between her leaving the library and the phone arriving home matched how long it usually took her to walk home. The other housemates were in and out at all hours and none could recall speaking to her. Her shelf in the fridge was almost empty, although nobody could remember the last time anything was eaten from it, and she wasn't a big one for fresh food with short use-by dates.'

'What about alibis for her housemates?' asked Warren.

'Limited,' admitted Wong. 'You know what students are like; they all claim to have been studying hard for their exams. We have a few snatches of them on CCTV from around campus, but not enough to provide satisfying alibis, and the location data from their phones is not much use. The university had a strict policy around mobile phone use in libraries and lecture halls, so their phones were turned on and off regularly. None of their handsets left the house on either of the two nights between Sinead's last sighting and her being reported missing on Friday the 11th, although even back then most people probably knew phones could be tracked, so I wouldn't read too much into that.'

Warren tapped his teeth thoughtfully. 'Let's assume, for the sake of argument, that she didn't disappear voluntarily. What do we know about her relationships with the other housemates?'

'According to the witnesses questioned at the time, they all got on very well. They'd known each other since halls in the first year, and this was their second year renting the house, so things can't have been too bad. I have a picture of them taken the day they moved in.'

'Wow,' said Hardwick. The image showed six smiling young people, crowded into the corner of a large kitchen. 'According to Stephanie, Ben was a "sucker for a pretty Irish girl",' she said.

'Then he must have loved living there,' said Sutton.

In the centre of the picture stood Louisa and Stephanie, dressed almost identically. Warren was hard-pressed to tell them apart. Flanking them were two more young women. They wore differing hairstyles, and the woman on the left was dressed in a flowing dress, rather than jeans and a T-shirt yet they too could have passed for sisters of Louisa and Stephanie.

'I think the one on the left is the woman I met leaving Ben Greenland's yesterday,' said Hardwick. 'Caitlin O'Shaughnessy.'

That meant that the one on the right must be Sinead. At either end of the line were two young men. Ben was immediately recognisable; his blue T-shirt was tight across his chest, with "University of Middle England Football Club" in white writing. The man on the opposite end was taller, with pale, acned skin and red hair, and wore the same T-shirt as Ben.

'At the risk of sounding like an old perv,' said Pymm. 'Ben was a very good-looking young man.'

'He still is,' said Hardwick, before blushing slightly.

'Louisa and Ben were probably together, at least casually, by this point,' said Warren, pulling the discussion back on track. 'But given what we've heard about him, I'd be interested to know what his relationship was like with his other female housemates, especially Sinead.'

'We don't really have much,' admitted Wong. 'There's nothing in the file to suggest she had any sort of relationship with any of her housemates. Outside of the house, Sinead had one or two boyfriends over the three years, but nothing serious. Obviously they were all questioned. Apparently, she was quite shy and wasn't one for picking up men in pubs or nightclubs, and was so focused on her work in her final year that her friends don't think she was dating. She never mentioned anyone special, or anyone she found a creep for that matter. But like I said, what we have is limited.'

Warren twisted his bottom lip thoughtfully. 'OK, this is a little too much of a coincidence for me. Let's track down these former housemates and re-interview them. This was only eleven years ago. If they were that close at university, they might still be in contact with the Greenlands, so if nothing else I want their insights on their current relationship.'

'Caitlin is due in later,' offered Hardwick.

Warren turned back to Wong. 'Who was the lead officer on the case? Can we speak to them?'

'He's retired, but still lives locally,' said Wong. 'I already contacted him, and he was very eager to speak to you. He describes it as the case that never left him.'

Chapter 10

George Rutherford had retired a little over three years previously. He arrived at Middlesbury CID within an hour of the briefing ending.

'When Camilla first called, I thought for a moment that she was ringing to say they had found her,' he said, over a cup of tea in Warren's office. He looked sad. 'Eleven years. Even if they found her body, it would be something, you know?' He cleared his throat. 'When I left the unit, I requested that if they ever found out what happened to Sinead, then – if at all possible – they let me be the one to tell her parents.'

'This was the case you couldn't let go of,' said Warren quietly.

'Yeah. Sinead was the same age as my youngest daughter, who was also away at university. Sinead's parents, Padraig and Alois, flew over from Ireland; neither of them had ever been to England before. I shouldn't have got so close to them, but they were completely lost; they didn't know what to do with themselves. I introduced them to Tania, my wife, who has family in Ireland, and pretty soon they were practically living with us. I guess I figured that if my little girl ever went missing, I'd want a kind face . . .' He cleared his throat again. 'Anyway, the days became weeks, and there were no sightings of her. It was as if she'd just vanished into thin air. After a month, the case started to wind down, and Padraig and Alois had to return to Ireland; they had left their son with his grandparents and had already stayed longer than they should have.

'I moved on to other cases, but we never closed it. I stayed in touch with her parents; they came over every year and I'd use someone I knew at the *Middlesbury Reporter* to run another story, but we'd never hear anything new. Eventually my contact left the paper and that was it.

'Padraig never got over it; he died of cancer a few years back, but I always thought it was the broken heart that did him in. After he passed, Alois applied to have Sinead declared dead – I couldn't blame her; she needed to move on. I visited her in Ireland last year for a memorial service on the tenth anniversary, and she still dreams that Sinead will walk through the door one day.'

It was a tragic story and one that clearly haunted the man years later.

'Why are you interested in her again?' Rutherford asked. 'Camilla told me you haven't got any new leads.'

Warren outlined Louisa Greenland's disappearance. 'It could all be a tragic coincidence,' he concluded, 'but I can't afford to dismiss anything. I'd really appreciate it if you could add some more detail to the case file.'

'Of course.' He settled back in his chair, and his eyes took on a faraway cast. 'I remember the house very clearly. It was an old family home – two floors with a loft conversion and an extension on the rear. Sinead was at the front, in what would once have been the living room; it was the biggest bedroom in the house – apparently, she won it in a card game. Behind it, the landlord had knocked through the old dining room into the kitchen and put a sofa and TV in there. That was where they did most of their socialising. There was a small shower room and toilet, and the extension at the rear had been converted into a bedroom. That was where Caitlin slept. The floor above had two rooms and a bathroom. The lads, Curtis and Ben, had a room each. Ben was at the front over Sinead as I recall, and Curtis was over the old dining room. The loft conversion had been divided into two, and the twins, as everyone nicknamed them, stayed in there.'

'So Sinead was on the ground floor at the front. What was access like?'

'They had double-glazing, and we found no signs of forced entry on either the main door, her bedroom door or the windows. We printed everything, but they were in and out of each other's rooms all the time, and it's not like the landlord cleaned all the door handles when he let the place to new tenants. We checked him out, obviously, but he was on holiday when she disappeared.'

'What about the relationships between the housemates?'

'Everyone we interviewed said they were all really good mates. They were even planning on going travelling when they graduated. They were all very worried about Sinead and felt upset and guilty that none of them had realised how much she was struggling with her mental health. But I'm guessing you really want to ask about Ben?'

'He is a person of interest in his wife's disappearance,' admitted Warren.

'Where to start? I know that by the time Sinead disappeared, he was with Louisa and I knew that they got married; they all came over to Ireland for the memorial service. But I also know he had a bit of a wandering eye back then.'

'In what way?'

'One of his friends, a big boorish idiot on the football team, referred to the house as "Ben and Curtis's harem". From what I can tell, Ben had a thing for pretty Irish girls and could really turn the charm on when he wanted to.'

There was that phrase again, Warren noted. Was it significant?

'Do you know if he had any sort of relationship with Sinead?' asked Warren.

'I honestly don't know. I'm sure you've seen the photographs of them all. I think Sinead would definitely have been his type, but I never heard anything concrete. By all accounts she was quite shy and the stereotypical good Irish Catholic girl, but then maybe he liked a challenge? It wouldn't have been too difficult to sneak into her room late at night if they were up to anything. The kitchen was between Sinead and Caitlin, and his room was above Sinead's, so they could probably have got away with it if they were discreet.'

'What about Curtis?'

'No idea. Again, I never heard of anything.'

'How would you characterise the housemates' reactions?'

Rutherford pursed his lips. 'Everyone reacts differently – you know that. Caitlin took it really hard. She was from Dublin and had gone to sixth form in England so she was a bit more street-wise than Sinead, who was from a very rural part of Ireland; I think she blamed herself for not realising how bad Sinead was. The twins had each other; Louisa was extremely upset, and Steph had to play big sister. Curtis was angry mostly. You know what young men are like; he desperately wanted to do something, but he couldn't.'

'And Ben?' prompted Warren.

'He was quiet. He was upset and worried, but if anything, I would say he was in shock.' Rutherford paused. 'I remember that after she had been missing for a month, he asked to speak to me. For an update. He kept on asking me why I thought she had gone and if I had heard of any reason she might have been upset and left. It was a little odd, as he was asking me the same questions I'd been asking him. He was convinced she had walked out and wanted to know if I'd heard anything. It was strange. In some ways he was acting guilty, but in other ways not. It wasn't like he'd killed her and it was eating him up inside, rather he felt that he'd done something that could have caused her to leave.'

'He chose Louisa over her?' suggested Warren.

'It's crossed my mind,' admitted Rutherford.

'OK, gut feeling. What do you think happened to Sinead?'

Rutherford gave a long sigh. 'I don't know, and that's the truth. On the one hand, her parents never believed she left voluntarily. She'd never do that to them. She'd never do it to her little brother; he was only eleven years old and she doted on him. Even if she did need a break to get her head together, surely she'd have contacted them eventually?

'And if she killed herself, where is her body? We're a town in the middle of the countryside. We're what, seventy miles from the coast? And there are no fast-flowing rivers that could wash her body out to sea. It's been eleven years. If her body hasn't turned up, you have to ask if somebody has hidden it. We did look into the people-trafficking angle, but it never really gained any traction.

'Then, on the other hand, I read her reports from the university counselling team and went back through all her social media posts and text messages. With hindsight, she was clearly on the verge of a major mental health crisis. But without concrete evidence of foul play, we didn't have the resources to trawl through thousands of hours of footage to see if she caught a bus or train to a suicide spot.

'And of course, she could have just decided to start all over again. Her parents put themselves into significant debt to fund her studies over here, and she was the first in her family to go to university; everyone back home was really proud of her. The counsellor said that Sinead was convinced she was going to fail her course and let everyone down, and I imagine the weed and booze hardly helped matters. Maybe she did just walk out? And once a few weeks or months have passed, it becomes harder and harder to go back.

'Honestly, Warren, I really don't know what happened to that poor girl. And it's bothered me for eleven years.'

Chapter 11

Warren decided to interview Caitlin O'Shaughnessy alongside Hardwick. DSI Roehampton had made no comment when he mentioned he was planning to partner Karen, and he took it as a tacit seal of approval. He'd decided when Roehampton first took over to continue running cases the way he always had; if she wanted him to start behaving more like a DCI and stay behind his desk, then he'd deal with it when she brought it up. The remaining housemate, Curtis Redmayne, lived just outside Paris – he was already on the Eurostar.

Caitlin O'Shaughnessy declined Warren's offer of a coffee. 'I don't imagine you serve herbal tea?' she'd said, her half-smile suggesting she could guess at the answer. Perhaps he should have brought Rachel Pymm instead; the two of them could have compared notes and maybe he'd have found out what on earth Pymm had been drinking all week. He'd caught a whiff of it and was none the wiser; it looked like she'd poured boiling water over the contents of her compost heap. He half-expected to see worms wriggling in it.

'I see you decided to stay in Middlesbury after you finished university?' said Hardwick.

'Yes, it's such a lovely town. The financial crash in 2008

happened just after we all graduated, which was rather bad timing. I had to decide whether or not to return to Ireland or stay in England. With Middlesbury on the express train line to London and so close to Cambridge, I figured there would be more opportunities to apply for jobs and internships here. These days I work remotely, freelancing for publications all over the world, but I've been here so long I can't imagine ever leaving.'

O'Shaughnessy still retained her Irish accent. Her hair was a shiny black, and her eyes a mixture of green and hazel. Even years after the group photo was taken at their house, she still bore a remarkable resemblance to Louisa and Stephanie. Was that significant? Warren found himself wondering what Sinead would look like today – or perhaps even did look like, given there was no definitive proof that she was dead.

'From what we understand of Louisa, her disappearance is very out of character,' said Hardwick. 'So we're concerned for her safety. We're trying to gain an insight into her state of mind in the run-up to her disappearance. Were you close to Louisa?'

'Of course, we lived together for three years; I was a bridesmaid at her wedding. We'd meet up when we had the time. Steph was Molly and Pippa's "official" godmother, but I was an honorary one, so I'd always get the girls a little something.'

'Did Ben meet with you also?'

'Sometimes he came. Not if it was just a girly catch-up, but we'd all get together for a meal every now and again, especially if Steph or Curtis were in town.'

'When did you last meet up with Louisa?' asked Warren.

'Longer ago than I'd have liked,' she admitted. 'Louisa was really busy with P@mper, and I'd been commissioned to write a book, so we found it hard to make the time.' Her lip trembled, but she managed to keep her voice steady. 'It's so easy to let things slip, you know? Weirdly, I think it was actually too easy to meet up. She was only ever a few miles away; in theory we could see each other at the drop of a hat. Because it was so little effort, we never went out of our way to *make* the effort. Do you understand what I'm saying?'

'I do. Sometimes it's too easy to put these things off,' said Warren. 'The last time you met up, was it just the two of you?'

She shook her head. 'No. We all got together on the anniversary of . . . well I'm sure you know.'

'The disappearance of Sinead McCaffrey,' Hardwick supplied.

'Yes. Eleven years this April. We mark it every year; all five of us from the house. Last year we went over to Ireland for the ten-year memorial, but we still came back to Middlesbury for a night.' She smiled at the memory, although there were tears in her eyes. 'We always book a table at the Abbot's Rest. It's just the way it used to be when we drank there. The landlord is even the same and he always reserves the back room for us. We kept on saying we should go back for karaoke night, just for old time's sake.' She gave a sad laugh. 'Back then Louisa, Sinead and I used to dress in matching clothes and sing as a threesome. Jesus, we were awful. We loved it though, Louisa especially. I bought Molly one of those karaoke kits you plug into the TV for Christmas. Ben always said Lou and the girls had way more enthusiasm than talent.' She wiped at a stray tear and gave a sniff.

'Poor Louisa. She didn't drink anymore, so she had to put up with the rest of us lot getting drunk and maudlin that night. She even played taxi, God love her, which is just as well. I'm not sure if an Uber would have picked up Curtis, the state he was in. It was just like the old days, although we don't get change from a twenty-pound note like we used to back then.' She paused. 'Even with one fewer person in the round.'

'Can I ask what you think happened to Sinead all those years ago?' said Warren.

O'Shaughnessy blinked, clearly not expecting to be speaking about events from so far back. 'I don't know. I never thought it made sense that she would just disappear. But then we never realised how bad things had got with her. Maybe she did walk away? Maybe she killed herself? Or maybe somebody took her? Since it happened, I've thought about it often. I read a newspaper story a few years back that said there were people-smuggling gangs operating in this part of England back then, so I've often wondered . . .' She shuddered. 'Sometimes I think it would be easier if she had committed suicide or even been killed by some psychopath. I've read about what those gangs do to girls like Sinead.'

'What was Louisa's state of mind when you all met last month?' asked Hardwick.

'God, now you're asking,' said O'Shaughnessy, clearly more comfortable talking about the present than the past. 'I don't think any of us were in a great place. The annual get-together was good for us for the first few years, but I'm not sure if it's really helping anymore. I think it might even be holding us back, especially now she's been declared dead. As to Louisa specifically? She was a bit quieter than usual, and she looked really tired. I know she was working silly hours, but it clearly wasn't healthy.'

'Did she ever mention anyone who worried her? Perhaps someone she thought was a bit creepy?' asked Warren.

'No, not really.' O'Shaughnessy looked at Hardwick. 'You know what it's like. Men making lewd comments, trying to cop a discreet – or not so discreet – eyeful when you bend over or wear a short dress. She was a good-looking woman and she got it as much as anyone, I guess. It's shit, but you kind of get used to it.' She paused for a moment. 'I know Ben's brother creeped her out. He creeps everyone out. I remember him at the wedding; I ended up having a dance with him and I had to keep his hands firmly in place.' She scowled. 'Dirty wee shite managed to grab my arse when everyone was kissing goodnight. I was single at the time and a bridesmaid, so he clearly thought I was fair game. Mind you, from what Louisa told me, whether you're single, or married to his brother, doesn't seem to bother him any. He's a junkie – not that that's any excuse.'

'What can you tell us about how things are at home? Between Louisa and Ben?' asked Warren.

'Fine as far as I know.'

Warren looked over to Hardwick, who took the silent cue. 'You said Louisa was no longer drinking. Why is that?' she asked.

O'Shaughnessy looked embarrassed. 'I imagine you already know the details, but Louisa was a bit of a party animal. She cut back when she was pregnant with the girls, obviously, but once they were born, she started again. I don't think anyone realised it was anything more serious than a couple too many on a girls' night out until she had her car accident. She was picking up Molly from nursey and had had a couple of large vodka tonics at lunchtime. Thank the Lord nobody was hurt. Anyway, that was a wake-up call. She got help and sorted herself out. As far as I know, she had been sober since.'

'And was it just alcohol?' asked Hardwick.

O'Shaughnessy shrunk into her seat. 'No,' she said eventually. 'Back at uni, she used to do a bit of coke, and I'll admit, we all smoked a bit of weed now and again.'

'Do you think she could have been using cocaine again?' asked Hardwick.

O'Shaughnessy said nothing for a few seconds. 'Shit,' she said finally. 'When we met up in April, she was very quiet. I assumed she was tired and a bit emotional. The rest of us were getting drunk and remembering the good times; Sinead loved the *craic*, so we always tried to honour that you know? Anyhow, you know how difficult it is when you're the only sober person – you feel a bit left out. Louisa disappeared off to the toilet.' She turned to Warren. 'You know what us girls are like – we never go alone, but this time she did. When she came back, she was full of energy and joined in with all the jokes and everything.'

'Do you think she could have been using it a little more regularly?' asked Warren, careful not to sound judgemental.

'I don't know,' said O'Shaughnessy. 'She never mentioned it. But back when we were at uni, we called her the queen of the all-nighter. Most of us used to make extra-strong black coffee, and I tried Pro-Plus once, but it gave me palpitations. She tried energy drinks, but they're full of sugar and she didn't want to get fat, so if she really needed to stay up late, she used coke. I always steered clear. I'm dyspraxic; my handwriting is bad enough as it is. If she was trying to stay up late every night to fill hampers, maybe she was using again?'

'Do you think Ben would know?' asked Warren.

O'Shaughnessy shook her head. 'No. I know they did a bit of weed now and again to chill out, but there's no way he would have tolerated her using anything stronger. Not after the accident.' She paused. 'Mind you, it makes sense now why she didn't apply for her driving licence again. I asked her why she hadn't; it would make their lives a lot easier if she could ferry the girls around. And it would be a lot safer than walking to and from that unit of hers late at night. She said she "didn't trust herself". I just assumed her confidence had taken a bit of a beating after the accident, but maybe she meant she didn't trust herself not to drive whilst high? And if she did have another accident, and they found traces of cocaine in her bloodstream, then that's a second offence. She'd be jailed right?'

Warren chose his next words carefully, knowing they could bring the interview to a halt.

'We've spoken to a few people who knew you all at university. There is a suggestion that Ben might have had a bit of a wandering eye?' That sounded less offensive than "was a sucker for pretty Irish girl".

'Away with you!' O'Shaughnessy laughed. 'He only ever had eyes for Louisa. That was just a bit of jealousy from some of the lads on the football team.'

'Of course,' said Warren. 'But I have to admit there have been some questions raised about his choice of housemates.'

'Pretty, dark-haired, Irish heritage,' interjected Hardwick, voicing sentiments that might sound dodgy coming from a middle-aged man.

'Just a coincidence,' Caitlin said firmly. 'There were about eighty of us in that block of halls in the first year. Ben was only a few doors down from Louisa. Sinead and I met through the Irish Students Association, and Lou and Steph used to come along on socials sometimes because they're half-Irish. Curtis was just down the corridor and played football with Ben.'

'We had to ask,' she said with a reassuring smile. 'But we've also heard suggestions Ben might have been unfaithful in recent years. Have you heard anything? Did Louisa ever mention any worries she might have on that score?'

'Complete shite,' said O'Shaughnessy forcefully.

'Thank you,' said Warren. 'Again, we needed to ask.'

Hardwick took over. 'I'm going to be honest, Caitlin, we're struggling to work out what has happened to Louisa. Do you have any suggestions? What's your gut feeling?'

O'Shaughnessy's eyes filled with tears again. 'I wish I knew. I really do. But gut feeling? She'd never leave those wee girls. When I went over yesterday, all they wanted to do was draw pictures of Mummy.'

With the interview clearly at an end, O'Shaughnessy picked up her handbag and finished her glass of water. She shook both officers' hands as they stood up.

'Oh, one more thing,' asked Warren, as she turned towards the door, 'was the meet-up to remember Sinead definitely the last time you physically met Louisa?'

'Yes, definitely,' she said.

'And have you met Ben since then?'

'No, of course not,' she said. 'At least not until I went around to see how he was coping.'

'Thank you for your time,' said Hardwick.

'We'll keep you posted, and if you hear anything or remember anything you think might be relevant, please don't hesitate to call,' said Warren.

Hardwick echoed him, handing over her business card.

After the woman had been shown out, Warren turned to Hardwick.

'Right, let's go back through the video and pick out the bits where she was lying.'

* * *

'The most obvious untruths were when we spoke about Ben's reputation as a ladies' man at university,' said Hardwick. 'She was far too quick to dismiss that, not to mention it flies in the face of everything else we've been told.'

'And the final question about whether she had seen Ben since they all got together to remember Sinead threw her off balance,' said Warren, taking over. 'She paused just a little too long and was then just a little too forceful in her denial.'

'So, what are your conclusions?' asked Roehampton, steepling her fingers, as she leaned on her desk.

The small office that Roehampton had inherited from John Grayson had changed significantly. Gone were the random pieces of golfing memorabilia and his expensive coffee machine, and in were pictures of Roehampton meeting various dignitaries. Photographs of her in uniform chronicled her career, ranging from a fresh-faced constable wearing an old-fashioned black uniform with chequerboard patterning, to her most recent formal headshot, her shoulders sporting epaulettes with a single super-intendent's crown just visible. Most striking was a photograph of Roehampton from the early 2000s, clad in full tactical gear carrying a carbine. She had left that unit some years previously but had kept up her certification and was periodically tasked as a gold commander in charge of armed operations.

The only hints of her life outside of the force were a couple of photographs of her with her daughter, now at university. Even her mug was plain white china.

'I have a few,' answered Warren. 'Some that may be relevant to Louisa's disappearance, some that are not. Some may even be relevant to Sinead McCaffrey's disappearance in addition to Louisa's.'

He referred to his notebook, where he had jotted down several ideas from the brainstorming session he'd held with the team before meeting Roehampton.

'First off, I'm going to strongly suggest that at the very least, Caitlin O'Shaughnessy holds a candle for Ben Greenland, and may have done so when they lived together.'

'No question in my mind,' said Hardwick.

'Which leaves a number of scenarios,' continued Warren. 'Most obvious is that Catlin was jealous of Louisa. She's killed Louisa and disposed of her body someplace.'

'Why now?' Roehampton countered immediately. 'Ben and Louisa have been together for what? A dozen years? They're married and have two kids. If Caitlin was so smitten, why wait until now? What changed?'

'Ben could have spurned her,' said Hardwick. 'Or, if they were already having an affair, broken it off or made it clear he would never leave Louisa.'

'Jealousy. Probably the oldest motive in history,' mused Roehampton. 'What else?'

'Louisa finds out Ben and Caitlin were having an affair,' said Warren. 'Things went horribly wrong when she confronted Ben. Perhaps Louisa even threatened to take the kids? If Caitlin was involved, or knew – or even just suspected – that's what happened, she could be covering for him.'

'Wouldn't be the first time,' agreed Roehampton.

'And it might not be the first time for Ben either,' said Hardwick.

'You're thinking Sinead McCaffrey?' asked Roehampton.

'Could be a bit of a theme here,' said Warren. 'He had been

with Louisa for some time when Sinead went missing. Perhaps Sinead and Ben had an affair, and she threatened to tell Louisa?'

Roehampton frowned. 'I get the whole thing could have been rather messy and awkward, and God knows university flings can be embarrassingly overdramatic, but murder? Seems a bit much. Where does Caitlin come in?'

'She doesn't necessarily have to,' said Warren. 'At least not directly. She could have had her suspicions or maybe figured it out herself? She might not even know anything about what happened at university.'

'Of course, if we want to get really Machiavellian,' said Hardwick, 'Caitlin could have forced Ben to get rid of Louisa by threatening to expose what he did with Sinead.'

Roehampton raised an eyebrow. 'Kill your wife, or I'll tell everyone you already murdered your mistress at university? That's quite the jump, Karen, considering we don't actually have any proof Caitlin and Ben were even having an affair, or that Louisa is dead. I don't doubt Caitlin might have had a crush on him. They might even have met up illicitly, and she isn't willing to admit it, since it looks bad, regardless of whether anything actually happened. But we're going to need a lot more.'

'OK, maybe a step too far,' conceded Hardwick. 'But consider this. Throughout the interview, she referred to Louisa in the past tense.'

Chapter 12

Ben Greenland played right-back for a pub football team. There was a league match the following morning, so Moray Ruskin and a couple of detectives from Welwyn spoke to his teammates after their training finished.

The team consisted of a rather motley collection of men aged between twenty-something and forty-something. By the time Ruskin spoke to the club captain, he'd heard every joke going about Greenland's footballing prowess, or rather lack of it, including that he'd be better off playing left-back – as in left-back in the changing rooms.

'Yeah, it's all true,' said Simon Linton. 'These days, the bloke has two right feet. Unfortunately, he's a leftie. But we need every man we have at the moment. Could use him tomorrow, to be honest. We're going to get hammered.'

'How long have you known him?' asked Ruskin.

'Seven or eight years now? We knew each other from the Albion; pub quizzes, darts tournaments, that sort of thing. He was one of the founding members of the team; in fact he even came up with the name: West Middlesbury Albion was too good not to use, even if we're based on the east side of town.'

'And do you know his wife – Louisa?'

'Yeah, she used to drink with us down the Albion. That all stopped when the kids came along, unfortunately, but she'd sometimes come and watch us play on a Sunday morning. We've all heard what's happened.' He shook his head. 'He must be going out of his mind.'

Ruskin chose his words carefully. 'We're trying everything we can to find her or work out why she may have left, so any insights you might have could be useful.'

Linton looked thoughtful. 'To be honest, I only knew Lou in passing, but I know things have been difficult recently. Lou started a new business and was working silly hours. He had to stop coming to the Wednesday night training to look after the girls whilst she worked. He still turns out at the weekend to play and the odd Friday night to train, but if he wasn't a mate and we weren't so desperate, I'd have probably dropped him.'

'How did Ben feel about that?' asked Ruskin.

Linton narrowed his eyes. After a long pause, he eventually gave a sigh.

'Look, he's a friend, and I don't want to speak out of turn.'

Ruskin said nothing.

'But I'm not daft. It's obvious why you're here; everyone knows the police always look at the husband first. Like I said, I don't want to speak out of turn, and I don't think for one second he's capable of hurting her, but things weren't great at home.'

'In what way?'

'I think he resented all the time she was spending at work. It wasn't that he didn't want her to succeed, and he's not the sort of twat who thinks looking after kids is women's work – he loves being a father, and he's always going on about the kids – but he misses his Wednesday night training with the lads, you know? He works all day and takes over the childcare as soon as he gets in, and usually does weekends as well. Lou works really hard obviously, but she gets a couple of hours to herself while the kids are at school to grab a coffee with her friends or go for a run. Which is fair enough – she earns it. Ben just wants one night a week for himself, but Lou insists she needs to work.'

Ruskin eyed the man. 'Is that all?' he asked.

Linton bit his lip. 'Look, you didn't hear this from me, but one of the reasons Ben liked his Wednesday night training is the pub visit afterwards. The visit *without* his wife, if you know what I mean.'

'I see,' said Ruskin, again leaving a silence that begged to be filled.

'And, er, we have an annual football tour. We visit a few clubs, play a couple of games, enjoy a few nights out . . .'

Again, Ruskin remained silent.

'Anyway, a lot of the lads share rooms, to keep the cost down. Ben always insisted on paying for his own room. He claimed it was because he snores. But a couple of times he'd skip the pub and have an early night . . .' Linton trailed off.

'You think he entertained visitors?'

'Could have done. That's all I'm saying.'

*   *   *

Moray Ruskin shared what he'd learned from Ben Greenland's teammates as soon as he returned. Warren and Sutton took the opportunity to also update Roehampton on other potential theories; it was important at this early stage not to become obsessed with one hypothesis to the exclusion of others.

She'd given a lukewarm response to the idea of a kidnapping for money, but agreed it was worth pursuing.

'I know it doesn't fit his offending history, but Russell Myrie is still a contender in my book,' said Sutton. 'We know he fancied his chances with her; he could have taken the opportunity knowing she's alone that time of night.'

'We need to rule him in or out,' said Roehampton. 'Pin down exactly what his relationship was with her and test his alibi.'

'So where does the Taser come in?' asked Warren.

'Maybe he used it to subdue her?' said Sutton. 'It doesn't sound like he'd have much luck getting her drunk; perhaps he used it to knock her senseless until he could tie her up, or whatever?'

'That's a hell of an escalation,' said Warren. He turned to Roehampton. 'Are Tasers easier to get hold of than handguns?'

'Depends who you know, I imagine, but to criminals, Tasers are tools to be used for a specific purpose,' she replied. 'Guns are more multi-purpose; you can wave them around just to make a point. Everyone knows what a gun looks like; Tasers look like bright yellow kids' toys.'

'That scenario might also fit Darren,' said Warren. 'He could be her supplier for the cocaine. He has a violent history, and it sounds as though his behaviour around women, including Louisa, is pretty suspect.'

'Or the two of them together,' said Sutton. 'They could very well know each other. For my money, it's already an unfortunate coincidence she has two such men in her life – I don't think it stretches the bounds of credibility for them to have realised they have a common acquaintance and teamed up.'

'I see nothing wrong with your logic, but we'll need more than a theory,' said Roehampton. 'We'll need evidence that they know each other. Check with their parole officers; see if they met in prison or are otherwise acquainted. Which brings us back to Ben. How strong a candidate is he?'

'I don't know,' admitted Warren. 'Everyone we've spoken to has said he seemed to love her. He certainly appears to be very upset and worried, and you could argue that if Louisa is dead, her business will die with her and leave him with a significant pile of debt.'

'But?' said Roehampton, leaving Warren to pick holes in his own theory.

'But . . . nobody knows what truly goes on in a marriage behind closed doors. The body language experts who analysed the press conference saw nothing to indicate he was putting on a show for the cameras, but couldn't rule it out. And we know his mother is wealthy; I'm sure she could be persuaded to step in if necessary to clear all the debts.'

'And there are plenty of good, old-fashioned motives,' said Sutton. 'Almost everyone we've spoken to says Ben has a wandering eye at the very least. If Louisa did discover he was playing away from home, she could have threatened to leave him and take the girls with her. He wouldn't be the first husband who killed his wife to stop that.'

'If it was so obvious to everyone else that Ben was sleeping around, why didn't she leave him sooner?' mused Roehampton.

'Could be that she was worried that she couldn't afford to,' suggested Sutton. 'Or maybe she still bears the scars from her own parents' divorce and didn't want to put the girls through that?'

'Or maybe he thought it was her having the affair,' suggested Warren. 'They're sleeping in separate beds, she's going out each night leaving him with the kids, and is alone all day. Rightly or wrongly, he could have thought she was carrying on behind his back. It could have been simple jealousy, or again, he could have been worried she was going to leave him and take their daughters.'

'He could even have found out that she lied about the bank loan,' said Sutton. 'She was sinking under a pile of debt. She had suppliers that needed paying and that big order was pay-on-delivery. We still haven't figured out what the second source of cash was she was receiving through that secure payment service, but her income still wasn't matching her outgoings. They'd already taken out a second mortgage. If she didn't manage to raise some more capital soon, or shift a load more hampers, he'd probably need to ask his mum to bail them out. Who knows how that might make him feel?'

'Men and their egos.' Roehampton sighed, her eyes rolling.

'I wouldn't dismiss it,' said Warren.

Chapter 13

Curtis Redmayne arrived late in the evening, coming straight from the train station.

'Thank you for dropping everything and travelling here. We really appreciate it,' said Warren.

'One of the perks of being the boss,' said Redmayne. The man sitting opposite Warren and Hardwick was dressed in an expensive-looking grey suit and equally pricey-looking black leather loafers, although in deference to the late hour, the top button of his cotton shirt was unbuttoned, and if he had started the day wearing a tie it had since been removed.

The slightly awkward-looking twenty-year-old in the house-mate photo had filled out, the traces of acne long gone. The mop of red-blond hair was now smartly trimmed, with the slightest hint of grey at the temples.

'We know you shared a house with Louisa back when you were students, but I'm afraid we don't really know the details,' Warren started.

If Redmayne suspected they were testing him, or had already been in contact with Caitlin, he gave no sign and willingly gave a detailed account of their relationship over the years. It matched what they had already been told.

'So, the get-together to remember Sinead was the last time you saw Louisa and any of the others?' asked Hardwick.

'Yes, although I have to admit things are a bit hazy towards the end of the evening. Louisa was good enough to drive me back to my hotel.' He looked a bit sheepish. 'I had planned on meeting up with them for a fried breakfast before jumping back on the train, but I'm afraid that I forgot I'm thirty-one not twenty-one anymore and didn't manage to make it. I barely made it to the train station, if I'm honest, and the last thing I wanted was a plateful of grease.' His face became sad. 'I wish I'd made the effort now.'

'And how was Louisa?' asked Warren.

'Tired and stressed,' he said. 'I'm sure you know all about her new business venture?'

'Yes,' said Warren, without elaborating.

'We had a bit of a chat about it. Between you and me, I promised I'd take a look at her business plan.' He looked a little ashamed. 'I might even have suggested I'd loan her a bit of money.'

'Didn't she have an extension to her bank loan?' asked Warren innocently.

Redmayne shifted uncomfortably. 'Again, in confidence you understand, she'd been turned down. When I looked at the figures she emailed me, I think the bank probably made the right decision. She'd already maxed out her credit cards, and they'd previously taken out a second mortgage. On the face of it, the deal with Holistics Gym looked great, but it was a gamble. If the stuff didn't sell, she ran the risk of a garage full of stock she couldn't get rid of and more debt.'

'What did you tell her?'

'I had to break it to her that I wasn't prepared to loan her the money. I'd have been happy to waive the interest – she's a mate after all – but it still would have been a bad idea.'

'And how did she take it?' asked Warren.

'Not well,' he admitted. 'The thing is, it's not even about me losing the money; God knows, I can afford it. It's that I worried she was gambling everything on this one roll of the dice. If it all went tits-up, she risked losing her house and everything.'

'Does Ben know about this, or the bank turning her down?' asked Warren.

'Not as far as I'm aware. But it looks as though she went ahead and signed the contract anyway. She was absolutely certain they would sell, but I think she was listening to her heart over her head.' A look of profound sadness crossed his face, and his voice took on a rough edge. 'That was the last communication I had with her. I'm so angry with myself, getting her hopes up like that. What was I thinking, discussing business after a skinful?'

'What was Ben and Louisa's marriage like?' asked Warren, casually.

'Sorry, do you mind if I have a coffee?' he asked. 'I've had a long day and I'm flagging a bit.'

'Of course,' said Warren. Hardwick jumped to her feet and went to the coffee machine. After a moment's hesitation, Warren accepted her offer; it was probably unwise this time of night, but now Redmayne had put the idea in his head, he felt a wave of tiredness sweep over him.

The machine gurgled away in the background and Warren discreetly watched Redmayne. The man's face was immobile, but his eyes were a swirl of conflicting emotions.

'This is what I wanted to talk to you about,' Redmayne said eventually, after thanking Hardwick for the coffee. She had wisely chosen decaf, Warren noticed.

'I'm sure you know all about Sinead's disappearance. About how she was stressed and at breaking point? About how we never figured out if she just upped and left or if something more sinister happened?'

Warren nodded.

'There's something I kept to myself at the time. It was only ever a suspicion, and I knew that if I opened that can of worms, there was no going back. If I was wrong, it would wreck everything. And even if I was right, it wouldn't bring Sinead back. So, I never said anything.' He took a long swig of his coffee, wincing at the heat. 'Ben was a bit of a player, if you know what I mean. I don't know what you've heard, but he wasn't completely faithful to Louisa.'

'I see,' said Warren, his own coffee forgotten. 'And do you think he had something to do with Sinead's disappearance?'

'No. Definitely not. At least not directly. If I thought for one moment he had done something to her, I'd have been straight down the police station – I promise you that, DCI Jones.'

'So how was he involved?' asked Warren.

'I never had any proof,' Redmayne cautioned them. 'But a couple of times when I was in the kitchen late at night getting a bite to eat, I thought I heard a man's voice, possibly Ben's, coming from Sinead's room. I couldn't hear what they were saying, but it sounded . . . intimate, you know? I knew Lou and Steph were on the top floor, as I'd heard them go to bed, so he could probably get away with it. Well, anyway, I figured it was none of my business, even if he was cheating on a friend.' He looked abashed. 'If I'm honest, I was slightly jealous.'

'You fancied Sinead?' asked Hardwick.

'No, nothing like that. Between you and me, I always preferred Caitlin.' He gave a wistful smile. 'Not that it ever came to anything. I think she was carrying a flame for somebody else. No, back then I just envied Ben's ease with girls. I was awkward and a bit useless.

'The thing is, after Sinead went missing, we were all very upset, but Ben seemed especially so. He never admitted having an affair with her, and I never asked, but a couple of times, when it was only the two of us and we'd drunk a bit too much, he used to get really maudlin and say things like: "What if it was something we did?" or "What if we upset her so much she felt she had to leave?" Looking back on it, when he said "we", I'm sure he meant "I".'

'You said you're certain Ben had nothing to do with Sinead's disappearance,' said Warren. 'What makes you so sure?'

'He couldn't,' said Redmayne, his tone firm. 'He just isn't that kind of guy. It's one thing to be unfaithful, and sleep with people you shouldn't, but that's completely different to hurting someone.

'There's something else I've never told anyone. A couple of years ago I was thinking about what happened. I should have said something when I remembered, but I was living in France and when I rang the Missing Persons Unit, DS Rutherford had retired and his number was no longer active. Sinead had been declared dead and the case was closed, so I never got around to saying anything.' He looked down at the table. 'Sorry. I really should have tried harder. But I think I know when Sinead disappeared.'

'What do you mean?' asked Warren, trying to keep the exasperation out of his voice.

'She was last seen on Wednesday the 9th of April,' said Redmayne. 'But nobody knows if she went missing that night, or in the following forty-eight hours. Well I was in the house a little after lunchtime on the Thursday, when Lou came home from uni. She'd been running late that morning for a tutorial and couldn't find her keys, so she'd just clashed the front door behind her. When she returned, she had to ring the doorbell to get let in. She kept on ringing, so I went downstairs to open the door.

'The thing is . . . Sinead's room was right next to the front door and she was always complaining how loud the doorbell sounded in her room. If she was in there, why didn't she let Lou in?'

Warren mulled over what he had just said. He'd pass it on and get them to update Sinead's file, but unfortunately, the information was over a decade too late; he didn't see what possible use it could be now.

'OK, Curtis. But what does all of this have to do with Louisa's disappearance?' asked Hardwick.

'The reason I wanted to speak to you, is because I don't believe a leopard changes his spots,' said Redmayne. 'I think it's quite possible Sinead left because on top of everything else, Ben was a bit of a shit to her. And now I think history might be repeating itself. I don't think Ben has hurt Louisa; I really don't think he has it in him. But I think he's been up to his old tricks. When we last got together to remember Sinead, he got really drunk. The ladies were off having a bit of girl talk and we were at the bar. He was quizzing me about my love life,' Redmayne's cheeks were tinged with pink. 'I mentioned I was seeing someone and that it might be getting serious. He started saying how I was still young, that I should enjoy life whilst I still could and not get tied down with a family. Which was weird in itself; it's the sort of thing you say to a twenty-year-old, not a thirty-year-old. But what was really strange was that he said: "Make sure they work odd hours, so they don't bump into your bit on the side." He was joking, but not joking, if you know what I mean?'

* * *

The photograph on WhatsApp made Warren smile, then feel guilty. It was ten o'clock and he was eating a pasta salad at his desk, the salad part of the meal deal already carefully deposited in the bin.

He got up and closed his office door, blocking out the hubbub from the late shift. The video call connected within seconds.

'Hello, sweetheart, I see somebody is up very late.'

'Ha, that somebody is busy teething.' The video lurched wildly as his wife Susan juggled the phone with a squirming ten-month-old. 'Say hello to Daddy,' she said.

Warren's heart melted as his son's face came into view. 'Hello, Niall,' he said, waving at the screen.

Niall's face was streaked with tears, but he perked up at the sound of his father's voice, a big smile spreading across his drooling mouth. A plump finger lurched toward the screen, promptly batted away by Susan. 'Oh no you don't,' she admonished.

Warren laughed. For some reason, the "end call" button was like a magnet to his son, and if Susan didn't watch Niall like a hawk, their video calls were regularly terminated early.

'How has your week been?' asked Susan. 'Are you still driving up tomorrow?'

Warren felt a stab of guilt. 'No, I'm sorry, sweetheart, I can't get away.'

He filled her in on Louisa Greenland's disappearance. By the time he finished, Susan's disappointed expression had given way to understanding. Somewhere out there was a missing young woman, whose life was potentially in danger.

'I'll see if I can pop up next week,' he promised, 'but until we get something concrete about which way the investigation is likely to go, everything is moving too quickly.'

Susan knew enough to realise that Warren meant whether the missing woman turned up, or the missing person investigation formally transitioned to a suspected homicide.

'Enough about me,' he said firmly. 'How's my favourite yummy mummy and our gorgeous offspring?'

'Not so yummy and not so gorgeous at the moment,' admitted Susan. 'I may as well be teething myself, the amount of grief it's causing.'

Again, Warren felt a flash of shame. He should be with her, taking his turn getting up to soothe their crying son. With hindsight, moving house with a small baby was a bad idea; moving into a house needing a new bathroom, kitchen and carpets was an even worse idea. In the end, Susan had taken Niall to her parents, leaving Warren to deal with everything.

'How's your dad?' he asked.

'Soldiering on,' she admitted. 'He's started getting up during the night. We're going to look into getting smart switches fitted to the appliances in the kitchen, so he doesn't burn the place down. He's still cooking and baking, but you have to watch him like a hawk.'

Warren could hear the exhaustion in her voice. Susan's father, Dennis, had recently been formally diagnosed with dementia. This was the other reason she'd decided to spend the remaining weeks of her maternity leave with her parents. The diagnosis had been hard for her mother, and Susan wanted to be there for her. Equally importantly, she wanted to build as many memories with her father as she could, before the inevitable progression of the disease cruelly robbed them of the man they loved. Until this case came along, they'd made the arrangement work, with Warren able to juggle his shifts to spend time with his family up north.

'And what about your mum?'

'Still a little in denial,' she admitted. 'She gets very frustrated with him sometimes.'

'She's scared,' said Warren quietly. 'And she doesn't know how to deal with that.'

'I know, but it makes things doubly difficult,' said Susan, and Warren could see they'd obviously had another argument.

Bernice was – to put it kindly – a force of nature. Those who didn't know the couple would see Dennis as henpecked, his persona in his home life a marked contrast to the respected and dynamic business leader he'd been before his retirement. In reality, it was far more complex. Where Bernice was forthright and even domineering, Dennis was quiet and diplomatic. The relationship between Susan and her mother could be fraught at times, but Dennis smoothed over the cracks and talked his wife down when she was being unreasonable. It was Dennis who had repaired the damage to the relationship between Bernice and her eldest daughter during Warren and Susan's lengthy, and at times heart-breaking, journey to start a family.

A staunch Catholic, Bernice had been vehemently against the couple's use of IVF. It had taken many months of unseen, gentle persuasion behind the scenes by Dennis before she finally accepted that her relationship with Susan and any future grandchild was far more important than adherence to an outdated and arbitrary rule seeking to govern situations that could never have been foreseen two thousand years ago.

'What about the driving?' asked Warren; he could see that

his son's eyes were drooping, the soothing voices of his parents hopefully lulling him to sleep for a few hours.

'I went out with him yesterday,' said Susan. 'I think he's safe for a while longer. His reactions remain sharp, he's using his indicators, keeping to the speed limit, giving cyclists plenty of space and following the instructions on the sat nav. As long as Mum or someone is with him so he doesn't get lost or flustered, I think he'll be OK.'

'Fifty years of muscle memory,' Warren reassured her. 'And you know how easy to drive hybrids are. They're like electric go-karts; no need to change gears or do hill starts.'

'I know, but it can't last forever. And then what will Mum do?'

That was a worry. Bernice had never learned to drive. The couple's home, whilst lovely and probably well suited to Dennis as his dementia journey progressed, was in a pretty little Warwickshire village with limited local amenities. Unfortunately, the decision to cut back on so-called "non-essential services" after government funding cuts for local councils, had reduced an already infrequent bus service, leaving residents reliant on cars or taxis to visit the nearby towns and cities. Needless to say, letters to local politicians asking how such a move squared with the government's environmental pledges had gone unanswered. With Dennis eventually unable to drive, and the inevitable passage of time reducing the number of her friends, Susan worried about how Bernice would cope.

'You'll need to teach her how to use the Uber app,' said Warren.

'I think that's beyond even my capabilities,' said Susan.

'According to the learned folks on Mumsnet, "there's no such thing as a poor pupil, just a poor teacher",' quoted Warren.

Niall promptly gave a squeal, making them both jump.

'Thank you,' said Susan to her squirming son. 'Tell Daddy he's talking bollocks again, and he needs to stay off forums populated by ill-informed—'

A pudgy finger aimed precisely at the big red button cut off

Susan's response, although Warren could guess how it ended.

He chuckled. 'Nice one, son. Impeccable timing.'

Warren leaned back in his chair, his spirits lifted by the conversation. It was a poor substitute for hugging his wife and cuddling his boy, but it was better than nothing. After the last couple of days, it was good to be reminded of everything he loved most in the world. Now if only Facebook could figure out how to transmit odours by WhatsApp, then he could drink in the warm baby smell that so calmed him. His nose wrinkled, as he remembered an odour of his son's that he wasn't so fond of.

'Yes, what can I do for you, Karen?' he asked as she appeared at the door. He frowned. 'Shouldn't you be home by now?' The past ten months had made him even more aware of the sacrifices parents like Hardwick made.

'I'll be off any minute,' she said. 'Mum and Dad are babysitting, and Robbie has a band rehearsal, so I figured I'd get a jump on the weekend.'

'Well don't overdo it,' cautioned Warren. 'Even officers with the dizzying rank of sergeant get to have a work-life balance.'

She blushed; her promotion was recent enough that the team were still enjoying teasing her along with Moray Ruskin, who was now firmly at the bottom of the pecking order, although Warren doubted he'd stay there for long.

Her face became serious, and Warren felt his stomach flutter.

'The DNA has come back on the bloodstain found in Louisa Greenland's unit. It's hers.'

SATURDAY 18TH MAY

Chapter 14

'Russell Myrie wasn't home the night Louisa Greenland disappeared,' said Hutchinson.

'Are you certain?' asked Warren. He slurped from his third coffee of the morning, taking care to hold the mug by its handle. The cuts on his hands had scabbed over and he'd decided to chance leaving them uncovered, but he'd accidentally picked up a hot drink earlier, and they were stinging again.

'That's what his neighbour reckons. The man next door came in from work a little after seven and Myrie's car wasn't there. He popped out for a cigarette a few times that evening, and the car hadn't returned. He also said there was no sound coming from Myrie's flat. Apparently Myrie usually watches the footie with the volume turned up full. He assumed he'd gone to watch it down the pub, but he didn't hear him come in and the car was still gone when he left for work early the following morning.'

'So he lied about his whereabouts,' said Warren. 'I'd say that's enough to justify a search warrant for his house and car.'

'And this might oil the wheels,' said Pymm. 'The preliminary search results are in for his garage. They haven't found Louisa's fingerprints anywhere in there, but you might find this interesting.' She handed over the scene report.

'Hmm,' said Warren after scanning the printed email. 'A coffee jar filled with drugs floating in the toilet cistern. Whatever will they think of next? I think it's time we had another chat with Mr Myrie. Let's get him arrested as soon as the paperwork is ready. Karen, what have you got for us?'

'I've just interviewed Angelina Greenland,' said Hardwick. The mother of Ben Greenland had been spoken to previously by the Missing Persons Unit, but given recent developments, it was time to speak with her again.

'She's now admitting Ben and Louisa's marriage was under a lot of strain,' said Hardwick, after chugging half a can of Diet Coke. 'She's clearly very worried. Her take on it was that Louisa may have bitten off more than she could chew with P@mper.'

'Does she still think Louisa has left voluntarily?' asked Warren.

'Outwardly yes, but it's clear she has increasing doubts. I don't think she truly believes Louisa would have left the girls.'

'What did she know about their financial situation?'

'She knows they've remortgaged the house and thought Louisa had extended her bank loan. I asked her if they had ever approached her for any help. She said she would have happily given Louisa a loan if she'd asked – she was quite open about the fact that she has plenty of money doing nothing useful. However, Louisa was determined to "stand on her own two feet".'

'Did you ask if Ben had requested any money?'

'She said he hadn't. She appeared to be telling the truth, so I chanced my arm and told her we were investigating the possibility Louisa may have been kidnapped for ransom. She was horrified, and I had to row back and tell her it was just one of a number of theories. She was adamant Ben hadn't approached her, but that if he did, she would pay the money in a heartbeat. For what it's worth, I believed her.'

'There are no suspicious transactions on her bank accounts,' offered Pymm. 'Do you think she'll tell us if he asks her for money in future?'

'To be honest, probably not, if he told her not to. I think the first we'd know about it is when her bank alerts us.'

'Did you get any more out of her about her own relationship with Louisa?' asked Warren.

'I started the interview with a general chat, and the impression I got was that she loves Louisa but perhaps thought Ben could have done a bit better.'

'In what way?'

'This is only my impression,' said Hardwick. 'But she did mention that they seemed very different. I probed a little deeper and she said, "Oh you know, different backgrounds. A different family set-up." I suspect she was hinting at Louisa coming from a broken family on a housing estate in inner-city Nottingham, rather than somewhere nice and leafy like Middlesbury.

'She admitted she was a little surprised when they first got together; apparently she didn't think it would last. She thought Ben would continue to "play the field" a bit more. My words, not hers.'

'Did you pursue that at all?'

'A little, but she sort of caught herself. I think she might have suspicions he could be a bit of a ladies' man, but she isn't going to admit that to a stranger.'

'What about his brother?'

'She changed the subject. I think she's a bit embarrassed, perhaps even ashamed of him. Whether she was trying to steer us away from him as a suspect, I wouldn't like to say.'

'We need to speak to him as a priority,' said Warren. 'Hutch, get a few bodies to canvass his neighbours. If and when we finally get him in for a chat, I want some ammunition in our pocket in case he tries to lie to us.'

'I think we can pretty much guarantee he's going to lie to us,' said Hutchinson. 'Whether or not it's relevant is another matter.'

Warren looked at his watch as he dismissed the meeting. 'I have a call to make.'

* * *

109

'Do you want to play I'll show you mine if you show me yours?' asked Warren, when DCI Carl Mallucci picked up his phone.

Mallucci was a drugs specialist working within the Serious Organised Crime Unit, based at headquarters in Welwyn Garden City. He and Warren had worked together several times over the years. It had been a frustrating experience initially; SOC played their cards close to their chest. Much of their intel was inaccessible to officers outside of the unit and they were often loath to share. Warren had felt like he was going to them with a begging bowl, hoping for whatever scraps they decided he could be trusted with.

But the two men had found themselves embroiled in a big case the previous year and forged a trusting relationship that was fast becoming a friendship.

'Hi, mate. Has Ash clipped your wings yet?'

'Not yet,' said Warren. 'But time will tell.'

'I'm still jealous,' admitted Mallucci. 'I haven't poked around a good crime scene in months. And how's the little one?'

'Teething,' replied Warren, 'although I shouldn't really complain. Susan has taken him to her parents for a few weeks whilst I try and make the house liveable.' He forced himself to sound upbeat.

'I wish I'd thought of that.' Mallucci chuckled. Warren remembered that he had four – or was it five? – kids, all under ten years old. The man must be an expert; Warren made a note to meet him for a pint to learn a few of the tricks they don't tell you in the classes at the community centre.

'I'll go first,' offered Warren, bringing the conversation back on track. 'Has Russell Myrie come across your desk?'

He could hear Mallucci tapping on a keyboard in the background.

'No, he's new to us. What have you got?'

Warren filled him in on everything they knew about the registered sex offender running the garage next door to Louisa Greenland's industrial unit, and what they'd found when they searched his premises.

'That's very interesting,' said Mallucci. 'He could just be a foot soldier, but it doesn't matter. It's who he knows that might be useful.'

'We're holding off on busting him for drugs until we've worked out if he has any link with Louisa Greenland's disappearance.'

'No problem, I totally get that,' Mallucci assured him. 'I might be able to throw in some info to help any arrest stick. Now what can I help you with?'

'Darren Greenland,' said Warren, filling him in on what they had so far.

'Yeah, he's one of ours,' said Mallucci. 'Most of what we have is accessible on the PNC, but we have a couple more burner phones linked to him on our system. None of them are active anymore, but if you're looking for past associations, his location history might be useful. I also have a couple of pubs and other places he's known to hang around. I'm going to hand you over to Sammy; she's had the pleasure of dealing with him in person.'

'He's really bad news,' Sammy said when the introductions were complete. 'Most of the folks we deal with are mouthy little gobshites, but he's also a proper creep and actually quite scary. Last time I arrested him, he was off his face on cocaine and the verbal he gave me was absolutely foul. We hear all sorts in this game, but he threatened to rape me and find my family and do even worse whilst I watched. I don't mind admitting it gave me a couple of sleepless nights.'

'Shit,' breathed Warren. This was not what he wanted to hear; they really needed to find him.

'Obviously, his solicitor claimed it was out of character, he had a bad reaction to the drugs, he was ashamed and sorry for any distress he'd caused, blah, blah, blah. But we all know that's bollocks. It doesn't matter how high on drugs you are, you don't say those sorts of things unless they're already in the back of your mind. Believe me, DCI Jones, he is a very, very dangerous man.'

Chapter 15

Russell Myrie vehemently protested his innocence from the moment he was arrested and officers entered his flat brandishing a search warrant, demanding his car keys. He handed them over with a glare when it became apparent that if he didn't, they might accidentally damage his pride and joy when they forced the lock.

'Did you enjoy the match on Tuesday night?' asked Sutton.

Myrie's eyes narrowed, but his voice was firm as he repeated "no comment".

'Where did you watch it?' asked Warren.

Myrie licked his lips. 'No comment,' he said eventually.

Warren gave a sigh. 'Are you sure you want to play this game?' he asked. 'We know you weren't at home Tuesday night; you lied to us. I'm telling you, Russell, it's not looking great for you right now. We have a missing woman, who's recently been in contact with a known sex offender. A sex offender who is lying about his whereabouts the night she disappeared.'

'No comment,' mumbled Myrie.

Warren looked at Sutton, before standing. 'Interview terminated.' He fixed Myrie with a stare. 'I hope you haven't made any plans for the next couple of days; I don't think we're going to have any problems getting an extension to custody, do you?'

* * *

'We're going to need more to get an extension to custody,' said Roehampton as Warren and Sutton left the interview suite. 'As I'm sure his solicitor has informed him.'

'Fake it 'til you make it,' said Warren. 'We've got him on the back foot. Whatever he was up to that night, it was obviously something dodgy. As long as he thinks we know more than we do, he's going to be sweating. Either he'll tell us what he was really doing and we can eliminate him, or he'll try and come up with a convincing lie. But with no contact with the outside world, hopefully he'll struggle to get anyone to corroborate his version of events.'

Roehampton didn't look convinced. 'I hope you're right.'

So did Warren.

* * *

'The CSIs have been splashing the luminol around,' said Sutton, addressing the afternoon briefing. 'Early days so far, but no traces of any bodily fluids in Russell Myrie's car, none in his flat and nothing obvious in his garage.'

'There wouldn't be if he strangled her, or he's stashed her alive somewhere,' pointed out Pymm.

'I agree,' said Warren. 'It's certainly not enough to rule him out yet. Have they found anything of interest?'

'Drugs,' said Sutton, a look of satisfaction on his face. 'In his flat there are packets containing more cocaine than could be reasonably dismissed as for personal use, and some vials of clear liquid that could be GHB, again in a watertight jar in his toilet cistern. He could be supplying the GHB to the clubbing scene, but given its other use as a date rape drug, I'd say he's back to his old tricks.'

'Shit,' muttered Warren. 'Any sign of a Taser?'

'Nothing in his flat or car, but his garage is heaving with boxes filled with vehicle parts and equipment. It's going to take some time to finish cataloguing it all.'

'The CCTV we've analysed so far would be consistent with him dealing drugs out of his garage,' said Richardson. 'You know the sort of thing; young lads on bicycles wearing grey tracksuits and hoodies coming in for two minutes, careful not to look at the camera above the door.'

'Which begs the question, was he Louisa's dealer?' asked Sutton.

'And if he is, does he have any links to Ben's dodgy brother?' asked Warren.

'They've seized a laptop, two mobile phones and a tablet from his flat,' said Sutton. 'That's in addition to the phone that was in his pocket when we arrested him. They're being prioritised. There was also five hundred quid in a coffee can in his flat and another two hundred taped to the back of the microwave in his garage.'

'He'll claim it's because he runs a cash business,' predicted Hutchinson. 'And if his accounts don't match, I'll bet he'll cop to incorrectly declaring his earnings and offer to pay the fine to HMRC. But added to the drugs, that'll never be accepted in court.'

'I'll speak to Drugs again,' said Warren. 'There's more than enough there to get him recalled to prison and a conviction for dealing, so we can take him off the streets for a while, if we want to. But before we make that decision, we still need to know if he had any involvement in Louisa's disappearance.'

*   *   *

'It'll be his arrogance that trips him up,' predicted Sutton as he removed his red bush teabag and slopped some milk into the mug. He and Warren were finalising their strategy before they interviewed Russell Myrie again. 'Those drugs are a case in point. Remember how he greeted us when we turned up at his garage? He was expecting us. Even if he has nothing to do with Louisa's disappearance, he had to know we'd probably end up searching his unit. Did he really think we wouldn't find his stash, or the cocaine and GHB floating in his cistern back at his flat? Or the cash? Anyone with a lick of sense would have moved all that someplace else quick smart.'

'Some things never change,' agreed Warren as he sipped his coffee. Unfortunately, John Grayson had taken his expensive coffee machine with him when he'd left, and Ashley Roehampton was an instant-coffee woman. Warren was contemplating treating himself to a machine, but they were eye-wateringly expensive, and the pods were an environmental disaster.

If he did purchase one, it would be securely locked in his office. He'd had little enough success persuading his colleagues to pop fifty pence in the honesty jar when they used the communal urn; they'd never cough up for the use of expensive coffee pods. Just this morning, he'd found that some cheeky sod had raided the jar for change for the vending machine, replacing the coins in there with some old pound coins that had ceased being legal tender in 2017; he'd have to get them changed at the bank. He had half a mind to ask Andy Harrison to try and lift fingerprints from them to see if he could nail the culprit.

'How are we going to tackle this?' asked Sutton. 'We're confident Louisa has been taken against her will, but she could still be alive, hidden somewhere. If Myrie is our man, then how do we get him to admit it and lead us to her before it's too late?'

Sutton wasn't crass enough to verbalise what they were both thinking. In a way, it would be easier if they knew Louisa was dead. Missing Persons were fast running out of leads, the investigation shifting away from tracing Louisa, towards identifying who might have taken her – CID's speciality. But whilst there remained hope she was still alive, they needed the cooperation of any potential suspects. Locking up the perpetrator could result in Louisa dying.

'He knows he is subject to recall if he's caught dealing drugs,' said Warren, 'so, we need to take that off the table for now. Let's not mention what we've found yet. I want him busy trying to convince us he had nothing to do with Louisa's disappearance, and for that we need him to give us an alibi. We can then probe that and release him on bail. I've spoken to Ash and she's trying to get funding to put him under surveillance. If Louisa's stashed somewhere he may lead us to her.'

Or to her body, he added silently.

* * *

'OK, Russell, we've given you plenty of time to reconsider,' said Warren. 'Where were you Tuesday night?'

'No comment,' he repeated, affecting an air of boredom.

Sutton gave his head a slow shake. 'Here's the thing; you're on the hook for a kidnapping at the very least. We know it happened Tuesday night, so tell us where you were and what you were doing. You lied to us, which tells me that whatever it is you're hiding is pretty serious. But ask yourself this: is it more serious than kidnap?'

'You're taking the piss,' said Myrie. 'You haven't got anywhere near enough to charge me, and you know it. You're just fishing.'

'You're right,' said Warren. 'We haven't reached the charging threshold yet, but we've got enough to persuade a magistrate to authorise your detention whilst we find what we need.'

'What the fuck?' exploded Myrie. He turned to his solicitor. 'They can't just hold on to me until they find something.'

'I agree, DCI Jones,' responded the solicitor, a deep frown on her face. 'Based on the circumstantial evidence so far, you don't have enough to justify further detention.'

'Why are you even looking at me anyway?' asked Myrie. 'Go and arrest her husband, the shifty little bastard.'

'Why do you say that?' asked Warren.

He gave a shrug. 'I saw him on telly – he hardly shed a tear. Nine times out of ten, it's the husband or the boyfriend. It'll be him, you mark my words.'

'We'll be pursuing all leads,' said Warren, masking his disappointment that Myrie's assertion appeared to be nothing more substantial than a desperate slur. 'But whilst we're on the subject, how well do you know Mr Greenland?'

Myrie blinked. 'Hardly met the bloke. I seen him a couple of times when she first moved into the unit. Just said a few words.'

'About what?' asked Sutton.

Myrie looked up at the ceiling in concentration. 'Christ, I dunno. I think he asked me how I got an internet connection and what type of CCTV cameras I used. Just practical stuff.'

'It's interesting that you know all about her security system,' said Warren. 'Given it was disabled a month ago.'

'What?' Myrie's mouth opened as he followed the same reasoning that Warren and Sutton had. 'Hang on, just because she had the same security cameras as me doesn't mean I broke it.'

'Nope, purely circumstantial,' agreed Warren.

'Remind me how well you knew Louisa,' said Sutton.

'Not very,' Myrie said, his tone suddenly cagey.

'But well enough to turn up unannounced, knock on her unit door, and bring her a cup of coffee on a Sunday afternoon? And then go inside for about twenty minutes?' said Warren.

'The door to Louisa's unit is outside of the field of view for both your camera and the garden tool repair business in the unit on the other side of her,' said Sutton. 'And of course, whoever disabled that camera ensured your visit wouldn't be recorded—'

'Hey now, hold on,' interrupted Myrie.

'—but Sunday afternoons in early summer are pretty busy when you fix lawn mowers and the like, so your visit didn't go unnoticed,' continued Sutton. 'In fact, it wasn't the first time you've been spotted. Just what was your relationship with Louisa Greenland?'

The CSIs had failed to find Myrie's fingerprints inside Louisa's unit, but that could simply mean he hadn't touched anything without gloves.

Myrie glared at Sutton. 'OK, I admit it, I fancied her.'

'And was the feeling mutual?' asked Warren.

He shrugged. 'Maybe. She definitely wasn't getting the attention she deserved at home; she's down there working all night, whilst hubby is home with the kids? Don't give me that modern man bollocks, something is wrong with that marriage. But I swear I never touched her. It was just a bit of harmless banter. I never met up with her and I definitely didn't see her Tuesday night.'

'So where were you, Tuesday night?' repeated Warren.

Myrie swallowed. 'No comment.'

Warren made a show of looking at his watch. 'Fine, play it your way. But I have a forensics team searching your flat right now. Believe me, if there is so much as a skin cell from Louisa Greenland in there, they will find it. And the same goes for your car. They'll take it apart piece by piece.'

The blood drained from Myrie's face. 'Wait, you can't do that,' he protested.

'I bloody well can!' snapped Warren. 'I have a missing woman, who may or may not still be alive, who has had previous contact with a serious sex offender. Believe me, we had no problem getting a search warrant, and we will not be pissing around. Right now, you are at the very top of my list, so unless you eliminate yourself from the inquiry, I will be focusing all my attention on you.'

'OK, OK,' said Myrie. 'I went around a mate's house to watch the footie. I ended up staying overnight.'

'Does this mate have a name. Or an address?' asked Sutton.

'Amanda Kirton. Flat 6 Landsdown Mews. On the Heathway.'

'That wasn't so hard, was it?' said Sutton.

Chapter 16

Amanda Kirton lived in a small, two-bedroom flat a couple of miles from where Russell Myrie resided.

'Yes, he was here Tuesday night,' said Kirton, a thirty-something woman with an impressive collection of piercings. 'We watched the football and he stayed over.'

Moray Ruskin remained silent. After a few seconds the silence grew uncomfortable and Kirton was unable to resist filling it.

'We've been seeing each other for a few weeks,' she supplied. 'Just a bit of fun, you know?' Her cheeks flushed slightly.

'How did you meet him?' asked Ruskin.

'At the pub where I work.' She smiled. 'He's a cheeky one. Whenever he got a round in, he'd tell me to get one for myself. Eventually we got to talking . . .'

'And he was definitely here all Tuesday night?' pressed Ruskin.

'Yeah, of course,' she said.

'Are you aware of his past convictions?' he asked. Beside him, Karen Hardwick looked sympathetic.

Her face hardened. 'Yes. I'm not a fool. He told me all about them.' She scowled. 'Everyone deserves a second chance. He made some mistakes when he was younger, but now he's grown up. He doesn't hang around with the people who got him into trouble back then. He has a successful business, and he just wants to put it all behind him.'

Hardwick cleared her throat. 'What did he say he went to prison for?'

Kirton looked defiant. 'Stealing cars, burglary and drug possession. But like I said, he's put all that behind him.' Her voice rose. 'You lot are all the same. You never forgive and you never forget. People like Russ are an easy target. As soon as anything happens, you just go and round up all the usual suspects and try and pin it on them. But you're wrong; whatever you think he did, he didn't, OK? Now, I'm busy and I have to get ready for work.'

'Why do you think we're here?' asked Ruskin.

'I don't know, do I? Could be anything.' She started to get to her feet.

'He wasn't in jail for stealing cars,' said Hardwick quietly.

'What do you mean? Yes he was, he told me. I even asked his mate Tyron. He laughed and said, "Yeah that's right, he was a bugger for taking what he wanted without asking first".'

'He was imprisoned for sexual assault,' said Hardwick, her tone gentle.

The blood drained from Kirton's face and she sat back down. 'What? I don't understand.'

'He was convicted of picking up three young women in bars, taking them home and performing sex acts on them whilst they were too drunk to give consent,' said Hardwick.

'There were several other accusations, including three rapes that were discontinued through a lack of evidence,' said Ruskin. 'He received close to the maximum sentence.'

'He's on the sex offenders register and is subject to a Sexual Harm Prevention Order,' continued Hardwick. Kirton had turned a faint green colour, and her breathing was ragged.

Hardwick reached over and took the woman's hand. 'It's a condition of his release that he has to tell the police about any

120

new relationship, and they will decide whether they need to inform his new partner about his offending history.'

It explained why Myrie had been so reluctant to tell them his whereabouts.

Kirton looked over at the framed photographs on the bookcase.

'Is that your daughter?' asked Ruskin.

Kirton gave a strangled sob. 'Oh, Jesus. She's only fourteen.' She forced her fist into her mouth. 'Russ used to take her swimming on a Sunday morning and pick her up from football training.'

'I'm going to put you in contact with a specialist officer,' said Hardwick. 'They'll speak to you and your daughter and support you. Has your daughter mentioned anything troubling? Any changes in behaviour?'

'No, nothing. Not really. But she's fourteen, you know what they're like . . .' She stood abruptly and went to her handbag, removing a pack of cigarettes. 'You don't think he . . .'

'I don't know,' said Hardwick. Russell Myrie's victims had been in their late twenties, and Louisa Greenland was thirty-one, but Myrie was a sexual predator known to groom vulnerable women. Where did he draw the line?

'Oh, Christ, this is a nightmare. How could I be so careless? I knew he had a past, but he seemed so sweet. I honestly thought it was a phase he went through. Why didn't I dig a little deeper?'

'He goes by his mother's maiden name,' said Ruskin. 'He was listed on the Police National Computer, but you'd never have found him with a Google search. He's a very devious man; it wasn't your fault.'

'And that bastard friend of his knew, didn't he?' Her voice became angry. 'No wonder he thought it was so funny when I asked about what he'd been done for. "Taking what he wanted without asking first". He fucking knew!' She took a furious drag of her cigarette and started pacing around the room. 'And then there was the drunken sex. I just thought it was spontaneous, but he probably planned it to feed his sick fantasies.' She stubbed the cigarette out in a glass ashtray and immediately lit another.

'Was he really here all night on Tuesday?' asked Ruskin.

She stopped pacing, as if suddenly remembering where she was. She slumped back down on the chair and bit her lip. Tears pricked at the corners of her eyes as she shook her head. 'No. Not all night.'

* * *

'They watched the football and then he got a text message a few minutes after the match ended,' said Hardwick, when they returned to the station. 'He told her it was a mate with a flat tyre. He said he'd go out and give him a hand. She went to bed a little after eleven and says she woke briefly when he returned.'

'Any idea what time that was?' asked Warren.

'No. She says she'd been sound asleep, so probably a few hours later.'

'I've checked the mobile phone number she gave us for him,' said Pymm. 'An unregistered pay-as-you-go texted just before eleven. Both his handset and the one that contacted him were then turned off. His stayed off until the following morning, when it reconnected near his garage. The unknown has remained off.'

'A burner,' said Sutton. 'Can you get a location for where it was before it contacted him?'

'In the car park of the KFC at the retail park. It's the only time it's been used.'

'There are two entrances there, if memory serves,' said Richardson. 'Only one of which is covered by cameras.'

'Did she say what she thought the text was really about?' asked Sutton. 'She must have had some suspicion for her to lie to you.'

'She admits she thought it was to do with drugs,' said Ruskin. 'They like to smoke weed and use a little coke at the weekends if her daughter is with her father. She claims she didn't think he was dealing or anything, but she wouldn't meet my eye.'

'To be fair, that sort of behaviour does fit with how drug dealers operate,' said Sutton. 'He could have been picking up a stash, especially given what we've found in his flat.'

'Or he could have been meeting up with an accomplice to go and snatch Louisa Greenland,' said Pymm.

'Pull all the CCTV and ANPR from the area surrounding the KFC,' ordered Warren. 'Even if they agreed to rendezvous elsewhere, I want to know who was driving around that part of town when the call was made. Rachel, we'll go and speak to DSI Roehampton to see if she'll back us in applying for a warrant to do a cell-tower download from the nearest masts. Whoever called him might have been careful enough to conduct their business on a burner phone, but that doesn't mean they thought to turn off their personal phone. That evidence could come in handy.'

'What are we going to do with Myrie?' asked Hutchinson.

'The bean counters have signed off on limited directed surveillance for up to three days,' said Warren, 'so I will authorise his release on bail as soon as that's in place. Hopefully, he'll lead us to her, or he'll meet up with somebody who knows where she is. There's not enough for the chief constable to authorise intrusive surveillance.'

'What if Myrie doesn't lead us to Louisa within those three days?' asked Ruskin.

'We'll review the decision then,' said Warren.

A lot could happen in three days in a missing person case. They would need to decide if Myrie remained a viable suspect or if their resources would be better used elsewhere.

*   *   *

They finally caught up with Darren, Ben Greenland's brother, shortly after the Feathers pub opened. He had an outstanding arrest warrant for not attending a court-mandated anger management course, so he was taken into custody and driven to the station.

'You're a difficult man to get hold of,' said Ruskin, after the warrant had been dealt with. He was technically free to leave but had grudgingly agreed to stay and give an interview about Louisa Greenland's whereabouts.

The resemblance between the two brothers was noticeable, but if he didn't know better, Ruskin would have assumed Darren was ten years older than Ben, rather than three years younger. The two men were the same height, and a similar weight, but where Ben was trim with a healthy glow, his brother could best be described as gaunt, his skin a sallow colour. A persistent twitch under his left eye signalled he was craving his next fix.

'I'm sure you've heard Louisa's missing,' said Ruskin.

Greenland shrugged. 'She'll turn up,' he said.

'Why do you say that?'

Greenland shrugged again. 'She's a drama queen. She just wants the attention.'

Ruskin bit his tongue. The whole team had spent the past three days becoming increasingly worried about the whereabouts of the missing woman, and Greenland's callous attitude grated.

'When did you last see her?' asked Ruskin.

He shrugged. 'Dunno. A couple of months ago? Mum's birthday.'

'What about Ben? Have you seen him since?'

Greenland shrugged again. Ruskin took a deep breath; the urge to get up and use his full eighteen stone to push the man's shoulders down, and dare him to shrug once more, was almost overwhelming.

He changed the subject. 'Louisa hasn't been seen since Tuesday. If she has decided to leave of her own accord, that's her business; she's an adult. But we want to be certain she's safe.' He forced a smile. 'I'm sure you understand. We're speaking to anyone who knows her to see if they can think of any reason why she might want some time alone. Do you know if there were any problems at home?'

Greenland snorted. 'What do you think? She's out working every night, leaving Ben to babysit, and she's sleeping in the spare room. Does that sound like a happy home life to you?' He shifted in his seat. 'But it doesn't matter. If you ask me, he could do better. She's more trouble than she's worth.'

'In what way?' asked Ruskin.

'No sense of humour; say the wrong thing and she loses it. It doesn't take much to set her off. Bitch gave me right mouthful at Mum's birthday party.'

'I see. Was that before or after you tried to slip a hand up her skirt?' asked Ruskin.

Greenland's mouth dropped. 'How did you . . .? Who the fuck said that?' he demanded.

'It wasn't the first time either, from what we've been hearing. An "accidental" hand on a breast at Christmas. An unwanted advance at a family barbecue.' Ruskin fixed him with a stare. 'Louisa never said anything to Ben – she didn't want to cause trouble. But you know women, they share everything with their friends. I believe the word she used was "sleaze".'

'Like I said, no sense of humour,' Greenland muttered.

'Remind me again. When did you last see her?'

'Mum's birthday. Back in March.'

'And she hasn't been to see you since?'

'You've just said she thinks I'm a "sleaze". She's hardly going to come over and have a cup of tea and a biscuit.'

'Is that a yes or a no?'

'A no, of course.' Greenland folded his arms and glared at the tabletop.

'How about something a bit stronger?'

'Don't know what you mean.'

'A bit of weed maybe? Just to relax at the weekend?'

'No comment.'

'Have you ever visited Ben and Louisa's house?'

'No. I've never set foot in the place,' he stated confidently.

'Never? Are you sure about that? Bearing in mind we can get a DNA profile from a single hair follicle these days.'

'No. Like I said, never.'

'What about the industrial unit she worked out of.'

'Nope, don't even know where it is.'

'So Louisa has never been to your flat to pick up cocaine?'

'No, never.'

'So why did your neighbours recognise her?'

Chapter 17

Darren Greenland had announced he needed a cigarette and toilet break. Ruskin had been reluctant to let him go; the revelation that his neighbours had seen Louisa at his flat had clearly shaken him and he was doubtless going to use the time to think up his response. Unfortunately, at present, they didn't have enough to arrest him.

To Ruskin's relief, Greenland returned. He'd been searched when he'd originally been detained, but his nose was reddened and his eyes were jittery. Ruskin tried not to think about where the wily man had hidden the cocaine he'd clearly just snorted, or how he'd managed to secrete it there in the moments between him spotting the uniformed officers heading towards him in the pub, and his bolting for the toilet before they arrested him.

'So, you were saying Louisa never visited you at your flat,' said Ruskin. In his experience, those high on cocaine tended to be motormouths. The question was whether Greenland had taken enough that he was hyperactive, or if he had used just enough to take the edge off his cravings to help him focus.

'She might have popped over once or twice,' admitted Greenland.

'Why?'

Greenland gave a leer. 'Forget the shit she's been saying about me, she was just keeping up appearances. She was well into me.'

'In what way?' asked Ruskin, careful not to put words into the man's mouth.

'She wasn't getting it at home, so she was coming somewhere she could.'

'Are you saying that Louisa Greenland and you were having a sexual relationship?' asked Ruskin.

'Yeah.'

'Were you selling Louisa cocaine?'

'Nope.' He gave a big smile and sat back with his arms folded.

Ruskin didn't believe him for one minute. If he and Louisa had been having sex, it was almost certainly as a means to obtain the drugs she needed. The problem was that Darren Greenland had now given a perfectly plausible explanation for why Louisa Greenland's DNA and fingerprints would be in his flat. From the smug look on his face, Ruskin could see he knew that.

'When was the last time she visited you?'

'Dunno, a week ago, maybe?'

'OK. Then let's assume that was the case,' he said. 'Did you ever visit Louisa at her home?'

'No, like I said, never been there.'

'What about her industrial unit?'

'I told you. I don't even know where it is.'

Ruskin had given him the perfect opportunity to explain away any traces of his DNA at the unit, but he hadn't taken it. Overconfidence, or was he truly not involved?'

'Where were you on the night of Tuesday May 14th, and the following morning?'

'At home,' he said.

'Are you sure?' asked Ruskin.

'Yes.' He fixed Ruskin with a stare.

'According to your housemates, you were out that evening.'

Greenland gave a shrug. 'My housemates wouldn't know if *they* were out that evening. Good luck with them on the witness stand.'

'Why would we need them on the witness stand, Darren?' asked Ruskin.

Greenland opened his mouth, before closing it again. 'Just an expression, innit?' he said eventually. He stretched his back and gave a lazy grin, although the smile didn't reach his eyes.

'So you were at home between seven p.m. on Tuesday night and, let's say, seven a.m. the following morning.'

'That's right.'

'Your housemates disagree, so is there anyone else who can confirm it?'

'Nope.'

'So what were you doing?'

'The cryptic crossword in *The Times*,' said Greenland with a smirk. 'Then I had a bubble bath before going to bed. You know what they say, "early to bed, early to rise, makes a man healthy, wealthy and wise".'

That was unquestionably a lie; Greenland smelled like he hadn't bathed all week.

'Is this your phone?' asked Ruskin, pushing a colour photograph across the desk.

'No idea. They all look the same, don't they?'

'Do you recognise this number?' Ruskin read out the number on the SIM card.

'Who knows their number these days?'

'Well the phone was found in the bottom of your wardrobe, and it has your fingerprints on it.'

'Probably is then,' said Greenland, clearly not bothered.

'It's locked with a PIN code. Could you give me it please?' asked Ruskin.

'Got a warrant?'

'I can get one,' said Ruskin.

'Go on then,' said Greenland. 'And when you do, feel free to ask again. Now, it's been lovely speaking to you, Constable, but I'm a busy man. I've told you where I was, and you have no reason to re-arrest me, so I'll be on my way. If you want to speak to me again, feel free to drop by anytime.'

He started to rise to his feet.

'Who did you go to meet on Tuesday night?' asked Ruskin.

'What do you mean?' asked Greenland, pausing halfway between sitting and standing.

'You went out Tuesday night,' said Ruskin.

'Bollocks. I was in all night watching TV.'

'You said you were doing a crossword, then had a bath and an early night,' Ruskin reminded him, keeping his tone neutral.

Greenland scowled, clearly annoyed that his flippant remarks were coming back to bite him. 'You know what I meant,' he muttered.

'So let's try again. Where were you Tuesday night?'

'Watching TV.'

'Where? You don't own one,' said Ruskin.

'Skags has one downstairs.'

'What did you watch?'

Greenland's eye twitched. 'Don't remember,' he said, a note of desperation creeping into his voice.

'The football?' suggested Ruskin, helpfully.

'Yeah, that's right,' said Greenland, relaxing slightly. 'West Brom and Villa. Went to penalties.'

'That's strange, because Skags said he watched the football alone. He might be a little, shall we say . . . forgetful, but I'm pretty sure he'd get that right. On the witness stand. Now, let's try *again*. Where were you Tuesday night? Your mobile phone left the house at eight-thirty. It was then turned off until the middle of the next day. Where did you go?'

'I want a solicitor,' said Greenland.

* * *

'So, he's not currently under arrest, and could get up and walk anytime,' said Warren. 'But instead, he wants a brief?'

'Sounds like he realises he's in the shit and wants to get his story straight,' said Sutton. 'He knows if he can't convince us he had nothing to do with Louisa's disappearance, we'll keep at him.'

'What do you want to do, Chief?' asked Ruskin.

'Wait until he's finished speaking to his solicitor, listen to whatever claptrap he feeds you, and then continue with the interview as planned,' said Warren. 'He'll probably go no comment, but hopefully he's too arrogant to do the blanket over the head, and face on the desk trick, so we can still see his reactions when you ask him the difficult questions.'

*   *   *

'My client, Mr Greenland, wishes to state he has nothing to do with the disappearance of his brother's wife, Louisa Greenland.'

Greenland stared into space, his face carefully neutral.

'He has no idea where Mrs Greenland is, or why she has left her husband. He admits he and Mrs Greenland had a casual, sexual relationship, but he had not seen her during the week preceding her disappearance. He was aware that her marriage was experiencing some difficulties, but does not know if this is the cause of her leaving.

'He admits he was untruthful about his whereabouts on the night of Tuesday May 14th. He left the house to deal with a personal matter that has no relevance to Mrs Greenland going missing and will therefore not be answering any questions or making any comment on that subject.'

'Are you sure? This whole thing could be cleared up here and now if you cooperate.'

Greenland turned to his solicitor expectantly.

'Mr Greenland does not wish to answer questions on his

131

whereabouts. Suffice to say, he believes it has nothing to do with Mrs Greenland's disappearance.'

'OK,' said Ruskin. 'When did you last see your brother?'

'I told you, at Mum's birthday party.'

'And was that the last time you spoke to him?'

Greenland paused. 'Can't remember.'

Ruskin waited for him to fill the silence, but he said nothing. He opened the folder that he had brought with him.

'Do you know this man?'

He pushed a headshot of Russell Myrie across the table.

Greenland's eyes narrowed. 'No comment.'

'This man is called Russell Myrie. Does that name mean anything to you?'

'No comment.'

'He is a regular at the Feathers pub, as are you. Do you drink with him there?'

'No comment.'

'Did you meet with Russell Myrie on the night of Tuesday May 14th?'

'No comment.'

'Do you know if Mr Myrie knows Mrs Greenland?'

'No comment.'

'Do you know if, or suspect that, Mr Myrie had anything to do with Mrs Greenland's disappearance?'

'No comment.'

Ruskin waited for a few beats. Greenland said nothing.

'Do you have anything else you wish to tell me?'

'No comment.'

Ruskin replaced the lid to his pen. 'Thank you for your time, Darren. Interview terminated.'

* * *

'No question, he was doing something dodgy Tuesday night,' said Sutton.

'But what?' said Warren. 'And with whom?'

'He definitely recognised Myrie,' offered Ruskin. 'But I can't tell what he was thinking when I asked if he met up with him.'

'Me neither,' said Sutton. 'I've re-watched the video on half-speed and once he got over the surprise of seeing the photo, he masked his expression.'

'None of the phones we seized from him match the burner that called Myrie from near the KFC,' said Pymm. 'So if it was him, he's tossed it.'

'But how would he have got to KFC?' said Richardson. 'It's too far to walk from his flat. There's no sign of him on any buses, and as far as we can tell, he has no access to a car. I'll put the word out amongst the cab firms, but you know what junkies are like. He won't have wasted drug money on a taxi unless he had to.'

'So somebody would have needed to pick him up,' said Warren. 'Which means a third person. What do you think about his denial when we asked him about his brother?'

'I wouldn't like to say if he was being truthful or not,' said Sutton.

'But he claimed he couldn't remember when I asked if he'd *spoken* to him,' said Ruskin. 'I reckon that means he has, and he's worried we'll catch him in a lie if we look at his call records. He'd been answering my questions up until then, so a no comment would have been a red flag. He only started no commenting when we showed him the picture of Russell Myrie because it caught him by surprise.'

* * *

'It's going to take time to finish processing Darren Greenland's room,' said Hutchinson. He'd been organising teams of door-knockers in the street that the house was situated on. Whilst there, he'd spoken to Meera Gupta, Andy Harrison's deputy, who was managing the search of the flat.

'It's a proper junkie palace. They're taking it extra slow to avoid needlestick injuries.'

'Anything interesting yet?' asked Sutton, although he knew Gupta would have contacted them if her team found anything significant.

'They've found a sweatshirt with a bloodstain that they've sent off for fast-track analysis,' said Hutchinson. 'But she's told me not to get too excited. It's in the crook of his elbow and seems to have seeped from the inside out. She suspects it's probably his from a leaking injection site.'

Warren wrinkled his nose in disgust. He'd searched plenty of drug users' houses back when he was in uniform with the West Midlands Police. They were almost always absolutely filthy, with all manner of unpleasant bodily fluids waiting to be discovered; he didn't miss that part of the job one bit.

'What else have the neighbours got to say?' asked Warren.

'An old boy across the road has taken it upon himself to record comings and goings from the house. He seemed delighted that we are interested in the place and handed us a dossier, complete with a USB stick he says is full of photographs. He's set a bloody camera up on a tripod in the front bedroom.'

'Jesus,' said Warren. 'Is he mad?'

'Frankly, yes. I'm going to get somebody down from the Drugs squad to see what he's got and persuade him to rein it in before they notice what he's up to. Anyway, he's seen Louisa a few times over the past couple of months. She stuck in his mind, as she looked a little more respectable than the usual visitors. And she arrived in a taxi, which is hardly normal.'

'Can he remember what time of day?' asked Warren.

'Early afternoon, usually.'

'Probably before she does the school pick-ups,' said Sutton. 'She could catch a taxi to Darren's flat, then either get another or catch the bus to the girls' school and nursery and walk them home.'

'What have his housemates said?' asked Warren, more in hope than expectation.

'Most have just given variations on "no comment", although not always that politely. They are not impressed we're conducting a search. The toilet was flushed the moment the front door was forced, and I suspect a few hundred quid's worth of Afghanistan's finest is currently making its way through Middlesbury's sewer system.

'But I may have one of them willing to talk if I can get her on her own. It doesn't look as though she's Darren's biggest fan. I'm thinking I might pretend to find something in her room and use it as an excuse to take her in so we can have a heart-to-heart. If that doesn't work, she was wearing a knocked-off replica Newcastle United shirt.'

'I thought your accent was a bit stronger than usual.' Warren chuckled. Hutchinson had lived most of his adult life down south, and his native Geordie accent was rarely noticeable, unless he'd been drinking or watching the football. But if their witness was from the north-east, then perhaps that might be enough to persuade her to open up.

'Are there any vehicles at the property?' asked Sutton.

'None that are registered, and our amateur surveillance expert has never seen any of them driving.'

'In that case, if he was involved in Louisa's disappearance, either he stole a vehicle or he had an accomplice,' said Warren.

SUNDAY 19TH MAY

Chapter 18

Four days into the hunt for Louisa Greenland and they had several potential suspects and even more theories, but little in the way of concrete evidence. Russell Myrie had been released under investigation. The search team had satisfied themselves Louisa was not in his flat and taken Myrie's devices for further examination, but had carefully replaced the drugs and cash after cataloguing them and taking samples for evidence, should they disappear.

It was a gamble, but it was decided that if Myrie was involved in her disappearance, they had more chance of him leading them to her if he thought he was in the clear. Anything he removed from the property would be retrieved by the surveillance team now tracking his every move.

Darren Greenland hadn't returned home. The search team in his flat hadn't yet finished; exactly where he had vanished to was a mystery. Warren could only hope that if they needed to find him again, they'd be able to do so.

All of Warren's decisions had been backed by Roehampton, but he was under no illusions where the blame would be pinned if they backfired.

What little sleep Warren had managed had been plagued with bad dreams.

By nine a.m. Warren was already contemplating googling to see if taking more than the recommended dose of antacids was likely to be dangerous, so the knock on his office door was more than welcome.

'We've just had an eyewitness report from one of the Greenlands' neighbours,' said Hutchinson. His face was flushed with excitement. 'And you are never going to believe this. She saw Louisa going back into her house on Tuesday night.'

* * *

Warren called an emergency team briefing and patched in Camilla Wong from the Missing Persons Unit on the speakerphone.

'The old lady on the opposite side of the road saw Louisa going into her house about eight-thirty p.m.,' said Hutchinson.

'How certain is she?' asked Sutton. 'It was nearly a week ago.'

'Adamant. She knows it was Tuesday, because she went into hospital for a few days the following morning. That's why she's only just come forward. Her eyesight isn't the best, but she was in her front garden watering the plants after watching *Emmerdale*, when she saw Louisa walking down the street, from the opposite direction to the industrial estate.'

'We don't have any CCTV footage from that end of the road,' said Richardson. 'That's why we won't have captured her.'

'And it was definitely her?' asked Warren.

'Yes, they've lived there since before the Greenlands moved in. She didn't speak to her, but she knows the couple quite well. She says she was wearing jeans and a blue jacket; she had a bag slung over her shoulder, although she can't remember any other details.'

'Louisa wasn't wearing a jacket earlier in the evening, when we saw her on CCTV, but a small coat could easily fit inside the backpack she was carrying,' recalled Richardson.

'If she's right, then that means Ben was lying about Tuesday night,' said Sutton.

'But why was she coming from that direction?' asked Hardwick. 'We have video of her walking towards the industrial estate earlier that evening. And doesn't the location history for her mobile phone show it never left her unit until it was turned off about midnight?'

'The witness says it looked like she waited briefly on the door-step before going in,' said Hutchinson.

'Could she have forgotten her keys?' asked Wong, her voice echoey over the speakerphone. 'She arrives, realises what she's done, and walks back home to pick them up? Then she needs to ring the doorbell to get Ben to let her in?'

'Then why was her phone located in her unit?' asked Hardwick. 'She must have been able to get in to leave it there.'

'Perhaps she went inside, put her phone down, and then for whatever reason went back out and the door locked behind her?' suggested Wong.

'I'm not sure how,' said Warren. 'It has a five-lever mortice and a padlock; it wouldn't just lock if the wind blew it shut.'

'I suppose her phone could have run out of juice, which is why it went dead at midnight,' said Hardwick. 'But we didn't find it or her keys when the unit was searched.'

'Ben could have taken those when he went to her unit the following day, before he reported her missing,' said Ruskin. 'How about this for a scenario? Louisa walks to her office, goes in, dumps her keys on the desk et cetera. Then for whatever reason, decides to nip back out – maybe she wanted some fresh milk or some biscuits to keep her going—'

'Or something stronger,' interrupted Pymm.

'Or something stronger,' agreed Ruskin. 'She puts her jacket on, grabs her bag and then closes the door behind her, closing the padlock, before realising she's left her keys and phone inside.

'She walks back home, rings the doorbell and Ben answers, clearly up to no good. Given what everyone has been suggesting, perhaps he has someone around since he isn't expecting his wife back? Everything goes pear-shaped, and he ends up killing Louisa. The next day, he takes the kids to school and goes to work as normal, which gives him an alibi. The nursery phones him unexpectedly, but that's not a big deal. He goes around to the unit and retrieves her keys and phone, then disposes of the body, before finally reporting her missing?'

'But what about the Taser? Why was it fired in her lock-up, if she was killed at home?' asked Warren.

'Maybe she wasn't killed at home? Maybe she went back to her unit again?' said Ruskin.

'Why?' asked Hardwick. 'And why haven't we seen her on CCTV walking back? And don't forget she was seen by her neighbour walking from the opposite direction to the industrial estate. Why would she do that?'

'Could she have caught a cab?' asked Ruskin. 'And it dropped her past her house?'

'Paid for how?' countered Hardwick. 'As far as we know her purse and phone were locked inside.'

'An emergency fiver in her backpack?' he suggested weakly. 'Anyway, going back to the Taser, what if he fired it to make it seem as though she was killed at the unit, rather than at home. To stop us looking too closely in the house, where she really died?'

'Then why remove almost all the AFID tags?' asked Sutton.

'He went to the trouble of disconnecting the camera weeks in advance, and I can't imagine he had a Taser just lying around,' said Hutchinson. 'That's premeditation, not spur of the moment.'

'Not necessarily,' said Pymm. 'He could have been thinking about killing her for months. Then she comes home unexpectedly, things escalate and suddenly he has to put his plan into action.'

'Did his neighbours actually see his car parked outside the house all night?' suggested Ruskin. 'He could have waited until he figured the rest of the street had gone to bed before nipping out to dispose of her body and stage the scene in her unit.'

'Presumably he'd have had to leave the girls unattended and his mobile phone at home,' said Sutton. 'But if he's just killed their mother, he's hardly a shining example of parenthood.'

'Does his car show up on ANPR?' asked Warren, in an attempt to remind them that they needed facts and evidence. The whole conversation was getting hypothetical, and rather far-fetched, in his opinion. But then again, he valued his team's creativity.

'Nowhere in the vicinity of their house,' Richardson replied. 'But there are routes out of that corner of town that wouldn't trigger any cameras. I can get Traffic to widen the search area.' She looked over at Hardwick and Ruskin. 'And I'll also check for any cabs around the time we think she returned home that night.'

'Do it,' ordered Warren. 'Unless he has access to somewhere like a garage that he could leave her, then we need to start thinking about potential dumping sites. If we can at least work out which side of town he headed to, it will narrow the possibilities.'

The area surrounding Middlesbury was semi-rural, with numerous farms and wooded areas. If it came down to a search, then they would need at least some guidance. A thought struck him. 'We haven't executed a warrant on the Greenlands' house yet. Is there any possibility her body is in the property?'

Hardwick answered. 'Unless he's placed her in the loft space, I can't see where,' she said. 'Kevin Lederer and the other FLOs have been there for the past couple of days. I'll check, but knowing Kevin, he'll have had a crafty look in every room as well as the back garden to see if there are any obvious signs of digging. There isn't a garage.'

'Well it looks as though Ben's not been entirely truthful with us,' said Warren. 'We definitely have enough to get a warrant to search the house properly.'

'Should we arrest him?' asked Wong.

'Not yet,' said Warren. 'I don't want to spook him. We'll bring him in for questioning under caution but downplay the significance of the search warrant. In fact, we'll see if he lets us in voluntarily. We'll let him think we're looking for reasons she may have left of her own accord. We'll also search his car whilst he's at the station. I'll speak to DSI Roehampton and get her to square it with the magistrate.'

There came a knock at the door, and one of the civilian support staff poked her head around the door. 'Sorry to interrupt.' Her face was grave.

Warren's stomach flipped.

'They've found a body,' she said. 'Farley Woods. A young woman, white, with dark hair.'

'Shit,' said Warren quietly.

* * *

'A group of ecology students, doing a woodland study, noticed a strong, rotting smell and a load of flies buzzing around a bush,' said Andy Harrison. 'The lecturer went to take a look and found the body.'

Warren had just finished climbing into a paper suit. Beside him, Moray Ruskin was zipping up one of the super-sized suits he carried in the boot of his car in case the CSIs didn't have one that fitted.

The three men ducked under the blue and white tape as Harrison led the way. A prescribed route of metal stepping plates had already been laid down and they took care not to slip and destroy any potential evidence.

'It's not my place to estimate time of death, but off the record, she's been here a few days.'

Warren braced himself. On Harrison's recommendation, he and Ruskin had smeared a generous amount of mentholated VapoRub under their noses.

The body lay on its back. Warren recognised the blue jeans and white T-shirt that he'd seen on the last CCTV footage of Louisa Greenland. A large, dark red patch was centred in her chest. A grey backpack was discarded a few metres away.

More stepping plates had been laid at regular intervals in a circle around the body, and Warren made a cautious circuit of the victim.

'I'm afraid there were quite a few students in the group, so we're going to have to eliminate all of their shoeprints before we can tell if the killer or killers left any useful impressions,' said Harrison.

Leaning forward to see her face, Warren confirmed it was Louisa Greenland; he'd been staring at photographs of the young woman for the past four days. He felt a wave of profound sadness. He wasn't surprised it was her, but it didn't make it any less tragic. The woman was just thirty-one, her whole life ahead of her. Someone was going to have to break the news to her husband and parents and sister, and then they were going to have to figure out how to explain to a five-year-old and a three-year-old that Mummy wasn't coming home. Warren felt a wave of empathy, as he imagined having to tell Niall . . .

'No attempt to hide her,' noted Ruskin, jerking Warren back to reality. 'I don't know if that's worse. She's just been . . . discarded.'

'The pathologist is due within the hour,' said Harrison, 'but it looks as though she's been stabbed.' His voice held a disgusted edge. 'And her hands are bound behind her. It doesn't look as though her clothes have been disturbed, but obviously the pathologist will need to determine if she has been sexually assaulted.'

'Any sign of a weapon?' asked Warren.

'Not in the immediate vicinity. Once the body has been recovered, and we've finished photographing, we'll do a fingertip search and retrieve the bag.'

'How did the body get here?' asked Warren.

'I'm only speculating,' said Harrison. 'But I'm not seeing any drag marks. Either she walked here under her own steam, or she was carried and dumped.' He pointed back the way they had walked. 'That access road comes within a hundred metres of here. Or . . .' he pointed in the opposite direction '. . . there is a dirt track a couple of hundred metres that way. It's quite overgrown but if she was walking, or there were a couple of people carrying her, it wouldn't be a huge challenge. We'll check her trainers for dirt and leaf litter.

'Unfortunately, both access roads are well used by forestry workers, students and Scout groups, so I don't know how much luck we'll have lifting tyre tracks.'

Warren thanked him, leaving him to organise his CSIs.

The post-mortem should reveal if she was killed elsewhere and her body dumped. But if her hands were tied then it suggested that if she had been killed where she was found, she had been forced to walk to her own death. He could only imagine her terror.

'We'd better get going,' he said. 'Before one of those students tweets about what they found in the woods today and the Greenlands find out about Louisa's death on social media.'

*   *   *

The discovery of Louisa Greenland's body had been a blow to the whole team. But unlike most such situations, where the finding was unexpected, the investigation was already well underway. After satisfying himself that Andy Harrison had everything in hand, Warren had left Tony Sutton in charge and returned to the station.

'The surveillance team assigned to Russell Myrie haven't spotted any suspicious behaviour,' said Richardson.

'It'll be interesting to see what he does and who he speaks to when the news breaks,' said Hutchinson.

'I agree,' said Warren. 'In the meantime, are we any closer to figuring out where he went that night and who he was meeting?'

'I've got the cell-tower data from the area surrounding the KFC when the text was sent to him,' said Pymm. 'It's on a retail park close to a residential area, and there are two more takeaways nearby, all of which were open until midnight.'

'So, lots of mobile phones,' said Warren.

'Yes. If whoever called him did leave their personal phone switched on, then it's in the mix somewhere. If we get a suspect, then we may be able to work backwards and place them there.'

'Did Ben or Louisa's phones show up?' asked Ruskin.

'No,' said Pymm. 'But then I wouldn't really expect them to. If the caller had any sense – and it looks as though he was at least switched on enough to use a single-use burner – then he made the call from the KFC, switched the burner off and then drove to the rendezvous point. All those restaurants are drive-thru late at night, so there are phones constantly arriving and leaving.'

'What about vehicles?' asked Warren.

'I have a list, but we can't link any to our persons of interest,' said Richardson. 'And you can easily dodge the cameras. There is ANPR half a mile away on the trunk road, but even that time of night there are too many vehicles to proactively trace without authorisation from a budget holder.'

Warren rubbed his nose wearily. 'OK, where are we with Darren Greenland?' he asked.

'No vehicle that we've identified,' said Richardson.

'He has a collection of burner phones and a more permanent handset,' said Pymm. 'I imagine he uses the permanent phone to keep in touch with family and his parole officer, but it so rarely leaves the house, at least when turned on, it may as well be a landline.'

'He probably switches it off whenever he's doing something or meeting someone he shouldn't,' said Hutchinson. 'I doubt he trusts his housemates enough to leave anything remotely valuable unattended when he goes out.'

'Speaking of housemates, have you had any luck with your new Geordie friend?' asked Warren.

'Yes,' said Hutchinson. 'She agreed to meet me in a local pub. She had some interesting things to say. I don't think she'd usually speak to the police, but Darren scares her. I think she's hoping that if we can pin something on him, he'll be out of her life.'

'Is she reliable?' asked Warren immediately. 'I'm guessing she's a drug addict and it sounds like she might have good reasons to lie to us. That's an easy win for the defence, especially if she won't come to court.'

'You're probably right,' said Hutchinson. 'But for what it's worth, I think she's telling the truth. She has just about managed to fund her habit so far – she didn't say how – but Darren has made it clear that if she's ever short of cash, she can borrow off him and pay him back in other ways.'

'I don't like the way this is going,' said Warren.

'Yeah, it's not good,' said Hutchinson. 'She says that she's seen Louisa a few times. It used to be a couple of times a month, but recently it's been a bit more frequent. She always went up to Darren's room, but was usually back down and out the door, quick smart. The last time she saw her would have been roughly a week ago, which matches what the old boy across the road says. She said Louisa was up there for about twenty minutes, and when she left, she was in tears.'

Chapter 19

By late afternoon, Tony Sutton had called to say that the pathologist had completed his initial *in situ* examination of Louisa's body and she was on her way to the morgue. He volunteered to stay out at the scene with Andy Harrison whilst the search began in earnest. That it meant he was unavailable to attend the post-mortem was just a coincidence.

'We've got a potential hit on the ANPR cameras nearest the industrial estate the night Louisa went missing,' said Richardson.

'What do you mean?' asked Warren. They had a complete download of all the vehicles photographed near Louisa's unit in the hours surrounding the disappearance but hadn't found any linked to persons of interest.

'We got lucky,' said Richardson. 'When her body was found in Farley Woods, I had the analysts scan ANPR and traffic cam records for cameras out that end of town. I figured vehicles seen in the vicinity of her lock-up that were later photographed on those cameras might include the killer's car. It could cut the list of potential vehicles if we end up having to investigate them all.'

'Good thinking,' said Warren. Richardson had worked Traffic before making the sideways move into CID. She was now the team's primary liaison with the Video Analysis Unit at headquarters, expanding her skill set to include all forms of video evidence analysis. 'Have you identified one?'

'Sort of. One of the analysts spotted a logical inconsistency. The same licence plate was snapped four times on two different cameras. Three times travelling in one direction – away from the unit and towards the woods – and once travelling in the opposite direction. The sequence in which the cameras were triggered would mean the car had to have left the industrial estate and been snapped, then somehow driven beyond the second camera without being photographed – which isn't impossible if they took a bit of a weird route – before turning back and being snapped by the second camera travelling back towards the estate, and then turning around *again* and being captured by it a second time. Then it would have needed to loop back, avoiding the camera again, to be photographed a *fourth* time travelling away from the unit.'

Warren blinked. 'You're going to have to draw it out for me,' he said.

Richardson handed over a printout of an annotated map. 'I thought I might. If you look, it is possible if the driver does a rat run down Parkland Road.'

'Yeah, that works,' said Warren. 'Granted, it's a bit weird, but maybe it was a taxi driver with multiple drop-offs or pick-ups? Or the driver forgot something and turned back?'

'That's what I would have thought. But look at the timings between the camera closest to the industrial unit and the first time the vehicle was photographed at the second camera.'

'Seven minutes,' said Warren. He frowned. 'How far are they apart?'

'Shortest possible route is nine point six miles.'

'Bloody hell.'

'That's an average of eighty-two miles per hour. And they'll have needed to do that rat run down Parkland Road, which is all narrow residential streets, at over seventy.'

'Even at that time of night, with blues and twos, I doubt a trained pursuit driver could manage that,' said Warren.

'And there are average speed cameras along parts of the trunk road,' said Richardson. 'Nobody was snapped travelling above the limit, which means that if they did slow down to fifty for those stretches, they must have been doing over a ton outside of them, on single carriageway with lorries and other vehicles present. There are no reports of anyone driving that dangerously; folks would have been ringing in left, right and centre. I can't imagine the killer would drive that recklessly with a kidnapped woman in the car.'

'So what's your interpretation?' asked Warren. He could only think of one explanation.

'I think same licence plate, two different vehicles. Then the numbers add up, with both vehicles travelling within the speed limit. It's a hell of a stroke of luck and a massive coincidence that they were both out on the road at the same time. But it would be an even bigger coincidence if one of these vehicles wasn't involved in Louisa's disappearance.'

* * *

The morgue serving Middlesbury, and the surrounding villages, was based at the Lister Hospital in Stevenage. The registered Home Office pathologist dealing with suspicious deaths was Professor Ryan Jordan, a pleasant-natured American, who'd worked in the UK since falling for an Englishwoman as a young man.

Strictly speaking, there was no need for attending officers to be inside the autopsy suite whilst the procedure was performed. A wall-length window, with a two-way intercom, allowed them to watch from afar. But as much as he disliked post-mortems, Warren felt he gained more if he scrubbed up and joined Jordan at the table. He also felt it was the least he could do for the victim. Jordan was a warm, compassionate man, treating the deceased with the same care and attention that he would a living patient. Warren found he could look a victim's loved ones in the eyes more easily, if he'd seen first-hand that no matter how their death had come about, they had been treated with dignity by someone who cared, before being handed back to them.

As always, Moray Ruskin had volunteered to attend. In another life, the young Scotsman could have been a pathologist; he certainly had the stomach for it. For his part, Warren had avoided eating since the body had been found.

'I've sent off for blood toxicology to confirm,' said Jordan. 'But judging by the scarring on her septum, and the traces of powder I've swabbed from the inside of her nostrils, I'm going to suggest she had been using cocaine in the hours before she died, and that she was a regular, if not habitual user.'

'What about alcohol?' asked Ruskin.

'Nothing in her stomach, and she had a blood alcohol level of zero. Her liver shows none of the signs I'd associate with chronic alcohol abuse, so either she wasn't a big drinker, or if she used to be, she'd been sober long enough for any damage to be repaired.'

'What about cause of death?' asked Warren.

'No big mystery. A single stab wound to the heart.' Jordan turned to a metal dish. Ruskin looked on in fascination, Warren with steely determination, as the pathologist gently turned the organ. 'As you can see, straight through the left ventricle. The blade was large, almost three centimetres wide judging by the width of the cut and the external wound. There is no serration, and only one sharpened edge, the other is a few millimetres in width. I'm going to suggest a large chef's knife with a sharp point, or similar.'

'Make sure the search teams catalogue the kitchens of any persons of interest,' Warren instructed Ruskin.

'Even with prompt medical attention in a hospital with surgeons on hand, the wound was probably not survivable. If it helps the relatives, it will have been relatively quick,' said Jordan.

'Was she killed where she was found?' asked Warren.

'I'd say so,' answered Jordan. 'The blood released from the wound has dribbled in a downwards direction, which indicates to me she was standing when the blade went in. I think she stood for a few seconds, then collapsed. The lividity from the blood pooling indicates she wasn't moved from that position after her heart stopped beating. There are also significant bloodstains on the surrounding soil, which will have come from a living person.'

'Andy Harrison said her hands were tied,' said Warren.

'Bound behind her back,' confirmed Jordan. He lifted a clear plastic evidence bag containing two, off-white plastic cable ties.

He lifted her wrists, one by one, chafing and bruising clearly visible. On the inside of her left wrist was a small tattoo of a broken heart, with the letter "S" in its centre; the matching half of the decoration worn by her sister.

'The ties were very tight. She'd have had no feeling in her fingers,' said Jordan. 'I've done a complete external examination.' He pointed to two circular bumps similar to mosquito bites on the side of her neck. 'From the distance apart, and what you found in her unit, I'd say these are from the prongs of a Taser.'

'So her attacker subdued her with a stun gun, then tied her hands behind her back to keep her immobilised,' said Warren. 'Are there any other bruises or cuts?'

Jordan gently lifted her hair; an ugly raised cut marked the right-hand side of her temple. 'From the swelling, I'd say she sustained this an hour or so before she died.'

'There was a spot of blood on the doorframe,' recalled Ruskin. 'A little over a metre off the floor. I'll bet she hit her head when she collapsed from the Taser jolt.'

'That interpretation would fit,' said Jordan. 'There are also some fresh bruises on her torso and legs. They don't appear to be from a beating.'

'Bouncing around in the boot of a car?' suggested Ruskin. 'They had to transport her to the woods somehow.'

'Again, that explanation would work,' said Jordan.

'Is there any evidence of sexual assault?' asked Warren.

'Nothing I could find,' said Jordan. 'And her underwear and clothing were undisturbed.'

'Which doesn't sound like Russell Myrie,' said Ruskin.

'I agree,' said Warren. 'Which leaves the motive wide open. If it wasn't sexual, then why?'

'If she was kidnapped for money, why kill her?' asked Ruskin. 'A dead body's not going to make the Greenlands pay up. If they were holding out, or Ben needed more time to raise the money, surely it would be better to keep her somewhere safe? Not to mention, a conviction for murder is a whole different kettle of fish to one for kidnapping.'

'Maybe they screwed up?' suggested Jordan. It was rare for him to overstep his role in the investigation, but Warren could see that the cold-blooded killing had touched him. 'If she saw their faces, or realised she recognised them, maybe they felt there was no choice? They couldn't risk her identifying them.'

'That's what I'm thinking,' said Warren. 'This was not a spur-of-the-moment thing. Taking her took planning and preparation, but what happened next? Did they keep her someplace whilst they contacted Ben?'

'Or whilst Ben tried to persuade his mother to pay up,' Ruskin reminded Warren.

'Her stomach contains traces of what could have been cottage pie,' interjected Jordan. 'Which her husband claims they ate about sixish. I can't use that to determine time of death reliably, but what I can say is that when she died, she wasn't dehydrated or malnourished. If she was kept somewhere for more than a few hours, then she was watered, and possibly fed.'

'Can you put any limits on when she was killed?' asked Warren. It was a big ask, and courts were increasingly sceptical of overconfident pathologists who tried to precisely calculate time of death.

Jordan was silent for a moment. 'Off the record, best I can give you is that judging by the state of the body, and that the blood was thoroughly dried, my gut feeling is she died more than twenty-four hours before she was discovered. But I'm not willing to speculate if she was killed the night she went missing or sometime later. The stomach contents might not even be from Tuesday night; they could be from later.'

The thought that Ben might have fed his captive wife leftovers from their final family meal made Warren's stomach clench. 'Well, regardless of when she was actually killed,' he said, 'walking her out to a remote part of those woods, hands tied, then killing her with a single stab wound wasn't a crime of passion. It was an execution.'

Chapter 20

'Sir, you are never going to believe what we've just found,' called out Pymm. She and Mags Richardson wore big, satisfied smiles.

'Tell me,' said Warren. They'd returned from the autopsy via McDonald's, at Ruskin's request. The constable had wolfed down his triple cheeseburger as if he hadn't been fed for a month, and had happily scoffed Warren's barely-touched meal too. The latter would eat later when his appetite returned.

'You go first, Mags,' said Pymm.

'You asked us to expand the ANPR search for Ben Greenland's car,' said Richardson. 'I found it. A single hit at 00.16 on Lester Road.'

'You're joking,' said Warren.

'It's only a partial; the licence plate was filthy, so there were a couple of digits missing, meaning we had to visually confirm using the photo. But the DVLA doesn't list any other Renault Espaces with that combination of letters, in that colour.'

'He said he didn't go out that night,' said Warren. 'What about you, Rachel?'

'I've been looking into the Greenlands' financials some more, and I noticed a change in one of their direct debits a few months back.'

'And?'

'Ben Greenland more than quadrupled the value of their life insurance policy shortly after Louisa signed the Holistics Gym contract. The payout on his wife's death will wipe out her debts, clear their second mortgage, and leave a tidy chunk of change left over. I think we've found our motive and maybe even opportunity.'

'Right, we need to bring Ben in and do a full search of their house and garden and his car,' said Warren. 'He's been lying to us, and I want to know why. At the very least, if he is innocent, then the threat of a murder charge might get him to start telling us the truth so we can figure out what really happened.'

He turned to Sutton. 'Fancy a bit of good cop, bad cop, Tony?'

'Do you need to even ask?'

* * *

'Sir, I've just brought Ben Greenland in, and he's being processed downstairs,' said Hardwick over the phone. 'But we have a problem with his solicitor.'

'Are they challenging the warrants?' asked Warren.

'No, nothing like that, they're completely kosher; the CSIs were in there the moment his mother took his daughters to her house. It's more a case of *who* his solicitor is.'

* * *

'What are you doing here, Stephanie?' asked Warren.

'I am protecting the interests of Ben Greenland, DCI Jones.' Stephanie Hellard pushed her chin out, her arms folded.

'You can't,' said Warren, dumbfounded. 'Your relationship with Mr Greenland and the deceased notwithstanding, you've been interviewed with respect to this case as a witness. You can't defend him – there's a clear conflict of interest.'

The whole affair was so surreal, he wondered for a moment if he was dreaming. Hellard was an experienced solicitor – she had even been made a partner in a respected law firm. Surely she must know there was no way she could represent her brother-in-law.

'I'm not defending him,' she clarified. 'I am making sure Ben is processed correctly and isn't tricked into making any admissions that might harm any later defence, should this nonsense ever get to court.'

'We have duty solicitors for that,' said Warren, amazed he needed to remind her. Ben Greenland would be treated the same as any other suspect, his rights strictly protected by an impartial custody officer well versed in the legal codes laid down by PACE.

Hellard gave a snort of derision. 'I am not trusting my brother-in-law's welfare to some overworked, uninterested duty solicitor who's only doing legal aid work because their firm isn't good enough to attract paying clients.'

Warren felt his jaw drop, before snapping it closed again. In all his years, he'd never heard a professional solicitor dismiss one of their colleagues in such an arrogant manner. And he couldn't believe he was about to defend a group of people who he had spent much of his career butting heads with. All police officers were at times exasperated, even frustrated, by the obstacles and objections thrown up by the persons representing the suspects they were trying to nail. But they recognised that for justice to be truly delivered, the accused had to have their rights guarded with as much vigour as the victim's.

For all its faults, Warren firmly believed that the British justice system was the best in the world, which was why, when a suspect was formally arrested, he would always try to persuade them to take the offer of a free, independent duty solicitor. The practice of encouraging or even bullying detainees to "voluntarily" waive their constitutional right to a lawyer, seen so often in true crime documentaries filmed across the Atlantic, made him sick every time he saw it.

He opened his mouth again to reply, unwilling to let the outrageous slur go unchallenged, before seeing her eyes. There was anger and defiance there certainly, but most of all, he saw pain. The raw pain of a woman who had just found out that her sister – her twin in all meaningful senses of the word – had been brutally murdered.

He consciously lowered his tone, trying to bring the temperature down.

'Look, Stephanie, I get that you want what's best for Ben, really I do, but I can't let you go into that interview suite with him. The whole case would be compromised. You must know that. Besides which, you know how cases like this play out. We're going to be digging into Ben and Louisa's private lives. What we find may not be pretty. Do you really want your memories of your sister tarnished?'

Hellard smiled tightly. 'Thank you for your concern, DCI Jones. However, I know what I am doing. As I said, I am here temporarily until his appointed solicitor arrives. She will be here in less than two hours, at which point she will take over.'

*   *   *

'This has the potential to become an unholy mess,' said Roehampton. She had been as gobsmacked as Warren when he relayed what had just taken place at the custody desk.

'I'm sorry, Guv,' said Hardwick. 'Ms Hellard was with Ben at the Greenlands' house when we arrived to arrest him and execute the search warrant. He was completely stunned and she kind of took over, inspecting the warrants and telling him to keep his mouth shut and answer "no comment" to everything. She told him to hang tight and she'd "sort everything".

'After then, we kind of lost track of her. She turned up at the custody desk shortly after Ben was brought in, claiming to be with him. She checked out, so they let her in. It wasn't until I went down there to see how everything was progressing and saw her that I realised what had happened.'

'Shit,' muttered Roehampton. She forced a smile. 'Hardly your fault, Karen. I've never come across this before.'

'Me neither,' confirmed Warren.

'What's our position on this?' asked Roehampton.

'Shaky, but according to Legal, it looks as though she's just about on the right side of the law,' said Warren. 'Are you certain she hasn't had any privileged communications with him since his arrest?'

'Definitely,' said Hardwick. 'He was still being booked in when she arrived. She spoke to him briefly, but it was just to remind him to say nothing. It was in full view of the custody area; there's no way it can be considered privileged. To be fair, Tony Sutton has reviewed the CCTV and at no point does she actually say she has been retained as his solicitor, she simply says that she is there to protect him. They just kind of assumed, after seeing her credentials, that she was his solicitor. They weren't to know who she was, especially given her different surname.'

'Hmm,' said Roehampton. 'Perhaps a little more rigour is needed at the custody desk?'

That was somewhat unfair, Warren thought, but now wasn't the time.

'What about the fact that her own firm will still be representing him?' asked Roehampton.

'Apparently, the appointed solicitor works for a different firm, and has been hired on a freelance basis. Stephanie will have no interactions with them, with all communications channelled through her partner. It's irregular, but as long as they maintain a firewall between her and the case, then legally it's not a no-no,' said Warren. 'Legal said they might be able to mount a challenge, but they weren't convinced it will work and it could take days to get a judgement. I think we're stuck with the situation.'

'They're lawyers,' said Roehampton, her distaste clear. 'You can bet there will definitely be a firewall – on paper at least. But we can be certain that Stephanie will know exactly what goes on in that interview suite.'

'That goes both ways,' said Warren. 'We are going to have to be extra careful about what we share with the family. Ben could easily get wind of whatever strategies we're planning.'

'I don't know about you two, but I think this whole thing was planned,' said Roehampton.

'I agree,' said Hardwick. 'She's a solicitor. She had to know that our attention would turn to Ben. Her precise use of language when she arrived at the station was clearly well rehearsed. You don't come up with that sort of strategy in a panic, when the police have just turned up with a handful of warrants.'

'And I'll bet the solicitor who's currently belting up the M11 from London will be far better briefed than you'd expect for someone who supposedly only got a call two hours ago,' said Warren.

A look of distaste crossed Roehampton's face. 'I hate being the one to say it, but isn't she awfully young to have been made a partner – even a junior one – in a respected law firm like that? Makes you wonder if she might have jumped a few hurdles . . .'

'I googled her,' admitted Hardwick. 'And found an article naming her as an up-and-coming star. The senior partner is a middle-aged man, big on family values, for what that's worth . . .'

'Aren't they always? Well regardless of how she got there, what I want to know is why she's doing this,' said Roehampton. 'Is she really that convinced he's innocent?'

'She was adamant she believed he would never hurt Louisa when I interviewed her,' said Hardwick.

'And that's been the assessment of everyone else we've interviewed,' added Warren.

'But still,' said Roehampton. 'She knows that for all our faults, the police don't simply arrest someone on a whim. And warrants don't get signed off unless there are sufficient grounds. You'd think that would raise at least some doubts in her mind.'

'Maybe there are doubts,' said Warren slowly. 'Maybe she isn't convinced that he's innocent.'

'What do you mean?' asked Roehampton.

'Her sister's just been murdered. She's spent enough time working in the justice system to know that from now on, the victim's family will only ever get a highly sanitised version of what's happening in the investigation. It could be a year before – if – this goes to trial, and even then, they won't see everything we have. Even with our commitment to openness and the support of the FLOs, the victim's family are at the bottom of our priority list. They get what we give them and no more. The integrity of the investigation comes before everything.' It was a harsh summation, but ultimately accurate. 'So aside from the investigation team, and the offender, the person with the most insight into what actually happened is the defence solicitor after the disclosure of evidence. Maybe she just wants to know what really happened? So she can decide for herself if her brother-in-law murdered her sister.'

* * *

Warren met with Tony Sutton for an hour before they headed down to the interview suite. Stephanie Hellard had finally left, after handing over her brother-in-law's representation to her colleague. As Warren had predicted, Josie Barton, the woman appointed as Ben Greenland's solicitor, had arrived with a bulging briefcase and her laptop. Her initial discussion with her new client had taken place privately, and lasted barely half an hour.

'She's been prepping for this for days,' said Sutton. The routine request for evidence disclosure had been politely rebuffed. There was no need for Warren and Sutton to reveal their cards this early in the interview process. So far, the search of the Greenlands' property had turned up one or two items of interest, but no smoking gun – or more accurately, bloodstained kitchen knife. All the utensils had been seized for detailed examination, but

162

none had any obvious blood traces, and the knife block had no suspicious gaps.

The smartly dressed solicitor was older than she looked – she had to be, otherwise she wouldn't have graduated from law school yet – but was still some years shy of her thirtieth birthday. She shook Warren and Sutton's hands firmly, but her eyes darted nervously about. Was this really Stephanie's idea of taking care of her brother-in-law? If Warren was in his shoes, he'd want a twenty-year-veteran duty solicitor, not whatever freelancer her firm could retain at short notice.

He turned his attention to Greenland. The man was silent, his head bowed, the initial shock of the arrest having given way to a dull listlessness. It had been five days since he first reported Louisa missing, and judging by his appearance he'd barely slept or eaten in that time. Now his wife's body had been found, the nervous energy driving him had vanished.

Warren had interviewed dozens of murderers over the years, and even more grieving loved ones, and had seen all manner of reactions. It was too early for him to decide which he thought Greenland was; the man could even be both.

Warren introduced himself and Sutton for the recording, reminded Greenland of his rights, then started with an expression of condolence for his loss. He carefully watched the man's reaction.

Nothing.

Was he too grief-stricken to fully process what had been said to him, or was he a calculating killer determined not to give anything away?

'I'd like to start by asking what happened the evening of Tuesday May 14th, the night you last saw Louisa.'

'No comment,' said Greenland, keeping his eyes firmly on the table.

'What time did you last see Louisa?'

'No comment.'

Beside him, Sutton stirred. 'It is going to be a very long night, Ben, if you refuse to confirm even basic information that you have already given in previous statements.'

Greenland looked towards his solicitor, who gave a minuscule shake of her head. He returned his gaze to the table and mumbled, 'No comment,' again.

It was obvious which way the interview was heading; Greenland had been instructed to answer "no comment" to everything he was asked. Warren knew from experience that open questions – requiring long, complex answers – would be more likely to be rebuffed. So he switched to the backup interview plan he and Sutton had devised, hoping short, simple questions might persuade Greenland to break his silence.

'Did you see Louisa again after she left your house on Tuesday evening?'

'No comment.'

And so it continued. For over an hour, Warren and Sutton worked their way through a list of pre-planned questions designed to test whether Greenland was sticking with his original statements. He refused to answer any of them. His solicitor remained as motionless as the Sphinx, not even taking notes.

Finally, Warren asked the most pressing question. 'Ben, did you kill Louisa?'

Greenland's jaw worked up and down and he briefly raised his head. His eyes brimmed with tears. 'No,' he said before lapsing back into silence.

With nothing else forthcoming, Warren decided to call it a day, and ended the interview. Greenland rose to his feet, zombie-like and was led back to his cell without a word.

'She didn't even demand to know on what grounds we had decided to arrest him,' said Sutton, once Barton was safely out of earshot. 'She was just there to listen and find out what we know. It was a fishing expedition.'

'She didn't catch anything though, did she?' said Warren. The two men had agreed that if Greenland no commented, then there was no point asking him anything that might reveal their strategy. Ideally, they wanted to sandbag Greenland with the inconsistencies they had found in his account.

In a way, it was a good thing. The longer Greenland held out, the longer the search teams had to find any evidence.

'We still have plenty of time before we need to apply for an extension to custody,' said Warren. 'We'll see what the CSIs find for us before then. In the meantime, I want to see what we've got on the other two upstanding gentlemen on our radar, and then I'm going to try and get home at a decent hour.'

MONDAY 20TH MAY

Chapter 21

The forensics team had worked through the night searching the Greenland family home.

'We'll get the metal detectors in this afternoon, but there's no obviously recently disturbed soil in the garden,' said Meera Gupta. 'And nothing in the shed or the loft space.'

One of the team's main priorities was finding the murder weapon. The lab had started testing the various knives seized from the kitchen for blood.

Warren wasn't too hopeful. The killer had been careful not to leave any trace evidence on Louisa's body. If she had been killed by her husband, in what appeared to be a well-planned attack, then he could have disposed of the knife anywhere. Even with blood dogs and metal detectors, it could take weeks to search the woods where her body was found, and whatever roadside verges he had travelled past on his way home.

'We've seized his wardrobe and are testing it with luminol. The bathroom and kitchen sinks are clean – no blood. We'll dismantle the sink traps and check the filters in the washing machine and tumble dryer later today.

'But we do have some good news. We found a second smart-phone, hidden down the side of his mattress. It's locked with a fingerprint and a PIN. As soon as we've had it fingerprinted and swabbed, I'll get it over to Digital Forensics and see what they can do with it. If nothing else, they should be able to get its number off the SIM card and the device's ID. They've already seized the house's Wi-Fi hub.'

'What about his vehicle?' asked Warren.

'Full treatment later today. They've already taken tyre impressions, although from what Andy tells me, the tracks up by the forest are a bit of a mess. But there's plenty of mud and leaf litter on the undercarriage, so we can get a soil comparison and a pollen expert to see if it has been to the forest recently.'

'Do it,' ordered Warren. The vehicle was the Greenlands' family car. Traces of Louisa's DNA, and even small amounts of blood, could be plausibly dismissed, however, evidence the car had been near the dump site would be more difficult to explain, especially if they were able to force Greenland into denying the car had been to the woods recently.

Mags Richardson had looked at the various routes leading from the Greenlands' house to where the body had been found in Farley Woods. She was confident that if Ben stayed within the speed limit, he could make the journey without being captured on any ANPR systems.

'We've also fingerprinted their home office,' said Gupta. 'There is an under-desk, metal filing cabinet marked "P@mper". It's locked with a key that is stuck to a magnet and fixed to the rear.'

'Sounds secure,' said Warren.

'To be fair, anyone could easily force it open. I suspect it's probably locked to stop the girls opening it and tipping it on themselves. Anyway, the key has Ben's thumbprint on it, as does the handle.'

'So he's opened it at some point,' said Warren. 'That doesn't mean he's been rooting through it recently. It could be an old cabinet they cleared out for Louisa's paperwork.'

'The plastic label tabs on the suspension files she organised her paperwork in have Ben's prints on them. It looks as though he lifted them out at some point.'

'That is interesting,' said Warren. 'What about the paperwork inside?'

'We've found his fingerprints on everything from invoices to bank statements. Including a letter from the bank declining her application for a loan extension.'

'Bingo!' said Warren.

✱ ✱ ✱

'The owner of the car snapped on ANPR has been tracked down,' said Richardson. 'Registered keeper is a Mr Karolinska. The vehicle is a white Ford Focus and he lives locally. According to his statement, he was out about that time. His daughter was at a house party and he agreed to stay up and pick her up when it finished, rather than have her call a cab. From his statement, I think his was the vehicle that passed the camera closest the woods travelling towards town at 01.09h, and then in the return direction at either 01.23h or 01.26h. Which means our suspect's vehicle was the one passing the camera near the industrial unit at 01.02h and the second camera at either 01.23h or 01.26h.'

'Brilliant,' said Warren. 'Rachel?'

'The phone Ben was carrying when he was arrested has been unlocked, and the analysts are going over it,' said Pymm.

'Good. We already know the phone didn't leave the house that night and didn't make any calls or receive any texts,' said Warren. 'What other messaging apps has he installed?'

'The usual. WhatsApp, Facebook Messenger. They should be able to retrieve anything he's deleted. I'll have a list of all his contacts, past and present, today. We'll get complete transcripts later.'

'What about photographs?'

'Lots, mostly of the kids. Unfortunately, the phone is pretty old, with very little memory, so he deleted a lot of images. But the good news is it synced automatically to a cloud storage service. It saves anything he deleted in the trash for thirty days. And with a warrant, we might even be able to access their backups and find anything he tried to get rid of earlier.'

'That could be useful,' said Warren. 'I can't imagine there will be any pictures of him stabbing his wife, but we might need to prove he had a prior association with other suspects. Have you anything from the phone found hidden in the bedroom?'

'They finished fingerprinting and it's definitely his. No traces of Louisa's prints or any unknowns; I'd say he kept it secret from her. It was locked with a fingerprint and PIN code. But here's the interesting thing. This handset is newer than the one he uses as his personal phone. It has more storage and its battery isn't knackered. They've had to keep his personal phone constantly on charge since they seized it. Now, if you had access to a better phone, wouldn't you use that, rather than a really old one on its last legs?'

'Not if you were skint and didn't want the wife to know you'd just spent money on a brand-new phone,' said Warren.

'My thoughts exactly.'

'Great work, Rachel.'

'I live to serve,' said Pymm.

'Before I waste my time walking halfway across the office, only to be called back, why don't you tell me what else you have?'

'Sir!' Pymm looked affronted.

Warren waited.

'It turns out he used the same PIN for this hidden phone as his personal phone, just with the digits reversed. Pete opened it on the second attempt.'

'And what have they found?'

'Early days; they haven't downloaded everything yet. But what I can tell you, is it's an unregistered pay-as-you-go, and its location and call history are staggeringly boring. It looks as though it hardly ever left the vicinity of the house in the two months since it was activated. The phone was turned on at home, the night she went missing. And before you ask, it has received no calls or texts in the previous month, and has a tiny 4G data allowance, which he barely makes a dent in.'

'And that's all we have from either phone?' asked Warren.

'That's everything we have so far on either phone,' said Pymm. 'Cross my heart.'

'Brilliant. Keep me posted on what the analysts find.' He turned and headed towards his office.

'One other thing,' called out Pymm.

He stopped in his tracks, and shot a glare at Ruskin, whose snort of laughter hastily became a cough. *One of these days . . .* he vowed silently.

'Make it good,' he warned her. 'You just told me that's all you had.'

'All I had from the *phone*,' she corrected him. 'They've downloaded the log from the house's Wi-Fi hub. It retains the unique MAC address of every device that accesses it, to make it quicker to connect.'

'Does it have timestamps?' asked Warren.

'No, unfortunately. However, they do have everything that has used the hub to access the internet within the past thirty days.'

She read from her screen. 'Two laptops, Louisa and Ben's. A tablet that we've already seized, a printer, the controller for their central heating and a smart TV. Ben's personal phone and the burner we've just found also use the Wi-Fi – that's probably why the burner has used so little data. We've also found four unknown devices – all smartphones judging from the manufacturer's code on their MAC addresses. Two of them match devices saved in the memory of the wireless router in Louisa's industrial unit. The other two are complete unknowns.'

'Is there any way to locate them?'

Pymm shook her head. 'No, their MAC addresses aren't sent

to cell towers, just individual wireless or Bluetooth networks, which can't be accessed without the correct tools and a warrant. The handset's unique IMEI code that identifies it on the mobile phone network isn't used on wireless networks.' She shrugged. 'Two entirely different systems, designed for different purposes, long before anyone thought a mobile phone would eventually become a minicomputer used to access the internet.'

'Well, I don't know about you,' said Warren. 'But I don't usually give out my Wi-Fi password to anyone, unless they are a trusted friend. We need to know who was visiting them recently. I'm assuming Kevin Lederer or the FLOs didn't take advantage?'

'I'll check, but that would be very unprofessional. It could be their parents, or Stephanie?' suggested Pymm.

'Should be easy enough to check,' said Warren. 'What about Ben's brother?'

'None of the devices we seized match.'

'That's a shame,' said Warren. 'He claims never to have visited their house; it would have been an easy lie to catch him out with.'

'He hasn't visited within the last thirty days,' Pymm corrected. 'That's how long the router stores its records.'

'I'd say her missing personal phone must be one of the ones that also connected to the hub in her lock-up, but are you thinking what I'm thinking?'

'Yeah,' said Pymm. 'Louisa had a second phone.'

Chapter 22

The child psychologist who interviewed the Greenlands' daughters phoned with her initial impressions mid-morning.

'Both girls are bewildered by what's happened over the past few days. At present, they just think Mummy is missing, but they are starting to get anxious.'

The simple statement cut to the heart of the tragedy.

Regardless of the outcome of the case, the two girls would forever be the children of a murder victim. At five years old, Molly would probably hang on to at least some memories of her mother, reinforced by photos and home videos, but would three-year-old Pippa retain anything more than fleeting impressions? And what if their father was the person responsible? They'd lose both parents in one cruel blow and have yet another label added to them: daughters of a murderer. How would they deal with that?

For the first time since the case had started, the father in Warren was fervently wishing the evidence was leading in a different direction. Ben was the prime suspect, and whilst bringing him to justice would be professionally satisfying, nobody would be celebrating that outcome. What those girls needed most right now was the love of their sole remaining parent. A parent currently sitting in a holding cell.

'Can they recall anything unusual from the night she disappeared?' asked Warren, forcing himself back into professional mode.

'Nothing, it was a normal night, from what Molly remembers. She says that when they got home, Louisa played with them for a bit before their father returned from work. They're too young to properly tell the time, so we can't be certain when he arrived home. But he took them to wash their hands for dinner as soon as he came in, which is their usual routine.'

'What other details do they remember?' asked Warren. If the two girls' accounts broadly matched, then it would strengthen the credibility of their recollections. If what they remembered from that evening differed from Ben's, then they would need that credibility to limit the likelihood of their testimonies being dismissed as unreliable.

'Both girls remember it was cottage pie for dinner. It's a favourite, but they don't have it very often.'

That was a promising start; it agreed with both Ben's initial statement and Jordan's findings.

'Molly remembers her dad staying in the kitchen to tidy up, whilst their mum played with them for a bit. She says they were trying to build a Lego castle. Pippa was colouring in.'

One of the FLOs had helped Molly continue building the castle whilst their father took a nap. Unfortunately, if these were favoured activities, then it was possible the girls were getting their days confused.

'Their mum took them upstairs to bathe them. They were both clear it was Louisa that night, as apparently "she's more fun". It sounds like Louisa wasn't so bothered about a bit of splashing and mess when it was Dad left to clear up.'

Despite the circumstances, Warren felt himself smile at the image. Niall had taken to the bath and the parent and baby sessions at the local swimming pool like a . . . well a fish to water. He had a suspicion his son was going to enjoy swamping the bathroom when he was a bit older. It sounded like the evening rituals in the Greenlands' home had been similarly loving.

'What happened next?' he asked.

'She got them ready for bed, then kissed them goodnight and told them she loved them both.' For the first time since the call had started, her voice lost its clinical edge. Warren felt the same; the last thing their mother had said to them was that she loved them and their final memories of her were horsing around in the bathroom. It was a small comfort.

After a moment, the psychologist cleared her throat and continued. 'Molly remembers the front door closing before her dad came upstairs. The girls share the same room, so she listened to her dad reading to Pippa, before they did some reading practice and he treated her with an extra chapter of the book they are reading for pleasure. Neither girl remembers waking up in the night. Their dad got them up for school and nursery as usual; Molly remembers hearing his alarm clock, so presumably it was their usual time. They know they have to be quiet because Mummy is sleeping, so they didn't see her that morning. That's their normal routine.'

'I don't suppose they can remember his demeanour?'

'No. I asked Molly what mood he was in, if he was happy or sad, but she just said "normal". Pippa couldn't remember.'

So far, the girls' accounts seemed to match Ben's and there were no obvious signs the evening had been any different to usual.

'What about their parents' relationship?' he asked.

'Molly said that sometimes her parents argued. Pippa said that Daddy was sometimes cross with Mummy and that Mummy was cross with him. She didn't really know why. But it's clearly bothering her; the nursery staff noticed she has been a bit "clingy" lately. They were going to ring home and have a chat, since it can be a sign of insecurity.'

'When did this start?'

'Two or three weeks ago. It's a bit subjective; kids go through phases and sometimes they copy each other. She could have been empathising with another child.'

'What about Molly? Does she have any idea what they were arguing about?'

'Possibly money, but she didn't sound sure. I spoke to her class teacher, and she said that she has been quiet over the past fortnight. The school safe-guarding lead was going to ring home for a welfare check, but Molly hadn't said anything, and she wasn't showing any of the usual signs of abuse or neglect. The school knew that the family's routine had changed, but generally speaking she seemed happy.'

Warren thanked her, before hanging up. It sounded as though the Greenlands had been undergoing some marital strains, possibly because of the situation with P@mper, and that was being picked up by their daughters. But their home life didn't sound especially difficult. The question was whether that strain had escalated recently to the point something had snapped.

*　*　*

The second interview with Ben Greenland started shortly after eleven a.m. He looked even more gaunt. The custody officer reported that he'd sat on the edge of his bed, head in hands, all night. He'd barely touched his breakfast and had to be cajoled into taking a drink when it was offered.

'He's in a bad way,' said the veteran sergeant. 'If he doesn't buck up, I'm going to get him assessed by a doctor and the mental health team.'

'What's your feeling, Ken?' asked Sutton.

'Could be racked with guilt. Could be grieving. Could be both,' he said eventually. 'Sorry, he's barely said a word.'

This time, the interview was opened by Greenland's solicitor, who announced she had a written statement to be read out on

Ben's behalf. He made no acknowledgement, fiddling with the plastic beaker of water he'd just drained.

The statement was detailed, and neither Warren nor Sutton spotted any inconsistencies with his previous account. The statement concluded with a repeat of his denial that he had anything to do with the disappearance, or subsequent death of his wife.

The solicitor closed her laptop and promised to email a copy to them immediately.

Warren thanked them both and suggested they take a break for an early lunch.

Sutton turned to Warren after Greenland and his solicitor had left. 'No way did he dictate that statement in the hour she met him before we resumed interviewing.'

* * *

Greenland's solicitor was as good as her word, and the statement was waiting in Warren's inbox. For the next forty-five minutes the team pored over copies of the document, devising follow-up questions. Whether Greenland would answer them or not, Warren had no idea, but they had to give him the opportunity. Importantly, the statement was now on the record and there were several provable lies.

'I'm not willing to take a wager on this,' said Sutton, as he struggled to peel an orange. 'Ooh, you little git,' he said blinking furiously as he received an eyeful of juice for his trouble.

'I'm laughing in sympathy,' said Warren, handing over a tissue. Sutton glared at him. 'But hey, if you aren't brave enough to risk a tenner on whether or not he goes "no comment", I respect that,' Warren said confidently.

* * *

'Thank you for your statement, Ben. If you don't mind, we'd like to ask you a few follow-up questions, just to clarify some details,' started Warren.

'Mr Greenland has said all he wishes to on the matter,' said Barton firmly. 'There is nothing justifying his further detention, and I demand that you release him, so he can support his children.'

'Of course,' said Warren. 'And the sooner he answers our questions, the sooner we can decide whether or not he can leave.'

Greenland remained mute. His solicitor scowled.

'You state that you stayed in all of Tuesday night. Louisa left at seven and that was the last you saw of her. Did you leave the house at any time that night, before you left for work the following morning?'

'No comment.'

'Are you sure you want to carry on playing this game, Ben? It's getting awfully tiresome,' said Sutton. The solicitor opened her mouth to object, but Sutton glared at her, and she remained quiet.

'No comment.'

Undeterred, Warren continued. 'I have an image, taken by an Automated Number Plate Recognition camera attached to a traffic light, showing a Renault Espace with the same licence plates as your car on Lester Road at a quarter past midnight. Is this your vehicle, Ben?'

Beside him, his solicitor stiffened in surprise.

Greenland paused almost three whole seconds, before muttering 'no comment' once more.

'Can you explain why your car was on the road that night?' Warren repeated.

'No comment.'

'Come on, Ben. Here's your chance to clear up what really happened,' said Sutton. 'Is that your car, yes or no?'

Greenland's voice was so quiet they could barely hear it. 'No comment.'

'You are making life very difficult for yourself here,' Sutton admonished him.

Warren took over. 'Did you see Louisa again after seven p.m.?'

'No comment.' This time his voice was more confident. Beside him, his solicitor visibly relaxed.

'Did Louisa return to the house Tuesday evening?'

'No comment.'

'Mr Greenland has stated repeatedly that the last time he saw his wife was when she left to walk to work,' said Barton, a note of exasperation creeping into her voice. 'Badgering him with the same questions repeatedly will not change his answer.'

Warren ignored the interruption.

'Did she or did she not return to your house?'

'No comment.'

His solicitor was frowning.

'I have here a statement from a witness who clearly saw a woman matching Louisa's description returning to your house shortly after eight-thirty.'

'What? That's impossible,' said Greenland, his eyes widening.

'How reliable is this witness?' demanded the solicitor, clearly unprepared for the disclosure.

'They know Mr and Mrs Greenland very well, and have given us sufficient detail for us to be confident that they are correct about the date and time. So, I ask again, Ben: did Louisa return home on the evening of Tuesday 14th May after she had already left for work?'

Greenland was silent for several seconds, his eyes darting around the room. He looked over at his solicitor, who still looked shocked. She shook her head again.

'No comment,' he said eventually.

'I think now would be a good time to take a break,' said Barton.

*　　*　　*

'She didn't see that coming,' said Sutton. The team had regrouped in the main briefing room.

'He's obviously not told his legal team what he was up to,' said Hardwick.

'Surely he can't keep on no commenting now?' said Ruskin. 'He must realise how bad it looks for him?'

'I wouldn't be so sure,' said Warren. 'If he did kill her, then either he has to come up with a plausible excuse as to why she returned, or he's going to shut down and hope it goes away. I wouldn't be surprised if he does just that. Lying looks bad, but at the moment it's all circumstantial, so don't get too carried away. Until we get some solid forensics proving his involvement, we won't have enough to charge him.'

'And without wanting to rain on our parade,' cautioned Roehampton, 'we still can't be certain he acted alone, or was even involved at all. Him being out and about could be a coincidence. For a start, why was his car only snapped once? Surely he needed to return from wherever he had been?'

'I can think of two explanations,' said Richardson. 'The simplest is that the traffic camera is a single, wide-angle lens on a pole, covering both sides of the road. It's in a crap position. Smaller vehicles can be blocked from view by larger vehicles, if they are travelling close behind one another. He might just not have been pinged on the return journey.'

'Plausible,' said Warren. 'What else?'

'He drove to that side of town, which was when he was snapped, did what he needed to there, then drove to her unit. Depending on the route, he could avoid cameras. Then he changed his licence plates and drove Louisa to the woods, which is when he triggered the two cameras. Then, when he returned from the woods, he came in from the west side of town and drove straight home. He wouldn't ping anything if he took that route.'

'So did he plan those routes, or just get lucky?' asked Sutton.

'All of the cameras are clearly signposted,' said Richardson, 'and there are websites listing their locations, and which ones store images or just record plate numbers.'

'So why did he travel out to that side of town before going to the industrial unit?' asked Warren. 'How does that fit with Louisa being seen entering their house at eight-thirty?'

'Are we one hundred per cent convinced it was actually Louisa that the lady across the road saw?' asked Roehampton. 'By her own admission, her eyesight isn't the best and we know of two women who could conceivably be mistaken for Louisa. I still can't work out why she would have returned home, coming from that direction, then gone back to her unit. That Taser AFID we found in her unit and the disabled CCTV smacks too much of premeditation.'

'A fair point,' said Warren. 'Moray, you were checking into Stephanie's whereabouts Tuesday night. Are we sure she wasn't here in Middlesbury?'

'She could have just about made it from her flat in south London,' said Ruskin. 'I called a mate who works for the Met. He took a look at the CCTV near the closest underground station to where she works. I've seen video footage of her walking towards the tube shortly after five; she even stops to chat to a homeless person selling *The Big Issue*.

'Her mobile phone travelled from there to home, which took about forty-one minutes with one line change. If she went straight back out and caught the next express train from King's Cross, she could have just about made it up here for eight-thirty p.m. or shortly after. If she drove, it's also possible, depending on traffic.'

'So it could have been her then?' interrupted Roehampton. 'Especially if our witness was a little off about the time – say she saw her just before nine, rather than just after eight-thirty?'

'Not really,' said Ruskin. 'According to her phone records, her mobile travelled straight back to her flat from work, and then didn't leave again all night. More importantly,' he said hastily, before somebody reminded him that phones could be left at home, 'she told Karen she received a call from a client Tuesday evening on the landline she uses for business calls. There was an incoming call from an unregistered pay-as-you-go at ten p.m. It lasted for forty-two minutes, until she terminated the call. To have been in Middlesbury at eight-thirty p.m. and receiving that call back in south London at ten, she would have needed to drive like a bat out of hell; there are no trains that could have done it. Her car wasn't pinged on any speed cameras or any ANPR, travelling either to or from Middlesbury.'

'Are we certain it was her who answered the call?' asked Warren.

'That's more tricky,' admitted Ruskin. 'We know she lives alone. None of her neighbours in the apartment block think she had a visitor, and as far as they know, she is single. The man in the flat next door could hear the TV until about eleven-thirty and is sure he saw her leaving for work the following morning.'

'Doesn't sound like it could have been Stephanie,' said Roehampton.

'I agree,' said Warren. 'I can't see how the woman across the road mistook her for Louisa. Which leaves Caitlin.'

'Who conceivably has a motive to harm Louisa,' Hardwick reminded them. 'If she and Ben were having an affair – or she wanted one – then she could have turned up at his house that night. If Ben spurned her, could she have gone around to Louisa's unit in a jealous rage?'

'She would have needed access to a vehicle to move the body,' said Richardson. 'I'll arrange an ANPR check for her vehicle, just in case that suspect vehicle we snapped using fake plates was a coincidence.'

'See if any of her neighbours recall her car being moved or her going out,' said Warren. 'Rachel, get hold of her phone records.'

'Should we bring her in for questioning again?' asked Hardwick.

Warren thought for a moment. 'Not yet. Let's do a little sniffing around first. In the meantime, before we go too far down this rabbit hole, let's not forget we have two other potential suspects. What do we have from Forensics?'

'The material Louisa's backpack is made from is the worst imaginable for lifting prints,' said Hardwick. 'They've not even managed to get a clear one of hers. Hopefully they'll get some contact DNA.'

'What about the contents?' asked Sutton.

'Her purse was in there, with cards and a bit of cash. It's made of leather, but the only clear prints are hers. Ditto with her keys.'

'If her keys were in there, that puts the kibosh on the theory that she locked herself out of her unit and returned home,' said Ruskin, visibly disappointed.

'Not necessarily,' said Warren. 'If Ben staged the whole thing, he could have chucked her keys in there to avoid awkward questions about why they were back at the house and not in her bag. Is there anything else of interest in there?'

'A packet of tissues, the wrapper off a tampon, and a few screwed-up receipts, for the supermarket and Mandy's Muffins in town. Again, only her fingerprints.'

'We'll load the receipts onto HOLMES anyway,' said Pymm. 'You never know.'

'I'm assuming you'd have told us if her mobile phone was in there?' said Warren, hopefully.

'No such luck,' admitted Hardwick.

'Have they looked at her clothing?' asked Sutton.

'Lots of blood, as you'd imagine,' she answered. 'There are a few spots away from the main stab wound that they're testing. We might get lucky and the killer cut themselves. Professor Jordan scraped under her nails and swabbed her wrists where she was bound, for contact DNA, although I don't know how much use it'll be if it comes back as a match for her husband.'

'We'll cross that bridge if we come to it,' said Warren.

'Her underwear has tested negative for semen and saliva,' Hardwick continued. 'Which matches the prof's belief she wasn't sexually assaulted. But her shoes have got mud and leaf litter consistent with her walking through the forest.'

'What about foreign fibres?' asked Sutton.

'They are still doing tapings, but there's nothing visible by eye.'

'How are they doing with the scene?' asked Warren.

'It's pretty compromised,' said Hardwick. 'The students had walked on the muddiest patches. There are several overlapping tyre tracks on the two nearest access roads. Andy Harrison reckons if we are lucky, and our killer's vehicle made one of the clearer sets, then we might be able to make a positive match. If not . . .' She shrugged.

Chapter 23

Caitlin O'Shaughnessy lived in a flat on the opposite side of town to the Greenlands. Depending on traffic, it would probably take her ten to fifteen minutes by car, or she could catch two buses and do it in a little over thirty if the timetables worked in her favour. They'd pulled security footage from buses on that route. The lady across the road said she had seen the woman she thought was Louisa walking from the direction of the bus stop, but she'd only seen her for a few seconds. Caitlin's car could have been parked a little further along the road.

The man in the next-door flat was surprised when Moray Ruskin rang the doorbell.

'She's a lovely lass, very friendly. She's looked after my cats a couple of times. What's happened?'

Ruskin gave him a practised smile. 'Just making some inquiries in the area. What can you tell me about her?'

'She works from home; she's a freelance writer, I believe.'

'Do you know if she's seeing anyone? Or has any regular visitors?'

'I think she might have a boyfriend. I sometime hear a man's voice coming from her apartment in the evening.'

'Could you describe him?'

The man paused for a moment. 'Thirtyish maybe? Dark hair, I guess medium build, quite fit-looking. I've only ever seen him from the back.'

'Would you recognise him?' asked Ruskin.

'No. Like I said, I've only caught a glimpse of him. I don't think they've been dating long – assuming it's even her boyfriend. Could just be a mate.'

'Do the flats have their own parking spots?'

'Yes.' He leaned over the balcony and pointed. 'That's hers there.'

'Do you know where she is at the moment?' asked Ruskin.

'She'll probably be at the leisure centre – she's a real gym bunny.'

'Do you know if she was in on the night of May 14th? Last Tuesday?'

He thought carefully. 'I think so; certainly her car was here. My boyfriend picked me up just before nine. He usually parks in whatever space is available, but he had to wait for me out on the street.'

'What about when you returned?' asked Ruskin.

'Just past eleven. I'm pretty sure there were no spaces then either.'

'One last question. Did Caitlin have any other visitors? Aside from her male friend?'

He pinched his lip thoughtfully. 'There was an older Irish couple that I bumped into once. I think they were her parents. Then there was another woman I saw a couple of weeks back. I think she stayed overnight.'

'Can you describe her?' asked Ruskin.

'Oh, that's easy; she was obviously Caitlin's sister.'

*   *   *

'Caitlin's car was apparently at her flat Tuesday night,' said Warren. 'Meaning if it was her the witness across the road saw going into the Greenlands' place, then she had to get there by some other means, and she left her phone at home.'

'Nothing on the CCTV from the buses,' said Richardson. 'Even if the old lady got her times a bit wrong, and she was coming from somewhere else rather than home, there is still realistically only one bus she could have been on that stops near the Greenlands' street.'

'It's a fair walk from Caitlin's flat,' said Ruskin. 'Maybe ninety minutes if she's quick? If she rode a bicycle it would be faster, but the old lady didn't see one. I suppose she could have been walking from somewhere else, rather than her apartment.'

'That leaves either a lift with someone, or a taxi,' said Sutton.

'Already on it,' said Richardson.

'Next question, who is this mysterious boyfriend?' asked Warren. 'From the description, it could be Ben. Do any other neighbours recall seeing him?'

'None mentioned it,' said Ruskin. 'We could do a follow-up with a photo,' he suggested.

'Whilst we're at it, why not also show a picture of Louisa and Stephanie?' suggested Pymm. 'If the woman spotted by Caitlin's neighbour two weeks ago wasn't her sister – if she even has one – then it could have been one of those two.'

'Which would mean either Caitlin or Stephanie is lying,' said Sutton. 'Both claim not to have physically seen Louisa since the April get-together to remember Sinead.'

'I think it is increasingly unlikely Louisa came home unexpectedly and was killed by Ben,' said Warren. 'I suspect our eyewitness is mistaken. I think we've ruled out Stephanie, which just leaves Caitlin.

'Rachel, can you find out if she has a sister, please? Hutch, I want you to get some decent headshots of Caitlin, Louisa, Stephanie and Ben, and Caitlin's sister if she has one; try social media. Also chuck in Curtis whilst you're at it and pad it out with a few unrelated photos. If we are going to be accusing Caitlin or Stephanie of lying, and Caitlin of having an affair with Ben, I want to be certain.'

He looked around the room, ready to dismiss them all. Hardwick looked as if she wanted to say something but was hesitant. He caught her eye and raised an eyebrow invitingly; it wasn't like Hardwick to be shy.

'I have an idea,' she said. 'It's a bit far-fetched.'

'Tell us anyway,' said Warren, intrigued.

'If the woman seen going into the Greenlands' the night Louisa was killed wasn't Stephanie or Caitlin or Louisa, then I can only think of one other person.'

There was a stunned silence as Hardwick waited to see if anyone else jumped to the same conclusion.

'Sinead,' said Warren.

Chapter 24

'Wow. That would be a hell of a twist,' said Roehampton, when Warren and Hardwick laid out her theory about Sinead. 'First question is what's her motivation for killing Louisa? And second, why now? She hasn't been seen for over eleven years.'

'It doesn't necessarily mean it was Sinead who killed Louisa,' said Hardwick. She'd alternated between confidence that the mysterious woman entering the Greenlands' Tuesday night was Sinead, and feeling like a fool for even suggesting it. 'All I'm saying, is that we should be open to the possibility.'

'What do you think, Warren?' asked Roehampton.

'I honestly don't know,' said Warren. 'Obviously, they never figured out what happened to Sinead. That leaves four possibilities. First that she was murdered – so where is her body? How was it disposed of in such a way it's never turned up? Second possibility is she killed herself – in which case, again, where is her body?

'Third, she was kidnapped. They found no evidence she was snatched by people smugglers or a random psychopath, but you can't prove a negative. But if that happened, why has she just resurfaced? Did she escape? Was she released? Why hasn't she turned up at a police station or found her way back to her family?

And of course, we still haven't ruled out Louisa being kidnapped, so there's a possible link.

'The final option is that she could have voluntarily left. Perhaps a mental breakdown? It sounds like Ben may have been having an affair with her; if he decided to choose Louisa over her, then that could have been a trigger. But again, why has she just reappeared in Middlesbury?

'I'll be honest, I've never been entirely happy with the explanations given by the housemates, and I know George Rutherford has his suspicions that they weren't one hundred per cent forthcoming. His feeling was that they felt guilty that they didn't realise she was struggling so much, but what if they were hiding something more significant? Curtis Redmayne has admitted he wasn't completely honest about Ben and Sinead's relationship and has suddenly said that he thinks he knows which night she actually went missing.'

'I know it sounds, far-fetched,' admitted Hardwick. 'But we have Sinead's DNA and fingerprints on file from the original investigation. I think at the very least, any unknown samples should be compared against them.'

'Let's just assume for the moment you are right, and whoever visited Ben Tuesday night was Sinead,' said Roehampton. 'Then was she also the person that Caitlin's neighbour saw?'

'I don't know,' admitted Hardwick. 'If it was, then the question is whether Caitlin has known where she was all these years, or if she only recently found out herself?'

'And if Caitlin has known, have the others?' asked Warren.

'It's been eleven years, though,' said Roehampton. 'She was what, twenty, twenty-one when she disappeared? What twenty-year-old has the foresight to plan something like this? Her family have been going out of their minds. Her dad has since died, and she abandoned her little brother who she was apparently devastated to leave behind when she originally came to England. Yet she has supposedly lived under the radar for all these years. How? Why?'

'I don't know,' admitted Hardwick again, beginning to regret ever opening her mouth.

'And again, why now? I know I'm repeating myself, but we've just become aware of this at the same time one of her old university friends is murdered. Is that a coincidence? Are the two events linked? Or has she been here in Middlesbury under our noses for years, and we just happen to have stumbled upon her because we're looking so closely at the Greenlands?'

'I don't know,' mumbled Hardwick. Tears started to well in her eyes and she felt a flash of shame at her weakness. Roehampton's tone was harsh – but then it should be. Extraordinary claims required extraordinary proof.

'Why don't we just add it into the mix of ideas,' suggested Warren, recognising how crushing Roehampton's dismissal of the theory was to the newly promoted sergeant. He knew Hardwick thought very highly of Roehampton, and rightly so. Her career was an inspiration to any officer, but especially to a young, single mother like Hardwick.

When he'd made the decision to withdraw his candidacy for John Grayson's former position, he'd been delighted that of all those considered for the role, Roehampton had been selected. And in his opinion, her promotion to superintendent was well earned.

But there were times when he thought she could be a little more tactful.

'I'll make Andy Harrison aware of what we've discussed,' said Warren. 'It shouldn't add any extra expense; it'll just stop any DNA matches being dismissed as spurious. I'll also speak to George Rutherford again; I'll ask him not to get the family's hopes up, but I'd like his perspective.'

'OK,' agreed Roehampton. 'But we have got to get a handle on this case – it's getting far too complicated. How many theories and motives have we got now? We've got to start whittling them down and crossing some suspects off the list. They can't all have been involved. I don't doubt we're uncovering a lot of hidden secrets here, but remember our remit is to find out who murdered Louisa Greenland. Let SOC deal with the drugs offences and let the probation service decide what to do with Russell Myrie.

'We also need to make a decision about whether we are reopening the case of Sinead McCaffrey or not. And if we are, whether it is being investigated in parallel, separately or as part of the Louisa Greenland murder.'

'Yes, Guv,' said Warren. Hardwick echoed his response.

The two officers left the office together, feeling like a pair of naughty schoolchildren.

'Thanks for the support in there, Boss,' Hardwick said when they were out of earshot.

'You did fine. Now let's have a late lunch, see what this afternoon throws at us, then get the gang together for a brainstorming session.'

* * *

Warren barely had time to unwrap his sandwiches before Janice snagged him.

'Sir, I've got Pete Robertson on the line. He says it's urgent.'

'Put it through to my desk phone,' he said. Strictly speaking, nobody, not even Roehampton had a dedicated admin assistant, but over the years, the pool of civilian support workers had divided up their duties between them. Janice had taken on Warren and he found her invaluable.

'We've decrypted Louisa Greenland's laptop. There are detailed business records on there that Rachel Pymm might want to look at. But I think you might be more interested in the contents of a folder we just found, tucked away where somebody nosing through her laptop would be unlikely to stumble across it by accident.'

Warren could picture Robertson folded behind his desk, in the tiny, airless office he shared with the rest of the Digital Forensics

Unit. He was amazed somebody as tall and ungainly as Robertson could move around the cluttered workspace without sending delicate bits of computer hardware flying.

'I'll email a few samples to you as zip file, along with her internet browsing history. Normally, I'd class these as NSFW, but I think you can be forgiven for looking at them on work time.'

'NSFW?' asked Warren, unfamiliar with the abbreviation.

'Not Safe For Work.'

*   *   *

'I wonder if Ben knew what she was doing late at night when he thought she was filling hampers,' asked Sutton. Warren had called him and Pymm into his office to show them what Robertson had sent him. He'd share the summary with the rest of the team, but his instinct was to preserve Louisa Greenland's dignity if possible.

'If he recently found out, it might have been a trigger,' suggested Pymm. 'At least we now know what that mysterious payment service is that she's been receiving money from.'

The files sent by Pete Robertson had been a series of JPEG images and short video clips taken on what Warren assumed was either a smartphone camera or the webcam on her laptop. Some of them were against a black dropcloth in what appeared to be her industrial unit. Others were recognisably located in the spare room she had been sleeping alone in since she started working late nights fulfilling orders for P@mper.

'The videos in the bedroom were taken during daylight hours,' noted Sutton. 'I imagine she took them on her mobile phone when he was at work.'

'There's a team looking through them all to see if there was anybody helping film them, but the unedited footage shows her using a Bluetooth remote to control the camera,' said Warren. 'I think this definitely confirms she owned a second smartphone. I can't imagine she would have used her personal phone – too much risk that Ben or one of the girls would stumble across them.'

He turned to Pymm. 'Have you found her page on the porn site?'

'Yes, it wasn't too difficult. It looks as though the website is relatively new; there are only a few girls on there. She goes by the name of "Secret Housewife". I've been looking at the money she's been receiving via the payment service and comparing it to the prices listed on her site. Assuming the hosts and payment provider take a hefty cut, and allowing for currency conversions, it looks like she sells a few pre-made photosets each week. Then there are some larger transactions that are either multiple purchases rolled into one, or custom sets for the more "discerning" client.'

'What about live chats?' asked Sutton. 'Could she have been interacting with someone on there?'

'There is that facility,' said Pymm. 'The good news is that the website is UK-based. We've had no problem getting a warrant for her log-in details, so I'll let you know as soon as they get back to us. If we're lucky, they'll keep records of clients' interactions with performers.'

With the meeting over, Warren offered Pymm his arm and they walked back to her desk. Ordinarily, people went to Pymm, rather than the other way around. It was a simple courtesy, but she hated special treatment. She was resisting using her mobility scooter at work, claiming it took longer to get in and out of it, and manoeuvre it in and out of her car than it took her to walk using her crutches. But by its nature, multiple sclerosis was progressive. The CID office had recently been given a long-overdue refurbishment, part of which included making the area more accessible. Warren only wished they'd also spent some money upgrading the building's elderly heating and air conditioning. A brief appearance by the sun a couple of weeks ago had thrown the air con into a complete fit, blasting icy air until it was turned off.

'You know I'm not one to judge a person's choices,' said Pymm.

'But this whole thing is really depressing. She signed up to that site after the bank had turned down her loan request, and Curtis refused to lend her the money. It looks as though she was working every hour God sent to make a success of her dream and provide for her kids, and she had a spiralling drug problem. I think she joined that website out of desperation.'

Warren nodded; Louisa's final Facebook post, a meme about every parent's wish being for their kids to have the freedom to choose what they want to be in life, seemed especially poignant now.

Pymm lowered herself carefully into her chair.

'The thing is, she was making a pittance from it. I've no doubt the site was fleecing her and the other performers on there, but just looking at the frequency of the payments she was receiving, she was selling hardly any sets. I'm no expert on the industry, but surely she could have made more money on one of the bigger, more established sites?'

'Are we sure she wasn't?' asked Warren.

'If she was, then I haven't found how she was being paid,' said Pymm.

'Cryptocurrency?' asked Warren. 'Could she have a Bitcoin account?'

'Perhaps, but even if she was being paid that way, she would have needed to cash the money out somehow, and I've not seen any transactions from currency exchanges. I suppose it could have been accumulating in a digital wallet somewhere for a rainy day, but looking at her bank statements, that rainy day has been happening for some time. It's practically a deluge.'

'Perhaps she didn't want to be on a more high-profile site in case someone she knew stumbled across the pictures?' suggested Warren.

'That would explain why there doesn't appear to be any social media links on her performer page,' said Pymm. 'She isn't going to want to risk pictures of her floating around Twitter or Instagram.'

'So the question is whether this is significant or not,' said Sutton, who'd joined them. He handed over a mug of coffee to Warren.

'Is that decaf?' asked Pymm.

'Of course,' said Warren.

'You're a lousy liar,' said Pymm.

'I agree with Tony,' said Warren, not willing to engage in another argument over his caffeine intake. He'd get no backup from Sutton, who had given up caffeine after his mini-stroke, four years previously. 'It could be a coincidence. She's earning a little extra money, no harm, no foul. It could even have Ben's blessing, or at least acceptance; needs must.

'But on the other hand, what if he found out? Given the stresses in their marriage already, it could have been the straw that broke the camel's back. I'd like to see his internet browsing history. We know he's alone each night after he's put the kids to bed, and we know he likes the ladies. Who knows how he's entertaining himself? He could have stumbled across her site.'

'I'll speak to IT,' promised Pymm. 'I'll also ask them to do a reverse image search on a few of her pictures and see if they've been shared anywhere else online. He might have found them on a different site. You know what the internet is like, once the genie's out of the bottle . . . Her pictures are perfectly legal, so there's no need for them to be squirrelled away on some seedy corner of the dark web. If they're out there, they're probably accessible via Google.'

'Good. Keep me posted about what else IT find on her laptop. Presumably she set up a separate email account to operate the website. If we can access it, we might find out if she's been interacting with any users. Her killer could be an obsessive who tracked her down offline. Or she could even have agreed to meet up with someone to earn some extra money.'

'Do we ask Ben about this?' asked Sutton. 'Or any of her friends? Or even her sister?'

Warren rubbed his eyes wearily. 'I think we'll have to eventually; it's a valid line of inquiry. If nothing else, I want to see Ben's reaction. And if she spoke to her friends about any unpleasant experiences she's had through the site, we need to know.'

'But if it was a secret, then we're potentially about to tarnish the poor woman's memory with her loved ones,' said Pymm. 'Who knows their views on pornography? It could completely change their opinion of her.'

Pymm was right, but Warren couldn't see any alternative.

Sometimes he really disliked his job.

Chapter 25

It was mid-afternoon before Warren finally managed to eat his lunch and snatch a few minutes on WhatsApp with his wife and son. But before long, he was standing next to Rachel Pymm's desk again. She had a veritable shopping list of new information that she needed to share with him.

'The memory dump of Ben's burner phone has been completed,' said Pymm. 'First of all, the phone has pretty much nothing saved on it, nor does it appear to have had much deleted. No photos or videos. It looks as though he used it purely for communicating.'

'How quaint,' remarked Sutton.

'Not that quaint. He didn't use it to send texts or make phone calls. Instead, he used the secure messaging app, Enkryp: end-to-end encryption, phone calls and messages, it can be used on phones and laptops. Years ago, you'd wonder if he was some sort of spy or involved in organised crime. These days you can download the app for £3.99 and use it to cheat on your wife.'

'I don't suppose you've accessed it?' asked Sutton.

'Unfortunately, no. It needs a PIN code – different to the one used for the handset – or a fingerprint.'

'What else have you found?' He could see Pymm wondering

if she could get away with holding something back for dramatic effect, but she saw the look in his eyes and decided against it.

'He had an app tracking Louisa's phone. Covertly. She wouldn't even realise it was installed on her handset.'

'Now that is interesting,' said Warren. He could think of several reasons why Ben might have installed such a piece of software on his wife's phone, and none of them were good. 'What else?'

'They've also cracked the password and encryption on Ben's laptop, and it's an interesting set-up, to say the least. For a start, he has a second, hidden user account.'

'You're kidding?' said Warren.

'It's nothing elaborate,' said Pymm. 'He's simply set up a second Windows account and mounted its user space on a concealed partition on the hard drive. It's not much more sophisticated than the way network managers set up work or school computers to stop users messing around with settings they shouldn't. Your work laptop has a similar hidden partition and admin account that IT access whenever they perform upgrades on it.'

'The last upgrade my laptop had was the type of coal it uses,' grumbled Warren. 'So why does he need it?'

'It's basically his porn account,' said Pymm. 'All the stuff he'd rather Mrs Greenland didn't stumble across. He can safely let her borrow his laptop logged into his normal user account and she is in no danger of finding anything dodgy. It also means he doesn't need to keep on using incognito mode when he surfs the web. His browser can store his search history to make things easier for him, which makes things easier for us.'

'So what have we got?'

'The analysts are still going over it, but the good news is his tastes are fairly mainstream; no child abuse or anything really dodgy. No inappropriate pictures of his kids. It looks as though he still has a thing for pretty, dark-haired girls though. His search history includes "pretty Irish girls" and other, more explicit variations.'

'Any evidence he came across his wife's pictures?' asked Warren. Just because Ben was a prolific user of pornography didn't mean he wanted to see his wife out there.

'None of the images from Louisa's laptop have been found on his hard drive using a reverse image search,' said Pymm. 'However, he was a member of a couple of online forums where users share pictures that they either find online or have created themselves. Unfortunately, he didn't let his browser save his password and login details, so we can't determine if her images are on there. If they are, and he found them, it doesn't look as though he downloaded them to look at in more detail. We also can't access the websites' browsing history for him, assuming they have one.'

'Damn,' said Warren.

'Don't lose faith completely,' said Pymm. 'If he did find her on there, his computer will have downloaded temporary thumbnail images to display the website correctly. Pete is going to try retrieving them.'

'That's great. Anything else from his browsing history?'

'Two things of interest. The first thing he does before accessing any porn sites is open a web version of the tracking software he's installed on Louisa's phone.'

'That makes sense,' says Warren. 'Stops him getting an awkward surprise if she leaves work early.'

'Second, he also uses the online version of that secure messaging app he uses on his burner. Again, he hasn't let his browser save his password. Unfortunately, what he hasn't done is performed any interesting Google searches, like "ways to kill your wife and get away with it". At least not that we know of.'

'Could he have used private browsing?' asked Warren.

'Yes, which is why I'm requesting his complete internet history from his service provider. Which comes with the added bonus, that unless he set up a Virtual Private Network, we should gain an insight into anything interesting that those unknown devices have searched for using their home Wi-Fi network.'

'And finally?' he said; some days he could read Pymm like a book.

'The website Louisa was sharing photos on has rolled over and given us access to her account and user history.'

'The look on your face suggests it was a rather satisfying experience,' said Warren.

'Oh yes. Some smug, greasy corporate lawyer told me they would challenge the warrant. He even gave me a lecture on privacy.'

'And your response?'

'I told him we were investigating a murder and by refusing to cooperate they were putting the lives of their performers in danger and allowing a sexual predator to roam loose on the streets. I suggested that wouldn't look good if the media found out. He got back to me in twenty minutes.' She gave an evil grin. 'Don't mess with Middlesbury CID.'

* * *

Warren decided to hold a final evening briefing before he and Sutton interviewed Ben Greenland for a third time. It had been a long day, but the influx of new information had injected the team with renewed energy, picking them up after the previous day's blow.

Roehampton was right: it was time to start prioritising. He'd wheeled in some whiteboards, on which he'd listed the various suspects and theories.

'OK, folks. Prime suspect at the moment is Ben. Why might Louisa's husband have been involved in her disappearance and then murder? Give me reasons for and against.'

'We're confident he is having an affair, right?' said Hutchinson.

The rest of the room signalled their agreement.

'In that case, she could have threatened to leave him, perhaps taking the kids with her,' Hutchinson continued.

'Alternately, he may have thought *she* was having an affair,' said Richardson. 'The tracking software he installed on her phone shows he was obviously keeping tabs on her.'

'And if he found out about her website, then that might fuel his jealousy,' said Ruskin.

'Even if he was already aware of it, that doesn't mean he was happy about it,' pointed out Hutchinson.

'We'll put it to him in interview and see what his reaction is,' said Warren.

'They were also struggling financially,' said Pymm. 'And it looks as though she wasn't entirely honest with him about the challenges they were facing. Taking out a second mortgage would have needed both their approval. But did she tell him the bank declined her loan extension to cover the upfront costs of her Holistics Gym deal, or did she lie to him and he found out she'd still taken the risk? I'd probably stop short of murdering him, but I wouldn't be impressed if my husband pulled a similar stunt.'

'The recent increase in her life insurance would wipe out that problem,' Hardwick reminded them.

'OK, so let's assume one or more of those scenarios are correct,' said Warren. 'What evidence do we have for and against?'

'His fingerprints are on the disabled CCTV unit,' said Ruskin.

'Circumstantial at best,' cautioned Sutton. 'He could have installed it.'

'We know he lied about staying in Tuesday evening,' said Richardson. 'He clearly didn't watch the football, and we have his car on ANPR at sixteen minutes past midnight. But we don't know what time he left or when he returned.'

'If he was gone for more than a few minutes, wouldn't their girls have noticed?' said Hardwick. 'If Robbie comes around late at night after a band practice, Ollie often wakes up and appears at the top of the stairs.'

'We probably shouldn't infer too much from them not

remembering waking up,' said Warren. 'They are so young, they might not know what night the psychologist was asking about.'

'The woman across the street believes she spotted Louisa coming home at about eight-thirty p.m.,' said Hutchinson. 'Which is after their bedtime.'

'I really don't think it was Louisa,' countered Sutton immediately. 'We know it wasn't her sister – she was in London – but we haven't ruled out Caitlin yet. Or even Sinead, if we go down that route.'

'Let's park Sinead for the moment,' said Warren. 'But Caitlin keeps on cropping up.' He started a second column on the whiteboard, headed with Caitlin's name.

'If Ben was having an affair, she'd be right at the top of my list,' said Hardwick.

'Her neighbour gave a vague description of a boyfriend that could be Ben,' said Ruskin. 'Can we get a search warrant for her place? If his DNA is present on the bedsheets, for example, that would resolve that question.'

'Let's continue laying out the reasons to suspect she was involved,' said Warren. 'Then we can see if it's enough for a warrant.'

'Jealousy,' said Pymm. 'She's either getting rid of her rival, or working with Ben to get rid of his problem wife so they can live happily ever after.'

'Loyalty,' said Ruskin. 'Ben killed Louisa and then involved Caitlin in the cover-up?'

'If it was her the neighbour saw,' said Sutton, 'she could have been minding the girls whilst he went out and committed the murder.' His face twisted. 'That's above and beyond, especially for an honorary godmother.'

'We'll need a lot more than that to get a search warrant,' said Warren. 'And even if we get one, she was Louisa's best friend. Any DNA or fingerprints found at her flat from Louisa and Ben could easily be explained away, as well as anything from her in their house or car.

'If we stick with Ben as the prime suspect, is there anyone else who could have helped him commit the murder? Leaving two small children alone for so long would have been a big risk. What if they woke up?'

'The obvious candidates are Darren Greenland and/or Russell Myrie,' said Sutton. 'We know Louisa had been visiting Darren. Probably for drugs, possibly for sex. But I'm struggling to square that with Ben going to him for help getting rid of her.'

'Ben might not have known about Louisa's relationship with Darren,' said Ruskin. 'In fact, given the likely fallout if Ben did find out, then getting rid of Louisa might have solved a problem for Darren. If their mother found out he'd been carrying on with her golden boy's wife, he'd probably have been disinherited. Perhaps Darren put the idea in Ben's head? Ben tells him he thinks Louisa's having an affair and he's worried she'll take the kids, or that she's basically risked their entire financial future. Darren says: "It sounds like you need to get rid of her ASAP."'

'But if the idea was originally Darren's, why involve Ben at all?' asked Warren. 'You know what they say about two people being able to keep a secret only if one of them is dead. It'd be better for him if he killed her himself and Ben knew nothing about it.'

'Maybe Ben doesn't know anything about it?' said Pymm. 'Darren would know Ben would become our prime suspect.'

Sutton disagreed. 'I can't see it. The whole thing about him potentially losing out on his inheritance is rather long-term thinking for a junkie. Would he really have decided to murder his sister-in-law just to cover up that he's been having sex with her in exchange for drugs? I still think that if he is involved, then it was with Ben's agreement or instigation.'

'Let's move on then,' said Warren. 'What are our thoughts on a kidnapping for ransom?'

'I'm not convinced,' said Pymm. 'The only plausible source for any money would be Ben's mum. But we've seen no suspicious transactions, and she appeared shocked when Karen interviewed her.'

Hardwick agreed. 'And Louisa was murdered. We don't know when that happened, but it can't have been long after she went missing. That wouldn't give Ben much time to get the money together. And once she's dead, that leverage is gone.'

'That could have been the plan all along,' said Hutchinson. 'Get the money and then kill her in case she identifies her kidnapper.'

'Or it could have been a mistake,' said Ruskin. 'But a clean stab to the heart of a bound victim, after walking them to their death, feels like an execution – not a chaotic situation that suddenly went wrong. And what about the lack of sexual assault? Given what we know about Myrie, I'd be amazed if he could keep his grubby hands to himself.'

'Maybe that's why Ben is refusing to speak,' said Hardwick. 'The kidnapper has proven they are willing to kill. He has two young daughters and his mother to think of.'

'The timing still bugs me,' said Hutchinson. 'There were several hours between us notifying him of Louisa's death and his arrest. You'd think the first thing he'd do is call his mum and beg her to release the money before they killed anyone else.'

Warren considered what they had said. 'I'm leaning away from the kidnap theory. Be open to any new evidence, but let's put a line through it for now.

'What are you thinking, Mags?' he asked, noticing Richardson's frown.

'I know we said to park Sinead, but what if she is involved? At least indirectly?'

'How do you mean?' asked Warren. 'Do you think she's still alive and somehow persuaded Darren or Ben to kill Louisa?'

'No, I think Sinead is dead,' said Richardson. 'But let's assume Ben was involved in her death eleven years ago. Who better to call and help him get rid of a dead body than his brother? He'd have been what? Eighteen? That's a big burden to place on someone so young. We all know drug addicts are often trying to deal with significant past trauma; I'd say a phone call out of the

207

blue from his big brother asking for help to deal with a murder would qualify.'

'They'd be forever linked,' said Sutton. 'If Ben goes down for killing Louisa, then he'd know there's a good chance we'd look into Sinead's disappearance again. Ben could have blackmailed Darren into helping him with Louisa by making it clear that if he didn't, then he'd be on the hook for his part in Sinead's murder.'

'Could Louisa have found out about Sinead?' asked Ruskin. 'That would make her potentially dangerous. Darren's housemate assumed they were having sex when she came around to get her drugs, but what if she was blackmailing Darren into giving her what she needed? That could easily be a twenty-minute conversation ending in tears if he said no.'

'If Darren was involved in her death, then he would have needed a car,' said Warren. 'And we've found no trace evidence from her attacker. This whole thing feels too sophisticated for him to be the mastermind. In which case, we're either back to Ben, who mysteriously left his house that night, or somebody else.'

'Russell Myrie would seem most likely,' said Sutton. 'We know he was out and about, doing something shifty. He could know Darren from the drug scene. He also had the exact same security set-up as Louisa, so potentially could have disabled it.'

'But again, it comes down to what we can prove,' said Warren. 'So far we have no forensics linking either man to Louisa's murder, and she was associated with them both, so her DNA and fingerprints can be explained away. There's no sign of the murder weapon or the Taser. We've not found her blood, there are no traces of Louisa in any of the vehicles we know they have access to, and we haven't linked the suspicious car with the cloned licence plates to either of them. All we really have on them is that they lied about where they were. Which for a couple of dodgy characters like these two is hardly surprising.'

'The killer must have stashed the murder weapon somewhere,' said Sutton. 'Or even that damn Taser. But Ben had at least twelve hours to ditch anything with her blood on it. It could be in the bottom of some stranger's wheelie bin on the other side of town or already buried in the local landfill.'

'We still haven't ruled out a stranger killing,' Warren reminded them. 'Or at least somebody we are unaware of. Rachel, what do we know about this website HotBritishHousewives.com?'

'Customers have to open an account with a credit card if they want to access anything more than a few non-explicit sample pictures,' said Pymm. 'There's nothing more than a few cheeky lingerie or topless shots in front of the paywall. Louisa's teasers were quite tame, and her face is partially covered in all of them. You probably wouldn't recognise her if you weren't looking for her.'

'That makes sense,' said Sutton. 'It was clearly just a means to an end, not a career. She wouldn't want recognisable pictures of her floating around the internet for the rest of time.'

'What about behind the paywall?' asked Warren.

'Members can browse through the different performers to see what they offer. The performers upload collections of images as sets. The system generates a contact sheet made of small, low-resolution thumbnails, censored with black banners. If the customer likes the look of a contact sheet, they add it to their shopping cart and download a folder containing high-resolution, uncensored versions of the images.'

'What was Louisa offering?' asked Richardson.

'Softcore mainly, which is why she earned so little. Performers set their own prices, but there are expectations about what the punters get for their money. Sets with more explicit content cost more. There's even a rating system customers can use to comment on "value for money". Let's just say the reviews are rather more to the point than Amazon.

'Her content has become more explicit over time. Either she became less shy or realised she had to offer more if she wanted to earn better money. Some of the performers grab the attention of the casual browser more than others, shall we say?'

'Have we got records of whoever downloaded her sets?' asked Sutton.

'In theory yes,' said Pymm. 'The user accounts should link back to a credit card; that's part of the site's age-verification system. We're compiling a list of all her customers, prioritising anyone who has downloaded more than a couple of sets or visited repeatedly.'

'People who may be infatuated with her,' said Warren.

'Exactly. The problem is that it's likely not all of the credit cards are legitimate. Stolen credit card numbers are traded freely on the dark web and used on porn sites to hoover up as much content as possible before the card is blocked and the user account deleted. If they are using a VPN to mask their IP address, they can open a new account with a different card, and the site won't know it's the same person they've already flagged as dodgy.'

Warren still thought Louisa's murderer was most likely her husband, or somebody else who knew her in real life, but it would be remiss of him to dismiss other possibilities out of hand. 'Then the obvious question is how did he go from stalking a woman on a website, who despite the site's name could presumably be based anywhere in the world, to killing her? How did he know where she lived?'

'Did she use the site's chat facility?' asked Sutton. 'Could somebody have tricked her into revealing some sort of clue telling them where she lived?'

'She did use it,' said Pymm. 'The site administrators keep recordings for four weeks before deleting them. If our killer did contact her through a live video stream, then we have a window of three weeks, since she last logged onto the site on May 13th. Unfortunately, it was a strictly one-way affair. Punters can type messages, but there is no voice or video function from their end, just the performers.'

'Surely she wasn't desperate enough to meet up with someone, no matter how much money they offered?' said Richardson.

Warren noticed that Pymm was frowning. 'Penny for them, Rachel?' he offered.

'I've got an idea,' she said. 'Can I borrow your laptop? It's quicker than going back to my desk.'

'Sure,' said Warren. 'Do you want me to keep it plugged into the projector?'

Pymm smirked. 'Probably better to disconnect it. We don't want to upset the cleaners.'

Passing it over, he watched as Pymm went to work, logging him off, then logging back on as herself. Opening a folder containing a sample of the images from Louisa Greenland's laptop, she selected one of the more innocuous pictures.

She hummed, nodding to herself, as she accessed some information about the file.

Next she logged onto the HotBritishHousewives website, entering the login details reluctantly provided by the website's administrators. She navigated to the page displaying the photoset containing the same image she'd just looked at offline. She clicked to download it.

'Not to nag,' said Warren nervously, 'but are you downloading pornography onto my work laptop?'

'It'll be fine,' said Pymm absently. 'It's only softcore.'

'OK, not a problem then,' said Warren, rolling his eyes. Around the room his colleagues stifled their laughter. All except Sutton, who didn't bother hiding his mirth. 'I'd phone IT,' he advised. 'Before they find it the next time they do a routine check. And probably best to give DSI Roehampton a heads-up, you know, just in case.'

'Ah ha, found it,' said Pymm, although her tone was more disappointed than triumphant.

'What?' asked Warren, unsure if he wanted to know.

'I know how the killer could find where she lives,' said Pymm. 'And the site administrators need to get their act together and fix this problem, before other performers are targeted by perverts and weirdos.'

'How?' asked Warren.

'The high-resolution images she uploaded to the website for punters to download still had the geolocation and timing metadata attached. Her smartphone recorded the exact GPS coordinates of where she took the photographs.' She spun the laptop to show an open window displaying Google Maps. 'Which includes her house and the industrial unit where she is alone late at night.'

'Shit, that's not good,' said Sutton.

'Contact the Sexual Exploitation Unit,' ordered Warren. 'Even if this has no relevance to our case it might be important to someone else. And tell them to contact the website to fix that ASAP.'

Dismissing the team, Warren sat back and rubbed his eyes with a groan. Sutton remained behind.

'I want you to review the original Sinead McCaffrey investigation,' said Warren.

'I thought you might,' agreed Sutton. 'But what about Ben Greenland? Ash signed off on his latest nine-hour custody review, but unless we come up with something new, we aren't going to get an extension.'

Warren nodded. 'We need to put the screws on him. If he doesn't stop no commenting, he's out the door.'

Chapter 26

Ben Greenland was pronounced fit to be interviewed by the duty doctor, but he looked positively ill when Warren and Sutton joined him. He was hunched over, his eyes red-rimmed from crying. Josie Barton was whispering in his ear as the two officers entered, but it was obviously words of comfort, rather than privileged legal advice.

Greenland remained silent, staring at the tabletop as Warren ran through the preliminaries. When he'd finished, the solicitor cleared her throat.

'I think it is time for you to stop this fishing expedition, DCI Jones. Mr Greenland is a grieving husband. In case you've forgotten, there are two small girls who have lost their mother in the most horrific circumstances imaginable. They don't yet know what has happened and it is only right their father be the one to tell them.' Her voice rose, and two pink spots appeared on her cheeks. 'Show some humanity here. So far you have presented absolutely no evidence my client was involved in this dreadful act; his continued detention is nothing more than an act of desperation.'

'I appreciate that, Ms Barton, but Mr Greenland's refusal to cooperate has left us no choice,' said Warren firmly, before turning back to Greenland.

'Ben,' he said, his voice softening. 'I know you want nothing more than to hold your daughters. I get that; both of us are fathers and we know that Molly and Pippa will be frightened and confused, but you have to help us here. Please, you must tell us; where were you going at quarter past midnight when your car was photographed in Lester Road?'

Greenland gave a sniff. 'No comment,' he whispered.

'Whatever you were doing that night, we can deal with it,' Warren pressed. 'The main thing is to prove to us that you were not involved in your wife's disappearance.'

Greenland shrunk into himself and shook his head.

'I remind you, DCI Jones, it is not his place to prove anything,' said his solicitor tartly. 'The burden of proof rests squarely with you. As yet, you have shown us nothing linking him to what happened to Louisa.'

'Tell us about P@mper,' said Sutton. 'Everybody we've spoken to has told us Louisa had got an extension to her bank loan to finance the upfront costs of her deal with Holistics Gym. However, that loan was refused. Were you aware of that?'

Greenland said nothing.

'We found your fingerprints on the letter from the bank declining her application,' continued Sutton. 'Did Louisa tell you this, or did you find it out for yourself when you went snooping through her filing cabinet?'

A brief look of surprise crossed Greenland's face. 'No comment.'

'How did you feel when you realised Louisa had gambled your home and financial security on a deal that might leave her – and you and the girls – with a mountain of debt and an industrial unit filled with unsold hampers?'

Greenland's jaw worked up and down, before he finally muttered no comment again.

Warren looked at Sutton and gave a tiny nod. Over the years, the two men had forged an effective double act. The shorter, more bullish Sutton would use his harsher Essex accent to play "bad cop", whilst Warren would be the kinder face, offering the interviewee a potential way out.

'Were you aware of how Louisa was earning additional money, in an attempt to keep her business afloat?' asked Sutton.

Greenland's eyes flashed briefly, too quick for Warren to tell if he was surprised or ashamed. Beside him, his solicitor appeared surprised.

'The Digital Forensics Unit have successfully unlocked your laptop, Ben,' said Sutton. 'And they have found, and accessed, the secret user account you use to hide your porn hobby.'

Greenland's cheeks flushed, but he maintained his silence. Sutton pushed on quickly, not wanting his solicitor to request a conference.

'Are you aware of the website HotBritishHousewives?'

Greenland looked away, the pink colouring spreading to his neck. Whether he recognised the site, or it was just obvious from its name what it offered, Warren couldn't tell.

'Did you know Louisa was posting pictures to this website that users could pay to download?'

Sutton spun his laptop around. They'd chosen one of the tamer images from her site. There was no need to hammer the point home.

'I don't know about you,' said Sutton. 'But I'd be pretty upset if I found out my wife was sharing intimate pictures with complete strangers. Or were you aware she was doing it? After all, your financial future was on the line. Sometimes we all need to make sacrifices for the ones we love. How do you feel about these pictures, Ben?'

Greenland covered his mouth with his hands, before closing his eyes and leaning his elbows on the table. His shoulders shook with silent sobs.

The solicitor glared across the table. 'I think a break would be in order, now.'

*   *   *

'We have got to get him to stop no commenting,' hissed Warren. 'I'm really struggling to read him; I can't work out if he's surprised at what we're telling him, or surprised we've found it out.'

'Then let's hope that damn solicitor of his stops advising him to no comment every bloody question,' said Sutton. 'She must see the strategy isn't working.'

The two men were at the communal urn. Warren was eating a banana and debating a second mug of coffee; Sutton was finishing a yoghurt.

'He's back,' Ruskin interrupted them. 'And he has something he'd like to say.'

'That was quick,' said Sutton, as the two men headed back to the interview suite.

The statement was stilted and formal, and had been crafted by his solicitor, rather than Greenland. It didn't matter; he had endorsed it with his signature.

'Like many people, Mr Greenland uses the internet to access adult entertainment. And like a lot of men, he chose not to share that with his wife. He wishes to stress that all the material he has viewed is entirely legal within the United Kingdom. As to the website HotBritishHousewives, he does not know if he has ever visited it, or viewed content downloaded from there. However, he is confident he has never seen pictures of his wife, nor was he aware she was uploading content to such sites. That is all he wishes to say on the matter.'

Greenland had composed himself during the break, his face now inscrutable, although his eyes remained reddened.

'OK let's move on for the time being,' said Warren. 'The Digital Forensics Unit have accessed both of your mobile phones. The one you use every day, which for clarity we shall refer to as your "personal phone" and the phone that we found hidden in your bedroom, which we shall refer to as your "hidden phone".'

The solicitor looked as though she was about to object at the

216

pejorative term they had deliberately chosen to provoke him. A glare from Sutton suggested she pick her battles, and she backed down. It was another example of when an independent duty solicitor would have spoken up, Warren thought.

'Why did you install covert tracking software on your wife's phone, Ben?' asked Warren. 'The matching app was found on your hidden phone and the website had been accessed regularly on your laptop.'

'No comment.'

'More to the point,' said Sutton. 'Why didn't you tell us about it? Your wife was missing. We may have been able to use it to find her. Surely, any husband worried that his wife had disappeared would have done anything he could to help the search?'

A look of shame crossed Greenland's face.

'Or maybe you didn't want her found too soon?' said Sutton. 'Perhaps you knew she was dead and wanted a bit of breathing space to cover your tracks?'

'No,' he said quietly, his voice cracking. 'I loved her.'

'Then why did you install that software?' pressed Sutton. 'Most husbands I know trust their wives; they don't spy on them.'

'No, it wasn't like that.'

'Perhaps it was to give you a warning Louisa was coming home?' Sutton said. 'In case she forgot to text you? It could be a bit awkward if she returned home to find you cracking one off, especially if you were on her website.'

Greenland glared at him. 'No comment,' he said, biting off each word.

'Did the tracker tell you she'd come home early, or did she catch you by surprise?'

'She didn't . . .' started Greenland, before clamping his mouth shut. 'No comment,' he said eventually.

'Or maybe it was something else,' said Sutton, as if the idea had just occurred to him. 'Were you having an affair?'

'No comment.'

'Look, Ben, we get it,' said Warren. 'Believe me, we've heard far worse. Were you having an affair with Caitlin O'Shaughnessy?'

Greenland acted like he'd been slapped. 'No!'

'Are you sure?' asked Warren. 'It's obvious she has strong feelings towards you. And a man matching your description has been seen near her apartment.'

'No comment,' he muttered again.

'Did Louisa arrive home unexpectedly and find you with Caitlin?' he pushed.

Greenland said nothing and looked down at the table again. Not for the first time, Warren wished there was a mirror on the table, or a camera pointing upwards to record interviewees' expressions.

'OK, Ben,' said Warren, allowing a note of impatience into his voice. 'Time to get everything in the open so we can start sorting out this mess. You are no commenting yourself into a whole heap of trouble. Are you having, or have you had in the past, an affair with Caitlin O'Shaughnessy?'

Greenland paused. Beside him, his solicitor delicately cleared her throat.

'No comment,' he said.

Sutton glared at the solicitor, who looked back impassively.

· Greenland folded his arms, the gesture a mixture of defensive and defiant.

'Why was the CCTV camera disconnected in Louisa's unit?' asked Warren.

Greenland opened his mouth but closed it again.

'The camera was unplugged from the rear of the digital video recorder on Monday 15th April,' said Sutton. 'Why were your fingerprints – and only your fingerprints – all over the cables and the rear of the DVR? That looks like premeditation to me.'

'No comment,' said Greenland, a bead of sweat on his forehead.

'Did you go to her unit that day?' asked Warren.

'No comment.' He wiped his brow.

'Come on, Ben, give us something to work with here,' said

218

Warren. 'All you need to do is tell us you weren't there and what you were doing, and you're off the hook. That camera was almost certainly disabled by the person who snatched your wife. Tell us how we can rule you out.'

Greenland shook his head.

'When was the last time you spoke to your brother?' asked Sutton.

A look of surprise crossed Greenland's face, but Warren couldn't tell if it was from the sudden change in direction or something else. Their strategy of jumping from topic to topic, keeping the suspect off balance, had proven effective in the past, but he'd obviously been told to default to no comment each time.

'Were you aware Louisa was visiting your brother on a regular basis?' asked Sutton.

This time the look was one of genuine surprise. 'No, why?' he responded, before remembering to say nothing.

'We believe it was to buy drugs, and your brother has alluded to a sexual relationship,' said Sutton.

'No, that's not possible,' said Greenland. 'She would never . . .' He broke off.

'Was that why you placed the tracking software on her phone?' asked Warren. 'Were you worried that maybe she was the one having the affair? Were you worried she might leave you and take the girls with her?'

'No, she'd never do that,' he said, a note of desperation in his voice.

Again, his solicitor cleared her throat.

'Would you like a throat lozenge, Ms Barton?' snapped Sutton, unable to help himself.

Greenland retreated into himself again.

'Do you recognise this man?' asked Warren. He pushed a photograph of Russell Myrie across the table.

Greenland clearly did recognise him but muttered no comment again.

'He runs the garage next to Louisa's unit.'

Greenland said nothing; it wasn't a question.

'He and Louisa had also struck up a friendship,' said Warren. He emphasised the word "friendship". 'And we believe he deals drugs. Was Louisa getting her cocaine from this man?'

'No comment.'

'You know what's interesting about your personal mobile phone?' asked Warren. 'There are very few messages to or from people that we would expect you to speak to regularly. Obviously, you could have deleted them. Fortunately, our Digital Forensics Unit can retrieve anything, given enough time. Now, you can continue to no comment, in which case this is going to be hanging over you until they get around to retrieving the files, or you can be upfront with us, and we can put this to bed now. Have you deleted any messages from your phone?'

'No comment.'

'Tell me about the Enkryp app on your hidden phone, Ben,' said Warren.

Greenland gave a start.

'You use WhatsApp and Messenger to communicate with family and friends. Why would you need another messaging app?' he asked.

'No comment.'

'Is it because you didn't want Louisa to be able to access it? To see who you've been speaking to behind her back? It has a separate PIN code.'

'No comment.'

'Louisa has used your phone, hasn't she?' said Warren. 'Her fingerprints are all over the touchscreen. Did you hand her the phone, perhaps to show her something funny on YouTube, or did she take advantage when you left it unlocked; to do a little snooping?'

'No comment.'

'Who were you contacting using Enkryp, Ben?' asked Sutton again.

'No comment.'

'Look, we know you have a, shall we say, wandering eye,' said Warren. Greenland blushed but said nothing. 'It's not gone unnoticed by your friends and family. If you were using the app to contact people you shouldn't, then I get that it could be embarrassing. But look at your options here; surely it's better you face up to your human failings and ask forgiveness, than continue as our prime suspect for the murder of your wife?'

'We will crack the PIN code,' said Sutton. 'But it could take ages. In the meantime, think about what will happen.'

'You won't be able to return to your family home,' said Warren. 'Visits with your little girls will be supervised. You won't be able to hug them or comfort them without a police officer in the room.'

A tear started to flow down Greenland's cheek.

'Who were you using the app to speak to on May 15th?' asked Sutton.

Greenland flinched.

'The family liaison officer heard you on the phone in the bathroom,' he clarified.

'No comment,' he whispered.

'Why don't you give us the PIN code. Let us take a look?'

Greenland looked over at his solicitor, before shaking his head.

Warren glanced at Sutton. 'Ben, have you been threatened?'

Greenland looked confused.

'Did someone demand money for Louisa's safe return?'

'No . . . no comment,' he amended. Beside him, his solicitor shifted, a canny look in her eyes.

'Because if that's what happened, we can help you. We can make sure your family is safe. If you tell us, we can track them down,' said Warren, looking at Greenland intently.

'No,' he said firmly.

Warren waited for a few moments, to see if Greenland would fill the silence.

He didn't.

'Interview suspended.'

* * *

'Nothing,' said Warren in exasperation. 'He's still being told to keep his mouth shut.'

'Do you think the ransom angle is still worth pursuing?' asked Roehampton.

'He appeared surprised,' admitted Sutton.

'I only really threw it in out of desperation,' said Warren. 'He's refusing to help us in any other way. It still all points towards him killing his wife. There's no evidence he's been approached for money, and it looks as though his mother hasn't been asked for anything.'

'I'm a little uncomfortable with the look in his solicitor's eyes,' said Sutton. 'I wouldn't be the least bit surprised if she comes up with some baloney about a mysterious voice demanding money to throw us off the scent.'

'We'll have to watch for that,' said Warren. 'It was always a danger it might give him ideas, but it's a valid line of inquiry.'

Roehampton's face was inscrutable. 'What about unlocking the app?' she asked. 'Is that possible or do we need his PIN?'

Warren puffed his lips out. 'I'll speak to Pete Robertson, but it was a bluff about being able to unlock it. All the public news articles I've found seem to think it's uncrackable.'

Roehampton looked uncomfortable. 'This isn't going well, Warren. Everything so far is circumstantial. I don't think for one minute Ben is in the clear, but I'm going to struggle justifying his continued detention. And magistrates are only human; they are going to see a grieving husband with two small girls who have lost their mother. They will need a damned good reason to keep him away from them much longer.'

She came to a decision. 'Hold him until the end of the current extension and see if any new forensics come back or we hear anything interesting from acquaintances. Interview him again, and if he still keeps his mouth shut, bail him. Let the Crown Prosecution Service know the state of play, but we're nowhere near the charging threshold.'

Warren nodded his assent. She was absolutely right. Without new evidence, there was nothing they could do.

TUESDAY 21ST MAY

Chapter 27

Ben Greenland's next interview took place shortly after seven a.m. The custody extension was due to run out within the hour, meaning they would either need to reveal some new information to secure a further extension from the magistrate, or he would be going home. Warren and Sutton decided not to put him out of his misery until the last possible minute.

Unfortunately, Greenland maintained his composure and continued no commenting until the very end. Finally, Warren had nothing left and they'd elicited no new evidence. His solicitor objected to the bail conditions they imposed, but was firmly rebuffed.

Thirty-six hours after his initial arrest, Ben Greenland walked out of Middlesbury police station.

Louisa Greenland's husband remained their prime suspect, but Warren couldn't help feeling they were back to square one.

*   *   *

Pymm started the morning briefing with an update on the customers who had accessed Louisa's pictures on HotBritishHousewives.com.

'Financial Crime have identified the owners of most of the

credit cards used to download content. Seven users downloaded more than two sets of Louisa's pictures, four of them on more than one occasion. Two have downloaded pretty much everything she ever uploaded.'

'Could they be obsessives?' asked Sutton.

'Quite possibly. They've been prioritised,' Pymm responded. 'We've also identified three registered sex offenders amongst her single-download customers, including one who is banned from using the internet to access pornography. He'll be getting a knock on the door today. We also have a stolen credit card used four weeks ago that downloaded everything she'd uploaded to that point, although it was blocked by the bank as soon as they tried to use it again. Cybercrime are trying to trace the user, but don't hold your breath. Downloading files is not like buying a TV; there's no need for the item to be physically delivered to a real-world address. It's child's play to mask the location of a computer.'

Warren still wasn't convinced that their suspect had singled out Louisa online, but he'd wait for the Financial and Cyber Crime units to report back.

'Do we know what other performers' pages these people accessed?' he asked. 'There could be more potential victims.'

'Unfortunately, no. The warrant had to be worded quite specifically to get the magistrate's signature. She said she had to balance our investigation's needs with users' privacy. But she was sympathetic and said if we can demonstrate that any of these users are potentially dangerous, she'll consider a revised application.'

It was the best they could hope for. Warren just prayed their killer – if they were still trawling for victims – didn't strike again whilst they gathered more evidence.

'The men we have identified are scattered across the country. I've called the nearest force to each of them to arrange interview suites and we'll send some specialists from Welwyn to speak to them. Mags has a team checking their vehicles on ANPR, but I can't get a warrant for their mobile phones. The website is perfectly legal, and aside from the gentleman who is banned from using the internet to look at porn, none of them have broken any laws.'

'Keep me posted,' said Warren. 'But remind the interviewing officers to tread carefully. The last thing we need is a complaint from some bloke whose wife has left him because we blundered in and told her what he was doing online.'

Next up was Mags Richardson, with an update on the search for the suspicious vehicle with cloned licence plates spotted the night Louisa had disappeared.

'Now we have some timings, I've had the analysts manually hunt through traffic cam footage that isn't linked to ANPR,' she said. 'They've found what we believe is the vehicle.'

She projected a still image on the briefing room screen. 'This is the clearest frame we have. You can just make out part of the licence number. As you can see, it is clearly not white.'

The vehicle was a dark-coloured, medium-sized five-door. The picture was grainy and black and white, taken via a night-vision lens from a distance. It was also obviously not the Greenlands' Renault Espace.

'So either Ben had returned home by then, he'd switched vehicles, or this is a wild goose chase and we're tracking someone else out and about in a stolen car.' Warren squinted at the screen. 'I don't suppose there's any way to work out who is driving?'

'The VAU have software that can combine all the useful data from multiple video frames and eliminate some of the noise. But it isn't magic; it can't conjure up photons of light that aren't there. We're not going to get a recognisable face.'

'Do what you can,' said Warren. 'Even an exact make and model, and the number of passengers could be useful. But one thing does puzzle me. They went to the trouble of cloning the plates on a car registered locally. Why didn't they choose a car the same colour?'

* * *.

229

Caitlin O'Shaughnessy looked exhausted when she attended the station for her second interview.

'We're very sorry for your loss,' started Warren. He'd decided to conduct it in a proper interview suite this time; he wanted her nervous.

'I'm sure you are aware by now that we brought Ben in to help us with our inquiries,' Warren could see from her body language that she understood the euphemism. Though not under arrest, she had been informed of her right to legal representation and had declined.

'There are some details of Ben's story that we need your help to clarify,' said Hardwick.

'Of course.' Her voice cracked. 'You don't really think Ben had anything to do with it do you? He couldn't.'

'Why are you so sure?' asked Warren.

'Well, he couldn't, he . . .' She paused. 'Well, he loves her and he's not that type of person. He's so gentle, he'd never be able to kill someone.'

'Remind me again, when was the last time you saw, Ben?' asked Hardwick.

'At our annual get-together. To remember Sinead,' she said.

'What date was that?' asked Hardwick, pen poised.

'The weekend of April 6th. The weekend before the date she went missing.'

'And what about Louisa?' she asked.

'The same weekend. Look, I told you this, already.'

'Sorry,' said Warren. 'We do so many interviews, that sometimes we forget what we've already covered. It's easier just to ask again.'

O'Shaughnessy said nothing.

'Just to be clear,' Warren continued, 'that was the last time you saw either of them?'

'Yes.'

'And you haven't spoken to either of them since?'

'No,' she said; her eyes dipped briefly.

'Are you familiar with Mandy's Muffins?' asked Hardwick. 'The little cake shop and café?'

'Sure,' she said. Everyone knew Mandy's Muffins; it was a Middlesbury institution.

'When did you last go there?' asked Warren.

'A few months ago? I treated myself after I landed a new commission.'

'And you haven't been there more recently?' he asked.

She frowned. 'I don't think so.'

'What were you doing on Tuesday May 14th. The night Louisa disappeared?' asked Hardwick.

'I was at home,' she answered firmly.

'All night?' asked Hardwick.

'All night,' she confirmed.

'Doing what?' asked Warren.

'Nothing much. I did some work, then watched a film before turning in for the night.'

'And you didn't go out at all?' asked Hardwick.

'No.'

'Was anyone with you?' asked Warren.

'No, I was alone. You can check my phone if you don't believe me; I never went anywhere that night.'

'We have,' said Warren, moving on without giving her time to react. 'What about your boyfriend? Did he come over?'

'I don't have a boyfriend,' she said.

'Oh? So who's the dark-haired man your neighbours have seen you with?'

O'Shaughnessy paused. 'Nobody,' she managed eventually. 'They must be mistaken.'

Warren and Hardwick said nothing.

O'Shaughnessy swallowed, then took a sip of water, before clearing her throat.

'I guess they must have seen a friend from the gym,' she said. Her cheeks flushed.

Again, the two officers said nothing.

'He comes over occasionally. You know, just to chill out.'

'Does he have a name?' asked Warren.

'I'd rather not say,' she said.

Warren said nothing, just raised an eyebrow.

'He . . . Well, it's complicated,' she said eventually. 'But he wasn't with me that Tuesday night, so it doesn't really matter who he is.'

'Perhaps let us be the judge of that,' said Hardwick.

'No. I can't give you his name,' she said, her voice firm.

'OK,' said Warren. He waited until she met his gaze. 'Are you having an affair with Ben Greenland?'

'No, of course, not,' she said. 'He was my best friend's husband. How can you even ask?'

'Have you had an affair with Ben in the past?' asked Hardwick.

'No, absolutely not,' she said, shaking her head vigorously. 'Ben is a dear friend, but we have never had an affair.'

'What about at university? Perhaps before he and Louisa got together?' asked Hardwick.

'No.' Her voice turned frosty. 'If you think I had something to do with my best friend's murder then come out and say it. I am here voluntarily; I want to leave now. If you have a problem with that, you can arrest me and then speak to my lawyer.'

Warren raised a hand. 'I'm sorry, Caitlin, please forgive us. Sometimes we have to ask difficult and upsetting questions. Why don't we start again? No more questions about Ben, I promise.'

O'Shaughnessy glared at the two of them, before finally slumping back into her seat. 'Go on,' she said eventually, folding her arms.

'Did Louisa ever speak to you about P@mper?' asked Hardwick.

'Of course,' said O'Shaughnessy. Her tone was still cool, but she had stopped scowling. 'She was my best mate. I bought hampers for all my friends and used to share her online ads on my social media.'

'Do you know how the business was doing?' asked Warren.

232

O'Shaughnessy gave a shrug but didn't meet their gaze. 'It was popular. I used her products myself and they were really good. Great value for money. You only have to read the online reviews; they're all genuine.'

'Do you know how it was doing financially?' he pressed.

'Not as well as it should have been,' she admitted. 'She had some great reviews, but only a few dozen. Some sellers have fifty times as many. I wrote an article a couple of years ago about these review farms. You pay a bit of money, and they'll write hundreds of glowing testimonials. I looked at some of her rivals; they all claim to be the same set-up, just one or two people working out of their garage, but they'd need practically every customer who ever bought one of their products to write them a five-star review to get that many ratings in such a short time. No chance. The platforms claim they do their best to stop it happening, but there's no incentive for them to do so. Products with more reviews sell more, and the platform gets a cut of each sale.'

'How did Louisa feel about that?' asked Hardwick.

'Frustrated. But she said she didn't want to go down that route.' Her voice softened. 'It's one of the things I loved about her. But anyway, that was all in the past. After Holistics Gyms offered her that deal, all her hard work was finally paying off.'

'Our understanding is the deal came with some strings attached,' said Warren. 'She needed to buy the materials up front and would then get paid on a sale-or-return basis. How was she going to finance that?'

'She asked for an extension to her bank loan,' replied O'Shaughnessy, her eyes flicking towards the table.

'And did the bank agree?' asked Warren.

O'Shaughnessy finally shook her head. 'No,' she admitted.

'Did Ben know about this?' asked Hardwick.

'No, I don't think so,' she said, still not meeting their gaze.

'Caitlin, how was Louisa funding the expansion of P@mper's business?' asked Hardwick.

O'Shaughnessy suddenly became very interested in a hangnail.

'Were you aware she was posing for an adult website?' asked Warren.

There was a long silence, before O'Shaughnessy finally nodded.

'Yes. Sort of. She mentioned she was considering it a few weeks ago.'

'And what did you say?'

'I told her it was a bad idea.'

'Do you know if she ever met any of the men who downloaded her pictures or watched her videos?' asked Hardwick.

'No, but I can't believe she'd be that silly.' She finally looked up, her eyes searching both of their faces. 'Do you think that might be who killed her? Some creep she met on there?'

'We're following all lines of inquiry,' said Warren. 'I'm going to ask again; did Ben know about the bank loan? Or how she was earning money to fund P@mper?'

O'Shaughnessy shrugged, but looked away.

'Caitlin?' said Hardwick. 'Did you tell Ben about what Louisa was doing?'

*   *   *

'Despite what she claims, I think Caitlin told Ben about Louisa's website,' Warren told the team.

'I agree,' said Hardwick. 'Her denial was a little too forceful, and she looked ashamed.'

'It would make sense,' said Richardson. 'We're all fairly confident Caitlin's having – or had – an affair with Ben. If she wanted Ben to herself, then I can believe she was whispering things into his ear when they were together. I'll bet she also told him about the loan refusal. That might be why he was snooping in her filing cabinet.'

'But why now?' asked Warren.

'Two reasons spring to mind for me,' said Hardwick. 'One,

she's in her thirties and to the outside world, doesn't appear to have a boyfriend. You can only withstand so many well-meaning aunties asking you when you're going to find yourself a nice man and settle down.'

'Amen to that,' said Pymm. 'Thank God I met Martin when I did. That shut them up.' Pymm's husband was over six feet, muscled and covered in tattoos and piercings. Unless you knew he was a special educational needs teacher, with a penchant for classical music and an encyclopaedic knowledge of fine wines, he could appear . . . intimidating.

'Second, the deal with Holistics Gyms,' continued Hardwick. 'Everything was on a knife-edge. Either she succeeded, in which case the Greenlands were going to pull themselves out of a financial hole and the future was bright, or she was going to crash and burn. A little push from Caitlin could be all it needed for their marriage to collapse.'

'How do we feel about Caitlin's denial that she knows Russell Myrie?' Warren asked.

'I'm leaning towards believing her,' said Hardwick. 'She wasn't in the best of moods by the time we showed her the headshot, but it felt genuine.'

'What about her repeated denials that she's met up with Louisa since the reunion?' Warren asked.

'The receipt from Mandy's Muffins was definitely for two people,' said Pymm. 'Two coffees, two rounds of sandwiches and two muffins. Lunchtime on a weekday, when we know Ben was at work.'

'But we have no proof it was Caitlin she met up with,' cautioned Richardson. 'The only CCTV is from over the till when Louisa placed her order. The waitress remembers serving Louisa and another woman, because she's heavily pregnant and Louisa jumped up to move some chairs for her. But she couldn't really describe who was with Louisa. It could have been Caitlin, or it could have been another thirty-something woman.'

'For what it's worth, none of Louisa's friends admit to meeting her there,' said Hutchinson. 'And Stephanie would have been working in London that day.' He didn't voice everyone's thoughts around the table; could it have been Sinead? Sutton's team were still working that angle, but it was far too early to throw it into the mix.

'Caitlin's car wasn't spotted on ANPR that day,' said Richardson. 'But she lives within walking distance of the café. Especially if she wanted to burn off the calories from one of those muffins.'

'We really need Louisa's phone,' said Pymm. 'She must have arranged to meet her friend somehow, but we have hardly any texts or calls from that week. She probably used WhatsApp, so we can't access the messages without her handset.'

'If Caitlin was using that meeting with Louisa to pump her for information she could funnel back to Ben, then she probably wouldn't admit it,' said Sutton.

Warren tried not to let his frustration show. 'Catch-22. All we have is supposition. There's nothing concrete to get a search warrant for Caitlin's flat. Without that search warrant, we can't find enough to prove that a search warrant is justified.' He turned to Richardson and Hutchinson. 'If we want to pursue Caitlin then we need to catch her in a provable lie. See if any of the businesses near Mandy's Muffins have external CCTV; if we can show Caitlin in the vicinity of the café when the food was bought, then I think that's grounds for a warrant.'

He turned to Ruskin. 'Any luck working out who may have been visiting Caitlin's flat?'

'Sorry, Boss. A couple of residents remember a dark-haired man about Ben's age and build in the apartment block a couple of times, but they couldn't swear it was him, or even be certain he was visiting Caitlin.'

'What about the woman her neighbour bumped into on the stairs?' asked Warren. 'The one that could be her sister?'

'She does have a sister. She's a couple of years younger than

Caitlin, but with the right haircut she looks like her. But I also showed him pictures of Stephanie and Louisa, plus a couple of other random women similar in appearance, and he suddenly became a lot less certain. Sorry.'

'Oh, well,' said Warren trying to sound upbeat. 'Eyewitness identification is dodgy anyway, even with trained observers. Anything new from Forensics?'

'Nothing in the Greenland family car indicates she was transported in the boot, and no suspicious bodily fluids,' said Sutton. 'The tyres don't match any of the tracks in the woods, or have soil consistent with that location. They've taken up the floorboards throughout their house and haven't found anything that could have been used in the kidnapping or murder. Same for the shed.'

'Does he have access to any outbuildings or lockers?' asked Warren.

'Nothing,' replied Pymm. 'No allotment or lock-ups, other than the one in her name. Nothing relevant in his file cabinet at work. There are no named lockers in the sports centre. The main bus station has storage; I've got some people going through the CCTV to see if he used it.'

'What about his mum's place?' asked Sutton.

'We would need a warrant,' said Hutchinson. 'But when would he have had the chance? Once he reported Louisa's disappearance, it became a three-ring circus. I don't know when he'd have snuck out. Either he gave his mum something for her to carry out with her under the noses of the FLOs, or he made a detour on the way home the night she was killed.'

'Is that possible?' Warren turned to Richardson.

She manipulated her tablet. 'Yes,' she said slowly, drawing out the word. 'He could avoid ANPR and traffic cameras by doing a rat run via residential streets.'

'He's a local lad; he's lived in Middlesbury all his life,' Sutton reminded them.

'Leave it with me,' said Richardson. 'I'll plot the most likely routes he would have needed to take. Perhaps we can get some residential CCTV?'

'Seize what you can, but hold off analysing it just yet,' decided Warren. 'That's a lot of resources for something that might not be relevant. We'll obtain a warrant for Ben's mother's place first. If she or her neighbours have CCTV, we may be able to rule it out completely. We'll execute the search on her car or property as soon as we get it in case she's looking to dispose of whatever he may or may not have handed her. Can you arrange a canvass of her neighbours, Hutch?'

'Will do.'

'Whilst we're on the subject, what's the situation with searching the woods where she was found?'

'Nothing in the immediate vicinity of the body,' said Hutchinson. 'But the area PolSA has been advising on a strategy for the next phase. She knows the woods quite well, and has a team ready to go; she's awaiting sign-off.'

'I'll speak to the guv,' promised Warren, wondering why Roehampton hadn't agreed already to the police search adviser's request. Searching an area that large wasn't cheap, but for a murder investigation it wasn't excessive.

He turned back to Richardson. 'Where are we with the taxi firms?'

'We've tracked down the firm Louisa used on rainy nights. She used their website but paid cash. They have no jobs logged for that night. We've looked at the drivers who picked her up on previous occasions and she never had the same one twice. They collected her from the street corner, not her actual industrial unit, so they wouldn't have known where she was working.'

'The drive is only a few minutes,' said Sutton. 'That's not long to build a relationship with a passenger. Although if she was high on cocaine, I suppose she could have been a bit more chatty than usual.'

'Do we know anything about the drivers, or the dispatcher?' asked Warren.

Pymm spoke up. 'Nothing on the PNC.'

'Could they have assigned an unlicensed driver off the books?' asked Hardwick.

'Possibly,' conceded Richardson. 'But the Abacus Cabs scandal last year has made local firms clean up their act. The council is a lot stricter on enforcement now.'

'It doesn't sound likely that she was taken by a cabbie,' admitted Warren. 'Rachel, feed all those names into HOLMES in case they crop up again. Mags, what about Caitlin?'

'Nothing,' Richardson admitted. 'None have a job for a Caitlin that Tuesday, or a pick-up or drop-off in the vicinity of either her flat or the Greenlands' house. Unfortunately, without accessing her phone or her bank records there's no way to tell if she used Uber or another app. We'd need warrants for each of them to tell us if she's a customer.'

'Catch-22 again,' said Sutton.

'Then let's move on,' Warren said. 'The Gruesome Twosome, Darren Greenland and Russell Myrie?'

'Forensics have found Louisa's fingerprints at Darren's flat,' said Hardwick. 'But we already know she was visiting him. The bloodstains on that sweatshirt we found don't match her blood type, so there's no point sending off for DNA. There are no more items of clothing with blood on them. There's plenty to keep the drug squad amused, but nothing that could be conceivably linked to Louisa's kidnap or murder.'

'Where is that damned murder weapon?' muttered Sutton to no one in particular.

'In other news,' said Warren. 'Carl Mallucci says they can't justify holding off on arresting Russell Myrie any longer. They're going in, so he'll soon be off the streets.'

*   *   *

239

'Can I have a quick word, Ash?' asked Warren, after knocking on Roehampton's door. It had been a year since she'd assumed the role, and Warren had known her previously when they both held the same rank, but it still felt strange addressing his senior officer in such a familiar way. Warren had worked with John Grayson for years before he felt comfortable addressing him by his first name at work. Roehampton insisted on first names behind closed doors, and the gender-neutral "Guv" at other times; a hangover from an early stint with the Met Police in London, where the term was ubiquitous.

Roehampton offered him a seat. This was the point Grayson would usually have fired up his coffee machine. Warren chided himself; he really needed to stop making comparisons between Roehampton and Grayson – it wasn't fair on her.

'The PolSA says she is waiting for your sign-off on expanding the search of Farley Woods.'

Roehampton frowned. 'Really? Are you sure?'

'Yes, she sent you an email with the details,' said Warren.

'How strange,' said Roehampton. 'I haven't seen it. Are you certain she sent it to me? She didn't use John's old email address?'

'I'll double-check and get her to send it again,' said Warren. 'But will you authorise it? We really need to find that murder weapon and we're running out of places to look.'

'Of course,' said Roehampton. 'As soon as I receive it, I'll deal with it.'

Warren saw himself out. John Grayson had been meticulous when it came to admin. There were many who felt he spent more time than he should down in Welwyn, or on the golf course with the senior brass, but to his credit, he had his phone switched on constantly, and would acknowledge and deal with emails at pretty much any hour of the day.

He was doing it again. Ashley Roehampton was not John Grayson; she was a decorated and experienced officer in her own right. She deserved to be judged on her own merits. He smiled to himself; if someone had told him seven years ago that he'd miss Grayson when he was gone, he probably wouldn't have believed them.

Chapter 28

Warren read the email Pete Robertson had sent him twice, before phoning him. The analyst picked up after two rings. 'I thought that might get your attention,' he said. The man was suffering from hay fever and his voice was muffled and nasal.

'Russell Myrie and Darren Greenland have the same encrypted messaging app on their burner phones as Ben Greenland,' stated Warren. 'Tell me that's not a coincidence.'

'Ha! Sorry, this particular app has been increasing in popularity for the past couple of years,' said Robertson. 'Drug dealers and other organised criminals have been getting wise to us using phone records. The first thing they do when they acquire a new phone is download the app.'

'Shit,' said Warren. 'I don't suppose there's any way you can access it?'

'Nope, not a chance.'

The news was mixed to say the least. Whilst it lent some more credence to the theory that Louisa's murder might have been a conspiracy between the three men, the popularity of the app meant its mere utilisation by them was not enough for that to be inferred. Warren had looked into whether or not he could demand Ben gave up his passwords or face prison. Section 49 of the Regulation of Investigatory Powers Act did provide for such a use, but it was politically sensitive. It would be unwise of him to start throwing that about without the weight of officers far higher in the food chain than either he or DSI Roehampton.

'Unfortunately, we aren't going to be able to tell if Ben Greenland stumbled across pictures of his wife online anytime soon,' continued Robertson.

'Is there any way to see if Louisa was featured on either of those closed forums he frequented?' asked Warren.

'No, in a word. To access the sites, we'll need to convince a court in the US to grant a warrant to us, and pornography is protected under their First Amendment as free speech. If Louisa was underage and there is probable cause to suspect her images are on their servers, then we might persuade the FBI to take an interest, but she was an adult.'

Warren pondered what he had said. The presence of Louisa's images on the site meant nothing unless they could also show that Ben had accessed them. Even then, unless he accessed them for the first time very close to the date she went missing, it would be hard to argue that they were a trigger for him killing her. However, it would allow them to make an informed decision about whether to continue committing resources to that line of inquiry.

'Could we join the forums as a punter and search for her pictures?' asked Warren.

'Joining is easy enough; you can set up a free account. But how would you search for her? One of the sites boasts that it has over 1.5 million pictures and videos, and the other isn't much smaller. Her images will be copyrighted, so whoever uploaded them probably won't have tagged her website's name, to prevent the site administrators removing them if they receive a takedown request.'

'What about reverse image search?'

'Not possible on a private database; they'd need to have already scanned everything on their forum, generated a digital fingerprint, and then committed server and processor resources to scanning the fingerprints. Sorry, Warren, unless we can find concrete evidence on his own computer's hard drive, I don't see how we can prove he's ever come across those pictures.'

* * *

'The VAU have completed their analysis of the video of the suspicious vehicle with the cloned licence plates,' said Richardson. She called up the image on her screen. 'They combined a dozen frames and got rid of some of the glare and reflections.'

The image was better than the original snapshot from the video, but still grainy and greyscale. The car's shape was slightly distorted, due to its changing angle relative to the camera in the different frames, but the model was clearly distinguishable.

'A dark blue or black Ford Focus hatchback,' said Richardson.

Warren placed his reading glasses on and squinted at the image. 'I can't make out any details of the driver, other than that there is one,' he said.

'That's the best we've got,' she said. 'They are reasonably certain there are no passengers, or at least no one of adult size sitting upright.'

'What have we got in terms of people of interest?' Warren asked.

'Nobody linked to the case is the registered keeper of a Ford Focus. I have a team expanding the search to known associates and family members, but they could easily have borrowed a mate's car for the night.'

'What about stolen vehicles or recent sales?'

'It's a popular vehicle, so there's a long list. We're prioritising any recently recovered vehicles from this area. As to recent sales or purchases, we're reliant on the previous owner and the new owner completing the paperwork. If it was a cash sale, then I wouldn't bet on the killer sending off the logbook. I've asked the DVLA to see if anybody recently sold one and it hasn't been registered to a new owner yet.'

'What about scrapyards?' asked Warren. 'If it was only needed to do this one job, an old banger could have been purchased and fixed up, then re-scrapped.'

'You're thinking Russell Myrie?' said Richardson. 'He probably has the skills, although he'd still need to sidestep the paperwork. Previous owners sign the car over to legitimate scrapyards. I can't see any yard dodgy enough to let him "borrow" a car willingly admitting to it.'

'No harm in asking,' said Warren. 'And I'll bet he knows someone who'll make up some new licence plates, no questions asked. He's just been arrested, and he'll be recalled to prison, so he's not going anywhere.'

* * *

The disappearance of Sinead McCaffrey was a cold case; it had been eleven years since she had vanished without a trace. Furthermore, with no evidence she had been killed, the investigation had been carried out by the Missing Persons Unit. Tony Sutton's first job had been to go back over the case file, looking for any fresh lines of inquiry.

'Sinead had a Facebook account,' he said, 'but rarely posted anything. If you can remember that far back, smartphones as we now know them were in their infancy, with only basic cameras. If folks wanted to share pictures on social media, they typically used a digital camera and uploaded them from their PC. Unfortunately, Sinead's account was closed years ago. However, her housemate, Caitlin, was a regular user and her Facebook account is still active.'

He switched slides. 'Caitlin received a new camera for Christmas 2007 and started sharing pictures on Facebook.'

He cycled through a series of images. The pictures were small and the quality poor, but there were numerous shots of the six housemates, in a variety of poses, mostly taken on nights out.

'These are the most interesting ones. What is the same in each shot?' There were three photographs, taken at different times and locations. The people in each picture varied and included others not in the household.

Hardwick noticed it first. 'That black car.'

The vehicle was in the background each time: a group shot of Ben, Louisa and Curtis at the beach, the car parked behind them. Ben, Louisa and Sinead on a picnic blanket, the car clearly visible in the background. Louisa and Stephanie next to a snowman in their front yard, the rear of the car just in shot on the road outside the house.

'None of the students in the house were registered keepers of a car,' said Sutton. 'And there is no mention of a vehicle in any of the statements taken from any of the housemates. But the DVLA and the Motor Insurance Bureau shows Angelina Greenland, Ben's mother, bought a nearly new black Vauxhall Astra a month before Ben went to university. It was insured in her name, with Ben as a named driver. And in November of 2007, the housemates' final year, a Louisa Keane was also added to its insurance.'

An excited buzz ran around the room. 'If Sinead was kidnapped, or killed, by one of her housemates, then they would have needed some way to transport her or dispose of her body,' said Hutchinson.

'Exactly, and because Missing Persons didn't uncover the connection, then the vehicle was never examined by Forensics,' said Sutton. He paused for effect, a grin forming on his face. 'And it's still on the road.'

WEDNESDAY 22ND MAY

Chapter 29

The morning briefing started with Hutchinson's report from the search of Angelina Greenland's house and vehicle.

'No sign of bloody clothes or the murder weapon,' he said, 'and no footage of Ben or Darren in the area since before Louisa went missing. Angelina stayed in that night. If Ben has disposed of any evidence, it wasn't around his mum's. If she smuggled something out of the Greenlands' house for him, she didn't stash it where it could be easily found.'

'It was a long shot anyway,' said Warren. 'How are we doing with the list of men who downloaded Louisa's nude pictures?'

Pymm pushed her glasses back on her nose and opened a new window on her screen. 'Slowly,' she said. 'They are scattered all over. At present, we're assuming somebody didn't fly in from overseas and are focusing on UK-based customers.'

'That's just what we'd need,' said Warren. 'An international manhunt. How many have been cleared?'

'Five of the seven we were able to identify,' she said. 'They all have alibis. Considering how far some of them would need to travel, it's easy enough to place them elsewhere in the time they would have needed to get down here, snatch her, dispose of her, and then return home.'

'Keep at it,' he said. 'I know it's another long shot, but we'll look like chumps if we had them on our list and didn't look into them.'

'Especially if they strike again,' said Pymm. 'You just know that somebody twisted enough to identify a total stranger on a porn site, figure out where she lives, and then kill her is dancing to a tune only they can hear.'

'Has HOLMES highlighted any similar cases?' asked Warren. The artificial intelligence underpinning HOLMES' Dynamic Reasoning Engine had been designed to find links between seemingly unrelated events.

'Nothing unsolved,' said Pymm. 'Although if we loosen the criteria, such as getting rid of the pornography angle, there are a lot of missing people who might have suffered a similar fate. We don't even know that her adult website is relevant; it could just be a coincidence. After all, there's no evidence she was sexually assaulted, which you'd expect from somebody who was infatuated with a sex worker.'

Warren agreed. His gut was telling him that Louisa's killing was personal; committed by someone close to her, rather than a stranger.

But his gut had been wrong before.

* * *

'Ben sold the Astra in February 2013,' said Pymm.

'So where is it?' asked Warren.

'At present, on the back of a low-loader, heading back to Welwyn,' she said. 'It's done fewer than 10,000 miles since the new owners bought it; it's just a run-around for the shopping and household chores. And the really good news is they've barely done any work on it.'

'That sounds promising,' said Sutton.

'Andy Harrison says not to get your hopes up,' said Pymm. 'It's been eleven years. But if Sinead was bundled in the boot, then it is *possible* there is still some trace evidence, especially if she was injured. If she was transported in the passenger compartment, forget about it; they'll never isolate anything from background contamination. And even if they did, Ben's defence team will point to the picture of Sinead at that picnic.'

'Well, it's all we've got so far,' said Warren.

*   *   *

'I've been looking into the mysterious car that we caught on camera the night Louisa went missing,' said Richardson. An exhaustive trawl of ANPR and other traffic cameras, across the country, had failed to find any other images of the car driving with its cloned licence plates. Whoever was driving the vehicle had either hidden it or, more likely, switched the plates back.

Warren took the seat next to her. He could smell a faint whiff of chlorine from her lunchtime swim and felt slightly guilty. With Susan and Niall away, he should be using the opportunity to get some exercise.

'Ford Focuses are popular with hire car fleets,' said Richardson. 'What if our killer hired a car, switched the plates, then handed it back?'

'That could explain why the colour was wrong,' said Warren. 'The killer took a punt and got plates made up for a white Ford Focus, then turned up and the car waiting for them was dark blue or black. Not a lot they could do about it.' He started to feel a stir of excitement. 'Even independents need to see a driving licence and will want a credit card they can place a ring-fenced damage charge on.'

'I'll get onto it,' said Richardson. 'But I'll need a team. If our killer was trying to stay under the radar, then they probably steered clear of the big companies and used a smaller business. And if they really wanted to hide their tracks, they could have picked the car up from a firm two hundred miles away.'

Warren gave a sigh. 'I suspect you're probably right. Hire the car from a one-man band in Manchester, say, drive to the outskirts of Middlesbury, switch the plates, take Louisa, then change the plates back and return the car to Manchester. Unless somebody reports a hire car with a load of blood in the boot, I can't see how we'd ever know.'

'If the killer did travel some distance,' said Richardson, 'then that might rule out Ben, or Russell Myrie. Neither of them would have had the time.'

Warren shrugged. 'For all we know, it could have been hired from our old friend Richard Latham at Middlesbury Rental Vehicles. The car whose plates they cloned was from Middlesbury, which indicates they are based locally, even if they did travel some distance to pick up a hire car. What do you need?'

'A few bodies to phone around rental places. Plus, I suspect we'll need somebody to draft warrants. We'll be asking for details of anybody who hired a dark Ford Focus and CCTV if they have it; you know how funny some companies are about data protection.'

'You've got it,' said Warren.

* * *

The house felt especially empty that night, his bed even emptier. Warren had left work shortly after speaking to Richardson. Aside from her flash of inspiration, the murder of Louisa Greenland seemed to be grinding to a halt. Tony Sutton had made some progress with the Sinead McCaffrey cold case, but there was no body, from an eleven-year-old disappearance, which might not actually be a murder.

He'd tried to distract himself with some TV and a beer, but he'd ended up turning it off and tipping most of the bottle down the sink. Warren worked long and often erratic hours, and Susan sometimes stayed up late to do schoolwork, so neither of them was a stranger to the spare bedroom, but this was the longest they had been apart since they first started living together. And what about Niall? Children changed so quickly at this age. What milestones was he missing? He vowed that when they returned, he would take a hard look at his working hours.

It was a stark contrast to his grandfather's generation, who married after the war. The night Nana Betty had died, Granddad Jack had revealed that in sixty-two years of marriage, they had spent only five nights apart. Warren could only imagine the loneliness Jack had felt over the past seven and a half years, going to bed without her each night. He at least could ring his wife, or even see her and his son's face on a video call.

He reached for his Kindle on the bedside table, determined to make the most of his time alone. The latest Lee Child was waiting for him on the device. A few chapters of Jack Reacher's unique brand of justice would take his mind off things, then he'd find a worthy but dull podcast on Radio 4 to lull him to sleep.

And he *would* go swimming in the morning.

THURSDAY 23RD MAY

Chapter 30

Karen Hardwick awoke alone for the first time in months. Her boyfriend, Robbie, had gone home to sleep at his own house the night before. He of all people would understand why she wanted to be by herself today.

She lay in bed, letting the tears flow silently, getting them out of her system before she made Oliver his breakfast. She was determined to make today a special day. Oliver wouldn't be going to nursery, and she'd booked annual leave. They were in the middle of a case, but DCI Jones had signed her leave request without hesitation. From the look of sympathy on DSI Roehampton's face, he'd explained why.

Despite herself, her thoughts drifted back to Robbie. She'd worked late the previous evening and he'd come around to look after Ollie. It was the first time she'd trusted him to do the evening routine and put her son to bed. She'd spent all shift with her mobile phone propped next to her monitor, the ringtone set to loud. To her relief, the only message had been a photograph of Ollie sound asleep in his bed, clutching his favourite stuffed T-Rex.

She'd been on the verge of giving up online dating, after it became apparent that most men who claimed they had no problem dating a widow with a four-year-old child and a demanding job, actually did have a problem. Then she'd met Robbie, a colleague of Rachel Pymm's husband. He understood her pain; he'd been there himself. His wife of only twelve months had died from breast cancer at almost the same time that Gary had been killed. The disease had struck before they had a chance to fulfil their dream of starting a family. An enthusiastic uncle to the children of both his sisters, he'd been a natural with Ollie, and pretty soon the little boy had come to expect him around the house.

'It was fine,' he'd said when Hardwick made it home. 'He behaved impeccably. He ate all of his dinner and was in bed on the dot of seven. He even cleaned his teeth properly.'

Hardwick had looked at him with a raised eyebrow. 'Are you certain that's my son you've put to bed, not some random kid who walked in off the street?'

Robbie had chuckled. 'You can go and check if you don't believe me. I assume you've got his fingerprints on file?'

Hardwick had kissed him, the tension she'd been feeling all evening finally draining out of her. It wasn't the first time Oliver had been put to bed by someone other than her. Both sets of grandparents were well versed in his routine, as was the teenage babysitter in the adjacent flat.

But letting Robbie do it was an important milestone in their relationship. As a police officer, she was naturally wary of strangers being with her child. But Robbie had been looking after his nieces and nephews for years. Furthermore, he was a special needs teacher. Checking to see if he had a criminal record, or there were any concerns lodged against him, was illegal. But she hadn't needed to. Without being asked, he'd presented her with the certificate from his latest criminal records check, updated just months previously when he'd taken on a new role at school as safeguarding lead. 'No secrets between us,' he'd said.

'There was one thing though.' He'd looked embarrassed.

Hardwick's heart had skipped a beat, a dozen different possibilities flooding into her mind.

'I was reading him a story, and well, he gave me a hug and a kiss.'

'OK,' Hardwick had said warily. Her son was naturally affectionate. It wasn't a problem, and in fact, she'd taken her son's ready acceptance of Robbie as a mark in his favour.

'And he said "goodnight, Daddy".'

Hardwick had taken a deep breath. 'How did that make you feel?'

'I'll be honest it flummoxed me a little; I wasn't really sure what to say. I told him that he already had a daddy, but he was in heaven. He seemed to accept that.'

Hardwick exhaled. She'd known it was a conversation she'd need to have with Ollie soon. The couple had decided recently that it was time to start thinking about a more permanent arrangement. Robbie owned the small house he'd shared with his late wife. Hardwick and Oliver still lived in the flat that she and Gary had shared, but the minuscule office she had squeezed a tiny bed into was rapidly becoming too small.

Leaving those homes behind, with all their memories, and buying somewhere together, was the next, logical step. But were they ready?

There was a cautious knock at her bedroom door, before a tiny head poked its way around.

'Are you awake, Mummy?'

'Of course I am, sweetheart.' She opened her arms and her son bounded into the room, clambering onto the bed.

'Do you remember what today is?' asked Hardwick clutching him in her embrace.

'It's Daddy's birthday in heaven,' her son said solemnly.

'That's right,' she said her heart breaking. 'So today it will be just you and me. We'll go and see him in the graveyard and give him his birthday card and his birthday cake, but you'll have to blow the candle out for him.'

She felt a stray tear and wiped it away with the corner of the duvet.

'Is Robbie coming with us?'

'No, sweetie, just you and me today.'

'Will he be coming over tomorrow?'

'Yes, I expect so.'

Oliver gave a yawn and snuggled into his mother's warmth. 'Good, I like it when Robbie stays.'

Hardwick kissed her son on the head. 'I do too,' she said.

＊　＊　＊

'It's Andy Harrison,' said Janice. She handed the phone over to Warren. 'He wanted to speak to DI Sutton, but he's not in until lunchtime.'

'What have you got for me, Andy?' asked Warren.

'The black Vauxhall Astra Tony Sutton sent for processing,' he said. The usually laconic CSI sounded excited. 'We gave it the full works and found fingerprints matching Sinead McCaffrey.'

'Where?' asked Warren his mouth dry.

Harrison paused. 'Some of them could have an innocent explanation. But I'd love to hear how they got on the *inside* of the tailgate, with the fingers pointing *upwards*.'

Warren pictured it. 'She must have been inside the boot.'

'That's the only way I can picture it. And it gets better. We tested with luminol. Small spots of blood, consistent with spatter, that have been wiped clean. And not just in the boot space.'

＊　＊　＊

'This is our best explanation for the presence of Sinead's fingerprints being in the boot of Ben's car, along with what we presume is her blood,' said Sutton. He'd arrived shortly after the call from Andy Harrison; his routine appointment with his cardiologist had finished with her usual caution not to overexert himself and get too excited. Harrison's phone call was making that a challenge.

'It may take a while for the blood to be confirmed,' Warren cautioned. 'An attempt was made to clean it up and it's been eleven years.'

'I'm all ears,' said Roehampton.

'None of the housemates or the neighbours reported hearing signs of a struggle,' said Sutton. 'So we believe Sinead was somehow subdued before being taken from the house. Her room was at the front on the ground floor, and the car was usually parked directly outside. It was your typical student place, so the distance from the front door to the garden wall was only a few paces, and the gate was missing. There were no streetlights within fifty metres, so the car would have been in shadow, assuming it happened after dark.'

'Makes sense.'

'Sinead was alive, as it would appear that after she was bundled in the boot, she scrabbled at the inside, leaving her fingerprints,' Sutton continued.

Roehampton shuddered. 'Poor woman.'

'That's the best we can do with the facts we have so far,' said Warren.

'The story is plausible,' said Roehampton. 'But even if the blood is a match, there are holes you could drive a lorry through.'

'I know,' said Warren. 'We still have no evidence she was killed. We don't even know the blood came from an attack. The fingerprints inside the boot could have been the result of horsing around. We have no witnesses who can tell us if the car disappeared in the middle of the night during the period we are interested in, and little chance of getting anything reliable eleven years on.'

'Keep plugging away,' suggested Roehampton. 'You've already uncovered more useful leads than the original Missing Persons investigation.'

'A different focus, and more resources,' said Warren, unsure why he felt compelled to defend the MPU.

'Maybe,' said Roehampton, but her face suggested otherwise.

* * *

If Tony Sutton heard one more Eighties power ballad, he was going to scream. He'd been on hold to the University of Middle England's student welfare department for over twenty minutes. In that time, he'd spoken to three different people and listened to scratchy renditions of six different pop songs. It was like being stuck in a traffic jam with Warren in charge of the car stereo.

'DI Sutton?' said a fourth voice eventually, cutting into "Total Eclipse of the Heart". 'I'm told you're looking for records into a former student from the early 2000s?'

'Yes, Sinead McCaffrey,' he confirmed, pushing aside his murderous thoughts, and injecting a positive note into his voice.

'Very sad,' said the voice at the end of the line. 'I remember it well.'

Sutton blinked in surprise. 'Wait, you were at the university back then. Ms . . .?'

'Joffre. Yes, that's why they routed the call to my desk. I've been here since, oh, 1995? Please, call me Sheila.'

Sutton resisted the urge to punch the air.

'Please forgive the delay,' said Joffre. 'I had to go and pull her file from the paper archive.'

'Thank you for making the effort,' said Sutton. 'I'm sure you're very busy this time of year.'

'Yes, exam time tends to bring everything to the surface.'

'I believe Sinead had dealings with the counselling service in the run-up to her disappearance,' said Sutton. 'DS George Rutherford of the Missing Persons Unit spoke to you.'

'Yes, that's right, there's a note on the file. May I ask what this is about?'

'I am reviewing Sinead's case, going back through the original records, to see if anything was overlooked. I wondered if you would be willing to let me see her file? Sometimes things get missed the first time around.'

Joffre sounded uncertain. 'I would need to ask my supervisor. I'm not sure where we stand with these new data protection laws. We might need a warrant.'

Sutton tried not to let the frustration into his voice. 'I fully understand,' he said. Before he could respond, Joffre spoke again.

'Oh, that's interesting.'

'What is?' he asked.

'The file has been updated since DS Rutherford requested it in April of 2008.'

'Updated? How?'

'There is a new record of an appointment to see an adviser from one of our partner services. It's marked "Confidential". Back then, every department used their own computer system and we swapped files via email. Very inefficient. At the end of each academic year, admin staff would spend the summer holidays printing out all the student records from each department and filing them together in the students' permanent paper file. We moved to a single system in 2011 but didn't have the budget to transfer former students' records to the new system. That's why she was still in the paper archive. DS Rutherford should have been told, but I guess it slipped through the net.'

'What was the appointment about?' asked Sutton, trying to contain the feelings of excitement.

Joffre's voice became muffled, as if she was trying not to be overheard. 'It's confidential, so I can't open it, but given the service she was accessing . . . I think it would be a *really* good idea if you got a warrant and requested her complete file.'

FRIDAY 24TH MAY

Chapter 31

Friday morning started with a nerve-racking wait. Warren had gone swimming before work, but rather than being relaxed by the forced isolation, he'd been anxious, worrying that whilst he pounded up and down the pool, his phone was vibrating in his locker.

'We have viable DNA!' had been Andy Harrison's triumphant opening sentence on the email he'd sent the previous evening. It was a testament to modern forensic technology. If it was Sinead's genetic material, it had been in the boot of the car for eleven years and attempts had been made to clean it up.

George Rutherford had been upset to hear that he'd failed to uncover that Ben had access to a car, although Warren had done his best to reassure him that nobody could have expected him to make such a connection. The man had lived with the mystery of Sinead McCaffrey's disappearance for over eleven years; it had become personal, and it was clear he felt he'd let both her and her family down.

He agreed with Warren that it was far too soon to share the lead with her family; raising their hopes, only to dash them again, would be too cruel.

Whilst they awaited the DNA match, their present-day investigation got an unexpected shot in the arm.

'Pete Robertson just called,' said Pymm. 'They've managed to recover the deleted data from that hidden phone of Ben's. It's all very well buying a new phone to use in secret, but it's no use trying to erase anything if the device's memory is only half-used. The phone doesn't write over it. He'd have been better off using his old phone; its storage is so chocka anything he deleted would have been written over with new data almost immediately.'

'Don't keep us in suspense,' said Warren.

With a flourish, she passed over a printout. 'Text messages. He was clearly worried that if Louisa ever found his secret phone and unlocked it, he might have some questions to answer. Hence him deleting these messages and installing that password-protected messaging app so he could continue his conversations in private.'

Warren scanned quickly down the messages. 'These are brilliant,' he said, passing them over to Sutton who'd overheard their conversation and walked over to take part.

'Now, give me the *really* good stuff.'

Pymm looked at him innocently.

He waited, an eyebrow raised, until she sighed. 'You used to be more fun,' she grumbled.

Warren's retort died on his lips when he saw the printout. He read through it at lightning speed.

'And we're certain this was definitely him?'

'No question,' said Pymm.

Sutton looked over his shoulder. 'Jesus. Let's see him explain that.'

* * *

'We've had a report through from Forensics about the kitchen knives retrieved from the Greenlands' kitchen,' said Hardwick. She'd spent the previous day with Ollie, visiting Gary's grave. On reflection, opening a bottle of Gary's favourite wine on a work

268

night had probably been unwise. Opening a second bottle had definitely been a bad idea.

'Don't tell me they've found Louisa's blood?' said Warren.

'Unfortunately, no. But it still makes interesting reading,' she replied.

She opened the file on her screen and focused her bloodshot eyes on it.

'The wooden knife block had five different-sized steel knives, all from a matching set.' She scrolled through the document to a photograph.

'There were no traces of human blood on any of the knives, or inside the block's slots. But when they examined the set, this one stood out.' She scrolled to a picture of the largest knife. 'The set is clearly well used. The blades are slightly blunted. But the knife expert who examined them is confident this one is much newer.'

A picture of the blades side by side showed that the knife in question was definitely different to the others. The metal was shinier, and there were visibly fewer scratches.

She switched to the handles. Again, side by side, under bright lighting, the black plastic handle appeared darker; less faded. The difference was tiny; but once you saw it, it was impossible to miss.

The observation was interesting, but Warren wasn't convinced of its significance. He said so. 'There's certainly a difference, but it assumes that all the knives were used equally and corroded to the same degree. They're different sizes and used for different jobs. We got a lovely set of chef's knives as a wedding present; I definitely use some of them more than others.'

'That's what I thought,' said Hardwick. She looked pleased with herself. 'So I contacted the manufacturer. They confirmed that these knives are sold exclusively through John Lewis. They can be bought as a set with the block, or they can be purchased individually.'

'So what are we saying here? That the original one in the block was replaced?' He frowned. 'Hang on, that doesn't make sense.

When would he have had the time to replace the knife after he used it to kill her? It's clearly been used a few times; you can see the scratches on the blade. Was he smart enough to rough it up a bit, so it didn't stand out? Or did he plan this whole thing well in advance?'

'I know, it's weird,' said Hardwick. 'Why not just kill her with the new knife? But either way, even if he bought it to replace the original, where is that knife now?'

*   *   *

'It's a match!' said Sutton, shortly after lunch. 'The sample in the car matches DNA from the hairbrush and toothbrush believed to have belonged to Sinead McCaffrey.'

Warren punched the air, then immediately felt bad about celebrating that they were one step closer to confirming that the young student had been taken against her will, and probably killed. But it also meant they were one step closer to bringing answers for her loved ones. And hopefully, one step closer to bringing someone to justice.

'Time to go speak to the guv,' he said.

*   *   *

Roehampton listened attentively. Her eyes were bloodshot, and she had a large glass of water next to her laptop. Scraps of foil from a blister pack of painkillers were on the desk next to her. She blew her nose on a tissue.

'Bloody summer cold,' she'd said by way of explanation. She leaned back in her chair after Warren and Sutton finished laying out the new evidence.

'I *really* hate no-body murders,' she groaned, a look of pain crossing her face. 'It's why I try to avoid cold cases.'

Warren sympathised. In an ideal world, if they didn't have

a body, then they should at least have a reasonable certainty that the victim had actually been killed. Evidence of an injury incompatible with life was a favourite expression used by defence and prosecution alike. Unfortunately, the blood found in the car wasn't nearly enough.

'Tony has moved the Sinead case forward, but there's not a lot more that Forensics can do,' said Warren. 'A sample of the blood has been sent for toxicological analysis. It is possible that a sensitive enough test might reveal any traces of sedatives, which would indicate it wasn't an accident.'

'And did the laboratory give you any indication *how* possible it would be to get a result?' asked Roehampton, fixing Warren with a stare.

'They were unable to say,' he admitted.

'And supposing they find traces of a sedating chemical. What about a concentration? Can they tell us with any certainty whether or not she had enough in her system to affect her, rather than a background level from whatever she took the night before to help her sleep?'

'It depends on the substance,' he said. He was seeing a glimpse of how she had earned the nickname "Ruthless Roehampton", early in her career. He wouldn't want to be sitting opposite her in an interview suite.

'And how long will the results take?' she pressed.

'Weeks.'

'Weeks. And it may not even tell us anything useful,' said Roehampton. 'Even if it emerges that she had enough tranquilliser in her to knock out a horse, we still can't show that she died. Or that Ben was the one who sedated her, killed her, or disposed of her body. We'll never get the CPS to back us in a charging decision. Bluntly, Sinead has been missing for over a decade. Why the rush to arrest?'

'Normally, I'd agree,' said Warren, trying not to sound desperate. He wasn't. Not really. But he and Sutton had discussed their options at length, and he suddenly felt as though he needed to defend himself. Ruthless Roehampton indeed.

'Look, the MPU did a pretty thorough investigation back then, all things considered. Tony has come up with some new approaches, looking through the prism of a murder investigation, but they should have been done back then. Realistically, we are unlikely to find any new forensics. Electronic data will be long gone. We could appeal for new witnesses, but it's eleven years ago. Curtis gave us a new nugget about the possible evening she was taken, but what use is it? Caitlin claims not to know anything more, but would she tell us even if she did?

'Aside from Ben, the only two housemates that haven't been interviewed again about Sinead are Louisa, obviously, and Stephanie. But we know that as soon as we ask Stephanie, it'll get back to Ben and we lose any element of surprise. If he did kill her, he's spent eleven years thinking he got away with it; when we question him, I want him off-guard.'

'Warren's right, Ash,' said Sutton. 'Ben knows we still think he murdered Louisa. He thinks he's *probably* got away with it, but he's savvy enough to realise that no matter what he may have read on the internet, he'll never know if we were bluffing when we said we'd be able to unlock that messaging app on his phone.

'Everybody watches *CSI* or true crime documentaries these days. Those who aren't dumb enough to underestimate our capabilities are paranoid enough to *over*estimate them. If he's guilty, he won't be sleeping easy.'

Warren took over. 'So imagine how he's going to feel when he's brought in again and instead of questioning him about Louisa, we tell him we've tracked down his old car from university and we've found Sinead's blood in it? And with what Tony found out yesterday from the university . . .'

Roehampton stared at the two men, frowning in concentration. Eventually a small smile tugged at her lips. 'So, this is the famous Jones and Sutton double act I've heard so much about. OK, gentlemen, you've made your case. Bring him in.'

*　*　*

Ben Greenland had been free for just three days when Warren, accompanied by a team of uniformed officers, arrived at his house.

Greenland didn't look any more rested than the last time Warren had seen him. It was hardly surprising; he'd spent the past few days trying to explain to his daughters what had happened to their mother and as a father – and human being – Warren could only imagine how terrible that must have been. And now he had arrived to take their dad away again.

Kevin Lederer remained the lead family liaison officer and had served as the escort when Greenland had his supervised visits with his two children. The two girls had moved back into the family home after the search concluded, allowing at least some sense of normality. Louisa's parents had taken it in turns to look after them, assisted by her sister, Stephanie. Ben was staying with his mother, who had accompanied him on his visits. Lederer had been there when Greenland had finally broken the news to his daughters the previous day.

'How are you holding up, Kevin?' asked Warren quietly as the uniformed officers arranged for Greenland to be taken to the station. He was relieved it had all gone smoothly. They'd told Greenland he was required for further questioning, and he'd acquiesced, so they hadn't needed to arrest him and handcuff him in front of his two daughters.

'Oh, you know,' said Lederer, his voice tired. 'It's part of the job, but it never gets any easier.' He gave a sad chuckle. 'I embarrassed both my kids by giving them a hug and telling them I loved them when I picked up from school yesterday. Public displays of affection are rarely appreciated by teenagers, but their mum told them I'd had a difficult few days at work, so they've been surprisingly understanding. No idea how long that will last.'

'Do you need some time away from it?' asked Warren, briefly imagining himself in Lederer's shoes.

Lederer shook his head. 'No, I'm fine. I'd rather keep at it. The girls like me and I'd probably keep checking in on them anyway. The more normal it is for them the better.'

Clapping him on the shoulder, Warren bade his farewells and returned to his car; he phoned the station to let them know he was coming in.

* * *

Greenland was formally arrested and cautioned when presented at the station. As Warren had hoped, finding out he was now under suspicion for the kidnap and murder of Sinead McCaffrey had knocked Ben sideways. By the time he had been fully processed, his solicitor was waiting for her initial consultation.

Warren and Sutton had decided to team up again for his interview but introduced Sutton as the lead investigator looking into the disappearance of Sinead. Hopefully, seeing that the eleven-year-old mystery was being given the same time and resources as his wife's murder would unsettle him still further.

'What can you tell me about the disappearance of Sinead McCaffrey?' Sutton started.

'No comment,' said Greenland.

'Seriously?' said Sutton, layering his tone with incredulity. 'Is this how you intend to duck every problem that comes your way? Just ignore it until it disappears? Like your wife and ex-girlfriend?'

'That was tasteless and uncalled for, DI Sutton,' snapped Greenland's solicitor.

Sutton apologised. Beside him, Warren noted Greenland's response. Was the flinch of surprise from the harshness of Sutton's words or the implication he had been in a relationship with Sinead?

'Is girlfriend too strong a word for the woman you were sleeping with behind Louisa's back?' asked Warren. 'Mistress seems old-fashioned. Perhaps "friend with benefits", as they say these days?'

'I hope you have some evidence to back up this slur,' said Barton.

'It was hardly the best kept secret, was it?' asked Warren. 'At least one of your housemates knew about it. And Sinead was certainly your type: dark-haired, Irish, pretty. A type you're still interested in, judging by your internet browsing history.'

Greenland flushed. 'No comment.'

'What did you mean by "was it something we did"?' asked Sutton. 'You've asked this a few times over the years. You know, after a few drinks, when everyone gets a bit maudlin.'

'No comment,' said Greenland. Was that fear in his eyes, wondered Warren?

'Did you mean "something we did" or "something *I* did"?' asked Sutton. 'What did you do, Ben?'

'No comment.'

'Did you kill her, or were you just the reason Sinead decided to leave that day?' asked Warren.

'I didn't kill her,' said Greenland. His lip trembled.

His solicitor cleared her throat, but Greenland ignored her. 'I didn't kill Sinead and I didn't kill Louisa.' His voice turned pleading. 'Why won't you believe me?'

'You know, I'd love to believe you,' said Sutton. 'Really, I would, but I can only go where the evidence leads us. And it's the same with a jury. Juries convict on *evidence*, Ben. Evidence we have put to you and asked you to explain, but which you are refusing to.'

Warren took over. 'We've been in this game a long time, Ben. And we've seen all sorts of explanations. All sorts of coincidences. Just because something looks bad, it doesn't mean the person was actually responsible. But innocent people try to explain. They don't sit there and no comment, when they could clear up everything by telling us the truth, even if it's unpalatable.'

'You know what, Ben,' said Sutton. 'You've clearly been a bit of a shit. You were shagging around behind Louisa's back at university and you didn't stop when you got married.'

His solicitor opened her mouth, but Sutton raised a finger and she remained quiet.

'But you know what? That's not illegal. There is nothing we can charge you with and nor would we want to. Your family and friends are probably going to think less of you. You are going to have to grovel and ask forgiveness. And you are going to have some explaining to do to your little girls. But what's the alternative? Trying to justify why they can only see you across a table for an hour, in a room full of other prisoners?'

'Do you really want to no comment yourself into a murder trial?' asked Warren. 'Even if Ms Barton here is telling you we don't have enough to convict – that a jury will never find you guilty – how confident are you? Seriously, are you willing to gamble on that, when she hasn't even seen all the evidence we have?'

'And do you want to put your family through a trial?' asked Sutton. 'Do you want all your dirty laundry aired in public, picked apart by the media and true crime fans? Unless somebody else goes down for the murders, even if you are acquitted, half the country won't believe you are innocent. Do you want to star in your own six-part series on Netflix?'

'OK, that's enough,' said his solicitor. The tears were flowing down Greenland's face. 'It's time for a break.'

'Were you sleeping with Sinead McCaffrey?' asked Warren, ignoring her.

Greenland was now crying freely, his fist stuffed in his mouth.

'Break. Now,' demanded his solicitor.

'Think about it, Ben,' said Sutton in one last parting shot as Warren suspended the interview.

* * *

'Bloody hell, boys, that was a bit 1970s, wasn't it?' said Roehampton. 'I'm amazed she didn't stop the interview sooner.'

'A calculated risk,' said Warren. 'We have to break him out of that no-commenting cycle, although I must admit I was a bit surprised at how far we managed to push it.'

'Yeah, it wasn't pretty,' admitted Sutton. 'But I think it had the desired effect. He must be questioning whether keeping his mouth shut is the right strategy.'

'We'll rein it in a bit now,' said Warren. 'I don't want an allegation of bullying further down the line.'

'Let's just hope his barrister doesn't try and get it struck out because his solicitor is bloody useless,' said Roehampton.

'Well he can't say we didn't offer him someone better qualified,' said Warren.

* * *

The break to confer with his solicitor lasted almost an hour. By the time they reconvened, it was getting late and both Warren and Sutton were feeling it. But the two men felt that Greenland was teetering on the edge. The last thing they wanted was for him to sleep on it and wake up in the morning refreshed and ready to go back to no commenting. They could legally speak to him for at least another hour before the custody officer insisted he get his eight hours.

Greenland's solicitor read out another statement on his behalf, and Warren and Sutton both felt satisfaction at the look of distaste on her face; she'd clearly counselled him to say nothing, but he wanted to set the record straight.

'So you admit you and Sinead McCaffrey slept together whilst you were both living at twenty-seven Potter Street?' said Warren, wanting to hear Greenland say it himself, rather than hiding behind his solicitor.

'Yes,' he said quietly.

'When did you first sleep with her?' asked Sutton.

Greenland swallowed. 'A couple of months after we first moved into the house.'

'And were you with Louisa at this time?' asked Warren.

Greenland flushed and stared at the table. 'Yeah. Kind of.'

'What does that mean?' asked Warren.

'Yeah. We were. She was my girlfriend.'

There were lots more questions Warren wanted to ask, but he sensed that if he pressed too hard, Greenland might close down again.

'And did this affair continue?' he asked.

Greenland nodded, his face a mask of shame. 'Yes.'

'Until when?' asked Warren.

Greenland's voice cracked. 'Until the end.'

'Was Sinead the only person you slept with?' asked Sutton. Greenland had broken his silence and admitted something he'd kept secret for the past eleven years. He was keen to see how much further he was prepared to go.

Greenland glanced towards his solicitor. 'No comment,' he said.

The lack of admission was frustrating, but the look on his face had told them all they needed to know.

'Did you sleep with Caitlin O'Shaughnessy?' asked Warren.

'No comment.'

His tone was firmer, as they moved back onto familiar territory. It was time to throw him off balance.

'According to the university counselling service, Sinead went to see them about three weeks before she disappeared,' said Sutton. Warren watched Greenland carefully; his face remained inscrutable.

'Tell me, Ben,' said Sutton. 'Did Sinead tell you she was pregnant?'

SATURDAY 25TH MAY

Chapter 32

Warren and Sutton decided to tackle Ben Greenland as soon as his eight-hour rest period was over, and he'd had a conference with his solicitor.

They'd decided to keep him off balance by not starting with the elephant in the room: Sinead's pregnancy. His response the previous night had been shock, followed by a no comment, the answer now an ingrained reflex. The interview had ended shortly after.

Warren wondered how the original investigation might have progressed if the university counselling service had kept better records, or if Sinead had kept the GP appointment that the counsellor had urged her to make.

'Are you the previous owner of a black Vauxhall Astra?' started Sutton. He read out the licence number.

Greenland looked surprised. 'Yes. But I sold it years ago.'

'And you drove it whilst you were at university?' Sutton clarified.

'Sure. It was an eighteenth birthday present from my mother.'

'Did anyone else drive it?' asked Warren.

'We added Louisa to the insurance in our final year, and then we both drove it until we got rid of it a few years later.'

'What did you use the car for?' asked Sutton.

'The usual. Shopping, moving things in and out of the house. Going to the cinema in Stevenage. A couple of camping trips and music festivals.'

'It was a nice car,' said Warren. 'Almost brand new. Quite impressive for a student.'

He shrugged. 'Mum got a good deal on it. It was ex-display and only had a few hundred miles on the clock. You know how car dealers take the piss with new vehicles: the moment you drive it off the forecourt it loses half its value. Mum figured it would be better to get me something almost new that would last for years, rather than an old banger that failed its MOT after twelve months.'

'You must have been very proud of it,' said Warren.

'I suppose so.'

'And you took good care of it, I assume?'

'Of course.'

'Didn't race around with your mates hanging out the windows or sitting in the boot?'

'No, of course not. I'm not a bloody idiot.'

'When did you get rid of it?'

He pursed his lips in concentration. 'In 2013? It was when we had Molly. We figured it would be easier to carry around all the baby stuff if we had a bigger car. Look, why are you so interested in my old Astra?'

'How did you dispose of the car?' asked Warren.

'Part exchange. It was only eight years old and I'd looked after it, so the garage gave us a good price.'

'Because you'd not let your mates clamber in and out the windows or the boot and hadn't driven it like an idiot?' said Sutton.

'Yes! It was an eighteenth birthday present. I was the only person I knew lucky enough to own one.' He looked frustrated. 'Not all teenagers are morons, you know. I respected it and drove carefully.' His voice caught. 'My dad was killed in a car accident;

282

the man who hit him was twice the drink-drive limit and racing his mate. The bastard hit my dad's car head-on, overtaking on a blind bend. He was going so fast Dad's steering wheel impaled him and killed him instantly. I lost my father before my tenth birthday; the fucker who killed him got away with a broken leg and ten years, out in six. Should have been life.

'That's why my mum bought me a modern car. Dad's car was a thirty-year-old "classic"; it didn't even have airbags. The fucker who killed him was in a Range Rover.' His voice softened. 'Dad never stood a chance.'

'I'm really sorry to hear that,' said Warren. 'I know what it's like to lose a parent so young.' He hadn't meant to be so personal, but Ben's story had triggered his own painful memories.

'I guess it taught me that life is short,' said Greenland eventually. 'Don't put off what you can do today and all that. It's why I encouraged Louisa to set up P@mper. She'd always wanted to run her own business.' He sniffed. 'It was hard work, but for the first few months, I saw the old Louisa again. The one I married; the happy, fun-loving Louisa. We couldn't go out much as money was tight and we needed a babysitter, so she'd host karaoke parties and Disney nights for the girls and their friends.' He wiped his eyes and his voice became quiet.

'After her accident – when it emerged she had been drinking – I was furious, you know? It was the lowest point of our marriage. But she was so upset, and she really embraced the treatment Steph was able to get her. I realised that we had been lucky. I'd already lost one person I loved through drink-driving. I couldn't bear to let drink-driving destroy my marriage as well.'

'I understand,' said Warren. And he did. But that didn't mean the man in front of him was innocent. Louisa's business venture was clearly placing at risk everything he loved again; was that a big enough trigger for him to take matters into his own hands? To stop his wife dragging their family into a financial black hole?

And what about Sinead? Ben was obviously a serial philanderer, sating his sexual appetite with other women, yet he was hardly unique. The university Pregnancy Advisory Service said she claimed an unnamed housemate was the father of Sinead McCaffrey's baby. They had been careful, but accidents happen. She had indicated to the counsellors she was scared of how her parents would react. A termination was out of the question, so they had advised her to speak to the father and see if it was realistic to pursue a long-term relationship. She'd been booked in for another appointment but had failed to show. A lack of communication, and poorly conceived privacy policy, meant nobody made the connection when she went missing.

One interpretation was that the stress of the unplanned pregnancy was what finally pushed her over the edge.

But it wasn't the only explanation for her disappearance.

'Ben, if nobody was allowed to drive your car, other than Louisa,' Warren said. 'And nobody rode in the boot. Then why have we found Sinead's fingerprints on the inside of the tailgate?'

Greenland's jaw dropped and his solicitor took a sharp intake of breath.

'What? That's impossible,' he stammered.

'I strongly advise no comment,' his solicitor interjected.

Sutton pushed a series of high-resolution photographs across the table. 'The vehicle is currently impounded in our forensics facility. The positioning and angling of the fingerprints indicated they were from a person physically inside the boot.' He paused for effect. 'Probably scrabbling to get out.'

'I don't understand. Why would she be in the boot?' he asked.

'You tell us, Ben. I can certainly think of one explanation,' said Sutton.

Greenland's eyes darted around the room. 'Maybe she was messing around with Louisa? Perhaps Louisa borrowed the car and Sinead got in the boot for some reason? For a joke, maybe?'

'I doubt that,' said Sutton. 'DS Rutherford interviewed numerous friends and family of Sinead, back when she first disappeared. Everyone described her as a sweet girl; a bit naïve, terrified of spiders and *enclosed spaces*. Do you really expect us to believe that somebody with claustrophobia got into the boot of a car voluntarily, and then shut the lid?'

'Regardless of the explanation for why her fingerprints were in that car – and I'll be asking our own experts to assess these findings – I see no evidence indicating that she subsequently came to harm,' his solicitor interrupted. 'Or a time when it could have occurred. It might have been months before she disappeared.'

Sutton pushed another photograph across the table. 'Do you recognise this item?'

Greenland shrugged. His solicitor was practically beside herself. 'Don't answer that.'

'Why? It's just a tyre iron.' A slow look of realisation spread across his face. 'Oh, no. No, no, no . . .' he started.

'This is the tyre iron from the Astra,' said Sutton. 'You'll be delighted to know that after you sold it, it went to a good home. One very careful owner; never had any problems. Not even a flat tyre. Your fingerprints are still the only prints on that tyre iron.'

He pushed a final photograph across the table. 'Alongside blood that we have positively matched to Sinead.'

* * *

Greenland had finally heeded his solicitor's advice and asked for a break.

'He's going to no comment again, isn't he?' said Ruskin.

'It's all he's got left,' said Warren. 'Either he tries to pin the blame on somebody else or he raises his hands and admits it.'

'That'll never happen,' said Sutton. 'We sweated him for thirty-six hours over Louisa, and he barely confirmed his name for the recording. He was happily chatting about Sinead because he had no idea we'd tracked down his car.'

'It's strange he kept it for all those years, though,' said Hardwick.

'Surely you'd sell it on if it contained evidence you transported a kidnap victim in the boot?'

'I think he was arrogant enough to think he'd got away with it and didn't want to raise suspicion,' said Hutchinson. 'It was his pride and joy; a present for his eighteenth birthday. Why would he fork out thousands for a new vehicle better than the one he was already driving? Besides which, it was still technically his mother's car. How would he convince his mum he needed to flog it?'

'Makes sense,' admitted Hardwick. 'I wish I'd got a car that nice for my eighteenth birthday.' She paused. 'To be honest, I'd settle for one that nice on my thirty-fourth birthday. Which is in eleven and a half months, by the way, if folks want to start saving.'

* * *

'Here's what I think happened,' said Sutton, when the interview recommenced. 'Feel free to jump in if I have anything wrong, or you wish to add anything.'

The solicitor scowled; Greenland closed his eyes.

'You met Louisa within days of starting university; she was on the same corridor in your halls of residence. Pretty, dark-haired, Irish heritage, just the sort of girl to catch your eye. Fair enough. You liked her; she liked you. You started dating, but not exclusively. At least not on your part. What were Louisa's feelings on the subject?'

Greenland said nothing.

'Either way, you were young, away from home, good-looking and making a name for yourself on the university football team. Louisa didn't usually come on the football socials, so when anyone showed an interest, you were free to pursue it.

'But Louisa and her sister had their own social lives. They'd joined the Irish Society, to honour their dad's side of the family. They made new friends – Sinead and Caitlin, who lived on their corridor. Your best mate was Curtis, who played football and also had a room in your halls.

'Pretty soon you were all hanging out, and by the end of the first year, you'd found the perfect place to live the following year, in Potter Street. Six bedrooms, a kitchen/lounge and space on the street for you to park. Stop me if I've got anything wrong.'

Greenland said nothing.

'I'll bet you were delighted, weren't you? Four pretty girls, and your best mate to boot. You and Curtis were the envy of half the lads on campus.'

'No comment,' he mumbled half-heartedly.

'Everything was good, wasn't it? Louisa was upstairs in the loft with her sister. Sinead and Caitlin were on the ground floor. You and Curtis were on the middle floor. It wasn't difficult to pop down and see Sinead with nobody knowing, was it? I'm sure she felt guilty about what the two of you were doing, but she was away from home for the first time as well, wasn't she? Curtis figured it out finally, but he's a mate; he wasn't going to say anything. In fact, he was probably a bit jealous. How am I doing so far, Ben?'

Greenland said nothing. He'd already admitted the basic facts.

'You were in the room above Sinead, so nobody would hear what was going on in her room,' said Warren. 'Which was pretty convenient. Louisa probably had no idea.'

'Wasn't Caitlin out the back in the extension?' said Sutton, as if the idea had just occurred to him. 'There was nobody above her either. Did you take advantage of that?'

'No comment,' said Greenland.

'Well anyway,' said Sutton. 'Everything was great on planet Ben. His girlfriend upstairs. A friend with benefits in the room below. Perhaps even somebody else in the back room?'

Again, Greenland muttered, 'No comment.'

'But then things started to get serious,' said Warren. 'It's the final year. Everybody is stressed, some more than others. Now you have to start making plans for the future. Unfortunately, twenty-seven Potter Street is an exclusively student property. You've had two great years there, but the landlord expects you to move out. Stephanie's already got her eye on London. Curtis fancies moving on also. Caitlin had yet to decide where she wanted to go. What was Sinead planning?'

'No comment.'

'Would Louisa have agreed to Sinead living with you two?' asked Sutton. 'That could have been convenient.'

'Not necessarily,' said Warren, turning to Sutton as if the two were simply discussing the situation over a pint down the pub. 'The set-up at Potter Street only worked because the house had three floors and the rooms had single beds, so Ben had an excuse not to stay with Louisa every night.'

'So what was the plan?' asked Sutton. 'Were you going to go your separate ways? Perhaps try and maintain the affair, or was it going to be the end of your relationship with Sinead?'

'No comment.'

'Did Sinead ask you to choose between her and Louisa?' Sutton pressed.

'No comment.'

'What about when she fell pregnant?'

'No comment.' He gave a sniff.

'Things got very real, very fast, didn't they?' said Sutton. 'The outside world is beckoning; time to find a job and a grown-up place to live. You were in a steady relationship. You'd had your fun at university. Maybe you could continue with your bit on the side? Perhaps there would be others? Perhaps you'd settle down and be the dutiful husband?'

'But Sinead threw a spanner in the works, didn't she?' said Warren. 'Did she insist you take responsibility for your unborn child? Did she ask you to choose between her and Louisa? Did she threaten to tell Louisa?'

'No, it wasn't like that,' said Greenland.

'What was it like, Ben?' said Sutton. 'Help us understand.'

'No comment,' he said eventually.

'Either way, that's your future screwed,' said Sutton. 'You lose Louisa and have an unexpected kid to care for. And probably a pissed-off set of in-laws.'

Greenland just shook his head.

'You had a problem that needed solving, didn't you Ben?' said Warren. He leaned across the table. 'Come on now, where's her body? It's been eleven years. Let her family give her a proper Catholic burial, with a headstone they can visit. Put everyone else who lived in that house out of their misery. They've spent eleven years wondering where their friend went. Wondering if they did something wrong. Or wondering if they let her down by missing how her mental health was declining. Do it for your friends.'

Greenland placed his head in his hands and started to sob.

*   *   *

Greenland had returned to his cell to eat, then had a lengthy consultation with his solicitor. Warren had taken the opportunity to squeeze in a half-hour video call with his wife, who looked even more exhausted than he was, and Niall, who was annoyingly perky.

Tomorrow morning they were supposed to be meeting the priest at the local church that Susan's parents and Granddad Jack attended, to discuss Niall's christening. They'd held off having the ceremony during the uncertainty of Dennis's diagnosis, and whilst Susan's favourite aunt recovered from a hip operation. But it was now only three weeks away. Susan's younger sister, Felicity, would be Niall's godmother, but Warren hadn't seen his brother in years and had no idea how to contact him. Tony Sutton, despite his troubled history with the Church, had been delighted when Warren and Susan had asked him to be Niall's godfather.

The priest had been very understanding when Warren explained why they wouldn't be able to meet that week, but Warren still felt guilty.

Furthermore, he hadn't visited his grandfather in a fortnight. The old man could use a mobile phone with his hearing aids, but attempts to video call the ninety-five-year-old, even with the assistance of the care home staff, were frustrating. As vitally important as Warren's job was, it didn't make these things any easier, and he ended calls feeling both guilty *and* depressed. Sometimes he wondered if it was worth it, now he had a family. He remembered John Grayson's advice, back when he was considering applying for promotion. *'The question you should be asking, is not "Am I the right person for the job?" but rather "Is this the right job for me?"'* Perhaps his old boss had a point?

Warren forced his attention back to the man in front of them.

'Did you kill Sinead McCaffrey?' asked Sutton.

Greenland was composed, but his solicitor had brought in some packs of tissues.

'No, I did not,' he replied.

'Then explain to us how the blood and fingerprints got into your car. The only other person with access to the keys was Louisa,' said Warren.

Greenland looked up in surprise. His face turned to disbelief. 'No way. I know what you're going to suggest, and no way was Louisa responsible.' He looked aghast. 'She could never do that.'

'Are you sure?' asked Warren gently. 'We know – *you* know – that Louisa was completely in love with you. Nobody has suggested that she ever strayed in your relationship back then. How do you think she'd feel if she found out Sinead was expecting your child? Angry and betrayed for sure, but she adored you. Would she have walked away from you? Or would she have decided to eliminate the competition?'

'No!' said Greenland, his voice rising in anger. 'No way. Louisa couldn't kill someone.' His voice become desperate. 'We don't even know Sinead is dead. She could have just walked away. Had her – our – baby in secret.'

'And remained hidden for eleven years?' said Sutton. 'Her

mother has been in agony all that time. Her dad died without ever knowing what happened to his little girl. Her brother grew up without the big sister he idolised. Do you really think she'd be that cruel? OK, her family are strict Catholics. She'd have been embarrassed and maybe even ashamed, but it was 2008 not 1958. Come on, man, as hard as it is to accept, we all know that she's dead.'

Greenland reacted as if he'd been slapped.

'Ben,' said Warren more gently. 'If Louisa didn't kill Sinead, then with the forensic evidence in that car, everything is pointing towards only one person it could have been.'

'There's a pattern here,' said Sutton. 'And it's not a pretty one. Two of your intimate partners are dead. Both of them had placed you in an untenable position. Both of them were a problem that needed solving.'

'How can you say that?' wailed Greenland.

'I don't like coincidences, and neither do juries,' said Sutton. 'Ever since this investigation started, you have refused to cooperate, forcing us to dig deeper into your lives. And what we've found is pretty damned ugly. Louisa's business was a ticking time bomb, wasn't it?

'You knew she'd lied to you about the bank loan; that they had judged the consequences from Holistics Gym breaking its promises to be too serious. Yet she signed on the dotted line anyway. And you also knew that you were jointly liable if she defaulted; you were married. The second mortgage was in both your names.'

'But you had a solution, didn't you?' said Warren. 'A plan B that would see you living happily after. Leave Louisa and run away with the only other person who had stuck with you. Who you'd been sleeping with since you were students at university. Who had also stayed in Middlesbury.'

'Caitlin,' said Sutton.

'No,' said Greenland, but his voice was weak.

'Don't bother denying it,' said Sutton. He pushed a stapled set of printouts across the table. 'These deleted text messages were recovered from the mobile phone you hid from Louisa. Steamy stuff – I can see why you hid them from your wife. But you got worried, didn't you?' said Sutton. 'You thought Louisa might be suspicious. You didn't want her snooping around and finding the phone, using your thumbprint to unlock it when you were asleep – you know, the way you did when you installed tracking software on Louisa's handset.' He reached across and pointed to one of the messages. 'So you sent Caitlin the link for a secure messaging app and urged her to install it. You need a PIN to unlock it.'

'No comment,' said Greenland. His face was alarmingly pale, and his voice trembled.

'But I think you used that app for more than just conducting your illicit liaisons,' said Warren. 'I think you were using it to plan for your future. A future without Louisa.'

'No comment,' he whispered.

Warren pointed to a different text message on the transcript, received a day before Ben sent the link to the app.

'Did you ever visit this website that Caitlin recommended to you?' he asked.

'No comment,' said Greenland.

Warren pulled out another pile of paper. 'We know you did; we recovered the browsing history from your phone. For the benefit of the recording, I am showing Mr Greenland a series of print-outs from a financial advice website called SolveYourWoes.co.uk.'

He turned back to Greenland. 'The website has an open forum where registered users can post questions. The advice is a bit rough and ready, and frankly anyone could be answering the questions, as users are anonymous. Are you familiar with this post, from March 23rd, asked by a user calling themselves "Prisoner1987"?

'"Hey guys, hope you can help. Wife has gone behind my back and I'm worried she's landed us in the shit. We've already remortgaged the house to support her business, and she told me she'd got an extension to an existing business loan to buy materials upfront to fulfil an order for a big company.

'"Turns out she lied. The bank said the terms of the contract are too risky, because if the company doesn't sell as many as it promises we end up with a load of unsold stock. They refused the extension. But she signed the contract anyway.

'"We have two small children and we're already pushing it with the mortgage payments. If this goes tits-up, we're fucked. The original loan is in her name, but the mortgage is in both our names. She has no other income. I work full-time. I've had enough. I need to know if I can protect me and the kids if I divorce her." Are you Prisoner1987?' asked Warren.

'No comment.'

'For the record, the password manager on Mr Greenland's phone automatically logs him into the site under the username Prisoner1987.'

Greenland closed his eyes. Beside him his solicitor winced.

'There are a number of replies to your post,' said Warren. 'The general consensus seems to be that if you were to divorce Louisa, as the primary breadwinner you would probably end up paying her maintenance, and child support if she won custody of the girls. She would be liable for the business loan, but you would both need to continue paying the mortgage.

'Now I'm not going to pretend to be an expert here, Ben. I've no idea how accurate that advice is. But it doesn't really matter, as you clearly believed it. This is your reply, the following day, again under the username Prisoner1987: "So basically, she's fucked us."

'There were a number of sympathetic replies. But this is the one that really stands out: "Yeah, bad luck, mate. If you stay with her you're fucked. If you leave her you're fucked. If I were you, I'd bury the bitch under the patio and move on."

'To which you replied: "It's a good idea, but I'd still need a loan to hire a builder."'

'Oh come on,' exploded Greenland. 'That was a joke. It was a plotline in some old soap opera from the Seventies. *Crossroads* or something.'

'*Brookside* and it was the Nineties,' Sutton corrected him, ignoring Warren's raised eyebrow.

'Well, whatever,' said Greenland. 'It was just a joke.'

'There was more than a nugget of truth in it though, wasn't there?' said Warren.

'What do you mean?' asked Greenland.

'If Louisa died, you'd be the beneficiary of her life insurance policy, A policy that recently had its cover increased. You wouldn't be rich, but it would more than wipe out her debts and clear the mortgage on the house.'

'That's madness,' said Greenland. 'We'd had the original policy years; it barely covered funeral costs. We've had two children since we first bought it.'

'Where's the knife, Ben?' asked Sutton.

'What knife?'

'The one from the knife block in the kitchen. The one you replaced. The one that is the same size as that used to stab Louisa through the heart.'

Greenland's jaw dropped.

Warren pushed a colour printout from a security camera across the table, and a copy of a bank statement, a single transaction highlighted in yellow.

'That's you buying the knife from John Lewis in Cambridge,' said Warren. 'The same weekend you were discussing killing your wife online. Where is the original, Ben? Where's the knife you used to kill Louisa?'

* * *

Greenland had slipped back into no commenting, and eventually they called it a night. Unless there were any unexpected revelations in the next few hours, they had done all they could for the time being. They had easily got an extension to his detention. The custody clock had resumed from his previous arrest, so they were now over sixty hours into the ninety-six they could hold him for, but Warren was confident they wouldn't be releasing him again.

'There's no sign of Caitlin, or her car, at her flat,' said Ruskin, his voice booming over Warren's desk phone. 'None of her neighbours have seen her.'

That was a worry. They needed Caitlin to confirm her relationship with Ben to tie everything up, and Warren was far from convinced she was an entirely innocent party to the whole affair. He ordered Ruskin to seal her apartment and authorised a couple of uniformed officers to stand guard in case she returned home; he filed a request for a search warrant to be executed the following morning.

Phoning the traffic department, he requested they search ANPR for her vehicle. If she had caught wind of Ben's arrest and decided to make a run for it, they didn't want her to get too much of a head start.

Next, he placed a call to Roehampton. Her voice was thick with sleep, her words slightly slurred. But she woke up fully when he apprised her of the evening's events and agreed to seek authority for an all-ports alert. Caitlin was an Irish national; the UK police enjoyed a close working relationship with their Irish counterparts, the *Garda Síochána*, but it was a further complication they could do without.

That done, Warren leaned back in his chair, suddenly too tired to move. Why did these things always happen at such ungodly hours? Forcing himself to his feet, he decided there was no need to stay at his desk any longer. He'd leave his phone switched on; if Caitlin was located, they could wake him. They had enough to arrest her on suspicion of conspiracy at least; she'd repeatedly denied having an affair with Ben. Most of the paperwork for the CPS had been completed as they went along. There was no point staying up even later to finish it, then bothering their twenty-four-hour on-call service; Greenland wasn't going anywhere.

Grabbing his jacket, he switched off the lights. It was too late to phone Susan, besides which, he was so tired he wouldn't make much sense and would probably fall asleep.

Waving goodbye to the night shift, he headed for his car. He knew that sleep would be elusive. They'd finally got their man.

So why did he still feel like he was standing at the bottom of a very steep hill?

SUNDAY 26TH MAY

SUNDAY 24TH MAY

Chapter 33

Warren awoke early, after a fitful night's sleep. Fortunately, he wasn't the only one up with the larks, and he'd spent an enjoyable few minutes watching Susan feeding their son his breakfast. Somehow, despite the fact that Susan was in charge of the tiny spoon, Niall still managed to end up with a face covered in whatever she was doling out of the jar. He left for work if not refreshed, then at least in a good mood.

'Caitlin's phone is turned off,' Pymm told the morning briefing after reporting that the final customer who had downloaded images from Louisa's website had been cleared. 'No network activity since yesterday evening.'

'ANPR records one hit on her car, heading out of Middlesbury at 21.32 on the A506,' said Richardson. 'No idea where she was going and no sign of her at any airports or seaports, so she hasn't jumped on a plane or a ferry yet.'

'We're still awaiting her bank records,' said Pymm. 'So I've no idea if she has bought a train ticket.'

'The warrant for her flat needs a signature,' said Sutton. 'I'm meeting the search team at eleven, so we'll be good to go as soon as we get it.'

'The CPS has almost everything they need,' said Warren. 'They want us to interview Ben again, to see if there's anything more. There remains the question of any co-conspirators for the murder of Louisa. We still don't have enough to point a finger at either Russell Myrie or Darren Greenland, but if Ben's brief is better than she appears, she must know the writing is on the wall now. Maybe the threat of being charged will get him to implicate them? Assuming they are involved, of course.

'The CPS will give us a charging decision once we've finished. No rush – we have plenty of time. If it goes our way, we'll get him in front of a magistrate tomorrow. In the meantime, a confession would be nice. It'll make things a lot easier.'

*   *   *

Unfortunately, a confession was not forthcoming. Greenland had vehemently denied any involvement in either Louisa or Sinead's deaths. Warren had given him an opening to see if he'd try and pin the blame, or at least share the burden, with others. But again, he'd continued to deny any involvement in the two women's deaths.

Warren had laid out his case to the CPS after interview, and they had called back within thirty minutes. It was much as he had expected.

'It's a go for murder for Louisa. Not enough to reach the threshold for Sinead,' he told the team.

'If he's got any sense, he'll admit to them both,' said Hutchinson. 'Get a reduction in tariff for admitting it at the earliest stage, and hope to serve the two sentences concurrently'

'Let's hope so,' said Warren. 'Tony, where are we with the search of Caitlin's apartment?'

'Briefing in half an hour,' said Sutton.

'Then do you have a few minutes to accompany me to the cells?' he asked.

'Try and stop me.'

*   *   *

Greenland had broken down again when he was stood in front of the custody desk, and the charges read out. His knees had buckled, and Warren had to catch his arm to stop him hitting the desk on his way to the floor. It had taken several moments before Greenland was able to confirm he understood what was going on, and he'd repeated his denials.

It was distressing to watch. Warren had seen many murderers charged in his time, many of them still protesting their innocence. But even though the man in front of him had been responsible for the deaths of one, or even two, innocent women, he'd never seen anyone crushed so completely.

'Look after him,' said Warren quietly to the custody sergeant.

He suddenly felt weary. In his job there were rarely happy endings, just the satisfaction of a job well done. No matter the outcome, nothing would change the fact that two little girls would never see their mother again. And he couldn't forget the part he'd played in taking away their father.

Too exhausted to trudge up the stairs, he took the elevator. The doors to the lift were adjacent to the desks of civilian support workers and it was Janice that he saw as soon as he stepped onto the floor.

'Sir, the front desk called,' she greeted him. 'Stephanie Hellard just walked in. She's demanding to see you. She says it's urgent.'

*　　*　　*

Warren decided to take a few minutes to clear his head before dealing with Ben Greenland's sister-in-law. Whether Stephanie Hellard liked it or not, she was not Greenland's solicitor and could not act in any formal legal capacity. He was not prepared to put up with her gate-crashing proceedings now that Ben had been charged.

Swiping through the side door into the reception area, he was struck once more by the similarity with her late sibling. It had been seven days since he had confronted her after she'd talked her way into the booking area, and he was shocked at her change in appearance. Her hair, immaculately styled before, was wild and unruly. What little make-up she was wearing looked to be at least a day old, and her mascara was smudged. Her smart blouse and skirt had been replaced with a shapeless tracksuit.

'Oh, thank God,' she said, crossing the room. Even from several paces away, Warren could smell the alcohol on her breath.

'Ben didn't do it. There's been a mistake.'

She started fumbling in her handbag and, for a moment, Warren wondered if she was going to pull out a weapon. Instead, she produced a mobile phone.

'I didn't see it until this morning,' she said, as she manipulated the device, her hands shaking so much it took three attempts to unlock it.

'Didn't see what, Stephanie?' asked Warren, his voice deliberately soothing. 'Why don't we get a cup of tea and talk somewhere a little more private?'

'No, you have to see this,' said Stephanie, thrusting the phone toward his face.

Warren squinted, the screen blurry without his reading glasses. Eventually his tired eyes focused.

The text message was from Caitlin.

'Tell Ben I'm sorry.'

Chapter 34

'The message came in yesterday afternoon,' said Hellard, her hands wrapped around a steaming mug. 'I've had so many messages from people wanting to know what's going on that in the end, I just figured I'd send a blanket text to everyone.' She shuddered. 'But I was so exhausted from trying to comfort the girls, that as soon as I got back to my hotel, I took a sleeping pill and went straight to bed.'

'Tell us everything you know about Ben and Caitlin,' said Warren. 'No holding back.'

He'd immediately called up to the main office to relay the news. DSI Roehampton was preparing to manage the coming storm. Ben hadn't yet been told about Hellard's appearance, and it didn't look as though she'd thought to contact his solicitor before arriving at the station. The prisoner transport van was currently parked outside, and the magistrates court had been told to expect a delay.

The first thing they needed to do was check the veracity of the message. Pymm was scouring Caitlin's phone records to check someone hadn't spoofed her telephone number.

In the meantime, they urgently needed to locate Caitlin. Richardson was on the phone to Traffic, trying to find any traces of her car, whilst Tony Sutton had accompanied the search team to her flat. They were due to force their way in any moment.

'Why would Caitlin harm Louisa – if indeed that's what's happened?' asked Warren. The text message could be seen as a confession – and they would be treating it as such until they could determine otherwise – but it didn't let Ben off the hook. It was possible the two of them had conspired to kill Louisa so they could be together. The text could be an apology to him because despite their best efforts, he had still been arrested.

'Caitlin was always sweet on Ben, even before we all moved to Potter Street,' said Hellard. 'It's no secret Ben had a wandering eye and I've wondered over the years if he and Caitlin ever did anything.'

'And what do you think now?' asked Warren. The revelations about Greenland's illicit communications with Caitlin had only been put to him late the previous evening. Had his solicitor relayed those to Stephanie?

Hellard looked down at the table. 'Now we know they did,' she said quietly, her voice coloured with shame. Clearly, she had been told.

'You need to be honest with me, Stephanie. No more games. Do you think Ben and Caitlin worked together, or was she solely responsible?'

Hellard met his gaze. 'There is no doubt in my mind that Ben is innocent.' She paused. 'And if Caitlin killed Louisa, then I'm certain she also killed Sinead.'

* * *

'We've found a note,' said Sutton, his voice urgent. Warren had been pulled out of his interview with Stephanie to take the call. A forced entry team had entered Caitlin's flat. As expected, there was no sign of her.

'There are several printed A4 pages. I've taken a photograph on my phone; I'll email it over. I can't see if there is anything on the rear of the sheets. I'll need to wait for the Evidence Recovery Team to arrive to turn them over, but I can read to you what is in front of me.'

'Do it,' said Warren; he could tell from Sutton's voice it was explosive.

My darling Ben,

Writing this letter is the hardest thing I've ever done. I am so sorry it came to this. I've loved you since the day we met. Those times we spent together were always so special. I knew I could never keep you to myself, and I told myself that was OK. I could share you with Louisa, if I had to. I knew you'd never leave her, but you were going to stay in Middlesbury, so I decided I would too.

Then Sinead told me she was pregnant. All she'd say was it was someone we were both friends with; and I just knew in my heart it was you. She didn't know about us of course – I never told a soul, and I had to sit there whilst she told me how much she loved you and how you loved her. Then she told me about how she had decided to keep the baby. She was going to ask you to raise your child together, back in Ireland.

I was devastated. All my plans were falling apart. I'd just signed up to do a postgraduate course at UME and I had no plans to move back to Ireland. The thought she would take you away from me kept me awake for days.

So I had to kill her. I had no choice – you must see that.

It wasn't hard. She'd been on anti-anxiety drugs and sleeping pills for months. I crushed a few into that bitter lemon she used to guzzle, and then walked her out to your car. I put her in the boot and then drove her to the woods.

You were devastated. It was so hard watching you seeking comfort with Louisa. When you told me you were breaking off our affair, I was heartbroken. But I knew it wouldn't last.

We're soulmates. For years I watched you and Louisa grow closer and have your girls, and all the while I waited. I met other men, but none of them were you. Louisa clutched you tighter and tighter and my heart ached.

I resigned myself to brief liaisons during football tours, or work trips, and then it happened. That night we bumped into each other as you celebrated your team's win, it was as if fate had finally intervened and told us to do what was right. We were both drunk, but that meant we spoke the truth. You told me how you felt trapped, tied to Louisa by the girls and that damned business of hers. That night in my flat, it was as if we were back at university. You had to leave after we finished making love, but I knew that things were finally changing. Those furtive nights in your bed as Louisa abandoned you to make those stupid hampers were wonderful.

I know you didn't want to hear what I was telling you about Louisa. Despite everything you were still loyal to her, but she was dragging you under. I knew I had to do something to break the impasse. I thought I could share you, but I couldn't.

And then she told me about your plans for the future. How you wanted to leave Middlesbury and start again. She was so excited about the future. I was devastated.

It was Sinead all over again.

I remember the argument we had that night when I confronted you. You could barely look me in the eye.

I realised that I was a fool. Louisa had dug her claws into you the moment she met you. You would never leave her. But we were destined to be together. So I had to get rid of her.

I had such plans for the future. I knew we would have to lay low for the next few months. To observe an appropriate period of mourning, but eventually we could be together. Man and wife, the way it was always meant to be, and one day perhaps, even a brother or sister for the girls.

But it all went wrong. I knew that the police would look

to you first. They always do. But you were innocent – they'd soon move on. Louisa was in such a dark place. The drugs, the website she was posing for to earn extra money, that creepy man who ran the garage next door, even your dreadful brother. They'd leave you alone.

But they didn't.

You could have saved yourself by telling them all about us. They'd have soon pieced it together, even though you were blissfully ignorant. We've never spoken about Sinead; I don't know if you ever had your suspicions. But you have remained loyal to me, keeping our secret. And I love you so much for that.

But now it's cost you. I love you too much to see you go to prison for something I did.

So this is my confession. The police will read it first. I just hope they share it with you.

I will always love you.

'She's signed and dated it at the bottom,' said Sutton. 'We're looking in her filing cabinet for an example signature to compare it to.'

Warren let out the breath he'd been holding; a weight had been forming in his stomach, growing heavier with every sentence.

Flashes of the hours he'd spent opposite Ben flooded his mind's eye. The shock and horror when he'd realised they thought he was guilty. The tears flowing down his cheeks as he'd tried to convince them of his innocence. His repeated no comments hadn't been the path of least resistance; he'd been fighting the urge to tell the truth. Warren felt a flash of anger directed at his solicitor. She'd urged Ben to no comment, convinced their case would fall apart. But she hadn't known the truth. He remembered catching Ben as he collapsed, when that strategy had backfired so spectacularly, and he was charged.

He took a calming breath. He could deal with that once they found Caitlin and wrapped up the case.

If they found her. If Caitlin was really serious about confessing, she'd have presented herself at the station, ready to face the music. But the letter and the text message both had a note of finality about them. Warren suspected that when they did locate Caitlin, she would already be dead.

Chapter 35

'What is it? Have you found her?' asked Hellard, when Warren re-entered the smart interview room. The team had just had a crisis briefing. The letter was damning, but there had been so much duplicity in this case they couldn't take Caitlin's signature at face value.

'No, there's no sign of her. Do you have any idea where she may have gone?'

Hellard shrugged. 'I really have no idea. Caitlin and I were friends at uni, but we hadn't spent much time together over the past few years.'

'Before I was called away, you were saying that if Caitlin killed Louisa, then she also killed Sinead. Why do you think that, Stephanie?'

'Little things,' admitted Hellard. 'I had suspected for some time that Ben might be sleeping with Sinead.'

'As well as Caitlin?' asked Warren injecting a note of surprise into his voice. 'And your sister?'

Hellard flushed. 'There had to be a reason a couple of the lads on the football team referred to twenty-seven Potter Street as "Ben's Harem". For the most part, I just figured they were jealous. You know what boys that age are like. But looking back at it, I have to admit there was a lot of sexual tension in that house. Some of it was obvious – we all knew Curtis had the hots for Caitlin, and obviously Ben and Louisa were an item – but when I remember some of the drunken nights we had . . .'

'I have to ask,' said Warren. 'Given Ben's . . . tastes . . . were you and he ever . . .?'

'No,' she said firmly. 'Louisa was my sister. And my best friend.'

'Of course, please continue,' said Warren, although a small, judgemental part of him wondered why she had chosen not to share her suspicions with her sister.

'Caitlin and Sinead were best friends. They told each other everything. Or at least I think Sinead did; she was so open and trusting. If she was sleeping with Ben, I can believe she let slip to Caitlin what was going on.'

'Were you aware that Sinead fell pregnant shortly before she disappeared?' asked Warren.

Hellard closed her eyes briefly. 'Shit.' She took a shuddering breath. 'Well, that would explain a lot. She was clearly upset in those last few weeks. You know, stressed out, not sleeping properly. But we all were – our finals were coming up. A couple of times I heard her being sick in the morning. I didn't think anything of it; Sinead liked the *craic* at the best of times, and like all of us, she was probably drinking a little too much to help unwind after a stressful day.'

'Do you think she told Caitlin?' asked Warren.

Hellard looked thoughtful. 'If she was going to share that news with anyone, aside perhaps from Ben, then I'd say yeah, she'd tell Caitlin. There's no way she'd tell her mum, and she could hardly tell me or Louisa.'

Hellard paused. 'You know, there's always something that's niggled me about the night before Sinead disappeared. We rarely locked our rooms; we had an unwritten rule that if the door was ajar, you could just go in. We were constantly in and out of each other's rooms, the girls especially – we used to borrow each other's clothes all the time. The night before Sinead was last seen, I saw Caitlin coming out of Louisa's room. She said she was looking for a skirt Louisa had borrowed. She clearly hadn't found it, as her hands were empty.

'Ben's mum added Louisa to his car's insurance in the final year and so she had his spare set of car keys. Caitlin could easily have swiped Lou's keys to get rid of Sinead's body.'

A memory from Warren's interview with Curtis surfaced. Hadn't he said that he'd known what night Sinead went missing, because Louisa had misplaced her house keys? If Caitlin had taken them the night she killed Sinead, she could hardly have returned them to Louisa's room that night if Louisa was in bed. Louisa had left the following morning without her keys and had needed letting back into the house.

'What was Caitlin like after Sinead disappeared?' asked Warren.

'Devastated. We all were,' said Hellard. 'I think we all felt we should have noticed the state she was in and done something about it.' She sniffed. 'If one of us had stepped in, could we have changed things? But now I think Caitlin saw Sinead as a rival. She had to get rid of her.'

'So why didn't she kill Louisa back then? Surely she was an even bigger rival?'

'Perhaps she was worried it would be too suspicious?' suggested Hellard. 'Two housemates going missing is a massive coincidence. Besides which, she'd just killed Sinead. Maybe she couldn't face doing it again?' She looked at Warren. 'You know how many murderers are so sickened by what they've done that they can't live with it. They certainly can't kill again.'

'But she did live with it,' said Warren. 'And it looks as though she did kill again. But why? Why did she decide to murder Louisa now, after all these years?'

'Perhaps something changed?' said Hellard. 'Caitlin continued living in Middlesbury, I guess to stay close to Ben. I did wonder over the years if they ever rekindled their relationship. When

311

Louisa started working those long hours and sleeping in the spare room, that would have been the perfect opportunity.'

Her eyes widened. 'Of course, that's what must have happened.'

'What?' asked Warren.

'A few weeks ago, Louisa told me she and Ben were thinking about moving to Leicester. His company are opening a new branch and he was considering applying for a promotion. House prices are cheaper than Middlesbury, and so are the rents on the local industrial estate. If Louisa or Ben told Caitlin this, then maybe she thought she had to act? To get rid of Louisa now, before it was too late?'

Warren thought back to Louisa's lunch date at Mandy's Muffins. Was that Caitlin? Was that when Louisa let slip to her old friend that she and Ben had plans to move? Had an innocent conversation over sandwiches, coffee and a muffin been the catalyst for this whole affair?

* * *

'We've tracked down the rental firm that the car with the cloned licence plates was hired from,' said Richardson, when Warren returned to the office. Stephanie remained downstairs. They still hadn't told Ben what was happening, but he imagined his solicitor would soon be up to speed. Roehampton was due a call with the CPS to decide what to do about the charges against Ben.

'It's a small, independent company based near Stansted Airport,' she said. 'They confirm they rented a dark-blue Ford Focus to a Caitlin McCaffrey on the day Louisa was murdered.'

'That matches a payment on Caitlin's credit card,' said Pymm. 'I spoke to the person working that day and he said his records indicate that he compared the photo on the customer's driving licence to the person renting the vehicle. It was booked online the day before.'

A new email alert popped up on Richardson's screen.

'That should be a link to the CCTV from above the till at the time the customer picked up the vehicle. I have somebody on their way out there to look and see what else they have.'

She opened the video and clicked play.

The camera was positioned to show a wide-angle view from behind the till, encompassing the server and extending a metre or so in front of the desk. The figure of a woman walked into shot. Wearing a red hoodie, with the hood pulled over a baseball cap, she looked to be about the same size and build as Caitlin. The woman handed over what appeared to be her driving licence. After a few seconds' scrutiny, the man turned to the computer and copied the details off it, before returning it. He offered the woman a card reader and she inserted her credit card, before typing in her PIN. A few seconds later, a laser printer spat out several sheets of paper.

'Damn, she was wearing gloves,' said Warren as the woman accepted a pen and scrawled her signature. The server opened a metal lock box on the wall behind the till and removed a car key with a large fob. Leaning over the till, he made pointing gestures. The woman turned, her face still hidden, and followed his directions, before walking out of shot.

The whole transaction took little more than a minute.

'Let's get that paper invoice,' said Warren. 'Even without fingerprints, her signature will tie it to her. I presume we have the vehicle's original licence number?'

'Yes, and it is currently in their lot,' said Richardson. 'I've arranged for forensic recovery. Their records show it hasn't been hired since it was returned early on the Wednesday morning.'

'Brilliant work,' said Warren. If the car had been used to transport Louisa to the woods, there may be trace evidence of her presence. And she had been stabbed to death; it would have been very difficult for her killer to avoid transferring blood to the car. Minuscule droplets could be detected by luminol and a UV light source, and blood dogs could sniff out traces that were otherwise inaccessible. Could they even find proof it was Caitlin driving?

'I've run the car's plates through ANPR,' said Richardson. 'We have her driving near the rental place and on the M11 travelling away from the airport, shortly after she picked the car up at eight-fifteen. Then we have hits travelling back towards the airport before the car was dropped off. But we have nothing between the car leaving the M11 and then re-joining it. So either she pulled off into a quiet country lay-by and didn't go anywhere for seven or eight hours—'

'Or she pulled into a lay-by, switched licence plates, and then carried on to Louisa's industrial unit,' finished Warren.

'Exactly.'

'That's great work, but we really need to get a stronger ID to prove our case,' said Warren. 'See if your team can capture a good face shot in that area. Rachel, I don't suppose she kept her phone switched on?'

'No, I'm afraid not,' said Pymm.

'She had to get to and from the rental place,' said Richardson. 'Either she drove herself there, caught public transport – which might be difficult given the time of night she returned the vehicle – or used a taxi.'

'Work your magic,' instructed Warren, taking his vibrating mobile out of his pocket. 'It's Tony,' he said.

'Warren, I'm with the Evidence Recovery Team at Caitlin's flat. You are never going to believe what we've just found.'

Chapter 36

'It was in a plastic crate underneath her bed,' said Sutton. He was live-streaming a CSI carefully laying the contents of the box on a sterile sheet for processing. He inventoried the items as they were removed.

'A five-pack of hooded plastic overalls, three missing.'

'They look like civilian versions of the ones CSIs wear,' commented Pymm, leaning towards the screen. 'You can buy them in DIY stores. Good for keeping blood off your clothes.'

'A box of small latex gloves, half empty,' continued Sutton. 'Cable ties – they look like the ones that were used to bind Louisa's wrists. Strong bleach and cleaning cloths. Oh hello, that's what we want.' The camera wobbled as he tried to position it more carefully to show the bright yellow, gun-shaped object. 'Unless I'm very much mistaken, this is a Taser.'

'Gotcha,' said Warren.

* * *

By the time the box was fully catalogued, they had uncovered everything necessary for Louisa's kidnapping and murder, including a set of licence plates matching the cloned ones fitted to the hire vehicle. Everything except one item.

'No sign of the knife,' said Warren, as he summarised the findings to Roehampton. 'Which worries me. Ben claimed the knife from their knife block was replaced after it was dropped and the blade loosened. He says he threw it away, but the bins are long gone, so we have no proof that's what really happened.'

'You're suggesting he could have kept it and used it on Louisa? That he might still be involved in her murder?'

'We only have that printed letter supposedly left by Caitlin that says she was solely responsible. She could be protecting him, assuming she even wrote it.'

'Is this your roundabout way of saying you don't want him released yet?' asked Roehampton.

'At least until we've verified some more details,' said Warren.

Roehampton sighed. 'I'm going to have to talk to legal and the CPS. We've charged him, so he's supposed to appear in front of a magistrate at the next available opportunity. I don't know if we can cancel the charges then keep him whilst the custody clock runs out. How long have we got left, potentially?'

Warren did the sums. 'Twelve hours,' he said.

'Then we'd better work out what the hell is going on quickly, because if he was involved, the moment he's out that door, he's gone.'

* * *

'Any sign of Caitlin?' asked Warren as soon as he left Roehampton.

'No sign of her car on any cameras, and her phone remains turned off,' said Richardson.

'Damn, we really need to find her,' said Warren. 'How far could she have driven without being pinged by ANPR?' he asked.

'A fair distance,' said Richardson. 'Her car was last seen on the A506. If she didn't trigger a speed camera, she could be anywhere between here and the outskirts of Cambridge. If she pulled off the 506 onto a side road, then the area becomes massive. She could even have doubled back and gone south. Half of Hertfordshire and large chunks of Essex and Bedfordshire are all accessible if you know where the cameras are.'

'And that's assuming she's even using her own licence plates,' said Pymm. 'She's already used fake plates once, she could easily have ordered a second set, and it's not as if whatever dodgy website she bought them from will have kept records.'

Warren took a calming breath. They were so close . . .

'Tony, get a bulletin out to the media,' he said. 'Photos, description of her car, all the usual. Maybe somebody will recognise her, or she might hand herself in? Keep it vague; say we urgently need to speak to her to assist in finding Louisa's killer. We'll warn members of the public not to approach. Karen, can you and Hutch organise a team to call all of her friends and acquaintances that we know of? Don't give them too many details; but make certain they know it is vital they tell us if they see her. Perhaps they know of somewhere she might have gone?'

The finality of the note and the text message gave valid reasons for suspecting Caitlin might be considering suicide, but it would be difficult to balance that with a warning for the public not to approach her.

He rang Sutton again, filling him in on what was going on. 'Any clues in her flat?'

'Nothing obvious,' said Sutton. 'The team have turned the confession note over, and there's nothing on the other side of the paper. The signature is similar to one we found on a copy of her flat's rental agreement. The fingerprint team are going to examine the Taser back at the lab under alternate light sources.'

'What about in the flat?' asked Warren. It was a big ask, given how little time they'd had to search.

'They've lifted them from the usual places – door handles, the bedside table et cetera. They'll let you know if Ben's or Louisa's turn up. They've taken comparators of what we presume are Caitlin's from her toothbrush and hairbrush, along with DNA.'

It was the best they could do; Caitlin had no criminal record.

Prints taken for exclusionary purposes during the original missing person investigation for Sinead would have been purged from the system years ago.

'Warren, I've just finished speaking to the CPS,' called Roehampton. From the tone of her voice, it wasn't good news.

* * *

Ben Greenland still looked shell-shocked as he clambered into his sister-in-law's BMW. With a signed confession from Caitlin, not to mention everything they had found hidden under her bed, the CPS had decided he no longer met the charging threshold. The dropped charges could be reinstated in future, but for now he was free to go.

In theory, there was still enough reasonable suspicion to re-arrest him as a suspect, but there seemed little point. The custody clock wouldn't be reset, so they could only ask a magistrate for a few more hours. Warren and Roehampton had discussed re-arresting him and then immediately bailing him, but decided against it.

When Warren had broken the news to Greenland, his solicitor had immediately advised that he make no statement – advice he had followed. As far as Ben was concerned, he had been fully exonerated. However, Roehampton had managed to convince the magistrate to grant a warrant to keep his personal phone under surveillance. An intercept for his calls and texts was out of the question, but she had agreed to real-time location tracking, and they could monitor his records. If he tried to contact Caitlin, or travelled anywhere, they would know about it.

As he watched the BMW pull out of the station car park, Warren chewed on a hangnail. This morning, it had seemed so clear-cut. Now, everything had turned upside down. On paper at least, they knew who was responsible for two murders.

So why did he feel like it wasn't over yet?

MONDAY 27TH MAY

MONDAY 17TH MAY

Chapter 37

Warren had tried his best to get some sleep, but it had been a losing battle, and he decided to go into work early. He wasn't the only one.

'The paper edition of the *Middlesbury Reporter* is out today, and they've printed Caitlin's picture on the front page, so perhaps we'll get some sightings,' said Warren, trying to start the early briefing on a positive note.

'Fingers crossed,' said Hutchinson. 'None of her friends or acquaintances could suggest where she may have run to. For what it's worth, the callers think everyone they phoned was telling the truth; they don't think they were covering for her.'

'No sightings of her car, phone activity or banking,' said Pymm.

'It looks as though Caitlin was very careful not to leave her prints on anything in the murder box,' said Sutton. 'At least her prints were on the confession.'

'Why did she type it?' asked Roehampton.

Warren shrugged. 'She told us she's dyspraxic with bad handwriting; she probably typed everything.'

'There are a number of purchases on her credit card from different DIY stores where she could have bought the kit,' said Pymm. 'We'll chase down the receipts and see if there is any

CCTV available. It looks as though she was planning this for some time; the credit card is only a month old, used solely for these purchases and the car rental. It's not with her usual bank, so I guess she thought that would stop us linking it back to her.'

'Well, let's see if we can piece together what happened,' said Warren. The evidence against Caitlin was strong, but it needed to be watertight. The case for killing Sinead would be far harder to prove, even with the confession, so they needed to show beyond doubt that she was capable of killing Louisa, her friend of many years. That way, her admission of guilt for the earlier murder would be more convincing at trial, even if she had a last-minute change of heart and tried to recant it.

He drew a timeline on one of the whiteboards. On a second board, he drew a question mark, under which he would list the remaining unanswered questions.

'We know she booked the hire car online the Sunday before Louisa was killed. It was waiting for her near the airport. She picked it up at eight-fifteen. How did she get there?'

'There's no sign of her car,' said Richardson. 'She could have been using cloned plates, but her neighbour thinks her car was parked in its usual spot that evening.'

'We need to verify that,' said Warren. 'Have a team scour the cameras for a Fiat 500; we'll look like fools if her neighbour got his nights mixed up. And see if there is any CCTV from businesses and properties in the streets surrounding her apartment block that night. How are we doing with public transport?'

'We're sourcing video from all the shuttle buses and the stops,' said Richardson. 'Fortunately, the security outside airports is almost as tight as it is within them. It might take us a while, but if she took a bus, we'll find her.'

'What about taxis?'

'None booked for a Caitlin through the usual companies,' she replied. 'But we're showing her photograph to local firms that might have done the job as a one-off. We'll check if anyone did a drop-off within a couple of miles of the airport. She could have walked the last bit.'

Finding clearer footage of Caitlin would help strengthen their case, but it wasn't their top priority. They would have weeks to find those small details between her being found and charged, and her trial.

'She picked up the car at eight-fifteen, headed up the M11 towards Middlesbury, before switching plates and continuing her journey,' said Warren. 'So what happened over the next few hours?'

'We can be fairly certain Louisa was snatched from her unit,' said Sutton. 'Finding that Taser yesterday proves the AFID tag they retrieved during the initial search hadn't found its way in there by some bizarre coincidence.'

'Clearly the woman across the road must have seen Caitlin, not Louisa,' said Hardwick.

'Then how about this,' said Ruskin. 'Caitlin parked the hire car near the Greenlands' house and went to see Ben, after Louisa left for work. Then, either she got into an argument with Ben, left and went to Louisa's unit, or she and Ben travelled together to Louisa's unit and killed her.'

'We know it wasn't spontaneous,' said Hutchinson. 'She bought that murder kit weeks beforehand, arranged a hire car, bought cloned licence plates, and acquired a Taser. Plus, somebody disabled Louisa's CCTV weeks beforehand. So either she and Ben planned it together, or she went to see Ben, perhaps having decided that if he didn't give her what she wanted she'd execute her own plan B. No pun intended.'

'Which is why we need that damned murder weapon,' said Sutton. 'That could be the key to this whole thing. Ben bought a new kitchen knife, he claims, to replace a damaged one. If the original knife was the murder weapon, then he obviously held on to it. The confession letter was desperate to make certain he doesn't take the blame, so she's hardly going to use a weapon that can be tracked back to him, when she could just buy one off the shelf. If Louisa was killed with that knife, then Ben was in on it.'

'And where did Ben go that night?' asked Richardson. 'If we accept that Caitlin used her hire car to transport Louisa to the woods, then why was Ben's car out and about at a quarter past midnight? We assumed he was no commenting in the hope everything went away, but what if it was because he *can't* explain where he was?'

'We don't actually know what time Louisa was killed,' Pymm reminded them. 'We only have the time her phone was switched off. A phone that's still missing.'

'Ben could have gone out to help with the clean-up in her unit. Or perhaps to dispose of the knife?' suggested Hutchinson.

'Could he have been the one in the hire car when it was caught on camera?' asked Ruskin. 'We're only assuming it's Caitlin driving it. Perhaps he killed Louisa, and then she drove his car and met him?'

Richardson was already shaking her head. 'It was probably too risky for him to go out for too long, in case one of the girls woke up. If they'd come downstairs looking for him, that's the first thing they'd have remembered when they were questioned. And if it was Aunty Caitlin sitting downstairs, that would have blown the whole thing out of the water.'

'We're starting to speculate,' cautioned Warren. 'Let's worry about what Ben was up to when we get him in for questioning again.'

'When should we do that?' asked Sutton.

Warren pinched his lip. 'Let's hold fire for the moment. We haven't got long left on the custody clock, so we need new evidence to justify further arresting him.'

Returning to the whiteboard, he refocused everyone on the timeline.

'We have the hire car travelling out of Middlesbury on its cloned plates after one a.m.,' said Richardson. 'Presumably that was on the way to the forest.'

'We don't see those plates again,' said Richardson. 'The next time we see the car again is when it's travelling back to the rental place on the original plates. Switching plates twice would make it almost impossible to make the link.'

'You said "almost".' Warren looked at her hopefully.

Richardson gave a sigh. 'There are hardly any traffic cameras on that route, and it's after dark, so we'll be dealing with black-and-white night vision on residential CCTV. We'll have to visually check every dark-coloured Ford Focus snapped that night. That'll take days. If you're hoping to identify those plates in case Caitlin has used them again on her own car, I think you'll be in for a long wait.'

'I had to ask,' Warren said, letting her off the hook. 'So we know that she eventually returned the car sometime after 03.52, when it was spotted on the M11, and dropped the keys in the out-of-hours box. Again, we could really do with some footage of that, and how she returned home.'

He stepped back a pace and looked at the two whiteboards. There were lots of gaps that needed filling and they still didn't know how, or if, Ben was involved. An initial forensics report was due on the hire car in a couple of hours, and another status update from Caitlin's flat. Perhaps they would yield something tangible. In the meantime, they could really do with knowing the present whereabouts of Caitlin. Every minute she was missing was a minute that she had to escape further. Or come to harm.

* * *

'Sir, I've just had a very interesting conversation with one of Caitlin's fellow gym users.' Ruskin shrugged off his coat, his brief wince reminding Warren of his injured shoulder.

Warren had almost forgotten that he'd asked him to try and verify Caitlin's claim that she was seeing someone from her gym.

'The front desk told me Caitlin was rather cosy with an Aiden

325

Price; they spend more time chatting than working out, apparently. I got a call to say he'd come in for a swim and snagged him after he finished.'

Warren leaned against Ruskin's desk.

'Price manages the Crazy Caterpillar bar, which is why he's conveniently free during the day. First off, he fits the description given by her neighbour. He's a similar build and age to Ben, with dark hair. He was a bit cagey at first, which is hardly surprising, given he was wearing a wedding ring.'

'I assume that if he works evenings, he isn't going to give Caitlin an alibi?' said Warren.

'Nope. Anyway, he eventually admitted the two of them were having "a bit of a fling". He'd pop back to Caitlin's flat sometimes for a bit of lunch; he blushed, so read into that what you will. His wife is at work during the day.'

'I see,' said Warren. 'And how serious was this affair?'

'He eventually admitted he's been thinking of leaving his wife for some time. He was building up to asking Caitlin if she wanted to make things a little more permanent, but he wasn't sure if she felt the same way.'

Warren raised an eyebrow. 'That would be an interesting turn of events, given her feelings for Ben.'

'That's what I thought,' said Ruskin. 'Perhaps he was her back-up plan if things didn't work out the way she wanted with Ben?'

'I can see what Alex sees in you, you old romantic,' joked Warren.

'Just saying it as I see it,' responded Ruskin with a lopsided shrug. 'But this is the really interesting thing. I asked him whether he thought Caitlin might be seeing somebody else as well as him, and he said the thought had crossed his mind. A few weeks ago, he even tried to have a look at her phone when she was in the shower. He took it out of her handbag.'

'And he saw the texts from Ben?' asked Warren.

'No, that's the thing. He'd seen her using her phone enough

326

times to know that her PIN code was ridiculously simple, 1234 would you believe? He put it in, and the phone wouldn't unlock. He's confident he hadn't made a mistake, because the next time she used it, she definitely typed in 1234. But she took it out of the front pocket of her bag, not the main compartment.'

'She had a second phone,' said Warren.

*   *   *

'Pete Robertson has confirmed that Caitlin's home router has several mobile devices registered to it,' said Pymm. 'Including one of the unknowns that used the Greenlands' wireless.'

'Then that confirms she was visiting their house regularly enough to have the Wi-Fi password,' said Warren. 'If that's the phone Caitlin installed the messaging app on to communicate with Ben, then we could really do with accessing it. I don't suppose the search team have found it?'

'No, and it's only a small flat,' said Sutton. 'If it is there, then God knows where she's hidden it. The place doesn't even have wooden floorboards she could pull up.'

'Then she's probably taken it with her,' said Warren. 'Are you sure there's no way to track the handset now we know its device ID?'

'No, it's impossible,' said Pymm, 'and she hasn't registered the SIM card.'

'What about a cell-site download to work out what phones regularly stayed at her flat?' asked Warren.

'Theoretically possible,' said Pymm, 'but her apartment is in the middle of a residential area. The nearest cell tower would pick up signals from hundreds of devices. We could compare them against lists of all the handsets frequenting the same locations we know she visits, but it could take days to narrow it down.'

Warren hissed in frustration. They needed to find Caitlin now, not in a week's time.

'But I may have an idea,' she said. She looked thoughtful. Warren raised an eyebrow, but she shook her head.

'Let me look into a couple of things – it might not even work.'

'Do what you can.'

Chapter 38

The initial forensics report from the hire car came in after lunch.

'They've found blood in the boot,' said Sutton, who'd taken the call. 'Tiny spots on the carpet covering the spare wheel.'

'There were smears on the doorframe to Louisa's unit,' recalled Warren. 'And a fresh laceration on her temple. If she hit her head when she was Tasered, there could have been transfer when she was bundled into the boot.'

'It was all at the left-hand end,' said Sutton, 'which would make sense if she was curled up in there sideways. Meera says they've sent off for fast-track DNA.'

'Brilliant. Now what about the driver?'

'They're sticky-taping the seats for fibre transfer. It's a bit of a mess, given it's a hire car, but they've already found a couple of red fibres that might match the hoodie she was wearing in the CCTV.'

'Any sign of that hoodie in her wardrobe?' asked Warren.

'No. So either she got rid of it, or she's wearing it now.'

'She might have been worried that some of Louisa's blood got on it,' said Hutchinson. 'Even the paper suits the CSIs wear at crime scenes aren't designed for a full blast of arterial blood. Some might have made it through the neck opening or up the sleeves of the cheap DIY suit she was using.'

'What about fingerprints?'

'Fewer than you'd expect for a hire car,' said Sutton. 'So she obviously took the time to wipe everything down, even though she was wearing gloves when she picked it up. Same for the key fob. What she didn't clean were the wheels. There is mud and leaf litter lodged in the treads and under the arches. The soil specialist is comparing it with the woodland where Louisa's body was found, and the tread patterns are being compared to the tyre tracks on the access roads.'

In his mind's eye, Warren could see the links forming. Louisa linked to the hire car through her blood. The hire car linked to the deposition site by its tyres. And if they could strengthen the connection between the hire car and Caitlin through a good face shot, to go with her driving licence and credit card, then they were nearly there. Now all they needed was evidence showing it was Caitlin who committed the murder or had worked with the person who had done so. The confession, whilst persuasive, needed to be definitively linked back to her. They'd shown it had been printed on Caitlin's laser printer, but a good defence solicitor might claim the fingerprints on the paper could have been from when she loaded it into the feed tray.

'We're getting there,' said Warren.

* * *

'Yes!' Pymm's yelp as she punched the air caught the attention of everyone in the office. 'I've identified Caitlin's second phone.'

'How on earth did you manage that?' asked Sutton, beating Warren to her desk.

'Magic,' said Pymm smugly.

'So that's what you've been brewing in your cauldron,' said Sutton snatching up her glass mug. 'I thought this smelled like the eye of a newt.'

'Funny man,' said Pymm.

The dregs sloshing around in the bottom did resemble something Harry Potter might cook up to ward off evil, Warren thought.

'I went through her bank records,' said Pymm. 'Caitlin had a contract with Vodafone. But I noticed she has also made a couple of small debit card payments to one of those cheap, SIM-only, pay-as-you-go companies. Presumably that was her second mobile phone. I contacted the provider and supplied her bank details. They traced it back to the account she was topping up, and voila, I have her mobile number. They are trying to link it to the handset's IMEI number, so we can still find it if she changes the SIM card.'

'I am definitely calling you Hermione, from now on,' said Warren. 'How long until we get her phone records and location data?'

'The warrant is already on its way,' said Pymm. She picked her mug up again and thrust it towards him. 'Fill that with boiling water, and by the time it's ready to drink, we'll be good to go.'

* * *

Pymm was as good as her word. By the time Warren returned with her noxious brew, she was already accessing the phone's location data.

'Damn, it's turned off.'

'Where was the last location it sent a signal from?' asked Warren.

Pymm transferred the phone's coordinates to a map. The circle was very large. 'It's rural, so there's only one cell tower in range,' she warned. 'It could be anywhere within this footprint.'

'We know she travelled up the A506,' said Richardson, pointing to the road bisecting the shaded area.

'It also overlaps with the edge of Barrington Woods,' noted Sutton. 'Everyone's favourite dumping spot for a body.'

Warren pointed to the timestamp for the last known location.

'It was stationary for over seventeen hours before it left the network. Either Caitlin switched the phone off or its battery died.'

Warren and Sutton looked at each other. 'Unless she chucked her phone out the car window as she drove up the 506, I think she's still there,' said Sutton.

'I'll tell the guv what's going on and organise a search team,' said Warren, already heading towards Roehampton's office; he continued talking over his shoulder. 'Tony, you and Hutch start sketching out the logistics so we can hit the ground running.' He paused. 'And make sure we have a paramedic unit on standby.'

* * *

'The SIM card was first activated a few days after Ben sent her the link to the secure messaging app,' said Pymm. 'She must have decided to keep their relationship a secret.'

'Moray said her boyfriend, Aiden Price, suspected she might be seeing somebody else,' said Warren. 'Perhaps she was worried he might stumble across those text messages with Ben?'

Pymm gave a sniff. 'It's funny how men who cheat on their wives still get jealous when the shoe is on the other foot.'

'It looks as though she only really used the phone's data plan,' said Warren. 'There are practically no text messages or voice calls. She must have been using that messaging app.'

Pymm switched to the phone's location history. 'The phone travelled from her flat to the Greenlands' the night Louisa was killed. It arrived at 20.36 and was then switched off. It was turned back on at her flat at 00.45. I reckon one of them dropped it back at her flat to build an alibi. It wouldn't be a huge detour from the industrial estate. Could that be what Ben was doing?'

'Now we know it was definitely her that the lady across the road saw,' said Warren. 'How did she get there?'

'By some sort of vehicle, judging by the speed her phone was moving.'

'What was the phone doing earlier that day?' asked Warren.

'Not a lot,' said Pymm. 'She only turned it on a few minutes before she left her flat. Before then, it was only on for a couple of hours the day before.'

'And the phone definitely went from her flat directly to Ben's?' he asked.

'Yes.'

Warren pondered for a moment. 'So, she kept it off whilst she picked up the hire car. That would be sensible. Her personal phone never left her flat either.'

'Which gives her another alibi,' said Pymm. 'If you remember, she claimed she stayed in and watched TV that night. Which we now know was definitely a lie.'

Warren turned to Richardson. 'The most likely scenario is that Caitlin drove to the Greenlands' in the hire car and parked it nearby. It wasn't captured on ANPR on either set of plates during that time, so either she drove there and didn't get pinged by any cameras, or she used another set of plates. Either way, we need to place the hire car in the vicinity of their house or her flat.'

'There are a couple of options,' said Richardson. 'We could try and identify if she used a third set of licence plates by comparing cars captured returning from the woods after we believe Louisa was killed, with cars near either residence, but that'll give us a bucketload of hits we'll need to visually verify as being attached to a dark-coloured Ford Focus.

'The other option is to look at the residential and business CCTV we've seized for a dark Ford Focus. Unfortunately, the witness said she was walking from the end of the Greenlands' street that doesn't have any properties with cameras, so we'll need to look at the whole area.'

Warren considered what she'd said. Both options would be resource-intensive, but they weren't time-critical; they would be used to strengthen the case for the trial. 'Do them both,' he instructed. 'I'll get the guv to sign off. There's no need to prioritise them, so that'll keep the bean-counters happy.'

He turned back to Pymm, who had continued scrolling down the location history.

'It looks like she went around to Ben's at least two evenings a week; more frequently over the last month. Each time, it was the same pattern. She turned the phone on during the afternoon, travelled there by vehicle, and then turned her phone off when she arrived. I'm guessing they contacted each other during the day. He then let her know Louisa had left, before asking her over for a bit of slap and tickle? She didn't need her phone when she arrived, so she turned it off.'

Warren smiled at her turn of phrase. '"Slap and tickle?" You've been watching *Carry On* films again, haven't you?'

'Martin's watching them with the kids; he says they need a rounded education.'

'Well, it's not ideal,' said Warren, his tone becoming serious again. 'It'd be better for the jury if she broke her usual pattern of behaviour that night.'

'I'll see what I can find,' Pymm promised.

Warren's phone buzzed.

'They've found her car,' Sutton announced, when the call connected. 'It was parked up a service road to the woods. Not really noticeable unless you were on the lookout for it.'

'Any sign of her?' asked Warren.

'No, but she's left her handbag behind, and the keys are in the ignition.'

Warren's gut tightened.

* * *

The search team had fanned out into the woods; a dog team, exposed to Caitlin's scent from clothing in her laundry basket, was expected within the hour.

'We've found both of her phones in her handbag,' said Sutton, calling from the scene, where he was supervising the loading of Caitlin's Fiat onto a low-loader. 'One in the main compartment, the other in a zip-up section in the front pocket. Both are turned off.'

'Get them to Welwyn ASAP,' instructed Warren. 'Prints and DNA first, then straight to Digital Forensics.' It was the Spring Bank Holiday, but the unit would still process priority crime scenes.

There were still a couple of hours of daylight left, but if Caitlin had trekked more than a few hundred metres into the densely wooded area, they might have to call it a night and start again at dawn.

*   *   *

By half-past eight, it was starting to get dark under the canopy of trees. Forensics had received Caitlin's car, and a team were looking for footprints around where the vehicle had been parked. Unfortunately, the ground was dry, and they hadn't had much luck.

Tony Sutton sat sideways in the driver's seat of his car, his feet on the roadside. David Hutchinson leaned against the closed rear passenger door, drinking a mug of coffee from a thermos. Sutton's bottle of water was still warm from the afternoon sun.

'We'll call it a day in a few minutes,' said Sutton. If nothing else, he didn't fancy going for a pee in the woods again. As if on cue, there came a crackle over the radio. He recognised the voice of the dog handler, Jan Adams. 'Barney's getting excited about something,' she said.

The search leader responded, asking her to stay put for the moment, whilst he sent a couple more officers to join her.

'Could be a false alarm,' said Hutchinson.

'Could be,' agreed Sutton. Nevertheless, he screwed the lid back on the bottle and replaced it in the drink holder. Hutchinson drained his coffee and flicked the dregs into the long grass by the verge.

'Barney's indicating,' said Adams. Over the open radio channel, they could hear whining and branches breaking.

Eventually, Adams' voice came over the airwaves. 'We've found her.'

TUESDAY 28TH MAY

Chapter 39

The forensics team had been at the site since the discovery, with a white crime-scene tent protecting the body from the elements and powerful lights so they could start an initial assessment before dawn. Warren accompanied Professor Ryan Jordan as they hiked through the undergrowth shortly after seven a.m.

'My wife and I loved camping when the kids were younger,' he was saying, seemingly unbothered by the whipping branches. 'We'd fly over to the States, spend a week with my family, then hire an RV and get ourselves lost for a few days trekking through the state parks.' He chuckled. 'Mind you, it was a little different back then. For a start we had no cell phone reception, and we borrowed Dad's hunting rifle in case we annoyed any bears.'

'Don't underestimate the vicious nature of the British squirrel,' joked Warren, noting he was rather more out of breath than the pathologist, who was at least ten years his senior.

They crested a small incline. Tony Sutton was already present, alongside CSM Meera Gupta. After dumping Jordan's bags of kit on a groundsheet the two men climbed into fresh scene suits; they didn't want to bring anything in with them that didn't belong.

'I'll do an *in situ* examination, then get her removed to the morgue,' said Jordan, all business now.

Warren accompanied him into the tented area; it was his first visit to the scene, having relied up until now on Tony Sutton's reports.

Caitlin was slumped against a tree, her head leaning forward. She was wearing the red hoodie seen on the CCTV from the car rental firm, with the sleeves rolled up, and dark-blue jeans. Both were caked in dried blood. Flies were already buzzing around.

'Pending a full exam, it looks as though she did both of her wrists, just to make sure,' said Jordan.

From what little Warren could see of the young woman's face, it was deathly pale; a faint green tinge already colouring it. The pungent odour told of the warm weather.

Leaving Jordan to his work, Warren exited the tent, taking deep breaths of the fresh woodland smell.

'The pill packets have been sent for processing,' said Sutton. 'Prescription sleeping and anti-anxiety meds. The printed label on the box is in her name.'

'And the bottle?'

'Vodka. Not much left; bagged and sent to Forensics.'

'What about the knife?'

Sutton held up his phone. 'A similar size, but different to the one missing from the Greenlands'. And a lot sharper, by the looks of it.'

There would be no arguments in court; the handle wasn't even the same material.

'So, either a different knife was used to kill Louisa,' said Warren, 'or she used the same one and Ben was telling the truth about the one in the knife block being an innocent replacement.'

'Sometimes coincidences happen,' said Sutton.

'Tell me about the flowers,' said Warren.

Sutton swiped to another image.

'A bunch of chrysanthemums. No packaging. The CSIs found fragments of a cut elastic band.'

The flowers were scattered around the body, in no particular pattern. Some had clearly been nibbled.

'There's no way to tell how they were originally laid out,' said Sutton. 'Wind and whatever critters found them have scattered them all over.'

'That's bloody weird,' said Warren. He'd heard of killers feeling remorse and returning to a body to lay a tribute wherever they buried them, but never a person killing themselves and bringing their own flowers.

'Makes you wonder . . .' said Sutton. He didn't need to finish the sentence for Warren to catch his meaning.

'It would explain why she's all the way out here,' said Warren. 'Why come out to the woods to cut your wrists? She lived alone; she didn't have any kids who could stumble upon her body. Why not do it in the comfort of her own bathroom?'

'Could Ben have done this?' asked Sutton.

Before Warren could reply, Jordan stuck his head out of the tent. 'Warren, Tony, you need to see this.'

The two men pulled their face masks back into place and followed him back inside.

Caitlin's body had been turned onto a plastic sheet, ready to be placed into a body bag. It took Warren a moment to see what Jordan had discovered beneath her body.

The flat stone was weathered, with patches of lichen growing across its surface. But the hand-painted crucifix remained visible up close.

Warren looked at Sutton. The flowers, the cross and the location all made sense now.

'Sinead's here,' said Warren.

*   *   *

The presence of Caitlin's dead body ruled out using cadaver dogs to search for any further remains; the whole area would be

341

saturated with whatever molecules the dogs' sensitive noses were trained to detect.

'The ground directly beneath where the body was found has sunk slightly,' said Dr Nina Hamley from the University of Middle England's Geophysics Department. The expert had arrived shortly after lunch. A ruddy-faced, middle-aged woman, she had been almost inappropriately gleeful at the opportunity to put her skills to use.

'There are lots of different ways to find a buried body: ground-penetrating radar, detection of volatile organic compounds and changes in the soil's resistivity,' she said. 'I can call on experts in all of those techniques, but they aren't cheap, or quick. My advice is to stick a spade in the ground there first and see if you find what you're looking for, before opening your wallet.'

The find made sense, in a perverted way. The spot clearly had some significance to Caitlin, and the flat stone was obviously a crude grave marker. Warren suspected Dr Hamley would be secretly disappointed if they found Sinead's remains so quickly, depriving her of an opportunity to try her expensive toys in a field setting.

Passing on her advice to Meera Gupta, he made his way back to Sutton and Hutchinson. They'd spread printed maps across a camping table a few paces from the tent.

'Rachel pulled this from Google Earth's archive,' said Hutchinson. 'It was taken twelve years ago. You can see here that the track Caitlin's car was parked on originally extended much further into the woods, coming to within just fifty metres or so of the body deposition site.'

'I wondered how she had managed to get Sinead so far from the road,' admitted Warren. 'She claimed in the confession that she drugged Sinead before placing her in the boot of Ben's car, and we suspect she clobbered her with the tyre iron. Sinead was the same build as Caitlin, so even if she was still on her feet, it would have been hard work getting her to walk all that way.'

'There are pictures on Facebook of Caitlin playing rugby in university,' said Sutton, 'so she was probably quite fit and strong. I can imagine her carrying Sinead's body in a fireman's lift that distance, but it won't have been easy.'

'It looks as though she refined her technique,' said Hutchinson. 'Louisa was walked to where she was killed, probably with persuasion from the Taser.'

'And she didn't go to the trouble of burying her,' said Warren. 'Assuming that's what's happened of course.'

Hutchinson and Sutton acknowledged the point. Unless Sinead's body was located, they were speculating.

*   *   *

The forensic team had started excavating the earth beneath where Caitlin was found. They'd know within the hour whether Sinead was buried there. Warren reasoned that by the time he got changed out of his paper suit, hiked back to his car, and returned to the station he'd be called back out again if they were successful. That was what he'd told Roehampton.

In reality of course, there was no way he was leaving the scene until they knew for sure if she was there or not.

'The till records show they sold a bunch of chrysanthemums Saturday night, at 21.38,' Ruskin told him. The constable was a little over a mile away at a filling station on the very edge of Middlesbury. Caitlin would have driven past it on the way out to the woods, and Warren had dispatched Ruskin there on a hunch.

'How did she pay?' he asked.

'Cash,' said Ruskin. 'She didn't buy any fuel, so didn't drive fully onto the forecourt and get picked up on ANPR. I guess if you're planning on killing yourself, a full tank of petrol isn't top of your list of priorities.'

'Any video footage?'

'Yes, she paid at the kiosk window. No face shot, but red

343

hoodie, baseball cap, blue jeans. From the height and build, it was definitely her.'

'What about the person serving her?' A bunch of flowers that time of night had to stick in the mind.

'Not available,' he replied. 'She's in Tenerife on a half-term break with the kids. She'll be back Friday.'

Warren sighed. They could always call the woman, he supposed, but she'd be back in a few days. There was no rush; it was obvious what had taken place.

'Get a message to her, tell her to call us as soon as she returns, and chase her if she doesn't get back to you by Saturday.'

* * *

It was Meera Gupta who announced the finding.

'We've found clothing, about a foot down. Looks like blue denim jeans.'

Warren and Sutton joined her in the tent. Hutchinson remained outside and phoned back to the station; it was crowded enough in there.

The two CSIs in charge of the excavation had switched to hand trowels, carefully placing soil into a plastic bucket. The dirt would be carefully sifted for evidence and, depending on the state of the body, fragments of bone or personal effects.

A body buried for such a long period of time would be largely skeletonised, but the body-recovery experts would ensure the coffin the deceased individual finally occupied would contain as much of their earthly remains as they could find. It was the best they could do for her and her loved ones.

Within half an hour, it was obvious that somebody hadn't randomly buried a pair of denim jeans. When they finally uncovered the torso, revealing a stained green T-shirt, with a barely visible logo from the University of Middle England's Irish Society, Warren had seen enough.

Exiting the tent, he relayed their find back to the station, before phoning George Rutherford. The retired detective broke down in tears, as Warren told him that Sinead McCaffrey would finally be returning home.

WEDNESDAY 29TH MAY

Chapter 40

Now that both Caitlin and Sinead had been found, the pressure was off slightly, but they still needed to confirm the sequence of events for the families' peace of mind.

'I'll say one thing about that bright red hoodie of Caitlin's,' said Richardson. 'It makes her a lot easier to spot on CCTV.'

Her screen showed video footage taken outside a café a few doors down from Mandy's Muffins, where Louisa had enjoyed lunch with a woman matching Caitlin's description.

'That's her,' said Sutton. 'The hood's up, but you can see her dark hair.'

'And that's definitely her handbag,' said Richardson.

'It gets better,' said Pymm from across the desk. 'The receipt from Louisa's bag shows that they had sandwiches, coffee and muffins. But I have a transaction on the same day for an amount equal to two more coffees on Caitlin's new card. They obviously made an afternoon of it.'

'She had her hood up at the till, which is why I didn't see her when I first looked,' admitted Richardson. 'She bought her round about forty-five minutes after Louisa paid for their lunch.'

'She probably didn't want anyone to see her and Louisa together,' said Sutton. 'But she should have paid cash.'

'She obviously thought that credit card was untraceable,' said Pymm. 'Which was sloppy.'

'Don't knock sloppy,' said Sutton. 'Sloppy criminals, dog walkers and nosy neighbours are how most crimes in Britain are solved.'

*   *   *

There was no hiding the heightened activity at Barrington Woods from the press, and so a statement had been released to the media mid-morning. It was brief, simply saying that a body had been found and they were waiting for the next of kin to be informed.

Fingerprints had been taken and matched to personal items in Caitlin's flat, and both Warren and Karen Hardwick, who'd interviewed Caitlin recently, were satisfied enough for the local *Gardaí* to have travelled out to see her parents.

No mention had been made of the second body. George Rutherford was preparing to travel to Ireland to keep his promise to Sinead's mother, but he wasn't going until a DNA match had been made. Nobody wanted to make a mistake after all these years.

'The knife found with Caitlin's body doesn't match the chef's set found in her apartment, which has none missing,' said Hardwick. 'However, there was a purchase from a cookery shop on the same credit card she used for the hire car for a sum matching that same brand of knife. It was bought on Monday 15th April.'

'A month before Louisa was killed and the same day they met for coffee,' said Sutton. 'Any CCTV?'

'None from the shop,' said Hardwick. 'Mags has a team seizing footage from surrounding businesses.'

'If she used the same knife to kill Louisa, then that's why we weren't able to find it,' said Warren. 'She must have had it in her apartment.'

'I wonder why she didn't dispose of it when she got rid of

her paper suit?' said Sutton. 'Surely she wasn't planning to kill herself at that point?'

Despite the search team's best efforts, they had yet to recover any bloodstained clothing or protective equipment from Caitlin's apartment.

'It's a lot easier to dispose of clothing,' said Pymm. 'Wrap them in a bin bag and chuck it in a random wheelie bin the day before collection and the bin's owner would probably never even notice. A big, heavy kitchen knife is more obvious.'

'Maybe,' said Warren. It was a small detail, but it nagged him. 'Any traces of Louisa's blood in her flat?' he asked.

'None yet,' said Sutton. 'Nor in the murder box.'

'The knife has been swabbed for DNA,' said Hardwick. 'I'll let you know as soon as we get a result back, but if it's a mixed profile from more than one person, it'll take longer.'

*   *   *

'How's this for sloppy?' Richardson called out. 'That red hoodie keeps on giving.'

Again, the video footage was from the pavement outside a row of shops. The familiar hooded figure walked briskly past the camera, head down, her distinctive handbag over her shoulder.

'This was taken less than ninety seconds before we believe a knife matching the one that killed Louisa was bought from the cookery shop. And this—' she switched windows '—is her walking back.'

Piece by piece, the story of what had happened to Louisa Greenland two weeks before, and Sinead McCaffrey eleven years previously, was coming together, but Warren was far from satisfied. If Caitlin really was responsible for the murder of two women she had once called friends, then her decision to end her own life had deprived their families of the chance to see justice done. There would be no trial, where she was forced to confront and atone for her actions, and no punishment, simply a coroner's verdict.

Her confession gave only the briefest of reasons for her heinous acts and left even more questions unanswered. Robbed of a jury trial, would Louisa and Sinead's families ever find peace?

Chapter 41

Ryan Jordan performed Caitlin O'Shaughnessy's autopsy at lunchtime. The body of what they assumed was Sinead was still being excavated, but she too would be making the journey to his morgue within a few hours. The state of her body, which appeared to be little more than a skeleton, would require the services of a forensic anthropologist.

Even with the air conditioning at full blast, the odour of Caitlin's partially decomposed corpse was noticeable in the morgue. Remembering Louisa Greenland's autopsy, Warren had smeared VapoRub under his nose before joining the procedure. Jordan hadn't bothered and therefore smelled the vodka after removing the contents of her stomach.

'There are pill fragments mixed in with what appears to be a partially digested meal of pasta with tomato sauce,' he said. 'I've sent them off for toxicology.'

Warren simply nodded. He doubted he'd be eating much himself for a few hours.

'I know what you're going to ask,' said Jordan, 'and there's no way to tell when she died. Over twenty-four hours, is the best I can give you.'

Caitlin had last been seen Saturday morning. Her main mobile phone had been turned off that afternoon, and her burner had arrived at the spot where her car was found that night.

'She could have died then, easily,' agreed Jordan. 'As for cause of death, that's a little more complicated.'

Jordan gently turned her left wrist over. 'These cuts were expert, no messing about. No practise cuts or signs of hesitation, she just went straight in. Both wrists. It's extremely effective and would cause death by exsanguination very quickly. But the volume of blood loss isn't as great I would expect.'

'You mean she didn't bleed to death?' asked Warren, with a frown.

'I'll need to do some more tests, and I want a second opinion,' warned Jordan. 'But I think her heart stopped before she fully bled out. That could have been due to the shock of the blood loss, or an underlying heart condition. But it could also have been caused by acute toxicity from her pills and the alcohol.'

Warren felt a chill pass over him. 'If she had taken that many pills, how was she in a fit state to cut her wrists so effectively?'

* * *

Warren made it back to Middlesbury CID in record time; he doubted even the notoriously heavy-footed John Grayson could have done it quicker.

'Ryan also found marks on her wrists that could have been from a restraint of some sort,' Warren informed the team, after telling them of the professor's concerns. 'They weren't from something as obvious as cable ties, and there is no abrasion on the skin from rope or rough cloth, but there was definite bruising. She could have been tied with a silk scarf or something padded to try and avoid leaving marks.'

'So we're saying she was murdered, and it was staged to look like a suicide?' said Sutton.

'Perhaps,' cautioned Warren. 'The toxicology results and the

354

cardiac specialist's examination could reveal that she had a heart attack, or she hadn't taken as many pills as we think. The marks on her wrists could be from a bit of harmless role-play in the bedroom, and the mud patches on her jeans and the bruises on her knees from her stumbling through the woods in the dark. But it's a possibility we need to look into.'

'But killed by who? Ben was in custody,' said Ruskin.

If Caitlin had been murdered, then where did it leave the investigation? All the evidence supported Caitlin being Louisa's killer, but did she have an accomplice who had decided she was a loose end? Had she been coerced into writing the confession letter?

Warren spied Janice making her way towards the group. She wouldn't interrupt them unless it was urgent.

'You placed a flag on Darren Greenland's name to alert you if he came up on the system,' she said.

Warren blinked in surprise. It seemed an age ago that Ben Greenland's brother had been considered a suspect.

'What's he been done for?' he asked. The man was a habitual drug user, with a string of offences primarily committed to feed his addiction. He'd probably been caught shoplifting again.

'He hasn't been arrested,' she said. 'He's in intensive care, after a drug overdose.'

Chapter 42

'He's in a coma,' David Hutchinson reported back, after speaking to the doctors treating Darren Greenland. He'd also spoken to the officers investigating the incident. If Darren didn't survive, then they would be opening an unexplained death investigation, so they were collecting evidence and witness statements with that in mind.

'The story his housemates are telling is that he went out to score some heroin last night and shot up in his room about eleven p.m., with the door left ajar. One of the housemates stopped by his room on the way to the bathroom and saw he was slumped over and had been sick down himself. By the time the ambulance arrived he was in cardiac arrest. They administered CPR and injected him with naloxone at the scene, but it's unclear how much brain damage he suffered.'

'Any indication whether it was accidental, deliberate, or if somebody staged it to look like a suicide?' asked Sutton.

'The housemates claim he was alone all night, although for obvious reasons take that with a pinch of salt,' replied Hutchinson. 'He has a few scrapes and bumps, but nothing to indicate he had been assaulted recently.'

'What about the injection site?' asked Warren.

'Single puncture wound; no evidence he was injected twice in close succession. We'd need a pathologist to do a full exam to see if there are any other fresh needle marks.'

That would be tricky. Assuming Darren didn't die within the next few hours, they'd need a court order to authorise a visit to a still-living patient unable to give consent. By the time that worked its way through the system, any additional injection sites would probably have healed sufficiently to make them indistinguishable from other recent track marks.

'Then let's put that aside for now,' said Warren. 'Which leaves accidental overdose or suicide attempt.'

'He has overdosed before,' offered Hutchinson. 'Both times apparently an accident. But he also has a history of mental illness and has reported suicidal thoughts in the past.'

'If the overdose was deliberate, then you have to wonder what the trigger was?' said Sutton. 'Why now?'

There was really only one obvious answer. Along with the revelations from Caitlin's autopsy, the team needed to cast aside their previous assumptions and rebuild their case.

'OK, folks, unless we have confirmation otherwise, let's operate under the assumption Caitlin was murdered,' said Warren. 'The possibilities as I see it are first, that Caitlin was definitely involved in the killing of Louisa – we have CCTV and bank records linking her to the car used to transport Louisa's body – and that she had an accomplice, or accomplices, one of whom decided she was a potential loose end.

'The second possibility is that she was not involved in the killing of Louisa, but is instead being framed, and a staged suicide is the final step. That flies in the face of the evidence, but we can't dismiss it. It could also be a combination of the two, with Caitlin only playing a minor part in the murder or the cover-up, and her co-conspirators attempting to shift all the blame onto her. Therefore, who were her accomplices?'

'Ben couldn't physically have done it,' said Pymm. 'God knows we still aren't convinced he wasn't involved in either Louisa or Sinead's murder, but Caitlin died after he was arrested. Could his arrest have been the trigger to kill her?'

'Whoever killed Caitlin must have also known about Sinead,' said Ruskin. 'Why else would she have been found where she was buried? That should narrow the suspect pool.'

'So, assuming there isn't somebody we haven't even considered, who does that leave us with?' asked Warren.

'The remaining housemates from Potter Street: Curtis and Stephanie,' said Richardson. 'The other three are dead.'

'And Ben's brother,' said Hardwick. 'We still don't know what he was doing the night Louisa was killed. If you remember, we established he was eighteen at the time of Sinead's death and still living in Middlesbury. We speculated he might have helped his brother dispose of her body. I wonder if he had access to his brother's car back then?'

'If all this is true,' said Sutton, 'then that means Darren has helped his big brother kill or dispose of three women. And perhaps not willingly; he could have helped with Sinead because his brother asked him to, then felt compelled to help him kill Louisa to stop his involvement with Sinead coming to light. Then he had no choice but to kill Caitlin because they needed her to take the blame for both murders and get the charges against Ben dropped. No wonder he's so messed up.'

'I wonder how well known he was to the other residents of Potter Street, back when Ben lived there?' asked Hardwick. 'Obviously, he'll have known Louisa. He would have been about sixteen or so when they first moved in, and it was his hometown. And let's face it, what teenage lad is going to turn down the chance to spend the weekend with four very pretty, older girls? If only for bragging rights at school?'

'Me,' said Ruskin, to general laughter. 'Although, when I was at uni, my housemate's parents thought she could be trusted to give her little a sister a taste of university life. As I recall, it was the seventeen-year-old who talked the twenty-year-old out of going home with a complete stranger, and sat holding her hair in the bathroom whilst she puked.'

'The same thing happened to me at university,' piped up Pymm. '*Obviously*, I was the responsible one.'

Everyone around the table chuckled, before Warren got them back on track. 'Given what we know about the drug taking in that house, it makes you wonder what else he was exposed to?' It was a sobering thought. Darren was hardly a sympathetic character, but one had to wonder if those early influences had started him on his downward path?

'We need to cover the basics,' said Warren. 'Hutch, I want you to take charge of finding out what Darren was doing over the period Caitlin disappeared. Speak to that housemate again; see if she has anything useful. Given the state he's in, she may even be willing to tell us more about what he was up to the night Louisa was killed.

'He must have got his heroin somewhere; work with Carl Mallucci and try and track down his dealer. Also, see if he had any contact with his brother, or any visitors. Given that he's shown no interest in reclaiming the mobile phones we seized when we first arrested him, I suspect he's already replaced them. Rachel, do a full location and history for whatever handsets he had on him or were in his room when he overdosed.

'Karen, I want you and Moray to look into Stephanie's whereabouts. We know she has been in Middlesbury over the past couple of weeks. Moray, talk to your mate in the Met again and dig a little deeper into her alibi for the night Louisa was killed. She was supposedly working that day and had a client call that evening placing her at home. If needs be, go down to London and speak to other residents in her apartment block and her workmates. I'll get DSI Roehampton to smooth things over with the Met and get warrants in place, in case anyone plays silly buggers.

'That leaves Curtis. He lives in France, but we know he has

family in the UK. Rachel, can you check his comings and goings with Border Force? See if you can obtain his phone records; you may need to liaise with Europol. It's a long shot, but if we can place him in this country or establish he had contact with any of our other suspects, we might demonstrate his involvement.'

'He told us he never had a thing for Sinead,' said Hardwick. 'But he admits he did like Caitlin back then. We've only got his word for that.'

'I'll speak to George Rutherford,' said Warren. 'I know he interviewed several of Sinead's other friends when she went missing. If we can track down some of them, maybe they can give us more details about what went on in that damned house?'

'It's like a cross between a bad reality TV show and a soap opera,' said Sutton. 'Was anybody not sleeping with Ben? Speaking of which, what are we going to do about him?'

'I don't know yet,' admitted Warren. 'We don't have enough to justify re-arresting him, and if we bring him in for voluntary questioning, he'll know we don't believe Caitlin killed both Sinead and Louisa. And if he is innocent, we're hounding a grieving husband and taking a father away from two traumatised little girls again.'

THURSDAY 30TH MAY

Chapter 43

The whiteboard in the briefing room had been refreshed with names of those who could have been involved in Caitlin and Sinead's murders, and any cover-up. Warren had added Russell Myrie as an outlier. He clearly couldn't have been involved in Caitlin's death as he'd been recalled to prison, and Warren couldn't see how he could be linked to Sinead's murder. But if Ben had accomplices, then he couldn't be dismissed.

'Curtis travels to and from the UK at least twice a month,' said Pymm. 'The business he works for has offices all over Europe, including London. He comes in on the Eurostar, sometimes just for the day; other times he stays over.'

'Don't tell me he was in the UK the night Louisa was killed?' said Warren.

'Yes, he came over on the Friday night before she died. She was killed on the Tuesday, and he returned to France on the Wednesday.'

'He didn't mention that to me and Karen when we interviewed him two days later,' said Warren. 'What about when Caitlin was killed?'

'Potentially. If she was killed on the Saturday, when the text was sent to Stephanie, he was in the UK, having come in on the

363

Thursday evening. He travelled back to France on the Sunday morning.'

'We need to know his movements when he was in the UK,' said Warren. 'How are his phone records looking?'

'Still waiting for them; it looks like he uses his French-based carrier when he's in this country. I couldn't get a warrant signed until Border Force confirmed his presence in the country and it tipped the scales towards reasonable suspicion. But if he had any sense, he'll have been using a burner.'

'Presumably, he was coming over here for meetings,' said Sutton. 'In which case, you'd expect his company to know his diary.'

'Speak to them,' said Warren. 'He's also here over the weekend sometimes. Was that business or pleasure? Where did he go? Rachel, look into his financials. See if he uses a hire car; we may be able to track his movements around the country. Mags, get onto Transport for London. Unless he used taxis, he probably used the underground or buses after he arrived at St Pancras, so he'll have needed to tap in and out with either his credit card or an Oyster card. Look for any CCTV confirming his movements. Did he go straight to work or are there any periods unaccounted for? Did he catch a train to Middlesbury?'

'I agree Curtis is a viable suspect,' said Roehampton. 'But what's his motive? If he was working with Ben, then it seems strange he'd suggest Ben was committing adultery, or he had been having a relationship with Sinead. That would immediately make us look at him harder.'

'Not necessarily,' countered Warren. 'If Ben's reputation as a ladies' man was as well known as it appears, then he probably assumed we already knew. Telling us makes it seem like he's being open and honest.'

'What if he's trying to frame Ben?' asked Hardwick. 'He may not have realised we'd already arrested Ben on Friday.'

'Why?' asked Roehampton.

'Jealousy springs to mind,' said Hardwick. 'By his own

admission, he was awkward with girls back then. He denied he had a thing for Sinead, claiming to prefer Caitlin, but we don't know if that was actually true. At the time of Sinead's disappearance, he was single, living in a house full of beautiful girls, and his best mate not only has a girlfriend, but he's also sleeping with other housemates that he fancies.'

'So why kill Sinead if he fancied her . . . sorry, stupid question,' said Ruskin.

'Because some men are so pathetic, they destroy what they can't have,' snapped Roehampton. She flushed at the sudden awkward silence.

'So does that include Louisa?' asked Warren, quickly.

'Could be,' said Sutton thoughtfully. 'Perhaps he made a pass at her and was rebuffed? She drove him home drunk from their annual get-together. Maybe something happened?'

'What about Caitlin?' asked Roehampton.

'Again, it could be jealousy,' said Sutton. 'He may have discovered she was sleeping with Ben – another woman he fancies taken by his best mate. Framing her for the two murders he committed would take the heat off him.'

'But all our evidence points towards Caitlin killing Louisa,' said Roehampton. 'Did he team up with her?'

Nobody had a ready answer.

Eventually, Warren broke the silence. 'We're speculating again. Let's follow the evidence. Karen, how are you and Moray doing with Stephanie?'

'We're going to London this afternoon to look into her alibi the night Louisa was killed,' said Hardwick. 'We're also going to visit her apartment to see her neighbours, and try and speak to her colleagues – if they'll agree; you know what solicitors are like. Moray and I are catching the express train down there in an hour.' She grimaced. 'I'm glad we get concessionary travel; an open return in cattle class at such short notice would cover my rent this week.'

'Have you managed to place Stephanie during the period when Caitlin was killed?' asked Warren.

'Most of the time she was at the Greenlands' helping look after the girls,' said Ruskin. 'Unfortunately, she's staying in a B&B without swipe card locks to log comings and goings. The only CCTV is over the reception desk and the front door; you could easily wander in and out the back door without anyone knowing. We're trying to track down any other guests who stayed there, but so far, nobody remembers seeing her.'

That just left Hutchinson.

'Darren's housemates claim they don't know who his dealer is,' he said. 'I guess they aren't going to rat out their supplier.'

'What about your Geordie friend?' asked Sutton.

'She barely remembers the night he overdosed. She took a pretty hard hit herself; she suspects it was either a dodgy batch or was a bit purer than usual. She's pretty shook up; it could have been her.'

'That lends weight to the theory it was an accidental overdose,' said Sutton. 'Unless Darren bought gear for them both, and he was deliberately given something to kill him.'

Hutchinson shook his head. 'She says not. She wouldn't trust him with the money to go and buy it, and even if she did, she wouldn't put it past him to cut it with something to rip her off. I spoke to Drugs, and they are a bit worried about a batch of heroin doing the rounds.'

'That doesn't mean he didn't try to kill himself,' said Warren. 'Do we know how he has been acting recently?'

'No, unfortunately, it isn't really that sort of household,' said Hutchinson. 'Even when they aren't off their faces, they tend to avoid each other. Nobody was surprised he'd overdosed.'

'Can anyone vouch for him the night Caitlin was killed?' asked Sutton.

Again, Hutchinson shook his head. 'They either don't know or don't care enough to risk getting themselves in trouble.'

'Phone activity?' Warren asked Pymm.

'Nothing; as usual, lengthy periods with it switched off, presumably whilst he was out scoring drugs or burgling. Pete Robertson has unlocked the handset he was found with, and no surprise, the address book was almost empty, but he'd installed the messaging app.'

Warren felt as though they were back at square one. A couple of days ago, it seemed as though he would get the opportunity to spend at least a few days with his wife and son before she started her phased return to school teaching. But it didn't look as though he would get the opportunity. Susan would return tomorrow to a house filled with half-built furniture, and she'd be starting her back-to-school preparation.

Sometimes, Warren wondered if the job was worth it.

*   *   *

Professor Nancy Whitmarsh had been friends with Ryan Jordan for over twenty years, which was why he was able to persuade her to take time out of her busy teaching schedule at Cambridge University to assist him in Sinead McCaffrey's autopsy. A short woman with bright purple hair and an easy laugh, she didn't fit the stereotype of a forensic anthropologist, but Jordan assured Warren she was the best in the business.

It was hard to reconcile the sad collection of bones laid carefully on the trolley with the vibrant young woman in the photos in Sinead's file.

'The soil is lime-rich and well drained, so soft tissue is better preserved than it might be,' Whitmarsh said. 'I'll take a wild guess and say the remains have been buried for at least five years. I'll send a sample to the lab for radiocarbon dating, but it'll have a large margin of error.'

'Does that mean DNA is possible?' asked Warren. So far, Whitmarsh had identified the skeleton as that of a female,

367

probably in her late teens to mid-twenties, approximately the same height and build as Sinead. The green T-shirt from the University of Middle England's Irish Students Society had the word "Sinead" just visible, across the shoulders, but he wanted to give her grieving family more concrete evidence. For them to fully move on, they had to be one hundred per cent certain it was her, and not some unfathomable coincidence.

'Should be,' Whitmarsh reassured him, 'or I can extract some from her bones or teeth, now we've done the dental prints.'

She pointed to the pelvis, speaking more to Jordan than Warren. 'As you can see from the pubic symphysis, the deceased had never given birth, but she was pregnant at the time of death.'

It wasn't a surprise, given what they had found out from the university counselling service, but a deep wave of sadness passed over Warren as the anthropologist gently removed the tiny foetus. He looked away for a moment, composing himself. The tiny, frail shape nestled within her hand barely resembled a baby, but still brought back painful memories.

'Approximately seventy millimetres from crown to rump, with some bone ossification,' said Whitmarsh. She rolled her Rs slightly, a throwback to the years she'd spent living in the West Country. 'Probably about twelve or thirteen weeks' gestation.'

'Can you identify the father?' Warren managed.

'There should be enough DNA for a parentage test,' she said.

Sinead had told the counsellors the father was one of her housemates. Ben was the obvious candidate, but this case had thrown up so many twists and turns, he wasn't going to assume anything.

Whitmarsh moved around the trolley. 'The most likely cause of death is a stab to the chest,' she said. 'There is a nick to the sternum that lines up with the hole in her T-shirt. The extensive blood on her clothing indicates she bled profusely from there, so was alive at that point. Assuming the blade penetrated deeply enough, it would have hit the upper left side of the heart, possibly even slicing the aorta. Not survivable without immediate medical intervention.'

'Can you tell what type of weapon was used?' asked Warren.

'I can measure the markings on the bone and get an estimate of the type of blade,' said Jordan. 'But without an intact organ, I can't tell you how deeply it entered, so I won't be able to give an accurate blade length.'

'Whatever you can get,' said Warren. Eleven years had passed since they believed she was killed, so the chances of retrieving the murder weapon were slim, but if they did find something, linking it to the injury would be a powerful piece of evidence.

Whitmarsh continued her journey. She leaned carefully over the skull and pointed to a crack on the left temple.

'Assuming this happened before she was stabbed, it didn't kill her,' she said. 'But with no brain to examine, I can't determine what damage was done. However, this is a depressed fracture from a blunt object, wielded with significant force. She would have been stunned at the very least.'

'Could it have been done by a tyre iron?' Warren asked, recalling the blood retrieved from the tool found in Ben's car boot.

Jordan peered closer using a magnifying glass. 'I'll take a cast and do a comparison, but maybe,' he said eventually.

'Caitlin's confession claimed she had drugged Sinead using her prescription anxiety and sleeping pills,' said Warren. 'She ground them up and disguised the taste with bitter lemon. Is there any way to detect traces of them after all this time?'

Jordan and Whitmarsh looked at one another. 'There are still some fragments of her stomach tissue,' said Jordan. 'I'll speak to the lab.'

Assuming all the tests came back positive, Warren had constructed a potential sequence of events. Sinead had been drugged and taken to Ben's car, after Caitlin had stolen Louisa's keys. The sedated woman had been placed in the boot, and taken to the woods, the vehicle driven up the dirt track perhaps within fifty metres of her final resting place. At some point, Sinead had been further incapacitated by a blow to the head with the tyre iron. Her fingerprints on the inside of the boot and the blood spatter indicated that perhaps the medication had started to wear off by the time they had arrived at their destination.

Still alive, she had been carried, or forced to walk, the remaining distance, before being stabbed through the heart and her body buried in a shallow grave. A flat stone, with a crudely painted cross, had then been placed as a marker.

But questions still remained.

Had Caitlin acted alone, or did she have an accomplice? The grave was almost two feet deep. Digging that, especially in the dark, was difficult. Did somebody else assist Caitlin, or had the hole been dug already? And what about the grave marker? Was that placed at the time of the burial, or did the killer return at a later date, perhaps feeling guilty?

One thing was certain; Caitlin wouldn't be answering any more questions or elaborating on her confession. Which meant it was up to Warren to finish the story and tell Sinead's loved ones what had happened that tragic night.

Chapter 44

It was obvious from the moment Moray Ruskin and Karen Hardwick entered the lobby of Brindstocke and Hellard, that none of their clients were funded through Legal Aid.

'Actually, she's DS Hardwick,' said Ruskin. The receptionist was hardly the first person to automatically assume the burly Scotsman was the more senior of the two officers and he could feel the satisfaction from his female colleague as she opened her warrant card. If the young man behind the mahogany desk felt any embarrassment at his assumption, he didn't show it.

'Smarmy git,' muttered Ruskin as the elevator doors closed. Immediately, the lift whisked them to the fourth floor.

Mason Brindstocke was outwardly polite, but refused to discuss the firm's relationship with Ben. Hardwick suspected he was somewhat uncomfortable with his partner's involvement in her brother-in-law's problems, even if – on paper at least – they had subcontracted his case to a freelancer.

Switching topics, Ruskin asked if it was normal practice for solicitors to receive out-of-hours calls on their home phones. Brindstocke replied smugly that their clients paid generously for such access. Judging by the furnishings and artwork in his corner office, Ruskin didn't doubt it. Unfortunately, Brindstocke refused to name the client Stephanie had been speaking to the night of Louisa's murder without a court order.

Within ten minutes of entering the building they were standing outside again, neither of them having touched their coffees.

'It was always a long shot without a court order,' said Hardwick philosophically. 'Well, judging by the number of photographs on his desk, Mr Brindstocke is an extremely happily married family man,' said Ruskin.

'Or he's overcompensating for a guilty conscience,' said Hardwick, recalling Roehampton's speculation about how Stephanie had made partner at such a young age.

'Cynic.'

She motioned towards the tube station at the end of the street; even at this time of day, a steady throng of passengers was entering and leaving. 'Shall we see how long it would take to get to Stephanie's flat from here?'

There were timetables for the underground network, but they were often a work of fiction. Hardwick wanted to see how long it would really take Stephanie to make it home on a typical evening.

'In a moment,' said Ruskin. 'I have an idea.'

He strode towards a young woman selling copies of *The Big Issue*. Fumbling in his pocket for change, he purchased a copy of the magazine, receiving a smile and a thank you in return.

'That's not a London accent,' he noted.

'Nae too different to yours,' the seller responded with a grin. 'Although I dare say you're from the posh end of town.'

Ruskin chuckled. 'Aye, guilty as charged.' He nodded toward Brindstocke and Hellard. 'Still, posh or no, not too many who sound like us in there, I reckon.'

'I wouldnae know – they rarely speak to me.' She said it lightly, but Ruskin could see it irked her.

'Is this your usual patch?' he asked.

'Yeah, I've got my regulars and there's plenty of folks coming in

372

and out of the tube station.' She smirked. 'Why? Are you thinking of stealing my business? You're dressed a bit smart.'

Ruskin chuckled again, before taking his phone out. 'Do you recognise this woman?'

She glanced at the screen, before looking away. 'Why do you want to know?' she asked, her tone wary.

Ruskin showed her his warrant card. 'I'm just doing a few routine inquiries.'

The young woman squinted at it. 'Hertfordshire Constabulary? And here was me thinking you were from Police Scotland.'

'Sorry to disappoint,' said Ruskin, noticing how, yet again, people automatically clocked him as a police officer. He may as well go back to wearing a uniform and save money on his dry cleaning.

'Anyway, what's happened to her? Is she OK? I haven't seen her for ages.'

'She's fine, Rosie,' Ruskin said, reading her name badge. 'Like I said, just doing some routine inquiries. Did you know her at all?'

Rosie paused, before answering. 'She used to buy from me sometimes.'

'And did you ever speak?'

'Just good morning. Look, these magazines are nae gonna sell themselves.'

'Of course,' Ruskin said. 'Thank you for your time.' He handed over his business card. 'If you think of anything I might be interested in, give me a call.'

Rosie shrugged and mumbled something dismissive. Nevertheless, the card disappeared into her coat pocket.

'What was all that about?' asked Hardwick, as they resumed their walk to the station.

'I'm not sure,' said Ruskin. 'Just a hunch. When I rewatched the CCTV of Stephanie leaving work that evening, I noticed she stopped and spoke to the *Big Issue* seller for at least a minute. She handed over something, but didn't receive a copy of the magazine in return.'

'Could it have been some food, or money?' said Hardwick.

'That's what I wondered, but Rosie claims to have barely spoken to her, which was clearly a lie. She also implied Stephanie buys her copy in the morning.'

'Do you think it's significant?' asked Hardwick. 'The homeless community don't always have a very high opinion of the police; she might not have wanted to answer your questions.'

'Maybe,' said Ruskin, thoughtfully.

* * *

The trip on the underground took Hardwick and Ruskin almost exactly the same length of time as Stephanie's phone on the night Louisa had been killed. The tube gods had been smiling on them, and they had waited only seconds between connections.

'Forty-one minutes, which matches the timetable,' said Hardwick. 'There's no way she could have made any detours without delaying her journey.'

'She could have handed her phone to somebody else to continue her journey and changed lines to King's Cross, then the express train to Middlesbury,' suggested Ruskin. 'But who? We know Caitlin was already in Middlesbury, as was Ben, as far as we can tell. Curtis perhaps?'

'Maybe,' said Hardwick. 'But it's getting complicated again.'

Exiting the underground station, they continued on foot to Stephanie's apartment block.

'Ever feel we work for the wrong branch of the justice system?' asked Ruskin. 'A nice-looking flat like this would be out of mine and Alex's reach in Middlesbury. Add in a tube station within a two-minute walk . . .'

'True, but we take scum off the streets. Brindstocke and Hellard put them back,' said Hardwick. 'I know who I'd rather work for.'

Stephanie's flat was number seven, on the top floor. Hardwick pressed the intercom for flat six. After a few moments, the speaker crackled into life.

'It's the police. We wondered if we could have a word?' she announced.

'Wait there, I'll come down,' said a disembodied voice.

A minute later, there was an electronic click; a security chain prevented the door from fully opening.

'Could we come in?' asked Hardwick. 'We want to speak to you about one of your neighbours?'

'Steph? In flat seven? I had a couple of detectives around here asking questions a week or so ago. Has something happened to her?' He released the chain and headed to the lift.

'Why do you ask that, Mr . . .'

'Polski. Matt. I haven't seen her for ages.' He looked anxious.

'She's fine, just a routine inquiry,' said Hardwick.

'Do you know Steph very well?' asked Ruskin.

Polski snorted. 'It's London, what do you think? I've been here two years and I only know her surname because it's on the buzzer.' It was clearly a well-practised lament. 'In Bolton, if you arrive at the bus stop two minutes early, total strangers know the names of all your brothers and sisters, what you do for a living, and what you had for tea last night, before you even take your seat. Try saying good morning when you get on the underground down here and see the looks you get.

'That's Steph's apartment,' he said, pointing to a door with a metal number seven. 'We share a living room wall.' He suddenly looked unsure. 'Um, if you're going to kick her door in, do I need to see a warrant or something?'

'Don't worry, there'll be no door kicking,' said Ruskin.

Polski opened his own flat and ushered them in, offering them both a coffee.

'Yeah, I can easily hear her TV, if she has it on,' he said as the kettle boiled. 'Not that she's antisocial or anything; it's just the walls are so thin, they may as well be made of paper like those Japanese houses.'

Hardwick took out her pocketbook. 'I wonder if you could go over the evening of Tuesday May 14th again?'

Polski shrugged and took them through what he'd told the Met detectives who'd visited him previously.

'You said you could hear her TV through the wall?'

'Yeah, not too loud, and I had mine on also.'

'And was it on all night, or was it turned on and off?' asked Ruskin.

'I think it stayed on. It went off about half-eleven.'

'Any idea what she was watching?' asked Hardwick.

'No idea. I could tell it wasn't the footie; I was watching that.'

'Do you know if she received any phone calls?' she asked.

He frowned. 'Now you mention it, I did hear a phone ringing. And I heard a voice speaking. It went on for quite a while.'

'Could you tell what was being said?'

'No, the walls aren't quite that thin.'

'Do you know what time it was?'

He stroked his chin. 'About ten? It was during extra time.'

That matched what Stephanie had told them.

'What about her apartment door?' asked Ruskin. 'Do you remember if you heard it at all?'

'No, but I rarely hear it anyway, unless she slams it.'

'Can you recall if she has any visitors?' asked Hardwick.

'No, not really. I only ever see her in the corridor if we happen to be coming out our flats at the same time.'

Ruskin showed him his phone. 'Have you ever seen any of these people?'

Polski swiped through the headshots of Ben, Darren, Russell Myrie, Louisa and Caitlin. He shook his head each time.

'One last thing,' said Hardwick. 'Does she have a car?'

'Probably, but I've no idea what she drives,' Polski replied.

'I don't suppose there's any CCTV?' asked Ruskin.

'Nah. The landlord's been promising to install it for ages.'

Thanking him for his time, the two officers left. There were no other apartments on that floor. The woman in the flat immediately below didn't recognise Stephanie, or any of the photographs

Ruskin showed her, and claimed not to be able to hear anything through the concrete floor.

'I'm not sure today's excursion really justified our time,' said Ruskin, as they settled back into their seats to travel back to Middlesbury.

He swore as the molten lava in his Cornish pasty incinerated the roof of his mouth.

Hardwick took a sip of her can of Diet Coke. 'Well be that as it may, I'm still claiming my subsistence allowance,' she said. 'I should have arrested that pasty seller in King's Cross for daylight robbery.'

FRIDAY 31ST MAY

Chapter 45

Warren was in a little later than usual. Susan had arrived home the previous evening, and by the time he'd returned from work, Niall was already asleep. He'd spent the morning playing with his son, before showering and heading to CID.

Warren had been full of apologies the previous night. Susan was supposed to have been returning to a freshly carpeted house, with a new kitchen and bathroom, filled with recently assembled furniture; all of which had been postponed.

'Listen, I understand,' she'd said. 'You could hardly take time off in the middle of a big case like this to supervise the fitters. Niall's room is finished and so is the office. We can build the rest of this furniture when we put him down to bed. Most of it needs two people anyway.'

If anything, her calm acceptance made Warren feel worse.

'I only need to physically be in work for two days a week; Caitriona is remaining as acting head of department until the end of the year, so the head has said I can work from home for one day a week and do next year's planning remotely.'

'But what about Niall?' he'd asked.

'I already contacted the nursery; they have enough space to take him on for an extra couple of days a week if we need it.'

'I don't deserve you,' Warren had said, kissing her on the lips. 'No, you don't.'

Karen Hardwick opened the briefing with confirmation that, as expected, the knife found with Caitlin had been covered in her blood. There were also spots on the handle matching Louisa Greenland. At least they could stop searching for the weapon now.

Mags Richardson was next to report. 'We've picked up some more footage of Caitlin from the area surrounding the car hire place at Stansted Airport. She chose well. It's a budget company so far from the main airport they offer a courtesy car to pick up people from the terminals and the bus station.'

'What have you found?' asked Warren.

'I have video of her walking across the car park towards the rental office just before she picked the car up at eight-fifteen and, again, walking away from there, after dropping the car off at quarter past four the following morning. There's no sign of her arriving in her own car. But, if she didn't mind a walk, the train and bus stations at the main terminal are less than thirty minutes at a reasonable pace.'

'Could she have caught the train or bus from Middlesbury?' asked Sutton.

'There is a coach service running twenty-four-seven picking up from Middlesbury, and regular train services during the day, although she'd have had to hang around until six a.m. to catch the first return. Alternatively, she could have caught a taxi to the airport stations so she wouldn't need to enter the terminal and risk being on camera.'

'Any footage of her getting on or off the trains or buses?' asked Warren.

'Not yet. Unfortunately, her bag was large enough for a change of clothes or a jacket to cover that red hoodie.'

'What about bank records?' asked Sutton. 'Any payments to train, bus or cab companies?'

'None, but you can buy tickets over the counter at the bus

station or the train station with cash. She could have done so weeks ahead; the timetables never change.'

'Is it worth searching CCTV at the bus and train stations and the airport?' asked Sutton. 'We've no hard evidence Caitlin used either route, or even left and returned from Middlesbury. If she was really devious, she could have come from Cambridge or elsewhere, wearing different clothes.'

'I'll see what the guv says,' said Warren eventually. Roehampton was ultimately in charge of the purse strings; he'd let her make the call. That's why they paid her ten grand a year more than him.

* * *

'The DNA results from Sinead's autopsy are in,' said Sutton. His face was sombre. 'Positive match to the DNA they retrieved from her toothbrush and hairbrush, and familial matches to samples they took from her parents and brother a few years ago.'

Warren gave a sigh. Finally, George Rutherford could travel to Ireland and break the news to her family. Unfortunately, until they had all the remaining pieces to the puzzle, he wasn't ready to point the finger at a possible culprit. But at least her loved ones could move to the next stage in the grieving process.

'There's more,' continued Sutton. 'The parentage test on her unborn baby doesn't match Ben.'

* * *

'According to what she told the university counselling service, the father of the baby was a housemate. She was very clear on that,' Sutton told the briefing. 'We naturally assumed it was Ben, given his reputation and after what we'd been told.'

'But if it wasn't Ben, that only leaves Curtis,' said Warren. 'He helped point the finger towards Ben in the first place, and it was him who claimed Louisa had been locked out of the house, leading us to assume the killer took her spare car keys. But if what Stephanie told us is true about the housemates' open-door policy, then he could have easily swiped them from Ben or Louisa's rooms himself.

'We know he was in the UK when Louisa was killed, and he didn't mention it when Karen and I interviewed him. He was also here around the time Caitlin is believed to have been killed.'

'So what's Caitlin's involvement?' asked Roehampton.

'Unclear,' admitted Warren. 'Curtis told us he had a thing for Caitlin, so she could still be involved in Sinead's killing, if there was some sort of love triangle going on. It's also possible Caitlin genuinely thought Ben was the father – she claims in her confession that Sinead was going to ask the father to be with her. If Sinead was circumspect about his identity, Caitlin could have put two and two together and made five.'

Roehampton rubbed her temples. Warren sympathised; he'd popped a couple of paracetamols himself.

'OK, let's assume he or Caitlin killed Sinead, probably for the same reasons laid out in the confession,' she said. 'But where does Louisa come in?'

'Most obvious explanation is that Louisa had figured things out, and she was killed to stop her talking,' said Warren. 'Another scenario is that Caitlin was jealous of Ben and Louisa's relationship and decided to kill her, just as it said in the confession. I'll admit that her involvement in Sinead's murder is based on what was claimed in there, and circumstantial evidence based on hearsay. But we have plenty of evidence she was a key player in Louisa's death. If Caitlin told Curtis that Sinead was pregnant, they could have conspired to kill her for separate reasons; Caitlin because she thought the father was Ben, Curtis because he thought he was the father. Afterwards, they'd have been bound together by their secret.

'Fast-forward ten years and Caitlin has decided to kill Louisa, and she contacts the one person who can't say no when she asks for help. A couple of weeks later, Caitlin feels remorse at what she's done, and the trouble she's got Ben into, and writes that letter confessing everything. Curtis somehow gets wind of it, so he kills her and hopes we see it as a suicide note.

'Or he decides to pin everything on Caitlin and stages her death to look like a suicide. He isn't mentioned in the confession; either because Caitlin left him out, or he wrote the thing himself.'

'For God's sake, it's not an episode of bloody *Love Island*,' snapped Roehampton. 'He shagged her, she screwed him . . . all based on rumours, hearsay and speculation. What's the *evidence* looking like?'

There was a shocked silence. Warren couldn't remember the last time a senior officer had raised their voice like that at a team briefing. He'd had his share of bollockings from John Grayson over the years – some of them even justified – but they had been in Grayson's office, the door firmly closed.

'Sorry,' said Roehampton. She gave an embarrassed smile. 'I've got a bastard of a headache and the Media Relations Unit are breathing down my neck for a statement to keep the press happy.'

'I've spoken to Redmayne's London office,' said Sutton eventually. 'Apparently, he was over each time for legitimate business, but he sometimes uses his flexi-time or leave to extend his stay over a weekend to visit family or friends.'

'I've received his phone records,' said Pymm. 'The company follows the French rules about work-life balance: no emails or calls outside business hours unless strictly necessary. When he's not on the clock, he turns off his phone and just checks in a couple of times a day. His phone location data doesn't place him anywhere near Middlesbury at the times we're interested in, but it doesn't rule him out either.'

'He travels around London on the underground,' said Richardson. 'He uses his credit card to tap in and out of stations. If he extends his stay, he usually hires a car. His company has an account with Hertz. Employees can use it for personal reasons as long as they pay for it. No sightings of any of the cars he's hired in this area on either of the nights we're interested in, but we know Caitlin had fake plates made up, so that's not conclusive.'

'He hasn't used his bank cards in this area either,' Pymm added.

'Well we certainly have enough to justify questioning him,' said Roehampton. 'Where is he now?'

'He's not in the UK currently,' said Warren. 'But he's expected to attend some shindig in London tomorrow afternoon; he's already booked tickets for the Eurostar. Failing that, do we have grounds for a European Arrest Warrant?'

'I'll look into it,' said Roehampton. 'In the meantime, arrange for someone to meet him at St Pancras. Bring him in voluntarily, if possible, arrest him if necessary. If Curtis is involved in either of the killings, is Ben is off the hook?' she asked.

Warren pursed his lips. 'I don't know,' he admitted. 'There's no shortage of motives, and he still won't explain why his car was spotted that night; that may explain why we haven't found any vehicles linked to Curtis. But Caitlin's confession seeks to absolve him of any blame.'

'If Ben was involved in some way, the conspiracy is even more complicated,' said Sutton. 'I'm not even sure where he'd fit into it.'

Roehampton rubbed her temples again, but her voice remained calm at least. 'I guess we just have to follow the evidence and see where it leads us, and hope somebody finally starts telling the bloody truth.'

SATURDAY 1ST JUNE

Chapter 46

Curtis Redmayne stepped off the eleven-thirty train from Paris and was immediately met by Karen Hardwick and a uniformed constable from Middlesbury. Officers from the British Transport Police were conspicuously present, as were two Metropolitan Police.

He acquiesced immediately to their request to accompany them back to Middlesbury, his face white with shock.

The drive took an hour, judicious use of the unmarked car's lights and sirens easing them through the capital's busy traffic.

'Thank you for agreeing to see us here, Curtis,' said Warren. He was accompanied by Hardwick in the main interview suite. Redmayne had declined the offer of a solicitor and had agreed that he was there voluntarily.

'I'm sure you've heard the news by now,' said Warren, deliberately ambiguous. He knew precisely what details had been revealed to the public and wanted to see if Redmayne knew more than he should.

Redmayne nodded. 'The body you found in the woods is Caitlin. She killed herself.' His voice cracked. 'After confessing in a letter to murdering Louisa. And Sinead.'

That could only have come from Ben or Stephanie; the press

conference hadn't given the cause of death or implicated her in the murder. Stephanie knew of Caitlin's confession to Sinead's killing, but neither she, nor anyone outside of the investigation, knew about the discovery of a second body. George Rutherford would be meeting Sinead's parents that afternoon.

'You knew them both, Curtis, and we are very sorry for your loss,' said Warren. 'We were wondering if you could suggest why this may have happened?'

Redmayne let out a shuddering breath. 'I just can't believe it. I mean Caitlin? I guess I'm not surprised she and Ben were having an affair; I was always a bit suspicious when she stayed in Middlesbury after we graduated. She could have gone to a lot better places than UME for her master's. It makes sense if she was hanging around because Ben was still here.

'But killing Sinead as well? She was her best friend. To think Caitlin was willing to kill two women because she was jealous of them . . . She just never seemed the type.'

'Were you aware that Sinead spoke to the university counselling service because she was pregnant?' asked Hardwick.

Redmayne's eyes widened. 'You are kidding?'

'Caitlin believed Ben was the father.'

Redmayne slumped back in his chair. 'Shit. Was that why Caitlin killed her? Because she was afraid that if Sinead was having Ben's baby, they could never be together?'

The man's surprise seemed genuine. Had Stephanie not told him this particular piece of news, or was he just a good actor? He'd had several days to practise his reaction.

'That's what she claimed in the letter,' said Warren.

Redmayne frowned. 'So why wait until now to kill Louisa? Surely Louisa was as big a threat as Sinead? If she'd killed Louisa back then, she could have had him all to herself for the past ten years.'

'Sinead wanted the father of the child to marry her and bring

390

up the baby in Ireland. Which would have been away from Caitlin,' said Warren, watching the man carefully.

'That might explain it,' said Redmayne, although he still sounded doubtful. 'Ben and Louisa had already decided to stay in Middlesbury after university, and Caitlin had signed up for her master's; I guess she figured she could keep sleeping with Ben, even if Lou was still on the scene.' He dropped his head into his hands. 'I always said Ben's dick would get him into trouble; and now three people are dead because he couldn't keep his fucking flies done up.' His voice was bitter.

'You told DS Hardwick and I in your last interview that you weren't really into Sinead; you had more of a thing for Caitlin,' said Warren. 'Do you still have feelings for Caitlin?'

Redmayne gave a bitter chuckle. 'No, that was a long time ago.' His face fell. 'Why? You don't think she told me about what she was going to do?'

Warren said nothing.

'I live in France, for God's sake. I see her once a year at our reunion. I hardly even speak to her.' He fumbled in his pocket and pulled out his mobile phone. 'Here, check my phone records.' The indignation seemed sincere. But then, if he hadn't used that handset to contact Caitlin, he was probably confident there was nothing incriminating on it.

Warren took it.

'Do you have any other phones?' asked Hardwick.

'Just my work phone, but I can't give you that – it has sensitive business information on it. You'll need a warrant.' Redmayne shifted uncomfortably. 'Look, I don't know why you think I'm involved. I really don't. Why have you brought me in?'

'On the day we found Caitlin's body, we also found a flat stone that appeared to be a grave marker,' said Warren.

Redmayne looked at him, his eyes full of confusion. Or was it fear?

'We dug into the soil underneath where we found Caitlin,' continued Warren. 'And found a second set of human remains.'

Redmayne gave a sharp intake of breath. 'You found Sinead?' It was half question, half statement.

'Yes, I'm afraid so.'

Redmayne looked stunned. 'My God,' he whispered quietly. 'After all these years. Have you told her poor mum?'

'We are in the process of doing so. DS Rutherford is breaking the news,' said Warren.

'Good,' said Redmayne. 'He was always so kind; it's only right that he does it.'

'We've confirmed she was pregnant,' said Ruskin.

Redmayne looked up; a shadow crossed his face, as he searched the faces of the two officers.

'Is this really why I'm here?' he asked.

'We believe it was your child,' said Warren. 'Curtis Redmayne, did you kill, or do you have any knowledge of the circumstances leading to the murder of Sinead McCaffrey?'

Redmayne's jaw dropped. 'No of course not!' he managed eventually.

Warren continued. 'Why didn't you mention to DS Hardwick and I that you had travelled to the UK shortly before Louisa Greenland went missing, and then returned to France immediately after? It was barely forty-eight hours before you travelled over to be interviewed.'

A look of dawning realisation crossed Redmayne's face. 'No comment,' he stuttered.

'Did you kill, or do you have any knowledge of the circumstances leading to the murder of Louisa Greenland?' asked Warren.

'No comment,' he said, his voice trembling. He'd started to breathe more heavily. Beads of sweat appeared on his brow.

'Why did you take personal leave between Friday 10th and Wednesday 15th May?'

'I want a lawyer,' Redmayne managed.

After suspending the interview, Hardwick accompanied Redmayne to the custody desk. Warren met Sutton in the corridor; Sutton was slightly out of breath.

'Ben Greenland's just walked into reception. He's in a right state, insisting that he needs to speak to you right now. He says the guilt's eating away at him and he needs to tell the truth.'

Chapter 47

Ben Greenland had been clear that he didn't want his solicitor. 'She'll just keep on telling me I have to "no comment" and I don't want that. I have to tell you everything.'

Warren made certain to get that on tape and was extra careful to ensure Greenland understood his rights.

'I know you think Caitlin killed Sinead and Louisa,' he said. His eyes were red-rimmed again. 'And when Steph told me that Caitlin had killed herself and confessed to everything, I was shocked. I couldn't believe it.'

He took a gulp of his water.

'Steph told me about how Caitlin had killed Sinead because she was jealous.' He looked at the tabletop. 'You were right. I did sleep with Caitlin . . . and I was also sleeping with Sinead.'

His neck had flushed red, the colour spreading up his face to the tips of his ears. His voice when he spoke again was rough with shame.

'I was a shit. I admit it. I loved Louisa – honestly I did – but I couldn't help myself.'

He wiped his nose with the back of his hand.

'It's not an excuse, but I was young, and I was at university. I went to an all-boys school; I didn't have any sisters, and all my cousins were boys. Girls . . . well they were just objects you know? I barely knew any until sixth form, and even then, there were only a handful, bussed in from the girls' school because they didn't offer some subjects.' He snorted derisively. 'They weren't even in any of my classes.' He let out a shuddering breath. 'I look back and I'm amazed any of them stuck it. It must have been horrible for them; it was like a bloody zoo. And the way we used to talk about them . . . if they turned you down, they were frigid. If they did date anyone, they were slags.'

He sipped his water again.

'I was short and skinny and had bad acne, so I never got a look-in. But by the time I got to uni, I'd had my growth spurt and the acne had gone. I hit the gym, and it turned out I was actually quite good at football. I joined the university team and it was just like being back at school. "Toxic masculinity" is the phrase they use today. It's a good description.'

He looked up, meeting Warren and Sutton's gaze. 'There was never any talk about violence or anything like that – I want to make that clear. But the football team were popular, you know? And we had a sort of league table . . . We called it being awarded a cap.'

He cleared his throat. 'I met Lou in my first week. She was on the same corridor in halls. She was lively and fun, and yeah, she was dark-haired, pretty and Irish, which I've always liked. Steph was quieter, and with them looking so similar, I suppose that made Lou seem even more bubbly by contrast.

'We got together after a few weeks. But there was pressure you know? Plenty of the lads on the team had steady girlfriends, but they were still getting caps. Sometimes they got away with it; other times they got caught. But it was just a laugh.' He looked embarrassed again. 'Except for the poor girls of course.' He fell silent.

'What about Caitlin and Sinead?' prompted Warren.

'They lived on our corridor as well. I'd never really spoken to them, although I'd noticed them of course. Then Lou and Steph joined the Irish Students Society and we started hanging out with them. Sinead was very quiet at first. She'd come straight over from rural Ireland and I guess she was a bit naïve; until she got a few drinks inside her. Caitlin was the opposite. She loved a party as much as Lou, and she took Sinead under her wing a bit.' He gave a sad sigh. 'But with Caitlin, it was a bit of an act. Deep down, she was quite insecure. I was getting some stick off the lads for not getting many caps, so when Lou and Steph went home for a week over Easter, I got drunk with Caitlin and well . . . you know. It was all consensual,' he added hastily. 'Anyway, the university rooms were tiny with single beds, so Lou and I often went back to our own rooms to get a good night's sleep. Caitlin would come into my room late at night, and she would end up staying. It was exciting; sneaking around late at night.'

He sipped his drink again.

'When it came to the second year, we found a great six-bed house down Potter Street. Curtis needed somewhere and Lou asked Caitlin and Sinead to join us.' A self-conscious smile crossed his face. 'Seemed perfect. Lou and I were getting more serious, but we still had single bedrooms, so again, we usually went back to our own rooms if we wanted a decent night's kip. Caitlin's room was a bit isolated at the back of the house on the ground floor, so I used to sneak down there sometimes.' He cleared his throat. 'The . . . arrangement worked well.'

'What about Sinead?' asked Sutton, his gaze boring into the man's eyes.

Greenland shrank into his seat and cleared his throat again.

'If anything, the lads on the football team got worse. They used to refer to the house as "Ben and Curtis's Harem". I guess I felt I had to live up to that . . .'

Warren and Sutton said nothing, just stared at him.

Greenland coughed. 'Sinead was a bit . . . unworldly. She wasn't a virgin, but she was still shy. And vulnerable . . .'

He raised his eyes to meet their gaze. 'I'm not proud of what I did, even though I acted that way around the lads on the team.' He gave a shaky sigh. 'It's been eleven years and I need to come clean. Sinead was a different person when she'd had a drink. Especially if she'd also been smoking weed. The first time it happened was the Christmas of our final year. Lou and Steph had already gone back to their parents – their folks were divorced, so they had to do the whole two-families thing. Caitlin had flown back to Ireland – I can't remember what Curtis was doing. Sinead wasn't due to fly back home until Christmas Eve. My family lived in Middlesbury, so I offered to keep her company, so she wasn't alone in the house, you know?' He broke off, knowing that neither of the two men opposite him believed his motivations had been so chivalrous.

'Anyway, one thing led to another . . .'

'And you were awarded another cap,' said Sutton.

Greenland winced. 'I just thought it was a bit of fun . . . I didn't realise it was more than that to Sinead. She was lonely; she missed Ireland, and I guess she was struggling even more than we realised.'

'And did you know that she fell pregnant?' asked Sutton.

Eventually, he nodded. 'She told me two weeks before she disappeared.'

'What did you do?'

He raised his eyes. 'I panicked. I was already looking to move in with Lou when we graduated. I didn't know what to do. I knew an abortion was out of the question. I felt trapped.'

'Did Louisa know?' asked Warren.

He shook his head vigorously. 'No. She had no idea. And I never told her.'

'What about Caitlin?' asked Sutton.

He let out a breath of air. 'At the time, I thought not. But in the days before Sinead disappeared, she was a bit strange around me. I started to wonder at the time if she suspected something, but then Sinead disappeared, and it all got sort of forgotten.

'What happened to Sinead was a wake-up call. For years, I

blamed myself for her disappearance. I genuinely believed she'd killed herself, and I thought it was my fault. I broke up with Caitlin and focused on my relationship with Louisa.'

'How did Caitlin take that?' asked Warren.

'Not well. She never said she knew I had got Sinead pregnant, but looking back, she was never quite the same with me.' He snorted. 'For years I was scared she'd say something to Lou. They were best friends; I knew she had stayed in Middlesbury because she thought we could be together behind Lou's back. At twenty-one, that seemed the perfect arrangement. After what happened to Sinead, she was a little too close for comfort.'

'Do you think Caitlin killed Sinead?' asked Warren.

'No,' he said, but his voice sounded uncertain.

'You do realise that you've admitted to the perfect motive to kill Sinead, don't you? Along with Caitlin?' asked Sutton.

Greenland nodded miserably.

'And that our forensics strongly indicate Sinead was taken away in your car.'

Again, he nodded.

Warren glanced at Sutton. It was time to shake things up a bit.

'Shortly after we found Caitlin's body, we made another discovery. We found a second set of remains that we have positively identified as Sinead. She was murdered by a single stab wound to the chest, in the same manner as Louisa.'

The change in Greenland's complexion was so sudden, Warren pushed his chair back, ready to grab him if he fell off his seat.

Greenland took a deep breath and gripped the table.

'You've found her?' he repeated.

When Warren confirmed it, he burst into tears.

*   *   *

Greenland finally came to his senses and asked for a solicitor. A duty solicitor this time. It broke the questioning cycle and

Warren worried he would go back to no commenting, but it was his right, and truth be told he'd feel safer knowing every box had been ticked. He honestly didn't know where the man was going, and he didn't want a future barrister questioning his procedure.

In the meantime, he and Sutton met up with the rest of the team.

'Curtis's solicitor is on their way,' said Hutchinson.

'What's your current hypothesis?' asked Roehampton.

'Ben didn't seem confident when he said he didn't believe Caitlin could have killed Sinead,' said Warren.

'Do you think *he* could have killed Sinead?' Roehampton pressed.

'Again, impossible to say,' said Warren.

'He went as white as a sheet when we said we'd found her body,' said Sutton. 'But if he is innocent, he's spent eleven years believing she killed herself because he got her pregnant. That must be a shock to the system.'

'If he did kill her, you'd think he'd have been all over Caitlin's confession,' said Warren. 'It pretty much hands him a get-out-of-jail-free card. Is he sophisticated enough to play hard to get? To make it seem more convincing?'

'Where does this leave Curtis?' asked Roehampton. 'He was on that same nasty little football team, as I recall.'

'He seemed genuinely shocked when we revealed Sinead's baby could be his,' offered Hardwick. 'But again, he's had eleven years to practise his response.'

'And we haven't even touched on Louisa and Caitlin,' said Sutton. 'We're assuming Sinead's killing is directly linked to Louisa's killing, with Caitlin's death following on. But what if they are distinct events? Ben, Curtis or Caitlin – or any combination – could have killed Sinead. Then perhaps Louisa could have found out about it?'

'I'm going to keep quiet about our suspicions that Caitlin was murdered,' said Warren. 'If the killer or killers thinks they've got away with it, they may slip up.'

'There is another possibility,' said Hardwick. 'What if Louisa killed Sinead?'

There was a long pause.

'We know she had access to Ben's car keys,' said Sutton.

'And she would have a hell of a motive,' said Warren. 'It seems everyone in on the secret believed the father of Sinead's baby was Ben.'

'And then what?' asked Roehampton. 'Ben killed her when he found out? Perhaps with the help of Caitlin? Who he then killed to cover his tracks? And pinned the blame for Sinead's death on Caitlin also?'

'The killer staged a suicide for Caitlin,' said Ruskin. 'Why not do the same for Louisa and not involve Caitlin at all? It just adds another layer of complexity.'

'Caitlin must have been a loose end,' said Sutton. 'These guys have all been meeting up every year since it happened, and by all accounts getting plastered. Could the killer have let something slip?'

'And Ben and Caitlin have been seeing each other,' Richardson reminded them. 'We know she was in the Greenlands' house the night Louisa was killed, and there is a ton of evidence indicating that if nothing else she helped the killer prepare.'

'All of this still works if Curtis was the killer,' said Sutton. 'Sinead's pregnancy would have upended his future plans also. We really need to rule him in or out of this.'

'I think we should give him the opportunity to explain himself, then verify,' said Warren. 'If we get a sniff that he's lying, we'll arrest him on suspicion of all three murders.'

'And what about Ben?' asked Roehampton.

'He's asked for a solicitor,' said Warren. 'We're on a sticky wicket, given that he's already been charged and then the charges were dropped. We'll need compelling evidence to justify arresting him again. We'll try playing him off against Curtis to see what his response is.'

Roehampton frowned. It was a risky strategy. Ordinarily, interviewers went in with a clear plan of action, their questions previously decided, often with an expected answer in mind. This case was completely open. They had no new forensic evidence pending; most of what they did have pointed towards Caitlin, who was not there to give her side of events.

'Do it,' she said.

* * *

Curtis had finished his conference with his solicitor.

'My client, Mr Redmayne, is shocked at the events that have taken place over the past fortnight and believes he can give you everything you need to clear things up.'

It was clear from the solicitor's tone of voice that she'd rather he no commented and made Warren and Hardwick do all the legwork.

'OK, let's start with Sinead, shall we,' said Warren. 'Was the baby yours?'

'It could be,' he admitted. 'Do you know how old the . . . foetus was?'

'We believe twelve to thirteen weeks,' said Warren. 'Probably conceived within the first or second week in January.'

'Yeah, that would be about right.' His voice caught. 'Sinead and I . . . well it only happened the once. But I guess that's all it takes.' He sniffed. 'I was having a difficult time. Work was mounting up, I was getting stick off the lads on the football team; it was all a bit much. Sinead – well she was also having problems. It was a weekend. Lou and Ben were away. I don't know where Steph and Caitlin were. I'd got hold of some really good weed, and Sinead had a bottle of Irish whiskey. We were just talking, you know? About stuff. Eventually, we went to her room, because it was more comfortable than sitting at the kitchen table. I don't know how it started, but we ended up in bed.'

He looked down at the table, embarrassed. 'Neither of us

ever said anything afterwards. Or at least I don't think she did. I never told anyone.'

'Did you claim your cap?' asked Sutton.

Redmayne flinched. 'How did you know . . .?' He shook his head. 'No. I was never a part of that.' His face twisted. 'I hated that team. I went to a mixed school; some of my best friends were girls and I have a sister. The way they spoke about women in the locker room or on nights out was disgusting. Rugby teams get a bad rep for their loutish behaviour, but they are perfect gentlemen compared to those throwbacks.'

'But you carried on playing anyway?' said Warren.

Redmayne flushed pink. 'I know I should have left. But I loved playing football; I always have. I still play now. I was going to quit and try and find a local team, but they needed a striker and Ben begged me to stay. He was my best mate . . .'

'And Ben took part in this *league*?' asked Sutton.

'Yeah. He really wanted to be one of the lads. I used to keep my head down, but he was fully into it. I can't remember how many caps he had, but it was well into double figures. Lou didn't really like the others on the team, so she only came out with us if we had a big win. Otherwise, we'd go clubbing after a match, and he could do what he liked. The lads on the football team were always popular you know?'

'Did you know Sinead was pregnant?' asked Warren.

'No. I swear I had no idea. I wouldn't say I forgot about our night together, but I never really thought anything came of it. It was a bit awkward for a couple of weeks, but that was it.'

'What was your relationship with Caitlin, back then?' asked Warren.

'Just friends,' said Redmayne firmly. 'If you're thinking she was jealous of Sinead, then you're barking up the wrong tree.'

'You realise it's difficult to believe you?' said Warren. 'After all, you lied to us about Sinead when we first asked, and admitted you preferred Caitlin.'

'I was confused back then, but I swear I never slept with Caitlin,' Redmayne admitted. 'Look, if it helps, I'm happy to take a DNA test,' his throat caught. 'To find out if the baby was really mine.'

'Who else's would it be?' asked Warren.

'Ben's. I told you before that I heard his voice in her room a few times. She never said anything, and he didn't either, but it was kind of obvious.'

'And what did you feel about that?' asked Sutton.

'Nothing really. Sinead and I really were just a one-night stand. It shouldn't have happened . . .' His voice petered out as the full ramifications of what had occurred finally hit. 'This is my fault,' he said, his voice filled with mounting horror. 'All these years, I've thought that if Sinead did kill herself, it was because Ben treated her so badly. But now I realise that if she was pregnant with my baby, maybe this was the whole trigger . . .'

'Why do you say that?' asked Warren quickly, not giving him time to think up a lie.

'It's obvious, isn't it? Caitlin must have thought Ben had gotten Sinead pregnant. Maybe Sinead even thought he *was* the father. Caitlin didn't want him to move to Ireland with Sinead, as she was planning on sticking around in Middlesbury to do her master's to remain near Ben. So she got rid of Sinead . . .'

'You realise we only have your word for this?' said Warren.

'I don't know what I can do to prove I didn't kill her,' said Redmayne, his voice desperate.

'I would remind you again that Mr Redmayne doesn't have to prove anything,' interjected the solicitor, who until now had been scribbling notes, saying nothing.

'Of course,' said Warren. 'Let's move on then, shall we?'

'Caitlin claims to have killed Louisa,' said Sutton. 'Why would she do that?'

'I have no idea,' said Redmayne. 'Perhaps she decided to get rid of her, so she could have Ben to herself?'

'But why now?' Sutton asked.

'I don't know,' said Redmayne.

Warren leaned back in his chair. 'We have a different theory. You see, we believe Caitlin was involved in the killing of both Louisa and Sinead, but that she may have had help. Sinead falling pregnant was inconvenient for you if you were the father, and Caitlin if Ben was the father. So getting rid of her solved both of your problems.'

'No, that's not what happened!' said Redmayne.

Warren ignored the interruption. 'Now, fast-forward to today. Caitlin and Ben are sleeping together again, but Louisa wants to move away from Middlesbury for a fresh start. Maybe she suspects something, maybe she doesn't. Caitlin knows that if they do move away, her cosy little arrangement with Ben will come to an end. But she needs a helping hand, so she calls on her old mate Curtis, the one person she knows is bound to help her, because he has a secret he shares with her.'

'No, no, no. None of that happened,' said Redmayne, shaking his head violently.

'Where were you the night Louisa was murdered?' asked Sutton. 'Don't claim you were in France, because we know you came in on the Eurostar on the Friday and left again Wednesday morning, the day after she was killed.'

'I was in Cheshire,' he blurted. 'I came over for meetings on the Friday. Then I caught the train to my parents'. It was their wedding anniversary that week. We had a family party on the Saturday, then I stayed over and took them to their favourite restaurant on the Tuesday night, which was their anniversary. I travelled back on the train Wednesday morning and was back in the Paris office by lunchtime.

'Look, give me my phone back. All my train tickets are electronic. I have photos from the whole weekend; I even WhatsApped them to my cousins. You can check them.'

Warren took the phone out of the sealed evidence bag, making certain he recorded what he was doing. 'You'll need to give me the PIN,' he said, not willing to hand the phone over in case Redmayne deleted anything or triggered it to wipe clean.

Redmayne recited the number.

It appeared to be as he'd said. Sutton noted dates and times.

'What about last weekend?' asked Warren. The time when they suspected Caitlin had been killed.

'My cousin's twenty-first. Again, a family party in Liverpool. I came in on Friday and left Sunday. We stayed over at the hotel; it was on the Saturday night.'

Again, train tickets and a glut of photographs.

Warren returned the phone to the bag and resealed it, before signing the evidence log. He looked at his watch. 'We will need to verify what you've just said,' he told Redmayne. 'I'd appreciate it if you don't leave the building.'

'Mr Redmayne is not under arrest at this time,' interrupted his solicitor.

'No, it's OK,' said Redmayne. 'The sooner this is all over the better.'

*   *   *

Warren arranged for Redmayne's phone to be couriered to Welwyn so the Digital Forensics Unit could verify the legitimacy of the train tickets and the photos. In the meantime, he tasked Rachel Pymm to organise a team to check the times matched his alibi. If they could rule Redmayne out now, it further narrowed the focus of the investigation.

'How are we doing with those other lines of inquiry?' Warren asked. He took a mouthful of coffee, scalding his tongue as he did so.

'I've got teams scouring the CCTV from the car hire,' said Richardson.

'Forensics have confirmed that Caitlin's fingerprints are only on the first sheet of her confession,' said Ruskin. 'It's not impossible to handle a sheet of paper without leaving prints, but it's awkward. The positioning of the print on one side of the first sheet could be from where she loaded a pile of paper into the printer's tray. But she supposedly signed the last page; I don't see how you could do that without leaving prints.'

'It doesn't make any sense that she would wear gloves to handle a confession,' said Sutton. 'Also, they have been unable to find the suicide note on her laptop's hard drive. Even if she didn't save the file when she finished writing it, autosave was activated, so there should be a temporary file on there. Pete Robertson reckons it's possible the confession was written on a different laptop, which was plugged into the printer with a USB cable, to ensure that the printer marks matched those found on the letter.'

'So who wrote it?' asked Warren.

Chapter 48

Ben Greenland spent less than an hour with the duty solicitor before signalling he was ready to speak again. Warren and Sutton re-entered the interview suite, fully expecting to be met with a wall of no comments.

To their surprise, Greenland had handwritten several sheets of notes. Warren was intrigued and decided to let him say his piece before they started working through their own questions.

Greenland cleared his throat several times before starting. He began by repeating his denial that he had anything to do with Sinead's murder, again expressing surprise that Caitlin had confessed. He then moved on to the subject of his wife.

'Our marriage was in trouble. When she started P@mper, I was pleased for her. We knew it would be hard work and that we would have to take some risks. We remortgaged the house to raise money to start the business and pay for the rent on the industrial unit. However, we had only been paying the original mortgage for a couple of years, so it didn't raise very much capital. It's a crowded market, with a lot of competition from sellers who pay for five-star reviews. Louisa was determined not to do that, and I fully supported her. After twelve months, P@mper was only just breaking even and it was difficult living on my earnings alone.

Louisa was sleeping in the spare room so she could work late, and our relationship was strained.'

He cleared his throat again and turned the sheet over.

'It was at this time I bumped into Caitlin on a night out after a football game. Although we had been seeing each other socially, it was always through Louisa, who was still her best friend. I thought that part of our life was over, and I hoped Caitlin wouldn't ruin her friendship with Louisa by telling her what had happened at university. Caitlin had a number of boyfriends over the years, but never really found "the one". That night we were both drunk and ended up back at Caitlin's flat. I thought it would just be a one-off, but she texted me a couple of days later. Louisa was at work, and I couldn't leave the girls, so Caitlin came over. She left before Louisa came home. It soon became a regular thing. Louisa usually texted me to tell me she was on her way home, but we had a couple of near misses.'

He coughed and turned to the next sheet.

'You are right. I was considering leaving Louisa.' He looked up and met the two officers' eyes. His voice caught. 'Despite what you must think, I genuinely did love Louisa and I wanted our marriage to work; to get back to the way we were before Louisa lost her job after her drink-driving conviction. The Holistics Gym contract seemed to be the answer. Louisa would need money to buy materials, and she claimed she got an extension to her business loan from the bank. I believed her at first, but she started acting strangely.

'When we all met for our annual get-together in April, she spent a lot of time speaking to Curtis. It was a really intense conversation. A couple of days later, he phoned her – I saw his name come up on the caller ID. When she left the room to take the call, I thought maybe they were planning something for my birthday. The girls were squabbling, so I couldn't overhear. When she came back, it looked like she had been crying, but she wouldn't say anything and she didn't hand the phone over so I could speak to him before she hung up, which was unusual.'

408

'Did you ever find out what the call was about?' asked Warren. Curtis Redmayne had claimed Ben didn't know about the bank's refusal; he wondered if Louisa had ever admitted she had asked him for a personal loan.

'No, but I have my suspicions.' Greenland took a deep breath. 'Louisa had been talking about moving to Leicester. My company is opening a new branch in a few months. I'd been given a nod and a wink that if I were to apply for the role of office manager, I'd be in with a very good chance. House prices are cheaper and there is a new industrial estate with better lock-ups and lower rents. The promotion would come with a significant pay rise. I was in two minds. On the one hand, it made perfect sense. On the other hand, I like living in Middlesbury. All my friends are here.' He looked away. 'Caitlin is . . . was . . . here.'

They gave him a moment to compose himself. His solicitor suggested a short break, but Greenland dismissed the suggestion. 'I need to do this,' he said.

'Louisa had become very secretive about P@mper. She would change the conversation every time I asked about it, so one night, I went into the office and looked through her filing cabinet. I found the letter from the bank. I couldn't believe she had lied to me. And that phone call with Curtis then made perfect sense. I think she asked him for a loan, as a mate, and he turned her down.' He sniffed. 'You've seen the letter with the reasons why they didn't give her the extension. I imagine that after he'd seen her figures, Curtis felt the same way.' He snorted. 'You don't become that rich without knowing a shit investment when you see it.'

He wiped his nose on his sleeve. 'I know that I'm a hypocrite. I have lied to my wife since before we were married; I couldn't tell you how many women I've slept with. And yes, I look at pornography when she is at work. And the worst thing is that I'm confident she has never been unfaithful to me; not once. No matter what my brother might claim.

'But this was a betrayal that could cost us everything. If those

409

hampers didn't sell, and Holistics Gym returned them, we'd be bankrupt. We'd have to sell our house; our daughters would be homeless. If Mum had to bail us out, it would tear our family apart. There's no way she could refuse to give money to Darren as well, and he'd be dead within weeks.'

'So what did you do, Ben?' asked Warren quietly.

'I didn't know *what* to do. I wanted to confront Louisa, but I was scared of what might happen, so I spoke to Caitlin. She urged me to consider all my options and sent me a link to a website giving free legal advice.

'I realise now that Caitlin was hoping this would finally destroy our marriage. She was becoming more pushy, and our text conversations were getting more intimate. I was paranoid Louisa would stumble across them. I heard about a man whose wife unlocked his phone using his finger when he was asleep. I then read about a secure messaging app that was better than WhatsApp, so I installed it. I suggested Caitlin did the same; I knew she was seeing someone else, and we didn't want him finding out about us and causing problems.' His voice became quiet with shame. 'I also installed some tracking software on Louisa's phone one night when she was asleep, so I would know if she left the industrial unit without texting me.

'The thing was, I felt frozen. It was like when Sinead told me she was pregnant. I didn't know what to do. Louisa had left us in a position where if I left her, we would be jointly liable for the second mortgage on the house. Louisa would be bankrupt, and as the main breadwinner, I'd probably have to pay her maintenance plus child support. The only way I could earn more money is to take the job in Leicester – but what about the girls? You know how the family courts are stacked against fathers. If Louisa gained custody, she could move halfway across the country; I'd never see them. I knew Caitlin wanted me to commit to her, but I wasn't sure I wanted to.' He looked down at the table. 'I cared for Caitlin a lot, and we had a lot of fun together. But despite everything,

I loved Louisa. She's the only woman I've ever wanted to spend my life with.'

Tears started to roll down his face, and this time when his solicitor suggested a short break, he agreed.

*   *   *

'Where's he going with this?' asked Roehampton.

Warren swallowed his final bite of banana. 'I don't know,' he admitted. 'I can't decide if he's being more open, now he hasn't got that bloody solicitor telling him to keep quiet, or he's laying the groundwork for his defence. And he's still not being entirely honest. He's made no mention of those clandestine meet-ups with Caitlin when he was playing away from home, so to speak.'

He walked over to Pymm's desk. 'Have you got those phone and financial records yet?'

'Just came through,' she said. 'I'll look at them now and see if Moray's hunch is correct.'

'How's the CCTV, Mags?'

'I've isolated several promising-looking frames and sent them to Digital Imaging. They'll clean them up as best they can. I called in a few favours; they'll do it as a rush job.'

'How's Curtis?' asked Warren.

'Still downstairs,' confirmed Hutchinson. 'Everything he's told us so far has held up to scrutiny.'

Sutton rejoined them. 'Ready when you are,' he told Warren.

'Let's go then.'

*   *   *

Warren was content to let Greenland continue talking.

'Caitlin's confession came as a complete shock,' he started. 'I didn't know what to make of it, but as soon as you let me go, I just wanted to be home. I spoke to Steph, and she basically told

411

me to let sleeping dogs lie. I'd been through hell and the girls needed me with them, not sitting in a custody suite.

'But it kept on nagging at me. It didn't seem right, and the timings didn't add up. You said you saw my car at quarter past midnight. You were right, Caitlin came around that night. She'd just landed a big commission and wanted to celebrate, so she caught a cab over and brought a bottle of wine. She arrived about eight-thirty. You've probably guessed I didn't watch the football, we . . . well we didn't watch TV. Louisa usually finished work at about two a.m. There were no cabs available for an hour, so I decided to drive Caitlin back to her flat at about midnight.' He looked ashamed. 'It's only a short drive. The girls always sleep through the night, so I figured it would be OK to leave them for a few minutes.' He cleared his throat again. 'I've done it before.'

'What route did you take?' asked Sutton.

'Erm, Bishops Street, then Lester Road.'

That was where the ANPR cameras had picked him up.

'What about the journey back?' asked Sutton.

He frowned in concentration. 'They were blocking Bishops Street off when we drove down there, a burst water main or something, so I went via Templeton Avenue instead. It's a little longer, but I didn't want to risk getting delayed on the way back, in case the girls woke up.'

'The thing is, I returned home and found that the tracker on Louisa's phone had been disconnected. Plus, I couldn't get to sleep and I knew Caitlin would still be awake, so I texted her using the app. I stayed up until about one-thirty, before I had to go to sleep for work the next day. If Lou's phone was turned off by her killer, then I don't see any way that Caitlin could have been involved.'

*   *   *

412

Warren and Sutton had a quick conference outside the custody suite.

'It's time for him to put up or shut up,' said Sutton. 'If what he says is true, then there should be a record of that conversation on the app. He needs to stop playing silly buggers and unlock it so we can see what's been going on.'

* * *

Greenland recited the PIN code for the messaging app without hesitation. Warren excused himself and relayed it to Pete Robertson. A few moments later, he received confirmation that the code had worked.

Returning to the interview, he placed Greenland's burner phone on the desk between them. The same courier who had taken Curtis' phone to Welwyn had returned Ben's two phones. Now Digital Forensics had made a copy of the data, there was no danger Greenland could wipe or alter the encrypted files, and they let him open the app.

Warren and Sutton scrolled through the exchanges. The first thing Warren noticed was that there were no conversations with Darren. At the mention of his brother's name, pain passed across Greenland's face; he was still unconscious in hospital, his prognosis unchanged.

'Darren and I have barely spoken in years except for family events,' said Greenland. 'If what you told me about Lou and him . . . it's the first I knew about it.'

Despite everything, Warren believed him. Whatever Darren Greenland had been up to the night Louisa had been killed, it had nothing to do with Ben.

After opening the conversation thread with Caitlin, they read through the entries. It was no surprise why the two lovers had wanted to keep their correspondence a secret. Warren skimmed past the intimate pictures Caitlin had sent. Across the table,

Greenland studiously avoided anyone's eyes. His solicitor maintained a professional poker face; she'd seen worse.

The exchanges were explicit, but aside from a few heavy-handed hints from Caitlin about wanting to spend more time with him, there was nothing incriminating from either of them. The night of Louisa's murder, Caitlin sent a text early in the evening to tell Ben she was on her way. Then there was nothing for several hours, until a message from Ben at 00.48 telling her what an amazing night he'd had. The back and forth became increasingly graphic, culminating in a photograph from Greenland at 01.32 sent to "tide her over" until the next time.

The final messages were an exchange on the day after Louisa was reported missing, followed a minute later by a call from Greenland to Caitlin. This must have been what PC Lederer had overheard coming from the bathroom. The texts seemed to show genuine concern and worry on the part of Caitlin, with offers of assistance in finding Louisa.

It would be up to Digital Forensics to determine if any messages had been altered or deleted, but on the face of it, it appeared Greenland was finally telling the truth. Which meant that however else she may have been involved the night Louisa was killed, Caitlin had an alibi.

The spontaneous nature of the interview meant that Warren and Sutton had little in the way of a "script" to follow. Warren looked over at Sutton and raised an eyebrow. The two men had conducted dozens of interviews together over the years. Sutton knew exactly what Warren was thinking – it was time to go with his gut instinct. He nodded his agreement.

'Ben, when we found Sinead's body, she was twelve or thirteen weeks pregnant,' Warren said carefully. 'We were able to perform a DNA test for paternity, and you are not the father.'

He let the revelation sink in. Greenland's face contorted as waves of emotion swept through him: shock, disbelief, confusion, then relief, tempered quickly by grief.

'Not mine . . .? Do you . . . I mean is there any way you can find out . . .?' He took a deep breath and started again. 'Do you know who the father is?'

'Pending DNA confirmation, we believe it was most likely Curtis Redmayne,' said Warren.

'What?' Greenland's jaw dropped. 'You can't be serious?'

'The pregnancy was most likely the result of a one-night stand. Curtis has confirmed that it is possible.'

'Shit,' breathed Greenland. He buried his face in his hands.

Warren debated briefly whether or not to give Greenland time to process the shock, before hitting him with even worse news, but he decided it would be better to get it all out in one go.

'I'm sorry to have to tell you, Ben, but an autopsy on the body of Caitlin O'Shaughnessy revealed inconsistencies. We believe she was murdered, and the death made to look like a suicide. Given what you've told us, that means it is likely her confession was also fake.'

Greenland seemed to shrivel. 'If she was killed, then doesn't that suggest she was murdered by the same person who killed Louisa – and Sinead?'

'That's what we believe,' said Warren. 'Or Caitlin worked with a second person, who then killed her to cover up his tracks, blaming both deaths on Caitlin.'

'But why?'

'Jealousy, perhaps?' suggested Sutton. 'Caitlin would have seen Sinead as a threat if the baby was yours. Curtis would have seen Sinead as a threat if he knew the baby was his. They both had a reason to kill her.'

'But that doesn't make sense . . .' said Greenland, almost to himself.

'Did you know Curtis fancied Caitlin when you were back at university?' asked Sutton.

'I don't know anything now,' said Greenland rubbing his face.

'Ben, we have to ask. Do you think Curtis and Louisa ever had an affair?' asked Warren.

'What? No! Why would you even ask that?'

'We know Curtis offered Louisa the money she needed. We also know he was extremely drunk when he did so, and Louisa drove him back to his hotel that night. Is it possible that offer came with strings attached? And that was why he reneged on their agreement – when Louisa turned him down?'

Greenland gave an incredulous laugh. 'You are joking right? Are you seriously suggesting that Curtis offered Louisa the money if she slept with him?'

'It's just a theory,' said Warren carefully.

'He hasn't told you, has he?' said Greenland, a look of understanding crossing his face.

'Told us what?' asked Sutton.

'He's gay, for fuck's sake!'

Warren thought he'd misheard at first, but the slight start of surprise from Sutton confirmed his ears hadn't betrayed him.

'He came out about a year after we graduated.'

'Are you certain?' asked Warren. 'What about Sinead?'

'He was confused,' said Greenland. He sounded weary now. 'I always had my suspicions. He never took part in the league, he never claimed any "caps", and I never saw him with a girl, even when they were practically throwing themselves at him. I don't think he really knew himself back then, or perhaps he just didn't want to admit it. That football team – it wasn't the most welcoming, you know?' He looked ashamed. 'Frankly, we were openly homophobic. We only got away with it because social media wasn't such a big thing back then. The rule was "what happened in the locker room, stayed in the locker room".

'But Curtis is footie mad. He lived to play, so he was never going to say anything and risk getting kicked off the team.'

'And Sinead?' prompted Warren.

Greenland gave a sigh. 'When he finally came out, I actually questioned if he was sure.' He blushed. 'I even asked him how he knew he didn't like girls, if he'd never been with one. Jesus,

I'm embarrassed just thinking about it. We were both pissed, but still . . . Anyway, Curtis took it well. He asked me how I knew I wasn't gay, if I'd never been with another man? Fair comment. Anyway, he admitted he had been with a girl once, to see what it was like. He said he'd only managed to perform by closing his eyes and imagining she was somebody else.' He cleared his throat. 'I didn't ask who; I didn't want to know. But anyway, he said he knew then that he could never be with a woman. He keeps it quiet; he only recently came out to his parents. But he has a partner now, back in France, and he wanted us all to meet him.'

Warren decided to request a brief break and exited the interview suite to confer with Sutton.

'If it's true what he says about Curtis being gay, then that probably scuppers the theory about him killing Louisa because she rejected him,' said Sutton. 'Especially if his alibi holds up.'

'Ben has supplied an alibi that effectively rules out Caitlin killing Louisa,' said Warren. 'And Curtis was up north the night she was killed. The killer knew about Sinead; that's why they left Caitlin's body on top of Sinead's grave, and linked Sinead and Louisa's murders in the confession. It doesn't rule out any of them being involved in Sinead's death, but it means there is definitely another person with knowledge of her murder.'

'I can only really think of one person,' said Sutton.

'I agree. But let's see if Ben voices the same conclusion,' said Warren, leading the two of them back into the custody suite.

As soon as they took their seats again and restarted the recording, Greenland took a deep breath. 'There's something else you need to know. This is why I came here today – I needed to get it off my chest. I couldn't let you destroy Caitlin's reputation, and I was worried that the killer is still out there.

'But now, after everything you've told me, I think I might know who it is. It's the only explanation that makes sense.'

*   *   *

Moments after Warren paused the interview with Greenland and headed back towards CID, he was met in the corridor by Ruskin.

'You are never going to believe who just phoned,' the Scotsman said. He continued without waiting for a response. 'Mason Brindstocke.'

'Stephanie Hellard's legal partner?' said Warren.

'That's the one. He gave me a whole load of pompous bullshit about being an officer of the court and compelled by his legal duty, blah, blah, blah, but he's shitting himself. He's trying to distance himself and his firm from Stephanie as much as possible.'

'What did he say?'

'After Karen and I left, he decided to check her call log and billable hours. They charge their clients by the hour, including for telephone consultations, which the solicitor records using an app. Stephanie's business line at her flat is paid for by the firm, so he looked up its records. She didn't record any billable hours for the night Louisa was killed.'

Warren stopped in his tracks. 'She said she was on the phone to a client that night.'

'She received a call at ten p.m., lasting for forty-two minutes,' said Ruskin. 'That much is true. And she definitely received it in her flat; there isn't a redirect to her mobile. I asked if she could have forgotten to update the log, what with everything that happened, and he dismissed it outright. She's very diligent and tends to log calls immediately. She's been correctly recording consultations for the past two weeks, even though she's technically on leave.

'Whoever phoned Stephanie wasn't a client.'

* * *

'The search warrants are with the magistrate,' said Ruskin, as he pulled his jacket on.

'Secure the premises,' said Warren. 'We'll get a paper copy

to you as soon as they're signed. DSI Roehampton is arranging support for when you get there.'

David Hutchinson joined them. 'There's a car waiting. We've authorisation for blues and twos, so it won't take long, even in this traffic.'

'Before we go,' said Ruskin. 'I got a call back from the woman at the garage who sold the flowers we found near Caitlin's body.'

'Go on,' said Warren, intrigued. Ruskin wouldn't be telling them this now if it wasn't important.

'Later that same night, probably about two a.m., she reckons the woman returned to the garage. She was dressed differently, but she's sure it was her. She didn't come to the kiosk and she wasn't in her car; she walked. She waited for a few minutes, then a car picked her up.'

'A taxi?' asked Sutton.

'She couldn't say. Unfortunately, the woman didn't come onto the main forecourt, so there won't be any CCTV.'

'Fantastic work,' said Warren, as yet another piece of the puzzle fell into place. 'Right, go and get this wrapped up.'

The two men hurried out of the office.

'I've got the cleaned-up CCTV stills,' said Richardson. The remaining members of the team gathered around her monitor. The images were from the car hire firm located near Stansted Airport.

'Are we one hundred per cent certain the image isn't reversed?' asked Warren.

'Definitely,' said Richardson pointing at the company's logo, printed on the rear of the T-shirt worn by the man behind the counter. 'The text is the right way around.'

She magnified the image. 'No question about it.' She pointed at the screen. 'You can see her right wrist as she reaches for the pen. Caitlin didn't have any tattoos.'

'But Stephanie does,' finished Warren.

*   *   *

'Met police officers have picked up Rosie, the *Big Issue* seller,' confirmed Sutton, hanging up his phone.

'Did she still have the phone?' asked Roehampton.

'Yes, she'd changed the SIM card but the IMEI number matches the handset that called Stephanie's business landline the night Louisa was killed. They're bringing her in for questioning.'

In the hour since Ben had voiced his suspicion that Louisa had been killed by her sister, yet more pieces had fallen into place. Curtis Redmayne had confirmed what Greenland had told them, even showing them pictures of him with his boyfriend. His parents and the hotel staff had verified his alibis for the nights Caitlin and Louisa were killed. When pressed, he'd admitted he had suspected for some time that Ben and Caitlin had rekindled their affair. The loss of Sinead had been a shared trauma and he'd been afraid that exposing the affair would destroy the group's friendship once and for all.

'Stephanie's mobile phone arrived back at her flat at 17.50, where it remained all night,' said Richardson. 'The rail companies and TfL confirm she would have had ample time to take the underground to Liverpool Street station and catch the Stansted Express to the airport, then walk to the car hire.'

'What about getting home after she returned?' asked Sutton.

'We know she made it into work at her usual time the following morning, and her phone travelled from her flat to the office by her usual route,' said Richardson. 'That's too early to have used the Stansted Express, so my guess is she caught the shuttle bus to Stratford, then used the underground to travel back to her flat.'

'Where she got changed, picked up her phone and went to work as though nothing had happened,' finished Warren. The cold-natured planning of the operation left him feeling sick. 'Any luck tracking her down?'

Hardwick shook her head. 'Her mobile phone has been switched off since just after Ben showed up at the station. The last location was the bed and breakfast she's been staying at, but that was hours ago; there's no sign of her.'

'What about the Greenlands' house?' asked Warren. If Stephanie realised the game was up and Ben had gone to the police, he worried about what she might do.

'No sightings,' said Hardwick. 'We've got officers there in case she turns up.'

'What about her car?' asked Roehampton.

'Gone,' said Richardson. 'No sign of it on ANPR, but she could have swapped the plates.'

'She's had a hell of a head start,' said Pymm. 'She could be halfway across the country by now.'

'Get in touch with her parents and tell them to be on the lookout,' said Warren. 'Also, contact the Metropolitan Police and ask them to post a few officers on the streets surrounding her flat and the underground station. Does anyone else have any suggestions?'

'She could be disguised as Caitlin again,' said Pymm. 'We should include that description and photo in any port alerts and press releases. I've placed a flag on the credit card she used in Caitlin's name as well as those in her own name, and her company AMEX.'

Sutton's phone vibrated with a text. 'That was Hutch,' he said. 'They're at Stephanie's flat.'

'I still don't get it,' said Hardwick. 'She killed her friend at university, then years later she impersonates another friend to kill her own sister. Why?'

'Jealousy,' said Warren heavily. 'That's what this whole thing has been about. And he—' he pointed angrily in the rough direction of the interview suite where Ben Greenland sat waiting '—is at the centre of the whole bloody thing.'

'We need to hear her side of the story,' said Sutton. 'But Ben admits he slept with Stephanie when they were at university. He claims it was because he was under pressure from those other cretins on the football team – to complete the set, as they put it – but you ask me he's just a horny little shit who thought he could do whatever he wanted. Plus, he's carried on meeting up with her clandestinely since they graduated.'

'I think we'll find the confession she left in Caitlin's apartment was actually Stephanie telling us the truth about her feelings,' said Warren. 'She just made it sound like Caitlin.'

'Was Stephanie aware of his relationship with Caitlin back then?' asked Hardwick.

'He didn't think so at the time, but now . . .' Sutton shrugged.

'So why the ten-year wait to kill Louisa?' asked Roehampton. 'If she wanted to be with Ben so badly, why didn't she kill Louisa back then? I know we keep on asking that same damn question, but why the massive gap?'

'We're not entirely sure,' said Warren. 'But Ben thinks it was the threat of him leaving Louisa and moving to Ireland with Sinead that may have triggered the first killing. Stephanie and Ben knew they could never really be together. Neither of them were brave enough to deal with the fallout from Ben leaving Louisa to take up with her sister. Ironically, if Louisa and Ben stayed together, then Stephanie would have an excuse to keep in touch with him.

'But after Sinead died, Ben vowed to mend his ways and broke off his relationships with Caitlin and Stephanie. Stephanie moved to London. When he and Louisa finally got married, Stephanie reacted by getting engaged herself to a man she'd only known for a few months. He thinks it was to try and prove that she was over him, although that was clearly not the case; the marriage only lasted a short time.

'When Louisa started P@mper, it affected their relationship quite quickly. We know Ben took up with Caitlin again and he admits to still sleeping with Stephanie. Apparently, it was Stephanie who told him about the secure messaging app.'

'So what was the trigger for her finally deciding to kill her sister?' asked Roehampton. 'Like you said, as long as Ben and Louisa were together, she had an excuse to see him.'

'Ben isn't certain,' replied Warren. 'But Caitlin's neighbour reckoned he saw somebody he assumed was her sister. A follow-up confirmed that she wasn't in the UK.'

'We assumed it was Louisa,' said Hardwick. 'But if it was Stephanie, maybe she was setting the groundwork with Caitlin? I have an idea. Let me make a call.'

Sutton's phone rang. 'It's Hutch. They've entered Stephanie's apartment. No sign of her. They're going to do a quick search for any clues to her whereabouts, then hand over to an evidence-recovery team.'

'Tell him I want to know the second they find anything,' said Warren. 'Rachel, how are her bank statements looking?'

'I have no transactions on any of her cards within the last twenty-four hours,' she said, scrolling through the records. 'But I have some large cash withdrawals over the past three weeks. Almost four grand in total.'

'She could be anywhere with that sort of money in her pocket,' said Roehampton.

'Here we go,' said Pymm. 'She transferred over a thousand pounds to a cryptocurrency exchange a month ago. Looks like funds for a shopping spree on the dark web if you ask me.'

'She had to buy that Taser somewhere,' said Sutton. 'And you can't just walk into Halfords and ask for several sets of licence plates without ownership documents.'

'She's been planning this for months,' said Warren. 'It was Stephanie who advised Ben and Louisa to increase their life insurance policies when she started P@mper. If she'd already decided to kill Louisa back then, she could have been making certain Ben started his new life without any debts hanging over him.'

'I've got some more enhanced CCTV stills,' Richardson called out. Again, everyone crowded around her desk. Sutton helped Pymm to her feet so she could join them.

'This is the footage from the till above Mandy's Muffins,' said Richardson. Now that they knew what they were looking for, it was obvious.

'I think she was wearing a wig matching Caitlin's haircut when she hired the car,' said Richardson. 'But that wasn't an option when she met her sister for lunch; Louisa would have been suspicious.' She magnified the image further. It was still blurred, but the dark smudge on the inside of her right wrist was clearly visible. 'Louisa's matching tattoo was on her left wrist, so we can be sure that's not her wearing Caitlin's red hoodie.'

'So it was Stephanie who Louisa had lunch with,' said Warren. 'What about when the knife was bought?'

Richardson opened another image, this one from the pavement outside the cookery shop where they believed the murder weapon had been purchased.

'Definitely the same hoodie,' said Richardson. She zoomed in on the figure's head. 'It's hard to be certain, but there are wisps of dark hair poking out the bottom of the hood. Stephanie's hair is longer than Caitlin's.'

'Get forensics to check the neckline and cuffs of Caitlin's hoodie for traces of foreign DNA,' said Warren. 'And tell Hutch and Moray to find Stephanie's toothbrush or hairbrush; if we can get some comparator DNA, that will go a long way towards proving it was her on the CCTV.'

'We'll need more than that,' cautioned Roehampton. 'She's a defence solicitor. I'm sure she's clever enough to know that if she claims she borrowed the hoodie because she was cold the last time she saw Caitlin, we'll struggle to prove otherwise.'

'If she tries that, we can prove she's lying,' said Hardwick as she hung up the phone. 'I just called Aiden Price, Caitlin's friend with benefits. He says that on the weekend before Stephanie and Louisa went to Mandy's Muffins, he and Caitlin didn't meet up for their usual morning gym session and lunchtime whatever session, because Caitlin had a friend from university staying. He had planned to tell his wife that he was going into work on Sunday afternoon, so they could meet up, but Caitlin begged off because she had – in her words – "the worst hangover of her life". She had no idea what the hell they'd been drinking as she couldn't remember anything after they returned to her flat from the fish and chip shop, but she was still being sick twenty-four hours later.'

'I'll bet Stephanie spiked her drink,' said Sutton. 'So, she had time to steal whatever she needed to impersonate Caitlin.'

'Including that red hoodie,' said Hardwick. 'I asked him if he could ever remember her wearing one, and he said she used to wear it all the time to the gym. But she was complaining she couldn't find it; she even wondered if she'd been so drunk, she'd left it in the chippy, but they hadn't got it.'

'Karen, we know Stephanie met Louisa in the middle of a Monday,' said Warren. 'Now that Mason Brindstocke has located his professional ethics, why don't you ring and ask for Stephanie's annual leave records. We need to prove she wasn't sitting at her desk when we believe she was in Middlesbury, dressed as Caitlin, lunching with her sister and buying the murder weapon.'

Hardwick smiled at the prospect of making the smug lawyer squirm. 'My pleasure.'

'You know the worst thing about all this, is that the real killer was at the centre of this whole affair from the beginning,' said Warren to Roehampton.

'It was Stephanie's idea for Ben to stick to no comment,' said Sutton. 'He reckons he was ready to tell us everything during the first interview, but she convinced him that if we knew he was having an affair it was motive enough for us to charge him. She must have figured that as long as we didn't catch wind of Ben's affair with Caitlin, we'd look at him and then move on. I wonder if she knew Caitlin was with Ben that night?'

Warren gave a mirthless chuckle. 'I feel almost sorry for that poor solicitor she subcontracted to do her dirty work. She was taken for a complete ride. I'll bet Mason Brindstocke is furious.'

Roehampton shrugged. 'Serves him right. He should have flat-out refused to get involved. Any truly ethical solicitor would have insisted Stephanie was far too close to the case. Makes you wonder if she had anything over him. I told you she was suspiciously young to make partner.'

'I wonder what Stephanie and Louisa spoke about when they met up for lunch?' mused Warren. 'She'd clearly already decided to kill Louisa by that point and blame it on Caitlin.'

'And I wonder how she found out about Caitlin?' said Sutton. 'She must have known before that boozy sleepover. I can't imagine Caitlin told her she was sleeping with her sister's husband, and I doubt Ben said anything.'

'Then let's hope we find her, so we can ask her,' said Roehampton. If Stephanie was as smitten with Ben as they believed, then she would probably see his turning himself in to the police as a betrayal. Would she harm herself?

Sutton's phone rang again. 'It's Hutch.' He listened for a moment, before handing the handset to Warren. 'You are never going to believe what they've found in Stephanie's flat.'

Chapter 49

'There was an old-fashioned answerphone in the bottom of her wardrobe,' said Hutchinson. 'One of those ones with a mini cassette tape – God knows where she got it from.' He gave a short laugh. 'It was a good job I was here. Mr Millennial thought it was a radio alarm clock.'

'Yeah, yeah, very funny,' Ruskin's voice boomed over the speaker. 'I'll remember that next time you ask me for help pairing your phone to your car's Bluetooth.'

'That's weird,' said Sutton. 'She's thirty-one – why on earth would she have one of those lying around? Surely her landline has voicemail or a digital recorder?'

'Because the cassette tapes are only about forty-five minutes long and stop recording and hang up when they run out,' said Warren. 'Bloody hell, that's clever. Have you played the tape yet?'

'Aye, we fast-forwarded through it, but there's only one message, recorded at 22.00, the night Louisa was killed,' said Ruskin. 'It sounds a lot like Rosie, the *Big Issue* seller. She appears to be reading articles from an issue.'

'That was her alibi,' said Warren. 'She gave that nice burner phone to her homeless friend, probably with a few quid as a

427

thank you, and told her to ring her landline and just speak until the tape was full and it hung up.'

'Also, the flat is full of smart plugs,' said Ruskin. 'Several table lamps and one connected to the TV.'

'So she came home from work, left her mobile phone switched on so that it showed her location as her flat, programmed the lights to come on and off in case anyone was outside, and switched the TV on,' said Warren. 'Then turned it off remotely at bedtime, so her neighbours thought she was in her flat all night. And to reinforce it, arranged for a fake call that she knew she could claim was privileged if we ever asked for details.'

'Diabolical,' said Roehampton.

'Moray, once you've finished there, I want you to speak to Rosie and see if she'll confirm all this,' said Warren. 'I can't imagine Stephanie told her she was planning to kill her sister, so she hasn't broken any laws. No need to go in heavy-handed.'

'Will do,' promised Ruskin. 'But would you like to know what else we've found?'

Warren rolled his eyes; Pymm hid her smile. 'Go on,' he said.

'The CSIs just emptied her wastebaskets. I think we know why she's doing this now.'

*　*　*

'Do you two have any idea where Stephanie might be now?' asked Warren. Redmayne and Greenland, the two remaining house-mates from the student house where the whole tragic affair had started, were sat in Interview Suite One. Warren's gut was telling him that neither man had been involved in Sinead's murder, and they had been ruled out of Louisa and Caitlin's killings.

For his part, Greenland looked both grief-stricken and ashamed. Caitlin, Sinead and Louisa had done nothing wrong. They had arguably made some poor choices, yet none of them deserved their fate. Nor the evisceration their memories would probably receive from some corners of the gutter press, who would fuel the righteous prejudices of their readers with salacious titbits and half-truths designed to maximise clicks and advertising revenue.

But ultimately, the real victims were the families and loved ones of Sinead, Louisa and Caitlin. And two little girls who had lost their mother, and whose trust in their father would be irrevocably damaged.

Redmayne gave a frustrated shake of his head. 'I'm sorry. I kept in touch with Steph, but really, aside from our annual get-together, we rarely spoke at great length. You seem to be looking in all of the obvious places.'

'Ben?'

'I wish I knew, really I do.' His voice was weary, the fight beaten out of him. Warren felt a twinge of guilt at his harsh judgement of the man. His actions might have been morally suspect, but nobody could have foreseen the consequences.

A low vibration started. Everyone in the room immediately reached for the pocket where that they usually kept their mobile phone; the twenty-first-century Pavlovian reflex.

The vibrating continued. It was coming from the folder sitting in front of Warren. He pulled it open quickly, revealing the handset sealed in a plastic evidence bag.

"Unknown Number", said the caller ID. It could be a telemarketer, a robocall, or just a wrong number. But if it wasn't, only two people had the number of Ben Greenland's secret second handset. And one of them was dead.

There was no time to formulate an interview strategy and so Warren followed his gut. He ripped open the evidence bag and answered the call.

'Hello, Stephanie,' he said.

There was a long pause, harsh breathing the only indication there was someone on the other end of the line.

'Is Ben with you?'

Out of the corner of his eye, he saw the door to the interview suite open. Karen Hardwick came in, her face flushed from running. She passed a piece of paper across the desk without a word.

Stephanie's phone had reconnected to the network barely a minute before. He looked at the handset's current location. It was only accurate to within a hundred metres, but Pymm's distinctive handwriting was emphatic. Within that radius was the only place that made sense.

'Yes,' said Warren. There was no point asking questions; he recognised the sound of someone on a precipice. She knew what she wanted to say, and he'd be better served listening than talking.

'I want to see him,' she said. 'I need to tell him, to his face, what happened and why.'

'We can arrange that,' said Warren. He could hear Sutton murmuring in Hardwick's ear to get Roehampton to mobilise an Armed Response Unit.

Greenland opened his mouth to speak, but Warren quelled him with a violent shake of his head, pressing a finger against his lips.

'Why don't you come here, and I'll arrange for you to speak to him?' he offered.

There came a low, humourless chuckle from the other end of the line. 'Really, DCI Jones? Do you think I'm that stupid? I know how the system works, remember? If I turn up at that dinky little station of yours, I'll be arrested on the spot. I'll never even clap eyes on him.'

'Then what do you suggest?' he asked.

'You bring him to me. I won't ask you to come alone; that'll never happen. But I'll only speak to Ben. And to you; you've earned the right to hear the truth. Then you can do whatever you want.'

'OK, where are you?' he asked.

'Oh, I think you can guess,' she said. 'I imagine you've already got armed response heading towards this handset. But when they arrive, tell them to stay outside. I will *only* speak to you and Ben.' Her voice turned cold. 'Any trickery and it ends now, and you'll never get the truth.'

The call ended.

'Where is she?' asked Curtis, his eyes wide.

Warren told him.

'Where it all started,' said Greenland, his voice bitter.

*   *   *

'We need to hear what she has to say,' argued Warren. 'Stephanie was quite clear she would only speak to me and Ben.'

'Surely we have enough to charge?' said Roehampton. 'I can't justify putting you and a civilian at risk.'

'It's not about the charges,' said Greenland. 'We all know she's going to prison for the rest of her life. It's about the truth,' he started to plead. 'I have to hear it from her own lips.'

'I'm sorry, I can't risk it,' said Roehampton. She'd already donned her high-vis jacket. She wouldn't be gold commander for the armed operation, but she was determined to use her rank and prior firearms experience to get as close to the action as they would allow her.

'Dammit,' shouted Greenland. 'I need to do this! I am a cheating shit and a coward. This is all on me – don't you see that? Three women I loved are dead, because I was a misogynistic, horny little bastard who only cared about getting laid.'

His voice turned pleading again. 'Do either of you have kids?' He didn't wait for an answer. 'Because I have two little girls who I have betrayed. Because of me, they have lost their mother. They've also lost their favourite aunty and another woman who they thought of that way. I don't know if they'll ever forgive me. But at least, when they're old enough, I can tell them the truth about what happened.'

He pressed on. 'Stephanie says she'll only speak to me and DCI Jones. Believe me, I've known Stephanie my whole adult life. If she says something, she means it. You won't change her mind. She promised that if we trick her, we'll never get the truth. You

431

won't negotiate her out of there. If you storm the place, she'll be dead before you break the door down.'

'It could be the only way to stop her killing herself,' said Warren.

Roehampton rubbed her temples and he could see the pain of her headache in her eyes. She really needed to get that looked at, thought Warren. Constant headaches couldn't be a good sign.

'Shit,' she muttered eventually. 'I'll contact the gold commander.'

* * *

'The landlord confirms that the place is empty,' said the super-intendent acting as gold commander. He'd been as sceptical as Roehampton at first, but she'd finally won him over. 'University finished for the summer last week and the tenants left before he charged them another month's rent.'

Greenland snorted. 'Some things never change. The tight-fisted bastard wanted us to cover Sinead's share of the rent when she disappeared.'

He was nervous, starting to babble, as an authorised firearms officer carefully tightened the straps on the ballistic vest he was wearing. 'You know, I used to drive past here now and again. The outside has never changed, no new paint or guttering. He hasn't even replaced that broken garden gate. I hope he's spent some money inside; that bloody boiler was on its last legs and there was a damn great damp patch on the wall next to Sinead's bed . . .' He trailed off.

'You know you don't have to do this, don't you,' Warren said quietly, as he adjusted the chinstrap on his helmet. There was no specific intelligence that Stephanie had a gun, but she'd success-fully purchased an illegal Taser off the dark web and some of her clients were the sort of people who could get you anything if you had the cash.

'Yeah, I do,' said Greenland, as he stood straighter.

'Ready when you are, Warren,' said Roehampton.

Chapter 50

The front door to the terraced house was ajar, the wood around its lock splintered. The buildings either side of it were either unoccupied or had been safely evacuated. Stephanie had left the hall light on.

Warren went first. *What the hell am I doing?* he asked himself for the umpteenth time. He was a detective chief inspector, not a hostage negotiator. Behind him, he could feel the nervous energy radiating off Greenland. In his earpiece he could hear the quiet murmuring of the armed response team, barely louder than the blood rushing through his ears. Both he and Greenland had been fitted with body cameras and radios broadcasting on an open channel.

The curtains to the front room – Sinead's old bedroom – were closed, but thermal-imaging cameras had identified a human-sized mass in the centre of the space. At this moment, two police snipers were trained on it. It was far from an ideal shot, should they need to take it, but hopefully they'd be able to distinguish between the two of them and Stephanie.

Warren gently pushed the door open.

The first thing that struck him was the smell.

Stephanie Hellard stood directly opposite, holding an unlit

plastic cigarette lighter aloft. A table lamp was the only source of illumination.

Warren let out a slow breath. 'There's no need for that, Stephanie – we're just here to talk, remember?' His voice was low and soothing, despite the fear sending adrenaline surging around his body. 'Why don't you put the lighter down, so you can tell us what you want us to know? Nobody needs to get burned today.'

The voices in his ear became insistent.

'Please confirm. Is the suspect armed? Is there a risk of fire or explosion?'

Either Hellard had very sharp hearing, or she was switched on enough to know that everything was being broadcast.

'Feel free to tell them what will happen if they try and shoot me through the window,' she said. 'A stray spark from a bullet and this place goes up like a bomb.'

'That's a yes,' said Warren, not taking his eyes off the woman. 'The room is doused in petrol. No sign of any firearms.'

'Why did you do it, Steph?' asked Ben. His voice cracked. Warren placed a calming hand on his arm, silently willing him to be quiet. Ben ignored him. 'She trusted you! How could you kill your own fucking sister?'

'Let her tell us in her own time, Ben,' said Warren, squeezing his arm firmly. This was *such* a bad idea. They'd discussed the need to avoid antagonising somebody who was clearly in a dangerous place emotionally; to let Warren take the lead. It appeared the instructions had either fallen on deaf ears, or Greenland had forgotten what they had agreed.

'I loved you,' said Hellard. 'Can't you see that? We were meant to be together.'

'But Louisa was your sister. She was practically your twin.' Ben's voice was incredulous. 'How could you betray her like that?'

She gave a bitter chuckle. 'You were her husband – how could *you* betray her like that?'

Ben opened his mouth to speak, before closing it again.

'Why don't you tell us everything at your own pace?' interjected Warren. 'I'm here to listen, not to judge.'

She ignored him.

'It should have been us,' she said. 'We were so perfect together.'

Warren's eyes had finally adjusted to the weak light from the table lamp. Once again, he was struck by Stephanie's remarkable similarity to her sister, and he could see how she had managed to convince a stranger she was the person depicted on Caitlin O'Shaughnessy's driving licence. Ben really did have a "preferred type" of woman.

'I . . . I'm sorry,' managed Greenland. 'I was a shit. But why did you do it, Steph? I'm not worth it. You're beautiful and funny and intelligent; there are so many men out there who could make you happy.'

Warren held his breath. Before they did anything else, they needed to defuse the tension in the room.

'You don't even remember, do you?' she said.

'Remember what?' Greenland asked, his voice desperate.

'The first day we met.'

'Of course I do,' he said, his voice becoming more confident. 'It was in the kitchen in halls. I even remember what you were eating. A pasta salad you'd made fresh.' He forced a chuckle. 'I was so bloody useless, I hadn't even left the water in my Pot Noodle long enough; it was still crunchy and the powder from the flavour sachet was all clumped together.'

'And then what happened?' she asked.

Greenland paused. 'I can't remember,' he admitted.

'Of course you bloody can't!' she shouted. 'Because Louisa came in and that was it. There I was, in jeans and a T-shirt, all sweaty from dragging my belongings up four flights of stairs, and in flounces Lou. Wearing a crop top so low and a skirt so high, you could practically see all the way through when she bent over.'

Greenland swallowed but said nothing.

'Don't you get it?' she wailed. 'I saw you first! All my life, I

435

was the big sister. I was the oldest in the year and she was the youngest. I helped her with her homework, comforted her when Mum and Dad were arguing, and even wrote her personal statement for university. And you know what? I didn't mind! I loved her so much.' She thrust out her wrist. 'We got these matching tattoos on holiday in Ibiza when we finished our A levels. Mum was furious – Lou hadn't even turned eighteen.'

Her voice became more contemplative. 'You know, everyone talks about how younger siblings have to live in the shadow of their older brothers or sisters. But nobody ever talks about the shadow that the older sibling has to live under. And when everyone thinks you're twins anyway . . .'

She gave a sniff.

'I'm so sorry, Steph. I had no idea,' Greenland mumbled.

She ignored him. 'When we got to university, I thought it was my time to shine. I'd be there if Lou needed me, but I was finally going to come out from her shadow. You know, everyone always commented on how we looked the same. Even I struggle sometimes to remember who is in old photos. But as soon as they started talking to us, they could tell us apart. Louisa, the scatty, fun-loving party girl, who'd made flirting an Olympic sport and whose laugh could be heard halfway down the corridor. Then there was Stephanie. Serious, clever Steph who was going to be a hotshot lawyer and who'd be so much prettier if she just smiled a bit more.

'That day in the kitchen, I couldn't believe what was happening. Ten minutes after I finished unpacking, the most handsome boy I'd ever seen walks in. And starts talking to *me*. Flirting with *me*. Do you know how long we were alone in there, Ben?'

'No,' he admitted.

'Forty-three minutes. There was a clock on the microwave. Forty-three minutes I had you all to myself.' She turned to Warren. 'Tell me, DCI Jones. Have you ever met someone and known there and then, that you've found the one?'

Warren thought back to the first time he'd clapped eyes on Susan – at a student party he'd gate-crashed with his best friend Griffo.

'Yeah,' he said.

Hellard turned back to Greenland. 'I know you have. Because I saw it happen. The moment my fucking sister walked in.'

She gave a short laugh. 'The thing is, I was almost used to it by that point. I couldn't compete with Lou. Nobody could. So I did what I always did; I pushed my feelings aside. I watched as you and Louisa became closer and closer. And then everything changed.'

Beside him, Warren saw Greenland close his eyes. 'I'm so sorry,' he muttered again.

'You remember that night, don't you, Ben?'

'Please don't,' he whispered.

'Louisa fell over in town when we were out celebrating Curtis's birthday. The hospital insisted she stay overnight because she was so pissed they couldn't tell if she had a concussion. We got back to halls at half past four in the morning. I was tired and emotional and still the worse for wear, and what did you do? You took me back to my room. Whilst my sister was in hospital, you fucked me!'

'I'm sorry, Steph, it shouldn't have happened. *I* shouldn't have let it happen.'

'You're missing the point,' said Hellard. 'It happened because it was *meant* to happen. I know that. You know that. Tell me I'm wrong! Because it happened again and again. And every time it felt so *right*.'

Warren eyed the distraught woman in front of them. The hand holding the lighter had fallen to her side, apparently forgotten. So far, Hellard had confirmed that she'd had an affair with her sister's boyfriend. But that wasn't why he was here.

'Tell me about Sinead,' Warren said.

Hellard laughed bitterly. 'Quiet, naïve Sinead. From the

backwoods of Ireland – even bloody Caitlin called her a bogtrotter! You thought you were so clever, waiting until the whole house was quiet before sneaking downstairs, whilst I was upstairs, hoping that I'd receive that tap on my door. But Louisa was sleeping in the next room and you only came to see me when she was so pissed she wouldn't wake up.

'The first time I followed you downstairs, you went into Caitlin's room.' Her lip curled. 'Hardly surprising – she always was a slut.' She paused. 'Isn't it funny how we label girls sluts? What do we call men who do the same? We call them players. Studs. Lady-killers. That's ironic . . . "Ben's Harem", wasn't that what that pathetic bunch of man-boys you played football with called this house? What were we? Just caps in that league table you all took part in?'

She laughed at the look of shock on Ben's face. 'Oh, please, every girl on campus knew about it. Some girls actually wanted to be a part of it.' Her voice turned bitter. 'The rest had too much self-respect. Well you'd already bagged three caps from the house; it didn't take a genius to figure out you'd be wanting to complete the set. And sure enough, one night I heard you get up and go downstairs. I knew Caitlin wasn't in, so that confirmed it.'

Greenland stared at the floor. Even in the dim light, Warren could see the redness that signalled when he was ashamed.

'And then, poor little Sinead comes to see me. Not her best friend, Caitlin, who hadn't got a sensible bone in her body. No, she comes to see *me*. Dependable, *sensible* Stephanie. She's got herself pregnant, the silly girl. When I ask her what she's going to do, she says she going to ask the father to marry her and move with her to Ireland. Of course, she wasn't going to tell me who the father was – how could she? But it wasn't difficult to figure it out. She was such a little mouse. I knew she wasn't seeing anyone outside our house, and she wouldn't want to marry someone she'd hooked up with for a drunken one-night stand. Curtis was obviously gay – we all knew it, even if he didn't – so that left you.'

Warren squeezed Ben's arm, willing him not to say anything. If Hellard found out she'd had it wrong all these years, that Ben wasn't the father of Sinead's baby – that everything that had happened since was the result of her mistake – then who knew what she might do? The smell of petrol still hung heavy in the air; the lighter still dangled from her hand.

'I don't know how I kept it together,' Hellard continued. 'Because I knew that if you broke it off with Louisa, then we were done. If you moved to Ireland, there would be no excuses to meet up. I couldn't ever be seen with you. The cheating ex of my beloved sister? It would tear our family apart.'

Her tone was incredulous. 'And you know what the irony is? I'm the reason you were able to keep having your affairs. Louisa wasn't an idiot; she suspected something. For weeks, I told her she was imagining things. That the cocaine was making her paranoid. I knew if she started digging it would all come out. Sinead and Caitlin for sure. And then some blabbermouth would mention the league and she'd start to think "well he's had three of the four . . ." I couldn't let that happen.'

'So you killed her,' said Greenland, his tone dull.

'Well I had to, didn't I?' said Hellard. 'The silly bitch would never get an abortion and her parents would demand to know who the father was. There'd be a shotgun wedding.' Her tone was matter-of-fact, as if it was the most logical course of action.

'How did you do it, Stephanie?' asked Warren.

'Like I said in the letter – the one I'm sure you've figured out wasn't actually written by Caitlin. Crushed pills in bitter lemon, enough to make her drowsy. I stole Louisa's car keys, walked her to the boot of your car, then drove her to the woods. You could drive a lot further in than you can these days. Unfortunately, I hadn't quite got the dose right. I'd wanted her so far gone she wouldn't put up a struggle, but not so out of it I'd have to drag her.' She shrugged. 'She came around in the boot of the car and was trying to get out, so I had to whack her with the tyre iron.

And then I had to drag her to the hole I'd dug anyway. I finished her off with a kitchen knife I'd bought second-hand for cash in a charity shop.'

'Where's the knife now, Stephanie?' asked Warren.

'God knows. I wiped it down, snapped the handle off and threw the pieces out the car window a mile apart.' She gave an infuriating smirk. 'The perfect murder; there's a reason I scored full marks on my criminology modules.'

'Not entirely perfect.' Warren was unable to resist. 'After all, I'm standing here now.'

'It kept you fooled for eleven years, didn't it? Be honest, DCI Jones. If I hadn't needed to kill Louisa, this would never have all come out.' Her smirk turned to one of frustration. 'It was just bad luck; not my fault,' she muttered to herself.

He decided it would be wisest not to respond to that. 'What happened after you killed Sinead?' he asked instead.

'Ha!' This time her voice was mirthless. 'That part of the plan didn't go so well.' She pointed a finger at Greenland. 'You had an attack of conscience, didn't you? Decided to mend your ways. You broke it off with me. I assume you stopped shagging Caitlin also?'

Greenland remained silent, just staring at his shoes.

'So now I had nothing.' She paused. 'You know, I was faithful to you, Ben.'

'What do you mean?' he managed.

'I was a virgin when you first slept with me. Did you know that? I was so confused afterwards. I'd just lost my virginity to a man who could never be mine. I should have backed away. It should have been a one-off, but every time it happened, I fell more deeply in love with you. There was never anyone else. I resigned myself to living off the scraps from Lou's table.'

She wiped her nose on her sleeve. 'I should never have agreed to move into that house, but how could I say no? Lou was my sister and my best friend. We'd insisted on sharing a bedroom when we were children, how could I say no to sharing a house?

'After Sinead, you made it *very* clear to me that you and Lou were going to get married and start a family. So I moved to London and decided to start again. I met Colin – big fucking mistake that was. Three years with a man with more money than personality and a clutch of bratty kids that put him off ever having any more. And now I'm stuck with his stupid, fucking surname, because my business partner changed all his stationery.' She scowled. 'I threatened to tell his wife why Mason agreed to make me partner, but the greasy bastard called my bluff.'

She returned her attention to Greenland. 'You know, I thought I'd lost you. I was divorced before I even turned thirty; and each year I had to meet up with everyone from Potter Street and mourn the passing of fucking Sinead. I thought that part of my life was over.

'But then you called me. You were in London for a work conference, and did I fancy a drink?' She wiped her eyes. 'And that was it. Once or twice a year, that was all, but I convinced myself it was enough.'

'I'm sorry, Steph . . .'

She cut him off. 'But then things changed, didn't they? Why don't you tell DCI Jones what happened in Ireland when we went to Sinead's ten-year memorial?'

'Steph . . .'

'Tell him!' she shouted.

'Lou had a relapse,' he muttered. 'She got blind drunk, and we had to take her back to the hotel and put her to bed.' He cleared his throat. 'Steph and I went back to her room.'

'And what did you say that night?' She didn't wait for his reply. 'That you loved me, and sometimes you wished you could tell the world.'

Greenland winced.

'Years I'd waited,' said Hellard. 'Years, thinking that the most special relationship in my life would never be more than an occasional hook-up. That was my lot. And then you started dangling it in front of me again. I figured to hell with the consequences. If I could win you back from Louisa, then I'd just suck it up. We could go and live somewhere far away and never see my family again. But there was another person in our way, wasn't there?'

Ben nodded miserably. 'Caitlin.'

'How did you find out about her and Ben?' asked Warren, trying to move the story on. They had been standing in the room for what felt like hours, and the smell of petrol was making him nauseous.

'Curtis, of course, back in September,' replied Hellard. 'He was supposed to be entertaining clients in London, but they called it off. So he called me out of the blue and we went for drinks and dinner.

'The thing about Curtis, is he was one of the few people who never really seemed to see Lou and I as a single unit, you know? And he loves a good gossip; I honestly think he forgot who he was talking to. He said, "I reckon Ben's up to his old ways again." I knew what he meant immediately, and I wanted to see if he knew about us. So I got him pissed. It's not difficult with him; doubles instead of singles when it was my round. He never could hold his drink.'

Her voice caught. 'When he said he'd seen you and Caitlin all cosy at Sinead's memorial – the same memorial where you told me you loved me – I couldn't believe it. It was Sinead all over again.'

'So you decided to kill her,' said Greenland, his tone incredulous. 'But why kill Louisa? If you got rid of Caitlin, and persuaded me to leave Lou, you'd have got what you wanted. Jesus, I can't believe I'm even saying this. You're fucking mad, you know that? You're an absolute bunny boiler.'

'Ben,' Warren cautioned.

'Because I saw what happened last time!' she cried. 'When Sinead disappeared, it drove you into Louisa's arms.' Her voice became earnest. 'And besides, it would have looked too suspicious. A second person you had an affair with gets murdered? The police would be all over you like a rash!'

442

'They *were* all over me like a rash!' shouted Greenland.

Hellard was shaking her head. 'No, don't you see? It was perfect. I knew that if I killed Louisa, the police would arrest you. Of course they would – they're so predictable. But when Caitlin kills herself and leaves a suicide note, that's it, case closed. And not only that, but they also have Sinead's killer. I made sure that you kept no commenting, so you couldn't give the game away. I knew exactly what I was doing. Even when they charged you, I got the charges dropped within hours.'

'This is crazy,' said Greenland, tears coursing down his face. 'You're crazy.'

'I love you! And you love me,' said Hellard. 'Don't you see what I've sacrificed for you? My sister. My friends. My family – do you really think they'd ever accept me getting married to my dead sister's husband?'

'My two girls have lost their mother. Murdered by their aunty!' said Greenland.

'We can bring them up together,' said Hellard. 'Lou was a shit mother anyway. If she wasn't trying to kill them by driving when drunk, she was whoring herself out on the internet. She was a fucking junkie, for Christ's sake! You can't tell me you didn't notice her red nostrils and her weird behaviour. At least this way they'll always believe their mother loved them – you could have told them whatever story you wanted to comfort them.'

Greenland recoiled as if physically slapped. 'You have no idea what you've done, do you? This whole thing is about you. What *you* want!'

'Ben, calm down,' said Warren. His eyes fixed on the lighter, which Hellard was gripping tightly. He had no idea if the petrol vapour had evaporated sufficiently that it wouldn't explode if ignited, but his nose suggested they'd be better off not finding out.

Greenland ignored him. 'Marry you? You have got to be fucking kidding. Yes I was a shit. I was an absolute bastard. In fact, I still am,' he shouted. 'I've lost count of the number of women I've cheated with. But here's the thing – judge me how you will, I don't give a fuck – I have only ever truly loved one woman. To think Louisa had got us into such a mess that I was even considering leaving her broke my heart. And I'll tell you another thing; she was the best mother those girls could ever have. There is no way you, or anybody else, could ever replace her.'

'I know that now,' said Hellard quietly. 'I know you were just stringing me – and Caitlin – along. But if I can't have you, then what's the point?'

'Whoa! There's no need for that,' said Warren, as Hellard lifted the lighter.

'You can leave if you want to, DCI Jones,' she said. 'But Ben stays.'

'I can't let you do that, Stephanie,' said Warren. Over his earpiece he could hear frantic instructions. The armed team by the front door were getting ready to pile in any second. The snipers outside were readying their shots, the danger of a stray spark from a bullet igniting the fumes now judged less of a risk than letting her use the lighter.

'Don't harm the baby,' he said in desperation.

Hellard blinked in surprise. 'Well, I didn't think you'd figure that out,' she said. 'I'm not even showing. What gave it away?'

'Empty boxes from pregnancy test kits in the bathroom wastebin,' said Warren. 'Two different brands; you don't do that unless the first one is positive, and you want confirmation.'

'You're pregnant . . .' Greenland swayed.

'Nine weeks,' she said. 'And yes, for the avoidance of doubt, it's yours.'

'Think about your baby,' said Warren. 'They're innocent.'

Greenland snorted. 'Believe me, I *am* thinking about them. Do you know how many young women I've seen get themselves pregnant in the hope that the judge goes lenient when they're sentenced? And do you know how many of those women I've seen give birth handcuffed to a hospital bed? Have you ever visited a mother and baby unit in a prison, DCI Jones? Because *I* have. And I don't want any of that.'

Her sudden movement caught Warren off-guard. He'd been so intent on the lighter, he hadn't noticed her other hand sneaking around her back. The knife tucked down the rear of her trousers was long and thin and extremely sharp.

Entrusting his fate to Kevlar body armour, he threw himself desperately towards her. He only made it two steps before she drew it across her throat.

Thrown backwards by his impact, she crashed into the flimsy, flatpack wardrobe, which collapsed around her. Struggling for control of the knife, Warren felt its blade, warm from her body, score its way down his arm.

And then he heard the snick of the lighter.

MONDAY 10TH JUNE

Epilogue

Tony Sutton pushed his hands into the pockets of the sombre black jacket his wife had dubbed his "funeral coat". It had been a lovely sunny day, but now the burial was over, the sun had retreated once more and a cool breeze had picked up, rustling the dozens of bouquets of flowers piled on the grave; his own, simple arrangement was barely visible.

It would be a few weeks before a permanent headstone was ready. Until then a wooden cross marked the spot; just name, date of birth and date of death. They were far too close together.

Such a tragic waste.

A shadow fell across the grave, interrupting his musing.

'The coach leaves for the wake in five minutes,' said Warren.

The two officers had been invited, alongside George Rutherford, to attend Sinead McCaffrey's final interment. Sinead's family had insisted Ben and Curtis also attend the ceremony. The two men had stood so awkwardly at the back of the church that Warren wondered if that had been Sinead's mother's intention all along – to kill with kindness.

Any chance of forgiveness for Stephanie Hellard from the family was a long way off, if ever. 'That evil woman hugged me just last year at Sinead's memorial,' her mother had said, a cold anger in her eyes.

Sinead's brother, now older than his big sister had ever been, had spat on the floor at Hellard's name. 'You should have let the bitch bleed to death, DCI Jones.'

Warren couldn't really respond to that, so had simply repeated his condolences. In his dreams, he could feel Stephanie's pulse, his hands slick with her blood as he applied pressure to the slice across her throat. She'd fought him every step of the way, and it had taken the combined force of both his and Ben's weight to stop her bleeding out before the paramedics made it into the room. When he'd jerked awake the previous night, the smell of petrol had lingered in his nostrils.

Despite the personal nature of the invitation, Warren and Sutton were conscious that they were representing Hertfordshire Constabulary. The previous day, he and Sutton had met with Assistant Chief Constable Mohammed Naseem and counsel from the Crown Prosecution Service, ostensibly to ensure both men were clear on what they could share with Sinead's loved ones without prejudicing Hellard's trial.

In reality of course, Naseem had wanted to hear the most intimate details of the case direct from Warren and Sutton's mouths. As soon as the prosecutor left, Naseem had produced the familiar leather-bound book he recorded notes in for his retirement memoirs. Warren was used to this by now; Sutton had been somewhat nonplussed.

'How long ago do you think Stephanie started planning to kill her sister?' Naseem had asked.

'Difficult to say,' said Warren. 'We know Curtis let slip that Ben and Caitlin were an item again back in September of last year. But from what Stephanie said when she was confronted, she had already made the decision to damn the consequences and try to get Ben for herself after he said he loved her back at Sinead's tenth anniversary memorial. She won't say if she was planning to kill Louisa that far back.'

Hellard had followed her own legal advice, and after being

450

pronounced fit to be questioned, had given only no-comment interviews.

'According to the doctors, and Ben's recollection, she probably became pregnant around the end of February. She had her girly night with Caitlin, when she stole her red hoodie, the weekend after this year's reunion in April. She won't say if she knew or suspected she was pregnant then. She only bought the pregnancy testing kits recently, so who knows if that was the catalyst to kill Louisa then? My gut feeling is she was already planning to kill Louisa and blame everything on Caitlin well before then.' He shrugged. 'I wouldn't even be surprised if she stopped taking her contraceptive pill on purpose.'

That was yet another tragedy. Tests had shown the baby was apparently unscathed, but what would happen to it, Warren had no idea. The child would be the offspring of a murderer, fathered by the man whose wife she had killed. They would have two half-sisters – the daughters of one of their mother's victims. Warren couldn't imagine how the child would deal with that once they were old enough to be told the truth, or how Molly and Pippa would feel towards their unexpected sibling.

Sutton joined in. 'It's all speculation, of course, but the favourite theory in the office is that by advising Ben to no comment, then suddenly producing evidence that cleared him and pointed the finger towards Caitlin, she was setting herself up as the hero. She'd successfully got rid of her rivals, saved him from prison, and was carrying his child. In her mind, he would be forever grateful, realise they were meant to be together, and they would live happily ever after.'

'But she didn't know what a shifty bugger Ben Greenland had been,' said Naseem.

'Exactly,' said Sutton. 'I don't think she realised what a can of worms she was opening – she probably had no idea how much evidence there was that Caitlin and Ben were together that night. Ben admits he had told Caitlin to keep quiet about their affair, even if she thought it would exonerate him. He placed all his trust in Stephanie to solve his problems.'

'For her part, Stephanie thought she was being clever, getting that easily manipulated junior solicitor to insist he no comment,' said Warren. 'But all it did was make us more suspicious. If he'd told us what he was up to the night Louisa was killed, we might have ruled him and Caitlin out sooner and continued chasing our tails trying to prove his brother and Russell Myrie were responsible.'

'Have you worked out how she managed to make those purchases and hire a car in Caitlin's name?' asked Naseem.

'We found a duplicate driving licence and a set of Caitlin's keys hidden in Stephanie's flat, along with a new credit card in Caitlin's name,' said Sutton. 'She'd also managed to pick up the exact same handbag that Caitlin used. The licence and credit card were applied for shortly after Stephanie spent the weekend with Caitlin, when we believe she stole the red hoodie. We suspect she got a set of keys cut when Caitlin was still passed out from whatever she spiked her drink with. According to her employer, she took annual leave around the time the DVLA and the bank posted the licence and card to Caitlin's address. Caitlin used to go to the gym or leisure centre every morning, so Stephanie could easily have intercepted the post using her copy of the keys.'

'Clever bugger,' muttered Naseem. 'What about the CCTV at her sister's lock-up? How did she disable that?'

'The day she met with Louisa for coffee, we have footage from a locksmith of her getting some keys cut,' said Warren. 'She did it about thirty minutes after Louisa bought them sandwiches, cake and coffee. We're guessing she pinched the keys out of Louisa's handbag when she went to the bathroom, then made some sort of excuse, like needing to pay for more parking. The cloud storage company have recovered some footage from six p.m. that same day that looks a lot like Stephanie disguised as Caitlin letting herself into the unit just before the feed was cut. The alarm code was the same as the Greenlands' house alarm, which Stephanie had known for years.'

Naseem shook his head again. 'She really put some thought into this. She'll not be able to play the diminished responsibility card at trial – too much premeditation. At least Sinead McCaffrey's family can finally lay the poor girl to rest.

'Eleven years . . . You know, I have a daughter almost the same age as she was back then . . . You send them off to university knowing it'll be a big adventure.' His mouth twisted into a grimace. 'And you know they'll probably get up to things that you'd rather they didn't share with you. But you pray every night that if they do get into trouble, they'll come to you first.'

'I know exactly what you mean, Sir,' said Sutton. His son was now studying for a PhD in history.

Warren could only agree with their sentiment. It would be many years before he and Susan would be faced with that, should Niall decide to go to university. He just hoped they raised a young man who had the strength to stand up for what was right and call out the sort of toxic behaviour that the Ben Greenlands of this world were too cowardly to challenge.

'How's the arm?' asked Sutton, jerking Warren back to the present.

'A little sore,' admitted Warren. 'I should have kept the sling on as a deterrent.' Handshakes at these sorts of events always seemed to be accompanied with a slap on the arm.

The two men approached the coach; a group of older men stood in a group, having one last cigarette before the journey to the community centre. The snick of their lighters made Warren flinch.

The cheap plastic one held by Hellard in the petrol-soaked bedroom had somehow failed to ignite. Before she had been able to try again, a vicious stomp from Ben Greenland's right boot had broken both the lighter and three of her fingers.

Sutton gave his friend's shoulder a squeeze and sought to distract him. 'Are we still on for the weekend?'

'Yeah, there's no way Susan and I will get those bookcases up, especially with this arm; they're solid oak and taller than both of us.'

'Don't worry, that's why I'm bringing Moray. And Mags has lent me her hammer drill to fix them to the wall, for when Niall starts climbing. We'll get that house of yours liveable before you know it. Now let's get on the coach. I'm dying for a pint of proper Irish Guinness.'

A Letter from Paul Gitsham

Thank you so much for choosing to read *Web of Lies*. I hope you enjoyed it! If you did and would like to be the first to know about my new releases, you can follow me on Twitter or sign up for my newsletter via my website.

Sometimes an idea comes to you unexpectedly, and you just have to write it! That's what happened here. The inspiration, as is often the case, came whilst my then fiancée (now wife) and I were watching a true crime documentary. A hapless suspect was in an interview room, being grilled by detectives. His solicitor was beside him, pen in hand, laptop open. And I started to think 'what if . . .'

As the credits rolled, I started pounding out ideas on my phone. Within minutes, I had a premise and a central idea.

Then came the frustration that every professional author is familiar with: the need to put the exciting shiny new idea to one side and continue with the book you are currently writing. However, over the next few months I continued to lay the ground-work, reaching out to fellow authors with legal expertise to make sure I could do what I wanted to.

Eventually, it was time to write. And boy did I write! From typing the first word to sending it to my beta readers took a little over three months. This included breaks for holidays and time taken out to edit the upcoming book. This is a personal best, and yet I never felt rushed or under pressure. It just flowed.

Writing this book gave me a lot of pleasure, and I sincerely hope that you enjoy reading it as much as I enjoyed writing it.

I hope you loved *Web of Lies* and if you did I would be so grateful if you would leave a review. I always love to hear what readers thought, and it helps new readers discover my books too.

Thanks,
Paul

Twitter @dcijoneswriter
Instagram @paulgitsham
Website www.paulgitsham.com
Facebook @dcijones

The Last Straw

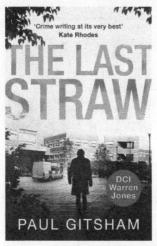

When Professor Alan Tunbridge is discovered in his office with his throat slashed, the suspects start queuing up. The brilliant but unpleasant microbiologist had a genius for making enemies.

For Warren Jones, newly appointed detective chief inspector to the Middlesbury force, a high-profile murder is the ideal opportunity. He's determined to run a thorough and professional investigation but political pressure to resolve the case quickly and tensions in the office and at home make life anything but easy.

Everything seems to point to one vengeful man but the financial potential of the professor's pioneering research takes the inquiry in an intriguing and, for Jones and his team, dangerous direction.

No Smoke Without Fire

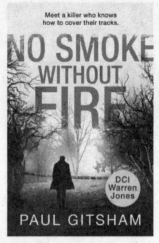

Meet a killer who knows how to cover their tracks.

NO SMOKE WITHOUT FIRE

DCI Warren Jones

PAUL GITSHAM

DCI Warren Jones has a bad feeling when the body of a young woman turns up in Beaconsfield Woods. She's been raped and strangled but the murderer has been careful to leave no DNA evidence. There are, of course, suspects – boyfriend, father – to check out but, worryingly, it looks more and more like a stranger murder.

Warren's worst fears are confirmed when another young woman is killed in the same way.

The MO fits that of Richard Cameron who served twelve years for rape. But Cameron never killed his victims and he has a cast-iron alibi.

Then personal tragedy intervenes and Warren is off the case. But the pressure is mounting and another woman goes missing. Warren is back but will the break he desperately needs come before there's another victim?

Silent as the Grave

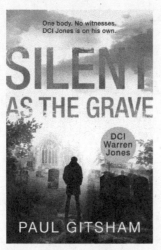

One body. No witnesses.
DCI Jones is on his own.

SILENT
AS THE GRAVE

DCI
Warren
Jones

PAUL GITSHAM

It's DCI Warren Jones' coldest case yet …

The body of Reginald Williamson had been well
concealed under a bush in Middlesbury Common
and the murder efficiently carried out – a single stab
wound to the chest. Reggie's dog had been killed just
as efficiently. With no clues or obvious motive, the
case is going nowhere. Then Warren gets a break.

Warren's instincts tell him that the informant is dodgy
– a former police officer under investigation. But when
Warren hears the incredible story he has to tell, he's
glad to have given him a chance to speak. Suddenly, a
wide criminal conspiracy, involving high-level police
corruption, a gangster and a trained killer, is blown wide
open … and Warren finds that this time, it's not just his
career under threat, but also his family – and his life.

Acknowledgements

Wow, another DCI Warren Jones hits the shelves! I can't believe
it's been twelve years since I started this journey. Of course, I had
many fellow travellers along the way, without whom this series
would never have been possible.

First and foremost as always, I have to thank my beta readers
– Mum, Dad and Cheryl – for all their support. Theirs are always
the first eyeballs to see what I've been up to in the office for the
last few months and their feedback is invaluable. The book you
are holding or listening to wouldn't be nearly as well polished
without the extensive notes that they send me.

I also need to thank my fellow writers. This was the year that
we finally emerged from our shells and started meeting in person
again. I'd forgotten just how enthused I feel after spending time in
their company, chatting about books, writing and life. One of the
best things about being part of the community of crime writers
is the friendship and support. Where else would you see people,
who on paper are direct rivals to one another, enthusiastically
promoting each other's work?

I want to specifically mention Lesley Jones and her husband
Chris, who generously worked through the legal implications for
the central premise of this novel. They confirmed that my initial

idea was unethical (the characters' actions, not mine!), but by doing so helped me craft a far more interesting twist. Naturally, this being fiction, I have stretched their advice to breaking point. If I've stepped over that line, chalk it up to artistic licence on my part.

As always, Team HQ and the folks at HarperCollins have done their job magnificently. It's easy to forget that the author is just the visible point of a very broad pyramid. In particular, it's always a pleasure to work with my editor Abi Fenton, and I feel the book takes a leap forward every time she makes a suggestion. Thanks for all your hard work over the years, it's greatly appreciated.

For those who prefer the spoken word to the written word, working with my long-time audio-narrator Malk Williams has become a joy. We have yet to meet in person – when I will buy him that long-overdue pint – but we've done several online video interviews and they've been an absolute blast (they are archived on YouTube for posterity, just search for me or Malk).

I also want to thank Nancy Whitmarsh, winner of the annual Young Lives Vs Cancer charity auction, for the use of her name (www.younglivesvscancer.org.uk). Your generous donation will make a difference to young people affected by this devastating disease.

And last, but not least, there are my readers. Readers are what make all this possible and worthwhile. Reading reviews, or speaking to people who have taken the time to tell me what they think of Warren and his adventures, is always pleasure. But just knowing that thousands of people have spent time in his company is a thrill. I hope that whether you are a long-standing reader of the series, or just decided to give a new author a go, the book lives up to your expectations.

Thank you once again for reading,

Paul

Dear Reader,

We hope you enjoyed reading this book. If you did, we'd be so appreciative if you left a review. It really helps us and the author to bring more books like this to you.

Here at HQ Digital we are dedicated to publishing fiction that will keep you turning the pages into the early hours. Don't want to miss a thing? To find out more about our books, promotions, discover exclusive content and enter competitions you can keep in touch in the following ways:

JOIN OUR COMMUNITY:

Sign up to our new email newsletter:
http://smarturl.it/SignUpHQ

Read our new blog www.hqstories.co.uk

🐦 https://twitter.com/HQStories

📘 www.facebook.com/HQStories

BUDDING WRITER?

We're also looking for authors to join the HQ Digital family!
Find out more here:

https://www.hqstories.co.uk/want-to-write-for-us/

Thanks for reading, from the HQ Digital team